THE
WIDOWMAKER

ALSO BY HANNAH MORRISSEY

Hello, Transcriber

THE
WIDOWMAKER

A NOVEL

Hannah Morrissey

MINOTAUR
BOOKS
NEW YORK

First published in the United States by Minotaur Books, an imprint of St. Martin's Publishing Group

THE WIDOWMAKER. Copyright © 2022 by Hannah Morrissey. All rights reserved. Printed in the United States of America. For information, address St. Martin's Publishing Group, 120 Broadway, New York, NY 10271.

www.minotaurbooks.com

Designed by Omar Chapa

Library of Congress Cataloging-in-Publication Data

Names: Morrissey, Hannah, author.
Title: The widowmaker : a novel / Hannah Morrissey.
Description: First Edition. | New York : Minotaur Books, 2022. |
Identifiers: LCCN 2022028689 | ISBN 9781250795977 (hardcover) |
    ISBN 9781250795984 (ebook)
Subjects: LCGFT: Detective and mystery fiction. | Novels.
Classification: LCC PS3613.O777928 W53 2022 | DDC 813/.6—dc23/eng/20220708
LC record available at https://lccn.loc.gov/2022028689

Our books may be purchased in bulk for promotional, educational, or business use. Please contact your local bookseller or the Macmillan Corporate and Premium Sales Department at 1-800-221-7945, extension 5442, or by email at MacmillanSpecialMarkets@macmillan.com.

First Edition: 2022

10 9 8 7 6 5 4 3 2 1

For Grandma. From whom I inherited my love of books.

THE
WIDOWMAKER

1
MORGAN

The key was a blackened talisman, tucked into her leather cuff. She'd gotten in the habit of keeping it there since it had become the only tangible thing she owned when, three months ago, her entire life was reduced to ash and ruin. The fire department had already come and gone by the time she arrived, her boots crunching on caramelized glass and stepping over hissing metal. Everything was wet and charred—mannequins with their faces melted in, the once larger-than-life Mylar tree shriveled to a root—which meant that whoever had left the key had watched and waited, like a tiger stalking its prey. But Morgan knew better. Only humans tortured their food before eating it.

A red balloon floated in the sulfurous haze, tethered to a small, coffin-shaped box set on a step of the smoldering staircase. A simple note scratched on the back of an envelope revealed it was for her: *My Ruin: All roads lead back to home.*

A puff of vapor escaped her lips—a silent scream, perhaps, at the omen from beyond the grave. The only person who would have used that moniker was dead. The last image Morgan had of her aunt Bern was of her lying faceup with her skull shattered on the concrete, mouth open to catch snowflakes. It was one of few childhood memories she hadn't overwritten. Rather, she kept it sequestered in a safe place so she could recall it at will, the way normal people preserved memories of their wedding day or the moment their first child was born.

Now, standing on the Reynoldses' back porch, she turned her wrist and pressed her thumb to the key, tempted to free it from its holster. The iron stung. The key would not fit, she determined, as she considered the aperture in the ornate metal plate.

All roads lead back to home.

This was not her home. If the sea glass–colored mansion at the top of the bluff hadn't tipped her off on her drive in, then the twelve-foot-tall gothic gate that swung inward to grant her entrance to the estate made damn sure she knew she wasn't on her side of the tracks anymore. This was Reynolds country, she'd thought, following the cobblestone path that wended past topiaries draped in white lights and a pair of concrete tigers, their faces frozen in mid roar and thick necks wrapped in festive, Fair Isle scarves. Then, she'd parked her salty little Honda Civic next to a newly waxed Land Rover and felt more than a little inadequate.

The Reynolds family was enshrouded in wealth, status, and mystery; and Black Harbor's entire eroding shoreline belonged to them. What remained of it, anyway. Over the past decade or more, Lake Michigan had eaten away the limestone as effectively as the city's grim atmosphere gnawed on people's morals. If they'd had morals to begin with. In her thirty-one years on this planet—most of them spent here in this frozen purgatory—Morgan had learned that some people were born purely and inherently evil. And Black Harbor was their breeding ground.

Morgan surveyed the snow-covered estate. Giant red bulbs hung from evergreen boughs, and three wreaths decorated the middle tier of a stone fountain. A lone lamppost wore a gold velvet bow and to her left, fairy lights twinkled as they wove through the crosshatched trellis that would work well for group photos. It was creeping up on two o'clock. The golden hour would be here soon, when the sun was low and its amber hues came alive to brush its subjects' skin tones with a warm glow. She raised her camera, snapped a test shot, and returned her attention to the door. Her worries melted away. It was just her and the keyhole. She felt the autofocus lock into place and took a photo. She could add it to her collection—the one she'd started since inheriting the key—of all the doors and their corresponding keyholes into which it didn't fit.

Not terribly unlike herself.

Pierced and gangly with a death stare that could intimidate a bull, Morgan didn't really fit anywhere, either.

Except The Ruins. She'd fit there. And then it all burned down.

Morgan considered the keyhole again and sucked in a breath. This wasn't home and yet, was it so wrong that she wished it was? That her childhood had been spent here, running free through an orchard and pushing siblings on a front porch swing; not curled up on the floor, left to lick her wounds like a dog and pray her door remained closed until morning.

A gust of wind came and pulled tears from her eyes. She repositioned her gear bag slung on her shoulder and, turning her back to the wind, slid the key out of her cuff. It didn't hurt to try. With the key pinched between her thumb and forefinger, she reached forward, when the door fell away. The woman who appeared behind it was so beautiful it hurt, Morgan thought, as she took in her verdant eyes and the short layers of russet hair that framed her face. She looked surprised, and Morgan suspected she hadn't anticipated someone who looked like her—dressed all in black, with a pierced septum and two studs in her bottom lip, skin pale as the Ghost of Christmas Past—to be standing on her doorstep.

"Oh!" she exclaimed. "You must be the photographer! Morgan, right?" She shifted the chubby-cheeked toddler she was holding to her other hip. It stared at Morgan in that unapologetic way that babies do. Morgan estimated 1.2 seconds before the drool on its lip froze into a "spitcicle."

She nodded and slid her key back into her cuff. Later.

"I'm Cora." The woman smiled, showing teeth brighter than fresh-fallen snow. Her lips were painted holly red, the same shade as her knit, short-sleeved sweater. Goose bumps stippled her arms. "And this is Charlie. We were just about to get Mamó some ginger ale, weren't we, Charlie?" Her voice pitched and fell. How easily some people could slip in and out of baby talk, Morgan mused, and she wondered, was *Mamó* some type of nickname for Mom? Grandma? Just like *Omi, Oma, Nana, Yamma,* and the cringey-beyond-all-get-out *Glamma*?

When Cora leaned over to grab a six-pack of cans resting atop a resin storage chest, Morgan stopped her. "I'll get them."

"Thank you," Cora said, speaking like an adult again. "Come in, please. My mom will be so excited that you're here. You're her gift," she added with a quick glance over her shoulder.

Morgan scrunched her brows. A gift? She'd never been anyone's gift before, and yet, perhaps that was how the people who'd paid her aunt had looked at her—a guilty little pleasure they'd never tell a soul about. Her throat felt dry. She licked her lips, tempted to suck down one of those ginger ales. Being back here had that effect on her. One breath of Black Harbor was potent enough to turn her devil-may-care armor brittle. She imagined watching it disintegrate and fall away like fish scales, leaving her raw and exposed while she served herself on a silver platter to the black widow of Black Harbor: Mrs. Eleanor Reynolds, whose husband, Clive, vanished twenty years ago. Eleanor was the obvious suspect, and according to the court of public opinion, she was guilty as sin. The eleven-million-dollar life insurance policy she'd taken out on Clive just weeks before his death had been, for all intents and purposes, her hand hammering the nail in his coffin. And he'd had an affair. Which meant he'd pounded the final nail in himself.

Morgan's ears pricked at the sound of the door closing behind her. Noting that Cora wore only Fair Isle stockings, she heel-toed her combat boots off in a mudroom she doubted had ever seen a speck of mud. Plus, it was larger than the space she'd recently moved back into at her parents' house. She set the ginger ale on a bench to straighten the tops of her stockings, making them even, and hung her jacket on an empty hook. Her glasses fogged.

"Mom," Cora called. Her voice carried through the kitchen, rose, and dissipated somewhere between the hardwood floors and the cathedral ceiling. "Morgan is here!"

Following cautiously in Cora's wake, Morgan set the cans of ginger ale on a granite countertop and waited. A current swam through the great room, fragrant with cloves and thyme and buttery croissants. It smelled of roast beef, too, and seasoned potatoes. The countertop boasted a trove of mini mince pies and single-serve sherry trifles. Adjusting her camera settings, Morgan took a few photos to show her mom the spread. Up until six months ago, when the highway construction shut it down, Lynette's Linzers—her mother's bakery—had been a beloved staple of Black Harbor, serving homemade cookies, tarts, and biscuits on the daily. Now, it was simply one of dozens of vacant storefronts.

Over the home's surround-sound system, a slow piano melody melted into a chorus of accordion, flute, and bagpipes. As the song picked up, Morgan recognized it as "Fairytale of New York," by the Pogues, and smiled.

Where was everyone, she wondered. Cora had gone and disappeared with Charlie down a corridor, and aside from someone who was clearly a caterer coming to check the oven, there wasn't a soul in sight. Had she gotten the time wrong? No, the email had stated two o'clock. She'd read it again this morning to be sure.

In a mansion this massive, there were a million places people could be hiding.

Morgan looked to her right and surveyed what appeared to be the living room. Overstuffed grey couches that could have swallowed her parents' dinky little sofa formed an L-shape around a glass coffee table. In the corner, between the stone fireplace and a large picture window, stood a tree that had to be fourteen feet tall. Its branches dripped with faux crystalline icicles; expensive-looking ornaments nestled in its boughs, and a glass Swarovski star twinkled at the top. Jesus, had they jacked this tree from Tiffany's?

Her gaze traveling upward and across the ceiling, Morgan noticed a lofted upstairs where all the bedrooms must be. Beneath it, in the wide hall down which Cora had previously vanished, floated a radiant, white-haired woman. She wore an emerald top cinched with a leather corset and flowy sleeves; her smile and socks matched Cora's.

"Uh, hello," said Morgan. "I'm . . . um . . . the photographer?" Her voice trembled. The sight of Eleanor Reynolds, here, in the flesh, had left her dumb.

"Morgan, what a delight." Eleanor beamed, revealing eyeteeth that were sharp, stark white, and perhaps a centimeter too long. Spreading her arms, she welcomed Morgan into a straitjacket hug.

"You must be Eleanor," Morgan said.

"The devil herself." Eleanor raised her hands as though holding up praise.

Eleanor's acknowledgment of her less than savory reputation put Morgan at ease. "Your home is stunning, by the way." Her eyes roamed the four-seasons room and the English-inspired kitchen with marble backsplash. A Prussian-blue china cabinet fit snug in a shallow alcove, holding stemware that undoubtedly cost more than Morgan's entire education. And yet, on the counter beside it was a red rotary telephone. It looked out of place here where everything was modern and cool-toned. Not to mention, who even had a landline anymore?

"Oh, thank you, darling."

"Mom was an interior designer for many years," chimed Cora, who had reappeared, sans Charlie. "A home stager. She even designed sets for Hallmark."

Eleanor rolled her eyes at Cora's praise; nevertheless, she grabbed her daughter's arm and gave an affectionate squeeze. "Puff pieces, dear, honestly. I should have done something important with my career. Cora is a child psychologist."

Morgan lifted her chin as though she cared. She couldn't tell if Eleanor and Cora were displaying genuine admiration for each other, or putting on a show.

"Help yourself, won't you, Morgan?" said Eleanor. "They're setting up food in the dining room. There's wine, beer, cocktails, coffee . . ."

"Nog," suggested Cora.

"Yes, nog," Eleanor repeated. "Make yourself at home, really."

Morgan smiled politely. She'd never heard anyone abbreviate "eggnog" before. The slang made these characters slightly more human. But then, she'd never been told to make herself at home while on the job, either. She was used to shooting cocktail parties and corporate events that took place in warehouses and banquet halls. Never someone's home, and certainly never in a murderess's mansion.

A gentleman between Cora and Eleanor's age swept in. Morgan watched as his hand grazed Eleanor's waist. Eleanor twirled gracefully, turning her body toward his. "Don, darling, this is Morgan, my *gift*. She's our photographer for the evening."

"Oh." Don looked impressed. He had a sophisticated, salt-and-pepper aesthetic. If Morgan had to guess, she'd put him at twenty years younger than Eleanor. *Damn lady, get it,* she applauded silently.

"Pleasure," he said, and offered his hand for her to shake.

The second Morgan offered her hand in return, jingle bells tinkled from down the hall.

The front door opened and Reynolds friends and family members filtered in, all toting decorated sacks and gifts wrapped in kraft paper and twine—ironically rustic. Morgan watched them with shameless fascination. They looked like they'd just stepped off the set of a photo shoot, so cozy in their chunky knit sweaters, moms and daughters wearing matching suede boots, gentlemen in flannel shirts that had never seen the elements for which they were intended. A little blond boy wore a marbled cardigan with elbow patches. Crouching, Morgan snapped several photos as he ran off with his cousins.

There had to be forty people once everyone arrived. Kids crawled beneath tables and thundered up and down the staircase. The clamor of conversation drowned out the Celtic Christmas music. The women clinked their wineglasses. Men guffawed and sipped dark beer. Morgan captured a photo of a freckled girl wearing angel wings and a tinsel halo eating a powdered cookie.

"You know you can eat the food, too. You don't just have to photograph it."

Morgan stood and turned to find the source of the suggestion. A man sat on the sofa, legs casually crossed, clutching a bourbon neat. He looked to be about her age. Early to mid-thirties? There was something about his eyes. Dark like his drink, and salient, they made her feel as though he was looking through her, not at her. She swallowed. What did he see, she wondered. Did her interior—dark and damaged beyond redemption—match her exterior? She hoped it did; enough, at least, so he would stay away. And yet, a quiet voice in her head pleaded for the opposite. Perhaps it was the way he stared through her, or the winsome smile that tugged at the corners of his mouth.

But, she was here on business. "Thanks. I might get a plate later. I was actually eying up the seven-layer bars."

"Want me to get you one?" The man shifted as though to get up. The natural light streaming in from the window subtly illuminated his face so she could see a shallow cleft in his chin, like a thumbprint.

"No, no, I'm good. Thanks, though."

"A drink then?"

She shook her head.

"You think this is one of those fairy places where if you eat the food or drink the wine, you'll have to stay forever?"

"Something like that." You didn't spend your childhood in Black Harbor avoiding cracks in the sidewalk only to be welcomed into the proverbial mansion and eat the food. "I don't drink on the job," she added.

"Because your pictures will be out of focus?" He lifted the glass to his lips. The corner of his mouth ticked upward.

Morgan nodded. "It's a risk I'm not willing to take."

Nor was it a risk she could afford. When she left Chicago with only the key and the clothes on her back, she'd used everything in her bank account to buy a one-way bus ticket to Black Harbor and a professional photographer starter kit—camera body, two lenses, off-camera flash, extra battery pack, the whole shebang. With the rest of her money, she'd purchased the only car her skimpy budget allowed. But, she was debt-free. Not everyone could say that.

"How 'bout after, then?"

Morgan tilted her head, sizing him up. "Anyone ever tell you you're a little forward?"

He laughed, the comment sliding off him like oil on a feather.

Searching for a distraction, Morgan turned and observed the photographs on the mantel, locking on to a portrait of a young Reynolds family. Judging by the scrunchies in the two girls' hair and Clive's color-block vest, it looked to have been taken in the early '90s. There was no denying that Clive was old-Hollywood handsome. He and Eleanor made an attractive couple. The frame was a touch out of line with the others. She nudged it forward, making it straight, when her hopeful suitor came up behind her. He stood close enough that she could feel the heat coming off his skin like she was sitting in front of a crackling fire; smell the sharp, evocative scent of his cologne: bourbon and black ice and a little bit of char. It was as though he'd simply selected them from a catalog and had them bottled into a quintessential male fragrance.

"Scary that that was twenty-five years ago."

Morgan did the mental math. "So, 1995?"

He pointed to Eleanor in the photo. "I can tell the decade by the height of my mom's hair. It was a sight to see in the eighties."

"I bet." Morgan pointed to one of the girls. She was nine or ten maybe. "Cora?"

He nodded, then drew her attention to the younger, fox-faced girl with golden hair, and a raven-haired boy who might have been thirteen. "Carlisle and David," he said, packaging them together. "It's a joke in our family, that David doesn't love anyone but himself. He loves Carlisle, though, 'cause she's his mini-me. They don't look alike, but trust me, inside they're made of the same stuff."

Morgan studied each of them in turn. They had the same stare. The way their eyes bored into the camera, it was almost as if they were challenging it. Daring it to call them out for something and yet not caring if it did.

"And who's this?" She pointed to a wild-eyed boy leaning over Clive's shoulder. He was wearing a striped T-shirt and a bulky Power Rangers wristwatch.

"The boy with the very unfortunate bowl cut, you mean?" He offered his hand for her to shake. "Bennett Reynolds."

"Morgan Mori," she said, though he already knew. He'd been the one to email her about the job.

"When do you get off the clock, Morgan Mori?"

She bit her lip. She could do this. "You tell me, boss. Though I believe the arrangement was for eight."

A wicked glint flashed behind Bennett's eyes. "Eight o'clock," he repeated. "You'll need a drink by then, trust me."

"Is that a bet?"

"It's a promise."

It was through Morgan's 50mm lens that she came face-to-face with each of the Reynolds clan. She led them out to the trellis, staging groups about four feet in front of it to capture the soft bokeh of the lights strung between the cedar boughs. She photographed Cora and her little family, adding in

Eleanor and Don, Carlisle, David, and Bennett, who stood at the edge of the frame, still holding his drink.

Carlisle was gorgeous in jewel tones, wearing a teal sweater dress belted at the waist and black tights. She looked like a snow angel come to life, her long golden ringlets cascading down her back. Morgan couldn't help but wonder if it was a wig. Everyone wore them these days, didn't they? David, on the other hand, was her antithesis, and that made him her complement. They were yin and yang together, light and shadow, dove and raven. When everyone else had dispersed, they posed to re-create an old photo from their childhood: Carlisle crossed her eyes and pretended to pick her nose while David looked on in animated disgust. Afterward, they huddled around Morgan's camera to see the photo appear on the LCD display.

"That's it, that's our Christmas card!" Carlisle laughed. They left Morgan to finish up before the sun went down, and later, when everyone was gathered inside by the fireplace, sleigh bells sounded.

Of course they got a freakin' Santa Claus, Morgan thought, as the children's eyes widened in excitement. They tumbled over one another as they ran down the hall, sliding in their socks when Santa Claus burst through the door with a festive "Ho, ho, ho!"

He was a convincing Santa—albeit nontraditional in a red patchwork robe trimmed with Celtic knots. A green beret with a shamrock perched atop his head. Toting a sack full of presents, he ambled in and plunked into the high-backed chair Cora had previously occupied. Then, he withdrew a pair of half-moon spectacles from an inside pocket and read the names off his list. Every single child received a present, which was damn impressive, considering how many kids there were.

Afterward, the kids took turns sitting on his lap and telling him what they wished for under the Christmas tree. Morgan captured every interaction, and when the last child had spoken, Santa gestured to her, bending his white-gloved finger. "And you, young lady. What do you want for Christmas?"

"Oh." Morgan gave him a dismissive wave.

"Come on, now." He patted his knee.

Morgan looked around. The chaos had quieted. The lights had dimmed. It had to be eight o'clock or close to it. She looked around, searching for someone to save her, but caught only Bennett's gaze. He sat at the end of the couch, a reflection of the firelight dancing in his green eyes. Morgan stared back, her brow raised, and lowered herself onto Santa's lap.

She bit her lip and prayed he didn't touch her.

"What's your name, young lady?"

"Morgan."

"Morgan." He sounded it out one syllable at a time. "What a lovely name."

"Thanks, I didn't choose it."

Santa chuckled. "What would you like for Christmas, Morgan?"

Sarcastic responses raced through her mind. A puppy? An Easy-Bake Oven? One of those fancy power lift recliners so her grandpa could hold on to a shred of his dignity instead of getting hopelessly stuck in the La-Z-Boy every night? That last one wasn't sarcastic. "A Butterfinger," she said.

Santa's eyes twinkled. "A Butterfinger?"

"King-sized."

"That depends. Have you been naughty or nice?"

Morgan froze. A shiver started at the base of her skull and trickled down her spine. It might have been the question itself, or the fact that his asking it made something pulse against the underside of her thigh.

Now finished and packed up for the night, and having said her goodbyes to the Reynolds family, Morgan stood on the porch where she'd stood hours earlier, contemplating the keyhole. She slid the key out of her cuff, and this time, as she approached the door, she heard a voice in the dark. "Looks like you're off the clock, Morgan Mori."

2

HUDSON

Jesus, Hudson, you sure know how to fuck up a crime scene.

Blue salt crystals dug into his knees, stuck to his palms as a final spasm racked his body. At the Fast Mart across from an empty furniture store, Investigator Ryan Hudson pressed his forehead to the cold concrete of the sidewalk. It grounded him, stopped the world from spinning out of control, if only for a few seconds.

Jesus, Hudson. He heard his friend's voice as clearly as though Garrison were standing next to him. It was something they'd said to each other often, during the decade they'd spent on patrol together. Never serious, and almost always accompanied by a ribbing or an elbow nudge, it was a deflection, a way of one placing his blame onto the other, like when they'd been called to Breaker's office after Garrison wrote forty parking tickets for the wrong side of the street. "Jesus, Hudson," Garrison had muttered. Or, the time Hudson had misheard an address over the radio, and when they arrived, the resident—believing her friends had gifted her male strippers for her birthday—ushered them inside. "Jesus, Garrison," Hudson laughed as he'd recounted the story back in the locker room. Garrison had unbuttoned his uniform then, revealing his black undershirt, and set his foot up on the bench in a mock striptease. Someone walked by and smacked his ass.

Wincing as though he'd been the one to get shot, Hudson cautiously rose to sit on his heels. He looked over his left shoulder, where across the street, Garrison's department SUV was parked. It looked like a dog waiting for its owner to come back.

A gust of wind tore through the lot, almost knocking him backward. The lake effect ripped the tears from his cheek, gnawed at the exposed skin of his legs. A plastic cone toppled over and rolled across the snow-scraped asphalt. His eyes followed it as it tumbled toward him and butted up against the curb.

Gingerly, Hudson stood. He swayed and planted his feet shoulder-width apart to steady himself. His throat burned. This was the first time in eleven years he'd thrown up at a scene. That was reserved for amateurs. *Baby cops.*

Even when Hudson had been a baby cop, he hadn't acted like one. He couldn't afford to. Wiry and spectacled, he looked more like an IT guy than a police officer. It didn't take much to pass the physical litmus test anymore. If you could manage twenty-five push-ups, run a mile in under ten minutes, and be of reasonably sound mind, you were hired. Because just like Hudson couldn't afford to act like a baby cop, the Black Harbor Police Department couldn't afford to be picky.

All around him, blue and red lights danced like the aurora borealis. Both Black Harbor and Wesson police vehicles were at the scene. Taking a deep breath and steeling himself for what he was about to walk back into, Hudson reentered the doorway he'd run out of a moment before, stepping aside as a patrol officer came through. The stink hit him again like a skid of bricks. It smelled like blood and shit and coffee.

With all the ins and outs, it was as cold inside as it was outside, though at least it was out of the wind. Camera flashes burst, yellow placards marked evidence, fingerprint powder saturated the contact surfaces.

Garrison lay on his back, staring empty-eyed and slack-jawed at his own blood spattered on the ceiling. The story of how he ended up like that was punctuated by the bullet hole in his neck. Two more projectiles were punched in his vest, dislodging the personal effects he kept in the center pocket: a picture of his wife and daughter, a couple of postage stamps, a twenty-dollar bill. Hudson stood over Garrison in a jacket and gym shorts, wearing socks and Adidas sliders. He'd been in bed when Breaker, his former lieutenant, called with the news. "Garrison's been shot," he barked, and before Hudson could process what he'd heard, the lieutenant rattled off an address Hudson immediately recognized as the store he and Garrison had been watching for robbery activity. Used to watch.

Guilt burned a hole in his stomach. He never should have gone upstairs. A promotion to investigator could have waited. After all, Hudson was staring down the barrel of another twenty years in law enforcement. He could have stayed with Garrison for his last few months before retirement. Had the tables been turned, Garrison would have done it for him.

Investigator Devine escorted the female witness outside, likely to find her a ride home, since the suspect had stolen her car. Hudson had observed Devine interviewing her earlier. She'd sat in the candy aisle with her knees tucked into her chest, rocking backward and forward, like a buoy stranded in a low tide.

Now, he heard Investigator Fletcher interviewing the cashier. According to the man's statement, he'd been held at gunpoint by a suspect clothed in all black: long-sleeve shirt, pants, and a balaclava, the fabric of which had been bunched up to expose a patch of light-colored skin. "Anything unique about him?" Fletcher asked. "Identifying features like scars, tattoos?"

"He had a mark on his neck," was all the cashier said.

"Anything else? Approximate height and weight? Eye color?"

Hudson stared at the floor. Saw the pool of blood becoming more viscous in the cold. Saw Fletcher's snakeskin cowboy boots. And he focused on them, anything to not look at Garrison. His eyes traced the outline of the pointed toes, scales carved in rounded diamond patterns, rivers of black that divided the continents of greys. Who wore cowboy boots in the city?

Fletcher scribbled something in his memo pad, shoved it in his back pocket.

Devine returned inside and joined his partner. "You got surveillance?" he asked the cashier.

"No. The camera's been busted . . ."

Their voices were drowned out by the blood rushing in Hudson's ears. Any other time, any other victim, he would have listened intently for any morsel he could pick up and file away for later to help solve the case, for when he built his own case to move to the Robberies Unit once Fletcher's or Devine's time was up. But tonight's victim was Garrison, and Wesson PD—the neighboring jurisdiction—would be taking over anyway. He was just here to stand watch until Medical Examiner Winthorp arrived and pronounced Garrison dead at the scene.

"Fuck me." Breaker stood beside him. His eyes were bloodshot. "You all right?"

Hudson set his jaw, locking in a sob. He tried to nod. He was all right, considering he still had a pulse. "You call Noelle?"

"I was just leaving to go over there. Did you want to come?"

Hudson swallowed. He couldn't imagine showing up at Garrison's house, ringing the doorbell, seeing his wife and daughter's faces when Breaker delivered the news.

Breaker took his silence as a no. He set his hand on Hudson's shoulder. "You should go home. Tell Miserelli to come sit with you. This is Wesson's investigation anyway." He left, then, to inform Noelle Garrison she was now a widow.

Hudson's stomach twisted. He could taste the bile making a resurgence up his esophagus. His mouth began to salivate and a cold sheen of sweat beaded on his neck and forehead only to be instantly wicked away by the cold. His eyes drifted to Garrison. He almost didn't look real, like he was made of wax. His skin was too ashen, his blood too bright. Shaking, Hudson knelt to examine Garrison's trauma plate. His uniform was unzipped; he'd undoubtedly been reaching into his vest's center pocket to pay for his coffee when the shooter entered the store. One bullet had chipped his ID card; it looked like a hole punch had bitten the edge from it. He saw the photograph of Garrison's family; it was worn, the corners rounded. A piece of faded red paper peeked out from beneath it. It looked like a raffle ticket, the kind torn from a roll at bars and high school football games.

He checked to see if anyone had eyes on him. No one did. They were all searching for casings and latent prints. Hudson tugged the ticket from Garrison's pocket. Crouched, he examined it, shielding it in his hands like a flame. The bottom right corner was singed. On the front, the words AD-MIT ONE were stamped, and on the back, a message:

Welcome to The Ruins
Where your true self dwells

"The Ruins," he whispered. The place didn't ring a bell. He stood and was about to google it when another whoosh of cold air assaulted him.

"Christ." ME Winthorp appeared next to him. Her black earmuffs looked like giant bolts screwed into her skull. "Why'd it have to be him?" She knelt beside the body, pressed two latex fingers to Garrison's throat. "Deceased. You got the time, Officer?"

He was "Investigator" now, but Hudson didn't correct her. He touched the center button on his phone. "Eleven forty-seven."

"December nineteen, twenty-three forty-seven hours," she said into her recorder. "You know how much longer they got?"

He didn't remember answering. Time crashed into him hard as a wave and when he broke free, it was around 2:00 A.M. and Garrison was stiff with rigor mortis. He watched as three men from the coroner's office arrived and lifted him into a black polyethylene bag. The zipper's teeth connected as the bag swallowed Garrison, and he felt the ugly, finite sound of it, like a serrated knife ripping him from bottom to top, gutting him like a fish.

3
MORGAN

"Sorry for all the pomp and circumstance." Bennett's gaze rose over the edge of his cocktail glass to meet Morgan's as he sipped his Manhattan. The drink was a lurid color, like blood in the water. "You must think we're some real grade-A snobbery."

Morgan smiled down at the bar. She did think that. But, after spending the last six hours with the Reynolds clan, she'd decided that they were nice snobbery, at least. If anyone had thought less of her with her Target leggings and Honda Civic, they'd kept it to themselves or discussed it out of earshot. It was all a whir, from walking up the cobblestone drive to being here, now, at Beck's Bar with Clive Reynolds's youngest son, who, with his good bone structure, white teeth, and eyes the color of money, was what her mother would call "a fine piece of man candy."

Christmas lights draped from the liquor case, bathing everything in a hellish red glow. Or a festive glow, depending on how you looked at it.

"It was quite the party." Morgan envisioned downloading the photos onto her computer as soon as she got home, seeing all the bokeh and smiles, the details of the champagne flutes with silver filigree entwining the stems, the garland that sprawled down the staircase and the crystal chandeliers. How many had she counted—seven? "Even Santa showed up."

"Who you seemed to have cast quite the spell on, by the way."

"He gave me his business card." As she stood from the old man's lap, he'd reached into his robe and extracted a card on which his name and business address were embossed. *Christopher Reynolds. CEO—Exos Labs. 101 Research Park Way, Suite 201.* Morgan was vaguely familiar with the place. They made chemicals or something. She used to see it every time she drove from Chicago to Black Harbor, which wasn't often, but the glass tower and never-ending campus made quite an impression. "My team's been asking for updated headshots," explained Christopher. "If you're interested."

Morgan had closed her fist over the card and held it to her chest as though she'd been given a golden ticket. Headshots for a company of that size could mean thousands of dollars. She'd have to buy some decent lights and new studio equipment, but for that kind of money . . . she could sell a kidney to get by in the meantime.

"I saw," said Bennett. "He's my uncle, you know."

"I figured. Same last name and all." Morgan took a drink of her Moscow mule. The ginger and vodka sparred on her tongue—the ginger prickling her taste buds as though urging her to retreat, while the vodka dared her to keep doing what she was doing. So far, the vodka was winning out. Some might call it flirting—leaning toward him with her elbow on the bar, her knees so close to his that the space between them felt charged. She bumped him gently and watched the light in his eyes intensify. "Were you watching me all night, or what?" She knew Bennett had witnessed the business card transaction, but there had been other times throughout the evening when she felt the weight of his stare. If she was being honest with herself, there was something exciting about it. Having inherited his father's Hollywood good looks, his penchant for fast cars, and his money, Bennett Reynolds was Black Harbor's most eligible bachelor. Not that that was saying a whole lot. A Black Harbor ten was a two anywhere else, and yet, here he was with her. Why? What were any of the Reynoldses doing with her, for that matter? She was not beautiful, even by Black Harbor's abysmally low standards, and she had no status; her mother was unemployed, and her father was an operator for a factory that made garbage disposals. But under the bar, Bennett's knee brushed hers.

"Not *all* night," he replied. "There were twenty minutes or so when I had to manage a scavenger hunt."

He didn't play coy. She liked that. She leaned toward him some more, pushing her knee against his.

"So, what the hell are you doing here, Morgan Mori?"

"You made me come out for a drink with you, remember?"

He laughed. "I mean Black Harbor. You seem talented enough. Intelligent enough. Why waste yourself in this gutter?"

"I could ask you the same thing, Bennett Reynolds. What's a guy who's got the world by the balls doing in a Black Harbor dive bar with me?"

The skin by his eyes creased when he laughed. "You first."

Morgan sighed. What the hell was she doing in Black Harbor? She must have asked herself the same question a thousand times since dragging her feet off the steps of the Amtrak. "It's home." Her voice caught on the second word. *All roads lead back to home.* "I got out for a while." She talked about Black Harbor the way everyone who left and crawled back did, like she'd completed a prison sentence and come back for more. "I went to college in Chicago."

"For photography?"

"Sociology."

"Interesting."

"Why?"

He shrugged. "I would have thought you'd have majored in photography, that's all. Or art. Something . . . related."

Morgan smiled to herself. If only he knew how related they were, she thought, because if sociology was the study of humans functioning as a society, then photography was the study of humans functioning as individuals. It was the best way to study people. To see who they really were, what lurked underneath. They welcomed her into their homes, their lives, to make sense of their world through her lens. And what had she concluded after her exploration of the Reynoldses' estate? That they were, in fact, a normal family—as normal as being filthy rich allows—who simply happened to be enshrouded in morbid mystery? Or had she discovered something more, perhaps something sinister, in the realm of a suspicious look, or two unlikely confidants engaged in conversation. All would be revealed when she processed the photos.

She had to admit, she was fascinated by Carlisle and David, how they hugged the outskirts of the party, always together and apart from everyone else. She'd seen them hold hands, once, and when Carlisle noticed her staring, she'd simply stared back, daring Morgan to say something.

Bennett turned, the reflection of a red Christmas bulb gleaming in his pupil like a hot coal. "So, why sociology?"

Morgan shrugged. "Because it was interesting," she said, playing his own word back to him. "And it seemed lucrative at the time."

"But photography is more lucrative now? I mean, I get it. It's a tough job market out there. You gotta make money whenever and however you can."

Morgan chewed a piece of ice, felt the cold slipping down her throat. What could he know of the means she'd gone to to make money? She had been an avid photographer since high school, when she first picked up a film camera and developed the negatives herself. She could still remember the smell of the chemicals—the fixer and the stop bath—and the feeling of a moment long gone being resurrected before her eyes on a sheet of glossy paper. A moment that she'd captured, preserved, immortalized. It felt a little like playing God, and for a feeling like that, who wouldn't come back for more? She'd lost sight of it in recent years, or perhaps not. Perhaps it was the pursuit of that feeling that set her on course for her latest venture. The one that had burned to the ground. Luckily for Morgan, she found photography to be a little like riding a bike. Once you knew how to chase light and bend shadows, it wasn't something you readily forgot.

"Are you slamming my career choice, Mr. Reynolds?"

"Not at all. In fact, if it weren't for you picking up that camera, you and I never would have met. So, I'd say that, to date, you've made all the right choices."

"To date" was a strong phrase. Since her previous life had burned to the ground just a few months ago, she'd been trying to make the right choices. Help her parents. Drive her grandpa to the senior home twice a week. Swear less. Smile more. It was hard, particularly the swearing and smiling part.

"I'm trying," she admitted.

Bennett touched his glass to hers and downed the last of his drink. He ordered another round for both of them.

As much as losing everything sucked, a part of her felt that she'd been reborn in that fire. A phoenix risen from the ashes and given a key to a new life. She hadn't stuck around for the results of the investigation and knew only what she read online. The fire department determined the culprit to be a branding stove whose flames caught on a curtain or a piece of artwork. Morgan had shaken her head as she scrolled through the article on her phone. The branding stove had been kept in a corner, no less than six feet from the walls. There were no curtains; the windows were painted black. Which meant that either the fire department was wrong, or someone had crept in and made a spark.

"You know, you're different without it." Bennett's voice punctured her reverie.

"I'm sorry?"

"Your camera. Not to sound critical—"

"—but you're about to criticize me?"

He laughed, looking down at the bar. "Never mind. I shouldn't have said anything."

Morgan scooted closer, her knee bumping his again. "Now, you have to tell me."

Bennett sighed, leaned back. As he did so, Morgan's eyes busied themselves with tracing the definition under his sweater. Whose stupid idea was it to make cable-knit sweaters so thick?

"It's just, I don't know how you do it. All those people at the party, how you pose them and take command of the scene." He shrugged. "If I didn't know better, I'd say you were almost an extrovert."

Morgan snorted. The ginger beer burned the inside of her nose. She was a recluse. But she was a dead shot with a camera. And that was enough to make her fearless. "Only when I need to be," she said. "With photography, it's all about focus. There might be a million things going on at an event, but it's okay. You just have to focus on taking the best picture you can of one thing at a time. So, I guess that makes it seem less . . . daunting."

Bennett nodded. "Well, I'm impressed by you, is what I meant to say."

Morgan felt blood rush to her cheeks. It was time to shift the conversation. She'd told him enough about herself. "So, what are you doing in the gutter, Mr. Reynolds?"

He laughed. "I'm in PE."

The bartender slid two new drinks toward them on flimsy corkboard coasters. Some of Morgan's slopped out of the mug and onto the counter.

"You're a gym teacher?" she asked, struggling to peel her attention away from the spill. She should wipe it up, or if she had a straw, she could suck half of it up and deposit it on the other side of her coaster; then they would at least be symmetrical. But that would lead to questions. It would be easier to just eradicate the spill altogether. Her gaze found the bartender, a grungy towel tucked in his jeans pocket as he stood with his back turned to them, arms crossed and neck craned to stare up at the basketball game on TV.

"Private equity," Bennett translated. "I'm the CEO of Reynolds Capital, my dad's business. Our main office is in the Loop, down in Chicago, but I've got an investment property in the area."

"Which one?"

"You know the old Burcowicz's Furniture Store on Sixth Street?"

Morgan nodded. She knew the one. It had been vacant for years. She always thought it would be cool to wander inside and photograph all that abandoned furniture. Cobwebs on chandeliers. A blanket of dust on a tufted chaise lounge. "What's it gonna be, a bank?" she asked.

The reluctant smile that spread across his face told her she'd hit the nail on the head. "How'd you know?"

She took another sip of her drink. "Because that's the irony of Black Harbor. There's a bank every square mile despite the fact that no one has any money." She paused. "Well, present company excluded, I guess."

Bennett laughed and she felt his knee press into hers again.

She didn't lean away. "So, CEO, huh? You must have stepped in after . . ." She caught herself. Bennett would have only been about thirteen at the time of his father's disappearance. Too young to run a company.

Bennett didn't miss a beat. "Christopher. He took over the business for a good twelve years after my dad left. Then I graduated with my MBA . . ."

". . . assumed the throne . . ." Morgan filled in.

". . . and Christopher became president of our largest portfolio company."

"Exos Labs."

"That's right."

In Morgan's mind, a battle raged. She imagined the Reynoldses as pieces on a chessboard. Christopher and Bennett made strategic moves while Clive, the king, sat in the corner.

But what about David, the eldest of the Reynolds children? Had he not wanted the multimillion-dollar enterprise? Or Cora? She seemed a capable career woman, being a psychologist and all. And why not Carlisle? She was younger than Bennett, but she could have gotten her foot in the family business by now, if she wanted. Morgan didn't know a whole lot about chess, but what she did know was that if Clive was king, Eleanor was queen; and while the king might technically be the most important piece on the board, the queen was the most powerful.

She filed the information away for another time. Tonight, her sights were set only on Bennett. And that damn spill on the countertop. She wondered if she was too far away to lean over and "accidentally" wipe it up with her elbow. "So, what's work like?" The question was a distraction. She didn't really care about the ins and outs of private equity.

Bennett swirled his drink. "Sometimes I feel like I'm playing *Zoo Tycoon*. Remember that for PC? You gotta keep all the animals happy and the people happy and try not to lose all your money."

"You make it sound exciting."

"I don't know if *exciting* is how I would describe it. *Invigorating*, maybe? See, there's only one kind of deal for me: the one that's gonna win me big. Coincidentally, it's the same deal that could potentially knock me on my ass and demolish everything I've worked for. I don't look at anything less than that."

Morgan held back a smirk. What could he possibly know about being knocked on his ass? For him, rock bottom was still probably a high-rise apartment and a trust fund. "Ah, a go-big-or-go-home kinda guy," she said. How ironic that the two of them were sitting side by side. Noting the expensive wristwatch, the sweater that probably cost more than everything in her closet, and the Porsche he'd parked across the street, Bennett Reynolds had obviously gone big. And she—well—she'd gone home. "You don't mind the shitty reputation that comes with private equity?" she asked, even though she knew better. Reputations could be shed like snakeskin.

Her gaze returned to the spill. Reflections of Christmas bulbs glistened in it, taunting her. She felt her nails digging into the worn cushion of her stool.

"I make a fuck ton of money." He said it like it should impress her. Suddenly, she envisioned him and his team tearing the guts out of a business, a pack of hyenas ripping at a carcass. Scavengers. "People come to us because they want to either sell the business that's bleeding them dry, or they want to invest in something that's gonna make a huge comeback and increase their investment tenfold."

"You sell pipe dreams."

If he took offense to her statement, he didn't show it. "Someone's got to. If you concern yourself with what others think about you, you'll never get anywhere." The bearded bartender walked past then, and Bennett flagged him over. "You got a towel?"

The bartender tugged at the terry cloth in his back pocket. He nodded.

"You know how to use it?"

When the man looked confused, Bennett pointed to the spill on the bar top, inches from where Morgan rested her hand. With one swipe, he cleaned it up. Morgan avoided eye contact with him and exhaled a sigh of relief. Things were even again. She could breathe. "So, you like what you do? Taming the zoo."

He shrugged. "I get to live in a high-rise in the city and drive a fancy car. Not too many people who grew up in Black Harbor can say that."

Morgan shrank a little, suddenly self-conscious about her rust-mobile parked outside. "You'll go back to Chicago . . . after Christmas?" Today was the nineteenth. Anyone who was planning on leaving the city for the holidays would have dipped out earlier this week.

"After New Year's, actually. It's a whole . . . thing," he started to explain when he noted her raised brows. "My family has a cabin up north. We used to go up there a lot, but, well, when my dad died, we stopped for a long time. Just locked the place up and didn't return for years. In case you couldn't tell, this two-week stretch of the holidays is my mom's favorite time of the year. If coming home and shacking up in the guesthouse is all it takes to keep her happy, well." He raised his glass to his lips, took a drink.

"She really goes all out," observed Morgan. "The food, the decorations, the Santa . . ."

"Did you see the Clydesdales?"

"The Budweiser horses? Yeah," she said, remembering the two chestnut-colored animals hitched to a white wagon with a horseshoe painted on the side. They were giving sleigh rides just as she and Bennett left the party.

"Christopher's friend has a farm just on the other side of town. He parks his car there and drives the horses over every year."

Morgan nodded, her brain stuck on what Bennett had said just a moment ago, about his family abandoning the cabin after his father . . . "You think he's dead?" she asked.

"Pardon?"

"Sorry, I was just—" She hadn't meant to blurt it out, but Clive Reynolds was Black Harbor's most famous unsolved mystery. Curiosity mingled with the alcohol in her bloodstream, quelling her inhibitions. "Your dad. You said after he died . . ."

"Oh." The shadow that had fallen over Bennett's face lifted. He pressed his fingertip to the rim of his glass, slid it toward the edge of the counter like pushing a chess piece across the board. The cherry clung to the bottom. "He better be."

4

HUDSON

The hush that descended upon Hudson's entrance into roll call was so portentous, so profound, he felt as though he'd been swallowed by a wave. The phantom current that knocked the breath out of his lungs pulled him toward Garrison's empty chair. He sat in the one next to it.

No one looked at him. Second-shift patrol officers, investigators, and command staff sat with their heads bowed, hands clasped, staring at their shoes or sneaking glances at the Wesson PD detectives who stood solemnly in the back of the room. Hudson did the same until, finally, Chief Stromwell cleared his throat. At a towering six foot five and 250 pounds, the chief was as large as the sand dunes he used to mow over in Iraq. And yet up there at the podium, he looked small. The reality of the past fourteen hours had made ants of them all.

"The hunt is on, but not for us. Wesson PD will be taking over . . ."

Stromwell's voice became lost to the storm that tossed in Hudson's head. His ears rang. A bolt of pain threatened to split his skull. He'd popped two Excedrin around seven this morning when he woke to feed Pip and let her out, then passed out on the couch for another couple of hours, trying and failing to convince himself he was trapped in a lucid dream; that he'd wake to a text from Garrison asking if he wanted to shoot darts after work. How long had it been since they'd done that? Three months? Hudson had been newly promoted to detective at the time.

"It's going to be brutal." Stromwell's voice rose to the surface again.

"Most of you have never been through something like this. And I pray we'll never have to again. Lean on your fellow officers. Find a quiet place if you need a break." He paused. His eyes landed on everyone in the room. "I think it's fair to say that Brix Garrison was a friend to everyone. Some of us, he taught a great deal of what we know."

Hudson clenched his jaw. The pain in his head seared behind his eyes. He took a deep breath, felt someone's hand rest on his shoulder. It hurt too much to look and see who it was.

After dismissal, Hudson trudged upstairs to the Investigations Bureau. He hung his jacket on the rack near the door, by the stainless-steel bench with shackles chained to the concrete wall.

"Hello, May," he said on the walk over to his desk. They were the first words he'd spoken all day.

"Good afternoon, Investigator Hudson." May Peters, the bureau secretary, looked up from her reports, her eyes magnified behind her red horn-rimmed glasses. She regarded him in the same manner as the rest of his colleagues had so far—with a sad, pitying look. She opened her mouth to speak, but thought better of it.

Hudson sat. He didn't like the looks, but he understood them. He'd doled out one or two himself in his time. Like in high school when a classmate's brother had jumped from Forge Bridge. At the funeral, Hudson remembered the brother's eyes being sewn shut. His hands, folded across his chest, looked like rubber. Layers of makeup covered the bruising and the busted capillaries. Shattered bones floated beneath the skin. When his classmate caught his eye after the ceremony, Hudson had given him the same despondent look May was giving him now.

He powered up his computer and extracted the contents of his messenger bag: his phone, memo book, water bottle. He stared at the black memo book. Tucked like a bookmark between its pages was the faded red ticket he'd discovered in Garrison's trauma plate pocket.

The Ruins.

He checked to ensure no one was near him before typing it into the search engine. Investigator Riley was already entrenched in her work, just her seafoam-green headset visible over the top of her computer. Rowe was in the alcove by Interview Room #1, pouring a cup of coffee. Devine and

Fletcher were in the Robberies office with the door closed. McKinley and Liebowitz hadn't returned from roll call yet. Sergeant Kole's office was dark, but Hudson could hear his voice, just barely, as he conversed with the Deputy Chief of Investigations down the hall, across from Interview Room #3.

He clicked Search.

A horror movie by that title occupied the top searches. He kept scrolling, and on the second page, found a restaurant in Seattle. He paused. Some years ago, Garrison had taken his bike out to Washington. He could have stopped to eat in the Emerald City, he supposed.

Hudson clicked on the website. It looked like fine dining with white-linen-draped tables and crystal stemware. A place Garrison wouldn't have been caught dead in. Unless he'd been meeting someone.

Who, though? A woman?

No. Garrison wasn't the type. He'd loved Noelle more than he'd loved summer nights and riding his motorcycle into the sunset.

Despite the distance that had inevitably crept between them when Hudson went upstairs, he hoped that if Garrison had been having marital problems, he would have confided in him. But then, who was he to wish that? He'd kept his own secrets from Garrison.

May walked past his desk then, carrying a stack of reports hot off the printer. Hudson closed out of the window and brought up Onyx, the PD's operating software. It took every ounce of will he had left to log in to the portal and open his latest case. When he'd come up to the bureau four months ago, he'd been assigned to Sensitive Crimes. The bureau's least-coveted position, it was where most newly promoted investigators landed.

He hated it. Hated reading the horrible things that happened to children. Hated standing behind the glass at forensic interviews, hearing the lies their parents coached them to say. Hated the never-ending caseload and the feeling that he was drowning, like he couldn't catch his breath, ever. How did you begin to prioritize them? To decide one person's trauma was more pressing than another's? Who was he to make that decision? He thought of Investigator Meyer on first shift, who'd been working this assignment for the past eight years. He didn't know how she coped. How she didn't go to sleep every night hating the whole world. Maybe she did.

Taking a deep breath, Hudson prepared himself to click on the first attachment, when at the bottom of the screen, a message from Sergeant Kole popped up: *See me in my office, please.*

The command hit him like a jab between the eyes. Was he in trouble? Maybe someone had complained about him vomiting all over the crime scene last night.

He pushed his chair away from his desk and walked the ten feet to Kole's office. It was open.

"Come in."

"Sir." Hudson closed the door behind him. His eyes took a moment to adjust to the dim ambient lighting. Although he didn't know why Kole always kept his office so dark, it was a welcome reprieve for the migraine that persisted.

Kole gestured to the pair of leather chairs in front of his desk. Hudson took a seat, feeling like he'd just traveled back in time to when he was in junior high, sitting in the principal's office. No matter how hard he went out of his way to not look for trouble, trouble sometimes found him—the occasional fallout of having a brother like he did.

Kole leaned forward with his hands clasped in front of him. The face of his watch illuminated, showing the time: 2:32 P.M. He said nothing, and Hudson wondered if he was giving him the chance to speak first, to come clean about spewing his guts on the asphalt. Hudson's tongue felt glued to the roof of his mouth. Sweat beaded along his hairline and he knew Kole noticed. The man was a legend in the interview rooms. He could read people's thoughts like they were neon signs floating above their heads.

Finally, Kole's voice punctured the thick, uncomfortable silence. "How do you like Sensitive Crimes, Hudson? Be honest."

The question caught him off guard. "It's . . ." How did he put this? Terrible? Soul crushing? The worst job he'd ever had? "I like it, sir."

Kole side-eyed him. "Listen," he said, and Hudson tried not to cringe as he waited for the blow. He was getting demoted. It was back to Patrol for him, where he'd have to explain to everyone that he couldn't cut it in Investigations.

"A Crime Stopper's tip came in last night—well, early morning, I should say—about a suspicious vehicle parked at the beach. We called in the dive team from the county. They went down to the lake—"

Goose bumps erupted on Hudson's skin. Just thinking about divers plunging into Lake Michigan's frigid, murky depths was terrifying. "They found the gun?" he managed. According to the ballistics report and the shell casings located at the scene, they were looking for a .50-caliber Desert Eagle.

"No. But they did find this." Kole turned his computer so Hudson could see an image of a classic car with a shiny black finish.

Hudson squinted. "Porsche 930 Turbo," he read off the screen.

"1978," Kole added. "The Widowmaker. Which is accurate, considering."

A good year. Garrison's badge number had been 1978, and he'd talked about it as though it were a bottle of Bordeaux. He liked to list all the things that were great about those four digits in history. It was, for one, a year when Jimmy Carter was president, when gas was only sixty-three cents a gallon, and the movie *Close Encounters of the Third Kind* was playing in theaters.

"Considering what, sir?"

"Considering it was registered to Clive Reynolds, who, you might remember, disappeared twenty years ago. It was listed as stolen back in July 2000. Clive was last seen about two weeks later."

Hudson reached back in his memory for what he knew about Clive Reynolds. The media loved to dig him up from time to time, obsessed with the fact that the wealthiest man in the city had simply vanished without a trace. There were endless theories concerning his disappearance, everything from him leading a double life to his wife having murdered him and covered it up.

"I remember," said Hudson. "He's still missing. Unless . . ."

Kole dropped a blue folder onto the desk between them. Photos of the submerged vehicle spilled out. It was hardly recognizable from the image he'd pulled up online a moment ago. For one, the black paint looked all but stripped away, the car bleached skeleton white. The leather seats had been gnawed on by fish and whatever else lived in the lake's watery limbo. The windows were frosted. Barnacles stuck to the door handles.

A chill grabbed Hudson by the spine and wouldn't let go. He tore his eyes away from the photos. Ever since he was young, he'd harbored an intense fear of water, likely stemming from the time he nearly drowned.

Kole laid three more photos over the ones of the car. Hudson squinted, turned one of the photos by pinching its edge. It was hard to tell what he was looking at. It looked like a mess of clothes—coveralls and a heavy canvas jacket. Skeleton hands poked out of the sleeves. The next photo depicted the same thing from farther away, and Hudson could see that it was indeed a dead body in the passenger seat. The third photo was a close-up of the skull—eye sockets now caverns that little fish could swim through, jaw unhinged in an underwater scream.

"That can't be . . ." Hudson's words dissipated into a breath.

"Clive? No." Kole slid out one picture. "Besides the fact that Clive filed an insurance claim for his stolen vehicle ten days before his disappearance, what's this guy wearing?"

Hudson adjusted his glasses. "Looks like a Carhartt jacket, or something similar?"

Kole nodded. "Are those the clothes of an elite businessman, Hudson?"

"No, sir. I wouldn't think so."

"I wouldn't either." Kole pointed to the empty driver's seat, drawing a circle with his index finger.

"The seat belt's been cut," Hudson offered.

"Whoever drove this poor bastard into the lake almost ended up right alongside him." Kole paused, and then added: "The car's in the impound lot. We'll get a warrant written up and search it tomorrow."

"We?" Hudson licked his lips.

"In the English language, that typically means you and I. Unless we're speaking French, in which case, *oui*." Kole's light-colored eyes locked onto Hudson's. His voice softened when he said, "You know Garrison was the first officer on this case?"

"He was?" Hudson knit his brows. How had Garrison never mentioned it in their 23,000 hours of working together?

"Yep. And me. He was my field training officer. I was fresh out of the academy, only been in uniform a few weeks when Eleanor Reynolds called to report her husband missing."

"Nothing ever came of it?" Hudson asked.

"You know how it goes in Patrol. Garrison took the report but then had to hand it off to Investigations. Guy named Gauthreaux had it for a while. Never managed to close it, obviously."

Hudson was familiar with the name Gauthreaux. The former investigator was an urban legend at the PD, the eponym of the phrase "Gone like Gauthreaux"—what people said about someone who slipped away unnoticed and unannounced. It was essentially an Irish goodbye, and yet, the Gauthreaux component added a note of disquiet. It alluded to the idea that the departed person would never be heard from again, like Gauthreaux himself, who one day had been here working the Clive Reynolds case, and the next he'd cashed out. Took a hit to his pension. Got the hell out of Black Harbor.

"You know, we don't always get to start what we have to finish." Kole scooped up the photographs and slid them back into the folder. "I know you were at recess drinking a juice box when this happened, but I was here. Garrison was here. And the discovery of Clive's car might finally add some solvability to this case."

"You think he was in trouble?" Hudson asked, already working through the fact that Clive disappeared ten days after reporting his car stolen. "That maybe he ditched the car for insurance money?"

"Possibly. Or someone was trying to kill him and he escaped. We don't know that the body in the passenger seat is a victim. But if we can get a positive ID on him, we might just be able to track it back to Clive. I think we owe it to his family, Garrison, and all of Black Harbor to figure out what happened to him. Don't you think?"

Hudson swallowed. "Yes, sir."

"Good." Kole bent over and set the box atop the desk. From what Hudson could tell, it was full of reports, some typed and some handwritten. There had to be over a thousand pages sorted haphazardly into faded manila folders.

"I've notified Investigator Meyer of the situation. You'll want to find a time when you can fill her in on your current cases; she's gonna take them over."

Hudson couldn't help it. He sighed with relief. But then he looked at the box filled with two decades' worth of questions, and his heart sank. "Sir?"

"Yes, Detective."

"Why me?"

"Because if anyone was going to finish what Garrison started, he'd want it to be you. And because I'm saving you, Hudson. From yourself." He looked up, noting the consternation written all over Hudson's face. "Listen. I know you want to hunt down the guy who killed Garrison. There isn't a soul within these walls who doesn't. But we can't. Not only did Garrison work for this department, he was your friend. The second you get involved, you taint the whole investigation. I know it sucks, but we have to let Wesson PD handle it."

Hudson chewed the inside of his cheek. He knew Kole was right, and yet, what had Garrison been doing with that ticket? "This is a diversion, then."

Kole slid the box toward him so that a sliver of it hung off the edge of the desk. "Figure out what happened to Clive Reynolds, Hudson, and you'll never have to work a Sensitive Crimes case again."

5

MORGAN

There was an attraction between them. She was sure of that, and yet, Bennett Reynolds had not tried to kiss her when they'd said goodbye on the curb, their skin illuminated by a single streetlamp, shadows elongated and stretching into the street. Although now that she was removed from the situation, perhaps his lips had brushed the soft spot beneath her jaw when he'd hugged her. She pressed two fingers to her neck, as though feeling for a pulse. Her skin tingled in response to her icy fingertips.

Would she have let him kiss her, she wondered. If he'd leaned in and pressed his mouth to hers, would the alcohol in her blood have persuaded her to kiss him back? She could do—and had certainly done—much worse than Bennett Reynolds.

But those memories were behind her now. Overwritten like all the others.

Houses zipped by on the road that would lead her back to her parents. Aside from a wind-beaten wreath clinging to every other door and the occasional string of multicolored lights hanging from gutters, the residents of Black Harbor had put very little effort into their holiday decorations. Eleanor Reynolds had more Christmas spirit in her backyard than the entire city combined.

Morgan was buzzed; she definitely shouldn't have been driving.

Which was probably why she suddenly had the courage to turn left onto Winslow Street, a road she'd avoided for as long as she could remember.

Her brakes screeched as she slowed to a stop in front of a small, slanted house. It was missing more shingles than it had left, and in the moonlight, the siding glowed bone white. A rectangular window was situated on each side of a front door that was either swung inward or gone so the house looked like it was screaming. Morgan stared at the pitch black of the doorway, paralyzed with a fear she'd all but forgotten.

She kept the car running with her foot on the brake. That way, should Aunt Bern's ghost come hobbling down the broken steps, she'd slam her foot on the gas and peel away. Her eyes drifted, then, to the spot where Bern's blood had soaked into the concrete. It was covered by three feet of snow.

The numerals on the mailbox were so faded they were barely legible: 604 Winslow Street. This was where it had all begun, and where it had almost ended more times than she could count. This was home, where all roads apparently led back to.

The skin on her left wrist burned. She dug her thumbnail under her cuff to scratch, and had the unsettling feeling she was playing the hot or cold game. This was where the note wanted her to go. The key opened something inside. But what? Her aunt's bedroom? Morgan had never been allowed in. To the kitchen cabinets? Bern had kept them locked.

Suddenly, Morgan's eyes flicked to the rearview mirror, where a shadow moved in behind her, a black shape blocking out the glow of the Christmas lights. It crawled to a stop.

An alarm dinged. Morgan jumped out of her skin, and when she looked down, noticed the gas pump icon glowed orange.

How long had she been sitting here?

It was time to go, anyway. Whoever had pulled up behind her wasn't going anywhere. Maybe they lived around here. Maybe it was a cop. But a cop would have turned his lights on by now, yeah? Watching the shadow, Morgan let out a slow exhale as she lifted her foot off the brake and stepped on the gas pedal. Her nerves calmed as she reached the end of the street and nothing appeared in her rearview mirror. She glanced at her clock and—never one to fall back or spring forward for daylight savings—automatically added an hour to its time. It was 10:46. The Fast Mart was only a mile from here. She could get gas and be home by 11:00.

Morgan turned left into the lot of the Fast Mart and coasted to a stop next to the pump. She got out and slammed her door. Frowned. A handwritten sign taped to the left of the credit card insert read *PRE-PAY ONLY!!!*

Her breath plumed in front of her as she heaved an annoyed sigh. Of course it was prepay only. Every gas station in Black Harbor was prepay only. Too many drive-offs. People couldn't be trusted.

She looked around. Hers was the only car here. Across the street, parked in the lot of the old furniture store, was a police SUV. She hoped he stayed over there. She really didn't need a ticket for expired plates right now.

Hands jammed into her jacket pockets, Morgan marched inside. Snow and salt crystals crunched under her boots. Jingle bells clanged against the glass, signaling her entrance.

Shit. The cop was inside.

Her instincts told her to run. Logic, on the other hand, told her to act casual, pay for her gas, so she could fill her tank and head home. Her sugar addiction told her to check out the candy aisle.

"Hello." The cashier smiled.

"H—" Morgan tripped, her boot catching the corner of the industrial rug. A strong hand suddenly cuffed her arm, caught her from smacking her head on the newspaper stand.

"Whoa, you all right there?" The police officer's voice was a warm baritone.

Straightening up, Morgan nodded. Forced a smile. "Thanks."

Something popped in his eyes then. A starburst. A camera flash. A spark of recognition, maybe? She'd never seen him before in her life and yet, he stared at her as though she was the final piece to a puzzle. Her legs felt like they might give out beneath her again as her mind grappled with the urge to flee. She ripped her arm away, perhaps a little too aggressively, and started down the aisle.

His gaze never left her, though. She'd felt the weight of people's stares enough to know when a pair of eyes were boring into her back.

Let him watch, she told herself. He couldn't do anything to her here. She'd taken care to exact her revenge outside his jurisdiction. And it hadn't been revenge so much as it had been justice in its most poetic execution. She'd be more worried if she were in Chicago, but Black Harbor—this was her home turf. Unless, what was that word? Extradition?

Just be cool. She crouched in front of a row of candy bars. It had been ages since she'd bought one. She grabbed a Butterfinger and was about to stand back up when the bells clanged against the glass again. Winter rushed in as behind her and to her left, the door opened. Had the cop gone, she wondered. No. Still crouched but peering over the red wire fixtures, Morgan could see the top of his head as he stood by the coffee machine.

Then, a chemical odor ensnared her. It smelled like spray paint. Her muscles locked up. Morgan fell backward onto her butt, her boot knocking loose a row of candy bars. Peeking through a fringe of dark hair, she watched as a person's shoes came into view. They were black, but when he took a step toward the counter, she could see that the soles were red.

"Give me the money," the intruder demanded.

"Off—Officer Garrison," the cashier stammered.

"Police, drop the gun!" the cop shouted.

The silence that cloaked the store was so intense, a pin dropping would have sounded like a window breaking. The hairs on the back of her neck stood at attention. She held her breath, her gaze focused on the gun in the intruder's gloved hand.

She heard the paper cup fall to the floor. Coffee splashed. An eardrum-shattering explosion rocked the store. And another one. And three more in quick succession. *Pop! Pop! Pop pop pop!*

Foil bags exploded. Potato chips rained like shrapnel. In front of her, the cop's body crashed to the tile. She heard the sound of bones snapping, a skull cracking, and then a ringing so terrible she clapped her hands over her ears and screamed as she braced herself for the bullets that never came.

The world wavered. She couldn't tell how many seconds passed before she summoned the courage to look at the cop lying on the floor. She could see him from the shoulders up, the dark, wet patches on his uniform. A sucking wound in his neck looked like a second mouth gasping for oxygen. Blood erupted from it and bloomed on the tile.

She pulled her knees into her chest, felt the wire fixture dig into her back. Her throat was shredded, but she couldn't hear herself, couldn't hear anything over the ringing in her ears. The cop's head rolled toward her. Morgan gasped, seeing that the light in his warm brown eyes had gone out. His pupils and irises were black as coal. She stared in horror, then, as his lips formed his last three words: "I found you."

6

HUDSON

Blades of lamplight leaked in through the row of skinny rectangular windows. They cast pearlish-white bars over Garrison's body, washed him in a strange, ethereal glow. He didn't look real. Dead bodies never did. Seated in the hard metal chair next to the casket, Hudson had stopped waiting for Garrison to wake up, to swing his legs over the edge, and lean over to land a punch into his biceps. *Jesus, Hudson,* he'd say. *You weren't cryin' over me, were you?*

The imagined scenario made his breath hitch. Hudson took off his glasses, scrubbed the lenses with his tie as fresh teardrops fell and stained his pants. His blurred gaze caught the edge of the American flag that stood at the foot of the coffin. It rippled slightly, as though someone were behind it, breathing, but he knew better: it was only the current from the heating vent above.

He stood, his joints snapping and popping, and began to pace. He'd been at the funeral home since just after 10:00 P.M., when his shift ended in the bureau and he'd come to relieve the young patrolman who was guarding Garrison's body. Garrison had watched their backs for over thirty years. They owed it to him to watch his now, as he ventured somewhere they could not follow. Not yet.

Hudson paused and faced the casket, his hands clasped in front of him. "I should have been there." He finally said it out loud. His voice was rough. He hadn't spoken for hours, not since he'd met with Sergeant Kole the afternoon prior.

There could mean a number of places, from sitting in the passenger seat of Squad #23 as they cruised along the vacant streets of Area 1, to being present in roll call when Lieutenant Breaker agreed to let Garrison ride out the rest of his career alone. But Hudson knew which critical *there* was haunting him. It was the Fast Mart at Sixth and Lincoln, where Garrison had been shot. Twice in the chest. Once in the neck. Three bullets. Six holes.

"Red dreads." Those were the two words the witness muttered as she rocked back and forth against the candy rack when Devine took down her information. She said them over and over, like a record with a scratch. The description did more than jog Hudson's memory; it ignited it.

Over the course of the last year, the convenience store had fallen victim to multiple armed robberies. Garrison and Hudson had worked the case hard, sitting in the busted-up lot of the abandoned furniture store across the street, waiting, watching for patterns to indicate when the perpetrators might hit next. They had suspects. Hudson scrolled through the camera roll on his phone now, and held on a screenshot of two teenagers who'd posted a "haul" on social media, fanning themselves with dollar bills and feasting on Swedish Fish. They wore hiking boots and hoodies that were too big for them. The one with Ronald McDonald–red dreadlocks had a gun tucked into his waistband.

Kai Steele. He was a frequent flyer around the police department; a career juvenile delinquent now old enough to buy guns and alcohol and hookers. It was only a matter of time until he cracked his threshold of petty thievery. Hudson wasn't surprised he'd taken it to the next level. But, did Kai Steele have a tattoo on his neck according to the cashier's statement?

Hudson zoomed in on the photo. He didn't see a mark, but that didn't mean he hadn't gotten one since.

Garrison had been on a mission to put him away before retiring in March. He'd have turned fifty-three. Time to hang up the duty belt. "I know it's not the sexiest coup de grâce," he'd told Hudson a few weeks ago when they'd sat in Garrison's basement bar with a couple of brandy old-fashioneds. "But I want to finish what I started. Give José some peace of mind."

Hudson had known he'd been referring to José Guerrera, the owner of the Fast Mart. He owned a few other local stops in Black Harbor as well. "Until the next thug comes around," noted Hudson. He couldn't help it.

But Garrison just flashed his signature smile, the one that could have charmed the habit off a nun. A puerile glint shone in his eyes. Dark-haired with a salt-and-pepper stubble, he was a Black Harbor Idris Elba, albeit a little worse for wear. "I'll be long gone by then." He set his lowball glass on the corkboard coaster. "Me and the Mrs. will be enjoying some sex on the beach. And I don't just mean the drink, son."

Hudson had shuddered theatrically. Thinking about Garrison and No-elle rolling around in the sand was the equivalent of imagining his parents doing the same thing. If his parents had ever been together. His mom was around; she lived on the other side of town. But his dad had never been in the picture. Perhaps that was why he'd gravitated so naturally toward Brix Garrison, the veteran patrolman who'd taken him under his wing when Hudson had been a yearling, fresh out of the academy, his legs not solid beneath him yet.

"What will you do?" Hudson had asked. While the question seemed to have come out of nowhere, it had been swirling around in his brain for some time, ever since Garrison had announced his intent to retire. He knew a lot of retired law enforcement officers who worked as school resource officers or mall security. But the only mall within fifty miles of Black Harbor had just closed its doors. Regardless of what his plans were, Hudson knew better than to believe Garrison would spend his retirement actually retired.

Garrison leaned back so his forearms were straight, his palms pressing into the edge of the bar. "I think I'm gonna take the bike back out to Washington for a bit."

Hudson furrowed his brows. There could only have been one thing out west calling Garrison's name, or so he thought at the time. Hart's Pass. It was the treacherous stretch of road on which, three years prior, Garrison had eaten asphalt, not to mention totaled his Harley-Davidson. He'd been transported via helicopter to the nearest hospital, where he'd been treated for a concussion, broken tibia, cracked ribs, and severe road rash on his right side. Hudson doubted this plan had Mrs. Garrison's seal of approval.

"You know me and unfinished business." Garrison said it as though it were ample reasoning for a return trip.

"You go together like peanut butter and shoe polish," Hudson offered, completing one of Garrison's signature sentiments.

"That's right." He took a drink and then stared forward at the glass bottles that lined the counter. Hudson couldn't tell if he was trying to read a label or staring at their reflection in the mirror, or neither. The pause was unusually drawn out. "And after that, who knows, I might start my own business. Just a small thing."

"Like what?" Hudson considered Garrison's interests: motorcycles, practical jokes, craft cocktails . . . Was that it?

Garrison shrugged as though the idea were hardly more than a fleeting thought. "A PI."

Hudson coughed and sputtered, choking on his drink. "PI? As in private investigator? You despise PIs."

"Only when they get in my way. If I'm the PI . . . well, I can't hardly get in my own way, can I?"

Hudson eyed him suspiciously. "What's bringing this on? You got some *unfinished business* I don't know about?"

"Let's just say I have an offer." He fixed Hudson with a look that said to leave it at that. And they had. There had been no more talk of Garrison's PI venture. He'd been so silent on the subject in the days and weeks that ensued, in fact, that Hudson had wondered if he'd abandoned the idea. Until now.

A smudge of makeup stained Garrison's starched collar. His skin looked to be caked with the stuff—foundation, or whatever it was called. His lips were too plum-colored; it looked like he'd borrowed his daughter's lip gloss, while around his eyes, the greyness of death crept in. Hudson hoped they would touch up his makeup before the funeral on Wednesday.

Jesus, Garrison, he thought. *What did you get yourself into?*

At the far end of the hall, the doors opened. The winter air stole inside, and the parlor felt more tomb-like than it had even a minute ago, when it had been just him and Garrison's corpse. Miserelli handed him a coffee from the gas station up the street and assumed the stance of a patrol officer—feet planted shoulder-width apart, left hand resting on the face of her flashlight that stood upright in her duty belt. "It's decaf," she said when he lifted the paper cup to his mouth. He lowered it, though, when the smell nauseated him. It triggered a memory of Garrison's coffee, spilled on the Fast Mart's tiled floor. The warmth was welcome, though.

"Thanks."

"When was the last time you slept?" She had to tip her head back to look him in the eye. At five foot two, Miserelli was the personification of a firecracker: small, compact, and explosive. Some people joked that she'd stand taller and walk straighter if it weren't for the chip on her shoulder weighing her down. Hudson didn't necessarily disagree. Miserelli was perpetually out to prove herself, but then, it wasn't a bad quality for a cop to have. Especially when the men on the force outnumbered the women twenty to one.

"Ryan."

"Huh?"

"I said, when was the last time you slept?"

Hudson thought, but the fog in his mind prevented him from coming up with an answer. He couldn't remember beyond the other night when he'd gotten the call that Garrison had been shot. He'd been in his bed then, hadn't he?

"I can tell," Miserelli said as though he'd given her a response. "You should get a nap in before your shift this afternoon. You look like shit."

"Thanks." His gaze drifted to the clock that sat above the row of narrow windows. It was ten after six. If he went home now, he could get about seven hours of sleep before having to get ready for work again. That was, barring any disasters or breakthroughs with the case. So far, he'd heard no updates from Wesson PD.

"Any updates?" he asked. Miserelli had just come from roll call. Perhaps there'd been news to share.

She shook her head, stared blankly at Garrison. Her eyes appeared to land on the same smudge on his collar. "I haven't heard any."

The disappointment didn't sting. It scraped at his insides, made the hollowness inside him more vast. He raised the cup to his mouth again.

The coffee was already lukewarm. Nothing was ever insulated from Black Harbor's bitter cold. He'd be willing to bet the police department had more reports of pipes bursting than any other jurisdiction in the world. A crumbling, crescent-shaped city, Black Harbor was the punching bag of its sister, Lake Michigan, who butted right up against it. The winds she hurled carried freezing precipitation, careening over the bluffs and slamming into brick walls of houses and vacant businesses. There were no lengths you could go to get away from it, and every year, the lake swallowed up more and more of the city, packing cops, civilians, and criminals tighter together.

"Heard you got handed a big case."

Hudson winced. He didn't like the way she said it. *Got handed,* as though he hadn't earned the Reynolds case. Perhaps he was sensitive because it was true; he hadn't earned it. What had he done in his brief stint as investigator to deserve a shot at solving Black Harbor's most notorious cold case?

Nothing.

And what was he doing, currently, to unearth new leads?

Nothing.

But how could he start anything until Garrison was laid to rest?

Excuses.

"You know Devine's gonna be on your ass now, right?"

He sighed. He knew that. Devine had made it no secret that he deserved the Reynolds case more than anybody, and "certainly more than this clown," when Hudson had emerged from Sergeant Kole's office yesterday afternoon. Hudson had said nothing, just sat back down at his desk and started forwarding his Sensitive Crimes cases to Investigator Meyer. Devine kicked his chair on his way out of the bureau and threw his leather portfolio against the wall. Papers scattered in his wake, settled to the floor like snowflakes. When he'd returned sometime later, he reeked of cigarette smoke.

Now, Hudson's phone vibrated with a message from Sergeant Kole: *Getting the search warrant signed for the Porsche. See you at the impound lot at 1315 hrs.* But Hudson didn't want to be late.

He sighed and felt himself being tugged in two different directions. Kole pulling on one arm to solve the Clive Reynolds case, and Miserelli yanking on the other to find out who killed Garrison. How could his world have imploded so completely in the past day and a half?

He looked out the window. Frost climbed up the glass, the way it had Garrison's eyes last night. Silence fell over them like a weighted blanket. But there was nothing comforting about it. It was a silence that intended to crush them—deflate their lungs, pulverize their bones to particles more minuscule than the powder cocaine that littered the streets and back alleys. Hudson was suddenly so tired he could barely stand.

He grabbed his coat off the back of the metal chair. "I have to let Pip out."

Miserelli nodded. A spring of titian hair came loose from her low bun. "Go on. You know Garrison always preferred my company over yours anyway." A corner of her mouth twitched, creating the faintest arrow-shaped dimple. He tried and failed to smile back.

She took over then, guarding Garrison's body as he had done for the past eight hours. It wasn't until he'd made it down the hall, his fingers gripping the door handle, that Hudson heard a small whimper escape from her.

He sat in his SUV, waiting for the engine to warm up before driving the few miles home. He should have started it ten minutes ago, while he was still inside, but he knew better. Luxuries such as remote-starting your vehicle were not afforded to residents of Black Harbor. A running vehicle was an invitation; it might as well have a "Free" sign slapped on the windshield. Look at what had happened to the woman at the gas station. The perp had driven off with her car. It was long gone by now, dumped somewhere across state lines and burned to a crisp, probably. But maybe not. If they found it, the case would become a lot more solvable.

Hudson unlocked his phone and studied the picture of Kai Steele again. The red dreadlocks behind the money fan. The gun in his waistband had a black grip, but he couldn't identify it beyond that. Not that it mattered. This wasn't his case.

And yet, he knew that if he was the one in the casket, Garrison would be on a manhunt right now. Slowly, his windshield began to thaw. He watched as the fractals of frost cleared away, white, wraithlike fingers receding. Perhaps it wasn't a manhunt at all, he thought, but a hunt for the woman who had witnessed everything.

7

MORGAN

Morgan shivered. Water droplets clung to her skin before evaporating. She wrapped a frayed towel around herself. She would never be warm again. Not after last night. Witnessing the murder of that cop, and the words he'd whispered to her in his final seconds, had left her chilled to the bone.

This was her third shower since finally arriving home at 1:00 A.M. A Black Harbor investigator had dropped her off after he'd taken her statement. He was fortysomething, she'd guessed, with brown hair and a five-o'clock shadow, and shorter than her. He said his name was Devine, or something like that. She sat in the back seat of his unmarked vehicle, behind the cage, while he followed the GPS coordinates to her address. It wasn't her first time in the back seat of a cop car. She remembered being eight years old, wrapped in a fleece blanket and hugging her Bart Simpson doll as two middle-aged investigators muttered things like "Jesus Christ," and "Goddamn house of horrors." That was when she'd learned that the back of cop cars wasn't just for criminals, but victims, too.

"Victim." She hated that word. Even "survivor" was starting to have a sour taste. Why not "endurer" or "outlaster"? She was more than a victim, wasn't she? And yet, she'd seen Investigator Devine mark her with a *V* on his paperwork last night. Technically, she supposed she was a victim. After all, the suspect had driven off in her car.

She wiped the steam off the mirror. The woman who stared back looked as though she hadn't slept for days. Purple half-moons cupped her eyes. Her skin was wan and snow white. Her mouth was open, just a little, as though she'd been frozen mid-speak, the words caught in her throat. A row of bottom teeth peeked from behind her bluish lip. They looked like piano keys.

Victim. An ugly word for an ugly person. *V* was for "vulnerable." It made her feel small and weak, which perhaps she was, but did it need to be broadcast to the world?

But *V* was for "villain," too. And she had been that, hadn't she? While she'd whiled away in Chicago in a little place called The Ruins. Yes, she'd had something of her own, once. Before it burned to the ground and the only possession she had to her name was a blackened key and a note.

My Ruin: All roads lead back to home.

Well, she was home now, standing naked in her parents' unfinished basement bathroom. Exposed two-by-fours stood behind her like prison bars, tufts of pink insulation stapled between them. Her eyes grazed the sink that had become her makeshift vanity, littered with her makeup: eyeliner, mascara, and a palette of red eye shadow swatches. She picked up a tube of concealer and dabbed it on her skin.

A message from Bennett Reynolds floated on her phone's steamed-up screen. She read the preview without opening it. *We should do that again sometime, Morgan Mori.*

It was just after 1:00 P.M. now, almost twenty-four hours since she'd stood on the Reynoldses' back porch. So much had happened since then. She was now carless, cameraless, and soon to be penniless when she returned his cash. *So you don't have to claim it on taxes, right,* he'd said as he'd given her the envelope of hundreds. Her stomach twisted into knots as the dread of explaining to the Reynolds family they would have no Christmas party photos settled in, and she wished, for the hundredth time, that she had never stopped at that gas station. That she had never gone out with Bennett. That she had driven directly home and not gone to the house on Winslow Street.

But alas, curiosity killed the cat. Or in this case, the cop.

I found you.

He'd spent his last words on her. And yet, she was certain she'd never seen him. Could he have remembered her from years ago, when she was a skittish eight-year-old girl with matted hair and bruises on her skin? Or had he been tracking her dastardly deeds at The Ruins?

Morgan finished her makeup, taking care to ensure perfect symmetry on the right and left halves of her face. Then, she left the bathroom and padded her way across the main area of the basement where she spent most of her time these days. It wasn't her childhood bedroom. That space belonged to Grandpa Teddy now. But she had pushed an old mattress up to an even older couch and had a comfortable enough area to sleep and watch TV. Her Bart Simpson doll lay on her pillow. Stained and faded to a shade of muted yellow, the white paint on his eyes scratched and all but flaked away, he looked—and smelled—like a stale french fry. She'd had him for as long as she could remember. Aside from the scars and nightmares, he was the only thing from her childhood that followed her everywhere she went.

She tossed her damp towel on the bed and grabbed the pair of black leggings and oversized T-shirt she'd crawled out of earlier. Her socks were thick, machine-spun wool—the kind only worn at cabins and in clammy basements. She put a sweatshirt on over it all and looked like a homeless person. Which, for all intents and purposes, she was.

Her parents let her stay, rent-free, as long as she drove Grandpa Teddy to the senior center twice a week for games and socialization. That was easy enough, especially because he'd stopped going about a month ago, when he'd ordered Morgan to pull into the beach parking lot. They'd just sat there in silence, watching the tide slam against half-sunk piers. Seagulls pecked at the salt. Black plastic bags occasionally wandered by, like tumbleweeds rolling through a tundra. The lighthouse, on its distant rocky perch, looked like a middle finger. They never spoke, just stared out the windshield at the darkening sky until the clock read 4:30 and he said, "Okay."

Now on Sundays and Wednesdays, Morgan didn't even plan on going to Silver Maple Assisted Living anymore. She knew she'd be driving straight to the beach. They'd have to take Grandpa's car today, since hers had been ditched God knows where. Along with her phone and all her gear.

The cops said they'd call her when it turned up. They'd said "when," not "if," as though the reemergence of her Civic was inevitable. Regardless of whether or not her vehicle came back into her life, her camera was long gone. She knew that for a fact, as she imagined her gear bag being rifled through like a fresh carcass being gutted by zombies. One hand would take her 70–200mm lens, another would snatch her 50mm. The camera body itself would be passed around. Someone would grab her flash, the 600EX II-RT she'd paid five hundred dollars for brand-new, and it would all be pawned. Except for the lithium-ion batteries—they would crack those open like oysters and drink the acid. Maybe the cops would recover her SD cards months or even years from now, lying on the table of a drug dealer's house, being used to cut cocaine.

She didn't have insurance on any of it. That would have been the responsible adult thing to do. She'd pay the consequences for that now, though. It would take at least five more jobs like the Reynolds party to recoup her equipment. Five more jobs for which she would need—and not have—her camera.

The envelope from Bennett lay on her computer desk. She had to return it.

Morgan sat on the edge of the mattress, her shoulders slumped under the weight of everything. How was she going to tell her mother she couldn't help with groceries this week? Or pay her portion of the phone bill this month? She couldn't bear to think about the moment when her mom would inevitably check the Nestlé tin and discover it to be empty. Although her parents had graciously refused her offer to pay rent, Morgan, after shooting family photographs, stuffed a few hundred dollars into the Nestlé chocolate-chip tin the night before she knew her mom was going to make cookies. No one ever mentioned the money, but it was gone the next day when Morgan checked, and so always, on the last Friday of every month, she refilled it. She knew her mother had come to rely on that income more than she would be proud to admit.

Morgan cradled her head in her hands. The scene from last night played on a relentless loop in her mind—another image that would haunt her every time she closed her eyes. She saw the cop's body buck with the impact of the first bullet. He'd danced, almost, his toes frantically tapping the tile as he'd fought to regain his footing. The fingers of his left hand were curled around the grip of his gun. His right hand reached toward her, grasping only empty air. And then the rest of the bullets had slammed into him and the surrounding area.

Pop!

Pop!

Pop!

Pop!

The clamor rang in her ears even now. She pictured him lying on the dirty floor, the spark of warmth in his eyes fading as something like terror took over.

No. Recognition.

I found you.

Goose bumps stippled her flesh. She felt compelled to crawl under the covers, drift out of consciousness with some Ambien and a few mouthfuls of the Absolut she stowed between the couch cushions. She crawled across the mattress and felt for the remote, when from upstairs, the muffled sound of knocking at the front door startled her. She heard her mom's hurried footsteps across the kitchen floor, and twenty seconds later, her voice calling down to her: "Mor-gan! A policeman is here to see you!"

Her fingers squeezed the corner of her pillow. Fuck. Found her indeed.

8

HUDSON

Hudson knew what she was thinking. That the man standing on her front porch didn't look like a cop. He was used to the reaction. The raised brow that nearly always preceded an assessment of his person and the conclusion: Too skinny. Too nerdy. Too meek to be a cop. Now that he no longer wore a uniform, more often than not when he arrived at a scene, he was mistaken for the medical examiner.

He peered beyond Mrs. Mori's head, her greying flyaway hairs that shot out like wisps, to look down the shallow, dark entryway. Framed photographs adorned the walls. A basket overflowing with laundry sat on the floor. The sounds of a daytime game show issued from the other room.

"Come in, please." Mrs. Mori stepped aside.

"Oh. Thank you." Hudson stepped up and over the threshold as a thin, dark-haired woman appeared. She looked like a ghost, pale as moonlight. A pair of clear-framed glasses occupied most of her face, encircled her jade-green eyes. He studied her, noting the silver hoop in her septum and the studs in her bottom lip. Water dripped from the ends of her hair that was chopped into a severe bob. Seeing her standing in a dim hallway, drowning in a black sweatshirt that would have been too large even for him, he recognized her as the witness from the Fast Mart.

She crept toward him as though he were a dog that might bite.

"Hello, Morgan," he said softly. It was the same tone he took with children, when he would sit down and build a rapport with them before the forensic interview. Sometimes the children spoke with him, told him about their day. Other times, they picked at their fingernails or just stared behind him, as though someone else were in the room. It always made him feel uncomfortable, like he was Bruce Willis in *The Sixth Sense*. Morgan was doing that to him, now.

She said nothing, just waited for him to explain himself. For someone so small and bird-boned, she was intimidating. Hudson bet she could play this silent game all day, but he had work to get back to. It was only a ten-minute drive to the impound lot from here, but Kole would have a signed warrant for the Porsche soon.

Finally, Mrs. Mori spoke. "I'm Lynette," she said.

"Ryan." He shook her hand and corrected himself. "Er—Investigator Hudson. I was wondering if I could speak to your daughter about the incident that took place at the Fast Mart last night."

"Oh." She brought her hand up over her mouth. "How awful. I'm sorry you lost someone from your department."

Hudson cleared his throat. His mouth twitched to smile a silent thanks. Mrs. Mori was sweet. If only she knew how much more Garrison had been than simply someone in his department, but the sentiment was appreciated all the same. Not everyone felt that way. He'd taken to avoiding social media and hoped that Garrison's wife and daughter had as well. For all the comments of sympathy and blue heart emojis, there were just as many *Fuck 12*s and *Smells like bacon*s. His blood simmered just thinking about them.

"I'd like to ask Morgan a few more questions about what she saw," he said.

Morgan's eyes darted to her mother. It was the most alive she'd looked since she'd materialized. "I have to take Grandpa."

"It's okay."

"This won't take long," Hudson promised. "I'm actually in the middle of another investigation. You were on my way, so I thought . . ." *Thought what,* he asked himself. *Thought I'd stop by and interrogate you?* "Is there somewhere we can talk?"

Hudson eyed Morgan slumped in the passenger seat of his car. She'd refused to grab a jacket, so she sat, now, wrapped in an afghan she'd snagged from the living room, feet shoved into unlaced combat boots. He turned the dial on the heat. "Sorry, the seat warmer's broken."

"Did you find my camera?" she asked.

He wished he had a better answer for her. "No. Sorry."

Nevertheless, it seemed to be the answer she'd expected. Her fingers tugged at the wavy edge of the blanket. Her maroon nail polish was chipped. "I have to drive my grandpa to the senior home in ten minutes."

He nodded. He'd heard her the first time. They were parked at a slant, on the slab of concrete that separated the Moris' modest ranch-style home from the road. Icicle lights dangled from the gutter. The wreath on the front door had seen better days. The light grey siding made the house blend in with the colorless sky.

"I guess you'd better get cracking then," suggested Morgan.

Hudson met the challenge in her eyes. "Red dreads," he said.

She twisted in her seat; the small movement of her torso revealed she wasn't wearing a bra.

"Those words mean anything to you, Morgan?" he pressed when she said nothing. "You talked to Investigator Devine, at the scene—"

"So why isn't he in my driveway?"

"He's tied up . . . with something else at the moment."

"You mean with a case that's actually in your jurisdiction? Because he said the Wesson PD guys were handling it. Shouldn't I be talking to one of them right now?" Her voice had gained an edge, a knife kissing a whetstone. She was aiming to unnerve him. And yet, her fingers kneaded the folds of the afghan.

Hudson felt heat rise in his cheeks. He had to admit, her knowledge of that surprised him.

But it shouldn't have. Garrison's death was currently the most covered story on just about every local media channel. The buzz would die down soon. They needed answers before it did. Before whoever killed him slipped back into the shadows. Before Garrison's death became another unsolved mystery in a stack of unsolved mysteries.

"You don't know anything about red dreads?" he said after a moment.

She fingered the vents then, turning the dials so they were all just so, an even amount of space between each blind. "Sorry to disappoint."

"Officer Garrison didn't say anything to you, give off any indication that he knew his attacker?"

"No." She said it quickly. Dismissively. A lie already queued up?

Hudson decided to change course. "It was after eleven."

"Don't worry, it wasn't a school night."

"Are you normally out that late?"

Morgan sighed. "I'm thirty-one years old, Detective. My parents don't enforce a curfew, if that's what you're asking."

"What were you doing before then?"

"Shooting an event, like I told the other guy. Thus the camera I no longer have." She tossed her arms up as though to demonstrate how empty-handed she was.

"Where?"

"On the lake."

"Where on the lake?"

"What's that got to do with anything?"

"Morgan, you're the one on a time crunch, not me." He hoped she didn't call his bluff. He should be on his way to the impound lot right now. "Where were you on the lake?"

She leaned forward to hug her knees. "At the Reynolds estate. They asked me to shoot their Christmas party."

Reynolds. The name caught him like a hook to the chin, though he tried not to show it. "You worked pretty late." If he kept tossing threads out, maybe she would pull on one and unravel a bit, he hoped. "The Fast Mart isn't exactly on your route home from the Reynolds residence. In fact, it's like six miles out of your way. You couldn't go the next day?"

"Look at you, throwin' down rhymes. And here I thought you was s'posed to be solving crimes."

"I never said I was a poet."

"At least you know it."

"Miss Mori."

She rolled her eyes. "I was out of gas. Almost. It's not good to let your car sit on empty in this cold, you know. It'll freeze your fuel lines."

"I do know that. But thank you." He tried to think of how Sergeant Kole might handle this conversation. How he might get her to talk. He tugged another thread. "Were you alone? You know, that isn't the safest part of town for a woman—"

"Whoa, sexist much? I can handle myself."

Hudson studied her, this fragile thing buried in a knit blanket. A child wearing boots too big for her feet. Piercings to make her look tough, untouchable. But she was scared; he could sense it. It was in the way she never looked at him. The way she chewed her nails, bounced her leg. She kept staring straight ahead, as though if she didn't acknowledge his existence, he would simply go away.

He wondered if that ever worked for her.

"I'm sorry. I didn't mean—"

"I have to go." He heard her pull on the door handle. Bitter air blew in.

"Wait!" The plea came out more forceful than he'd meant for it to. He hadn't realized he'd shot his arm out and had her by the elbow. The door closed softly, didn't connect with the frame.

She raised an eyebrow and Hudson realized he'd been better off before when she'd avoided looking directly at him. Her irises were the shade of sea glass, but her pupils were infinitely dark, like the hollow of a tree. Her stare froze him from the inside out. He let her go. "I'm sorry. It's just—"

"I don't see how me shooting an event at the Reynolds place has anything to do with . . ." She paused, a question suddenly entering her mind. "What's your deal? Don't cops die all the time?"

The verbal slap made Hudson flinch. "Yes and no." In Black Harbor, criminals outnumbered cops twenty to one; and yet, the police department hadn't suffered a line of duty death since 1985. This was uncharted territory for everyone. "He was my best friend," he said after a breath.

Morgan bit the inside of her cheek. "I have to take my grandpa." She pushed the door open again.

"Sixty-two thousand dollars," he blurted.

Morgan paused. She sat so still and it was suddenly so quiet, he half expected her head to spin completely around, the rest of her body facing away. But she just looked so her chin was parallel with her shoulder. She had a pretty profile, perfect as a doll's. "What?"

"The reward for information leading to the arrest of Garrison's killer is at sixty-two thousand dollars—and climbing. It's yours if you can help me identify the man who shot him." He pulled up the photo of Kai Steele on his phone and held it in front of her.

"Why don't you just claim it?" she wondered.

"Cops are exempt. It's our job to solve crimes." Except not this one. He was way beyond his parameters here. He hoped she didn't notice the beat of his pulse quickening in his neck.

Her fingers grazed his as she took the phone. She was cold, like a corpse. But there was a buzz of electricity beneath her skin. He felt charged as he watched her study the screen. Her eyes shook as she scanned the details of the photograph. Finally, after a moment of deafening silence, she handed it back to him. "I said treads, not dreads." She opened the car door and stepped out. "The soles of his shoes were red."

9

MORGAN

Waves tumbled and crashed against the crags. Sharp silhouettes against the horizon. Teeth jutting upward, spearing the clouds' underbellies. Her grandfather's Oldsmobile groaned in the wind. Morgan stared at the windshield as she had twenty minutes ago in Investigator Hudson's vehicle, tripping over the tumult of thoughts that raced and roiled in her mind, no different from the waves she watched now.

From the corner of her eye, she stole a glimpse of Grandpa Teddy. He sat as stoic as a bent old man can, hands lightly clasped between his knees, looking out at the lighthouse. A charcoal tweed fedora rested on his head, perched atop bristles of white hair that matched his whiskers.

He'd been quiet since Grandma Daisy passed away, hardly speaking more than three words at a time. She wondered, fleetingly, what it was like to miss someone so much, to love them so deeply that when they died, you lost the will to talk. Did she ever want to love someone like that? Was it really worth the pain? Choosing to love someone was a fifty-fifty gamble. You bet on dying first so you wouldn't have to bear the agony of the other's absence. Grandpa Teddy had lost the bet.

"What'd he ask you?" His gravelly voice startled her.

"Huh?"

"Detective."

Morgan couldn't remember the last time he'd said something directly to her. In fact, she couldn't remember the last time she'd heard him speak at all. Their coexistence under the same roof was narrated with the occasional nod, a slight pressing of the lips, and passing the mashed potatoes at dinner. Which was fine with her, by all counts. There was something about simply being able to sit quietly with someone and not feeling pressured to speak. She supposed he felt the same way, which was why he preferred to sit out here on the lakefront with her instead of going to Silver Maple where he'd be forced to play cribbage and make small talk.

"Um . . . he just . . . wanted to know what I saw last night."

Grandpa Teddy nodded but didn't look her way. Morgan side-eyed his profile. He used to be a boxer, back in the day. His neck was corded with ropey veins that now lay dormant but for a subtle, almost imperceptible twitch here and there beneath his crepey skin. His nose had always reminded her of Italy, with a strong dorsal hump from having been busted so many times. His eyes were foggy, like the vastness that enveloped the Oldsmobile.

"Did you tell him?"

Morgan nodded. "I already gave a statement last night, but yeah. I told him the guy had red-soled shoes. He wore a mask. Black gloves." Despite the heat blowing at her from the vent, her blood chilled.

She'd been honest with Investigator Hudson about what she'd seen. Or thought she'd seen. Although, she'd omitted the part about having been with Bennett Reynolds earlier. But what would that possibly have to do with the officer's death? Bennett Reynolds, of all people, did not need to rob a gas station for a few hundred bucks.

A black plastic bag rolled by, catching on the pillar of a rusted water fountain. She watched as the wind picked it up and tossed it toward the snow-covered beach. As her eyes followed the bag, her mind drifted back to twenty minutes ago when she'd gotten into a police vehicle and willingly walked away. How many times had she imagined the opposite? Being driven to an institution—a jail, a mental facility—where she'd be searched and hosed down and pumped full of nullifying substances. But, she'd walked free. And that was something. Perhaps, in some strange way, the pieces of her ruined life were falling into place to create a better mosaic. Maybe that was why she'd suggested talking in his car—to prove she could do it. Or, because she knew it was best to keep him at arm's length. Hudson didn't fit the bill for a cop any more than she did for an innocent photographer. He was a misfit, like her, and damn if she didn't automatically like him a little for it.

But he was still a cop.

"Watermelon jollies," said Grandpa Teddy.

Morgan turned, wondering if the statement was his dementia kicking in. "What?"

His eyes followed the same empty bag as it twirled and pitched. "Daisy. She smelled like watermelon jollies."

Morgan smiled, remembering the crinkled yellow wrappers often strewn about her grandparents' house when she was young. He was right. Her grandmother's purse, even, smelled like artificial watermelon. After she quit smoking in the late '90s, she sucked on hard candies instead. Her favorite was watermelon-flavored Jolly Ranchers.

"They say the thing you remember most about someone is their scent," said Grandpa Teddy. "And it's true. If I catch even the slightest whiff of anything watermelon . . ."

Morgan dared a glance at him. His eyes were teary. She knew if she mentioned it, he would blame it on the warm air blowing out of the vent.

"I'm glad you're okay, Morgan," he said, and she felt her own eyes burn. A teardrop raced down her cheek. She discreetly wiped it away with her sleeve. She nodded. *Thanks* was what she wanted to say, but her tongue felt glued to the roof of her mouth.

Just like it had Saturday night, when she recalled the clang of the bells against the glass.

The rush of frigid air and the sound of his footsteps on the tile. She remembered the nausea that gripped her; could taste, again, the bile rising in her throat, feel her stomach lurching in response to the smell that he'd brought in with him.

"Spray paint," she whispered.

"Pardon?"

"He smelled like spray paint," she said, a little louder this time. "The perp at the gas station."

"You sure? Not gasoline?"

Morgan shook her head, perhaps a bit too fervently. To an untrained olfactory, the scents of gasoline and aerosol might smell similar. But to her, the discrepancy was as stark as real sugar cookies and an artificially scented wax candle. "Aerosol," she said again. "Spray paint. It was tacky, too. Like it hadn't dried all that long ago."

Now that she said it out loud, Morgan knew all of those things to be true. Suddenly, she was transported back to the convenience store floor, crouched in the candy aisle, waiting for the nausea to pass, listening to his shoes stick to the tile.

The red treads. She remembered them more vividly now. Their imperfect edges. The smudges of black they left in their wake. "He spray-painted his shoes," she said.

Grandpa Teddy made a noise deep in his throat. His eyebrows scrunched toward the middle of his forehead. "Why would someone do a thing like that?"

Morgan shrugged, though she'd watched enough *Dateline* and *America's Most Wanted* to know that criminals covered recognizable features on their clothing all the time. "Could have been covering up a logo," she offered. "Or maybe the shoes were too distinctive."

Grandpa Teddy wet his lips. He drew in a breath as he looked to the lighthouse again. Finally, for the first time since they'd been sitting here, he turned to Morgan. "Sounds like you've got something else to tell that detective now, huh?"

Morgan sighed. She could feel Hudson's business card burning a hole in her jacket pocket, and she allowed herself a moment to fantasize. A reward for $62,000 was a lot of money. If this information led to the arrest of the cop killer, she could travel, actually get out of Black Harbor, not just a ninety-minute drive across state lines. Maybe she'd fly to another country, another continent. Leave her past behind. Live anonymously.

Unless it was all just a ruse to get her to talk. Whatever the fine print was, Morgan doubted she would meet all its requirements. She never measured up to what people expected. Although, she had nothing more to lose at this point. She exchanged looks with Grandpa Teddy, the quiet acknowledging smile they'd grown accustomed to. At the very least, she might get her camera and her car back.

10

HUDSON

The Porsche was hardly recognizable from the photos kept in Clive Reynolds's file. That car had been sleek and jet black. It *looked* fast with its streamlined silhouette and whale tail spoiler. *This* thing looked like something that had been dug out of its watery grave. The once fire engine–red interior was faded to the color of the Ruins ticket, and its headlights were opaque. Patches of verdigris sprawled across its hood. Through the open driver's side window, Hudson noted the severed seat belt and the empty passenger seat. The human remains had been transported to the medical examiner's office.

"It's like online dating, right?" said Kole. "The pictures and the real thing don't have a lot in common."

Hudson smiled and allowed himself a momentary time-out from the investigation to wonder how much experience Sergeant Kole had with online dating. Everyone knew he had been involved with a transcriber a few years ago, who no longer worked at the PD. The relationship had only surfaced because it was entangled in an officer-involved shooting and the downfall of one of Black Harbor's most notorious drug dealers, the Candy Man. It seemed uncharacteristic of Kole to have a relationship under the microscope like that. He was reserved and sure of himself. No, Hudson decided. He would not have an online dating profile.

"Has the body been ID'd yet?" he asked, knowing the answer. It was just an attempt to get the ball rolling, to show that he had been focused on this investigation rather than concerning himself with the mystery of who killed Brix Garrison. *Red treads, red treads.* The words ran on a loop in his mind ever since they'd left Morgan's lips.

"Not yet. Winthorp's got the bones at her office. Last I heard, she submitted a request for dental records."

Hudson nodded. Identification through dental records could take six to eight weeks, maybe longer. It was possible they could get authorization to push it along quicker, but not unless something came along to make the case more urgent. A word that never applied to cold cases. However, it was clear they were dealing with more than a disappearance; the mystery of Clive Reynolds's fate involved at least one homicide. Nevertheless, the homicide was twenty years old. He knew what the state's perspective would be: that the identity of the drowned man in the car had waited two decades. It could wait another two months.

"You see that, don't you?"

Hudson looked to where Kole was pointing. He wore black latex gloves; they both did. The bitter December air seeped in at the wrists and got trapped. His hands felt like blocks of ice. He bent and peered through the driver's side window to see inside the cramped interior. The back seat was so small, it looked like it could only fit a fridge pack of soda, possibly a child lying across it. And this was not a vehicle for children, as Kole mentioned when he first introduced Hudson to the dive team's photos. Built to accelerate to sixty miles per hour within five seconds, the Porsche 930 Turbo had a nasty habit of killing its owners, earning the moniker the Widowmaker.

But the back seat wasn't what Kole wanted him to see. It was the rusted rod with a bulbous head that lay across it. Hudson sized it up. It was too short to be a golf club. "Torque wrench?" he guessed.

Kole looked mildly impressed. "Didn't peg you for a car guy."

"I'm not, but I've watched a few *How It's Made* episodes in my time."

"Good show. What's funny, is—well, it's not funny," Kole said as he took his phone out of his coat pocket, "was that the passenger's right eye socket was busted. Winthorp sent me this."

Hudson glanced at the image on Kole's phone. It was a picture of a skull set on a white cloth. A hand held a ruler next to the broken orbital bone. No, it wasn't just broken, it was gone. Apparently, it had been pulverized so severely that pieces had torn away and floated to the bottom of the lake.

"He was dead before impact."

"Or close to it," Kole acknowledged.

Hudson stepped back to broaden his depth of field. "The driver's side window. It was rolled down."

"Or smashed out completely."

He approached the car again and reached inside the square opening. His right hand found the window crank. It was stuck at first; immobilized by water and two decades of debris. But with a little elbow grease, the crank turned and a panel of glass slid upward.

Glad for the brief exertion that thawed him, if only slightly, Hudson looked at the severed seat belt again. Threads hung loose from it. Turning on his phone's flashlight, he scanned the floor for a jackknife or something that could have cut the restraint. But he didn't see anything. If a knife had been used, it could have fallen to the lake bed or the person who escaped could still have it in their possession. Doubtful, but not impossible.

"You think they're alive?" Hudson posed to the universe.

Kole tipped his chin in the direction of the driver's seat. "It's possible. They made it out of a drowned vehicle. Leave it to Black Harbor, though, for them to catch a stray bullet in the throat or something." He stopped abruptly, apparently realizing the picture he'd just painted. Garrison had caught a bullet in the throat. Two more in the vest.

Hudson focused on the open window again. Whoever had driven the Porsche into the lake had known enough to wait until the vehicle was fully submerged to roll it down. He'd have to measure it, but the opening looked large enough for a grown man to crawl through. He grabbed the door handle. His gloved hand stuck to the stainless steel. It felt like he was touching a bar of dry ice. The hinges groaned as he pulled the door toward him. On the other side now, Hudson thrust his arms through the open window. The frame dug into his shoulders, but he managed to get his torso completely out.

He heard shoes crunching on snow and looked up to see Kole wielding his phone. "Say 'Cheese.'"

It was something Garrison would have done. Hudson rolled his eyes, but couldn't help smiling, just a little.

"That's going up at your retirement party."

"If I make it that far." Hudson bit his lip, concentrating. "I figure if I'm roughly Clive Reynolds's size and can wriggle my way out . . ." Carefully, he backed out of the opening and stood next to Kole again.

Kole was nodding. "You're dead on, almost. What are you, six three, six four? A buck eighty?"

"Something like that."

"That's how Winthorp ruled out Clive being Joe Blow in the passenger seat," said Kole. "The femur's too short. That guy, we're looking at five eight, five nine. Husky boy."

Hudson felt color rise in his cheeks. Kole was testing him. He'd seen the email from the medical examiner's office, but he hadn't had a chance to review it. Correction: He *had,* but he'd chosen to spend his time prodding Morgan Mori about an incident entirely unrelated to this one.

Or was it?

Morgan had been at the Reynolds estate the same night Garrison had been shot by a man with red-soled shoes—who could be anyone from Kai Steele to a random thief who'd heard through the grapevine that the Fast Mart was easy money. And yet, the urge to tell Kole about Garrison's side business as a PI gnawed at him.

Let's just say I have an offer.

As he'd come to learn within the past twenty-four hours, Garrison had been the first officer to connect with Eleanor Reynolds regarding the case of her missing husband. Could he have picked the investigation back up, all these years later?

"Clive Reynolds filed a claim on his car missing in July 2000," he said, thinking out loud. "And he disappeared ten days later."

"Yes," said Kole. He shoved his hands in his pockets, braced himself against the wind that suddenly rolled through the impound lot. "You insinuating that Clive dumped the car himself? For the insurance money? After he bashed some poor bastard with a tire iron?"

Hudson exhaled. A puff of fog hung in the air for a second, suspended. "Stranger things have happened, no?"

"This is Black Harbor. You know what we call it when strange shit happens around here? Tuesday."

Hudson laughed, dug the toe of his shoe into the snow. He looked into the car again and frowned. "The victim was wearing a canvas jacket. I wonder what Clive Reynolds was doing with a guy like that. Doesn't seem his type."

"Blue-collar, you mean?"

"Yeah." His mind flipped through the mental Rolodex he kept of Clive. Family photos, newspaper clippings, magazine articles. He was always wearing a suit, or at the very least, business casual, such as when he went to car shows or the golf course.

"That's a *you problem* to figure out." Kole clapped him on the shoulder. He waved to the community service officer in the little outbuilding, signaling his departure.

The weight of Kole's hand translated to the weight of the case pressing down on him. The first step in identifying the driver was identifying the victim. Because if he identified the victim, he might be able to answer the question of why someone would drive a $40,000 Porsche into the lake.

In 1978, when the vehicle would have been purchased new, $40,000 was a lot more money than it was today. Remembering his college economics class, he knew that the U.S. historically experienced an average inflation rate hovering between 3 and 4 percent, and it was higher back then, closer to 8 percent. That meant that in 2000 when the car had been dumped, it had a buying power of over $100,000. And today, he was looking at what would have been a $160,000 collector's car rusting away in an impound lot.

Hudson had work to do. And it started by diving into that box of records on his coffee table.

Kole was walking back to his Impala.

"Wait," Hudson called.

The sergeant turned. Another gust of wind tore through the lot, blowing Kole's blond hair across his forehead. This was how cops got weathered, Hudson realized. Standing in the harsh elements, investigating drowned cars in below-freezing temps.

"Where would you start?" he asked. "Without the dental records."

"I wouldn't."

Hudson furrowed his brows.

"I'd wait. And listen."

Hudson winced as the wind bit into him. He wanted to ask what Kole meant, but for fear of giving off the impression he didn't know what he was doing, he kept silent.

"I'll have Atchison release it to the media. Set up a tip line. There's no sense keeping it quiet anymore. This thing's been an anchor for the past twenty years. God only knows what other secrets have been stuck down there with it."

Hudson nodded. Sergeant Atchison was the department's public information officer.

"Then, I think we should send the dive team back down there to search for Clive Reynolds's remains and the knife that was used to cut the seat belt. Who knows, you could have two mysteries wrapped up with a pretty little bow before Christmas."

Hudson's breath hitched with excitement, until he realized that Kole was referring to solving Clive's disappearance and the identity of the victim in the passenger seat, not Garrison. He couldn't help it. "Or three," he suggested.

Kole paused. "What are you talking about?"

Hudson swallowed. He'd gone and done it. His hand shook as he handed Kole his phone, a tremor that could be chalked up to the cold. But Kole would know better. He stared at the image from Hudson's camera roll: the screenshot from Kai Steele's social media. Even though Morgan had clarified "red treads" instead of "dreads," it didn't rule him out as a suspect.

"Ah yeah, this SOB," Kole muttered. "Let me guess. You think he robbed the Fast Mart and killed Garrison."

Hudson shrugged. "It's possible."

"A lot of shit's possible, Hudson. What isn't, though, is you working this case." There it was, the cool edge he'd expected. "You can text me that pic if you want and I'll forward it to Wesson PD. But no more. I put my ass on the line for you to have a chance at solving *this* case, the Clive Reynolds case." Steam puffed from his nose. He gave Hudson his phone back. "Don't fuck it up. For either of us."

Hudson wet his lips. They were chapped, cracked. A subtle tinge of blood hit his tongue. "You're right. Sorry, sir."

"Don't be sorry. Just be focused." He tipped his chin toward the drowned Porsche, then turned and walked toward his Impala. Hudson listened as he slammed the door, started the engine. His tires crunched on packed-down snow as he ambled out of the impound lot and onto the street.

The walk back to his own vehicle felt arduous. He'd thought handing off the picture would make him feel lighter, but it had the opposite effect. It felt as though he'd given up something that didn't belong to him, taken the solving of it from Garrison and given it to someone from Wesson PD who might never complete the case. Unfinished business. Garrison would be rolling in his casket.

Behind the wheel with the engine on, he gave his car a minute to warm up. He ripped the latex gloves off and threw them on the passenger seat. His fingers were almost too frozen to grip his phone when he took it out of his pocket again and pressed the Home button. A new email message popped up from Morgan Mori.

Can we talk? Off the record.

11

MORGAN

Investigator Hudson wasn't one of those renegade cops like you read about in books or see on TV, she thought as she'd crawled into bed last night. He was the type no one gave a shit about, the type who followed rules, who dotted his i's and crossed all his t's. She'd emailed him yesterday to meet, but he didn't get off work until 10:00 P.M. As if that were a reasonable response. What kind of guy had an opportunity for information regarding his best friend's murder, and then asked the informant to save it for the morning?

But, at least he knew what "off the record" meant; he'd asked her to come over to his place, not the police department. Perhaps he had a rebellious bone in his body after all. It might only be his pinkie bone, but still.

Morgan popped an Ambien into her mouth and washed it down with a swig of vodka. Tucking the bottle back in the couch cushions, she aimed the remote at the TV, powering it up for another night of *The Simpsons* reruns. The news was on. A police officer with steely hair spoke into a mic held by a reporter just out of view of the camera. A bar at the bottom of the screen read SGT. ATCHISON, BHPD.

"*. . . recovered at the bottom of Lake Michigan,*" he said. "*We have reason to believe it's been down there since July 2000. If anyone has information regarding Clive Reynolds's 1978 Porsche 930 Turbo and/or the human remains located inside, please call our tip line.*"

"*Thank you, Sergeant Atchison.*" The camera shifted to the reporter, a petite woman in a red wool coat who posed a stark contrast against the grim, colorless backdrop of the police department. Snowflakes fell and melted in her hair. *"For viewers just tuning in"*—Morgan felt called out—*"the vehicle of Clive Reynolds, former CEO of Reynolds Capital who has been missing since July 2000, was located in Lake Michigan when the sheriff's department dive team was searching for the gun that shot Officer Garrison of the Black Harbor Police Department."* The screen changed to show a portrait of Officer Garrison dressed in his patrol uniform, in front of the American flag. Morgan's insides turned to ice. Her hand had gripped the remote so tightly the plastic groaned as she remembered his empty eyes and the spark of recognition that had lit in them, remembered the soundless words his lips had formed. *I found you.* She remembered the blood that had pooled around him, then reaching toward her like crimson fingers, and she'd recoiled with her back up against the candy shelves, paralyzed by fear and straight-up *what-the-fuckery.*

The news continued with Morgan hardly paying attention, until another image appeared on the screen. It was a mug shot, showing a man in an orange jumpsuit. She expected to see the man with the red dreads that Hudson had shown her earlier, but this guy was older. His grin revealed one silver eyetooth, and his head was shaved close to the scalp. On his neck was a tattoo of a geometric snowflake.

"Since opening the tip line this afternoon," said the reporter, *"police have identified one person of interest in the shooting of Officer Garrison. Tobias Shannon, also known as 'Hades,' previously incarcerated for delivery of cocaine and armed robbery, has been connected to several homicides in the city, but never convicted. Multiple tipsters have confirmed they saw Shannon walking away from the area of the Fast Mart on Sixth and Lincoln shortly after shots were fired. Anyone with information regarding where Shannon might be staying is encouraged to come forward so police may question him regarding his whereabouts that night. All tipsters will remain anonymous . . ."*

The Ambien had taken effect. Morgan closed her eyes, the image of Tobias Shannon's tattoo blinking like an optical illusion.

Morgan approached the stoop and rolled her eyes as her gaze landed on the iron nameplate above the entrance: HUDSON HOUSE. Not only was he a nerd posing as a cop, he was a pretentious nerd posing as a cop.

She stood on his doorstep now, her hands balled into fists and shoved in her armpits. Unlike Hudson, who had waited at her parents' front door some twenty hours prior, she didn't look like she'd just exited the stage of *The Book of Mormon*. She wore black tights that had a run down one leg, combat boots with scuffed toes, and an oversized black sweater she'd repurposed as a dress. Her beanie was red, though. How festive. After all, Christmas was just three days away.

Damn. He'd mentioned he lived close to the police department, but close was an understatement. If it weren't for the pothole-ridden street cutting between them, his house would be in the department's front yard. In the corner adjacent from City Hall, she observed the black-and-white SUV parked on the snow-covered lawn. The blue marker on the signs for Officer Garrison had all but washed away. Deflated balloons flopped on their strings like fish that had been yanked out of the water.

She pressed the doorbell and took half a step back. That's when she noticed the keyhole. Morgan sucked in a breath. A house this old might have a lock that fits a skeleton key. Rolling up her baggy sleeve, she finagled hers from her leather cuff, inserted it, and turned.

Nothing.

She pulled it out a notch, jiggled it.

Still, nothing.

At the sound of footsteps coming from inside, she concealed the key in her fist. Hudson opened the door. "Good morning, Miss Mori."

It was 9:00 A.M., too early for formalities or niceties. Nevertheless, Morgan invited herself inside. She was met immediately by a small cinnamon-colored puff.

"Pip, let Morgan in."

The yippy dog bounced backward, nails clacking on the hardwood floor. Morgan knelt to pet it as the door shut behind her. The kitchen smelled like toast and something sweet. Jam or honey, maybe? The white walls had a bluish tint to them, like hoarfrost or a duck egg. On the far side of the room was an alcove with a built-in table. The chairs might have been rescued after fifty years of chilling in someone's attic—metal frames, leather mustard-colored cushions. A ceramic butter dish with a peacock painted on its side sat in the middle of the table, next to a plate with crumbs and a swipe of strawberry jam. She narrowed her eyes at Hudson. She would have pegged him as more of an avocado toast guy.

"You find my camera?" she said. "Or my car?"

Hudson scratched the back of his neck. She'd unnerved him in his own home. She liked that. "Unfortunately, not yet. We've got an ATL on it and we're combing the database for any cameras that match yours showing up at pawn shops in the area. No word so far, though."

Morgan clenched her jaw. The news was what she'd expected, but it was still a kick in the teeth. Tears brimmed in her eyes and she told herself it was from the wind a moment ago when she'd stood outside. She wiped one away, silently swearing at the fact that she probably smeared her eyeliner. *Shit.*

"I wouldn't give up hope," said Hudson. "It's only been—"

"Almost forty-eight hours. Isn't that the cutoff?"

"Not always. Sometimes articles turn up months later."

Months. She couldn't go months without work. And her camera was more than an article. That camera was her life, her livelihood. It was the only way she could make money. Without it, she was fucked, destined to keep leeching off her parents, who could already hardly afford to live. Destined to stay here, in Black Harbor, forever. She sighed. "Well, he couldn't have gotten too far. I practically coasted on fumes to the pump."

The slight but visible quirk of Hudson's brow told her this was new information to him. "You hadn't filled up yet?"

She shook her head. "Had to pay inside first."

Hudson was quiet as he digested this new morsel of information. Morgan watched his eyes move behind his glasses, the stark light from the kitchen windows reflected in his lenses. He looked like a robot, processing lines of code. The sound of her setting her purse on the countertop snapped him out of his trance. "Can I get you something to drink? Coffee, water?" he asked.

"Peppermint mocha, extra whip." When his mouth twitched in a nervous smile, she added, "Kidding. Coffee's fine."

He didn't have any brewed. Which was surprising. She thought all cops drank coffee. Coffee and donuts, wasn't that the shtick? By the looks of his thin frame, Hudson didn't look like he put down too many pastries.

Or maybe he was a smoker with a high metabolism. His house didn't smell like a smoker's house, though. Having lived with Bern, she was all too familiar with the way the tobacco infiltrated the fabric of everything, coated it in sticky grime so the place appeared to be under some vintage film filter.

He brought the empty decanter to the sink and began to fill it. Morgan seized the opportunity to peruse his house, which, by the way, didn't look like it belonged to him at all. A floral blanket sprawled over the back of the couch and decorative plates hung on the walls. A glass mosaic lamp was perched on an end table, and there was a corner cabinet displaying ceramic peacock figurines.

"You like peacocks," she stated.

She heard a click as he set the coffeepot to brew. "Nan did. She grew up on a peacock farm."

"Is she dead?"

She saw him blanch but wasn't sorry for it. What was the point of beating around the bush? He'd been the one to use past tense, after all. "Yeah. She died two years ago."

"From what?"

She watched his jaw tighten. "Accident."

"Sorry," Morgan offered. "My grandma died last year. Now my grandpa lives with us. He's totally lost. He's got dementia and . . ." She shrugged. Why was she telling him this? There was something about him. He was like her. Adrift.

"The grandpa you take to the senior home on Sundays." There was something about his tone, relief, perhaps, at steering the conversation away from his life and back to hers.

"And Wednesdays. He's the one who convinced me to come talk to you, actually."

"I owe him a thanks, then." Hudson poured her coffee in a mug. She noticed he didn't prepare one for himself. "You take cream?"

"How much you got?"

He smiled like she'd made a joke, but went to the fridge and extracted a carton of heavy cream.

"Sugar?" Morgan asked, her gaze skipping over the countertops, searching for a sugar canister like her mom had.

Hudson opened a cabinet and took out a glass sugar shaker with a silver top. She took it and began to pour, watching the crystals dissolve like snowflakes on asphalt.

"Would you like to sit?" he asked. "We don't have to stand in the kitchen."

Morgan let him lead the way into the living room. The hardwood floor creaked beneath her feet, protesting her presence. Loneliness was an entity in this house, and it was used to having Hudson all to itself.

"This is an old house," she said.

Two main pieces of furniture—a couch and a love seat—were arranged in an *L*. Hudson walked over to the love seat. He waited for her to sit on the couch before sitting down himself. "Built in 1889," he offered. "You should see the basement. It's a dungeon. Dirt floor, no windows."

"You film horror movies down there or what?" Morgan clutched her cup. It was too hot to drink.

"No, but I could probably lease it out if there were any promising filmmakers in the area. You know any?"

Uncrossing her legs, Morgan gathered up some of her sweater and used it as a makeshift coffee collar, showing off the tops of her thighs. "I'll let you know if I come across anyone. Everyone thinks they're either a photographer or filmmaker these days. You could have a sweet side hustle." She watched Hudson avert his eyes from her legs; his cheeks colored. And then just as she hoped, his gaze slid back for one more look.

She seized the opportunity to study him, too. A fleeting thought caught her by surprise: She would like to photograph him. Just as he was, his profile illuminated by the cold light streaming in through the window. Her eyes traced the imperfect slope of his nose, the indent between his lips, the curve of his chin. It was moments like this when the reality of her stolen camera hit hardest. When she noticed something gorgeous in this grotesque world and couldn't capture it.

The TV was on, barely audible. Obnoxious yellow and red shapes flashed on-screen, advertising a going-out-of-business sale. Pip hopped up on the cushion next to her and curled on a pillow. There were loose papers and manila file folders stacked on the coffee table. She squinted. They could be police reports. "You take your work home with you?" she asked.

Hudson looked a little guilty. "Sometimes."

"You need a hobby, Detective."

"Got any recommendations?"

"We could start a book club." The word "we" surprised her. Had she used that pronoun before, ever? Why, then, had she just used it with him?

"Let me guess. The first rule of book club is we don't talk about book club," said Hudson.

Morgan smiled—a real teeth-showing smile—and stared down at her coffee. "Exactly. That could be our first book, I guess."

Hudson laughed quietly to himself, the precursor to a story. "When I was in college, my roommate worked at the campus dining hall. Every night, he'd have me send in an order under the name Tyler Durden. And every night—surprise—Tyler Durden never came to pick it up."

"So . . . he got to take it home?"

Hudson nodded. "I ate a lot of shitty pizza that year."

"I still eat a lot of shitty pizza," Morgan admitted, and felt a tiny shift in the cosmos. It was the first time she'd sat with a cop and not been questioned. For the first time, maybe, she could let herself believe that he was here to help her, or even just get to know her. Not hunt her down or mount her on his wall like a trophy.

Maybe.

She stared at the table. At the uneven stacks of paper. Her fingers itched to cut the decks, make them even. But it might mess up his work. She took in a deep breath and settled for picking at her cuticles.

"Do you read?"

The question shook her. She felt like an eight ball as her thoughts rattled and ricocheted. She used to read. A lot. She'd spend whole days immersed in stories and characters' lives. Because characters didn't judge her for how she dressed or whether or not her facial expressions showed an appropriate amount of emotion; they just let her be a silent observer. But real life was different. People weren't characters. There was no linear narrative, no central plot. Everyone just slogged through life trying not to get murdered or hit by a bus.

"No," she said after a moment of awkward silence. Not books anyway. She read people.

He raised a brow, but not in judgment. "Kinda tough to have a book club then."

Morgan shrugged. "Don't people just drink wine and gossip at those anyway?"

"I wouldn't know." The quiet began to settle again, disturbing the once perfectly frozen particles in the air. Morgan could see the conversation withering before her eyes. He wasn't a trained interrogator, she knew that. It was part of why she'd agreed to sit with him in his car yesterday. She'd wanted to see what he was all about. What lay beneath the badge and the button-down shirt, the practiced composure. His lack of confidence bled from his pores like ink.

"Do you?" she asked, commanding the equilibrium to stay put. Pulling on threads as he'd done with her. "Read, I mean."

"I do." He looked a little sheepish, and she caught a glimpse of who he might have been in his college days, eating pizza his friend brought home from work. She didn't figure he'd changed much in those—what—ten years? How much nerdier and devoid of self-esteem could he have been?

"I mean, other than these." Coffee cup in hand, she pointed at the stacks of reports. She didn't look directly at them. The asymmetry was driving her crazy.

Hudson laughed. "I used to. When I was on patrol. Some nights, Black Harbor was a ghost town." He paused, furrowed his brows. "Less than a ghost town. Ghosts are smart enough to leave."

"Unless they have unfinished business," said Morgan. "Then they're stuck here forever."

Something about that statement struck him. He looked as though someone had just turned a screw in his back. All around them, Morgan felt the air particles shake. The sphere that had been protecting them from the outside world shattered, like the windows of the Fast Mart. She heard a car alarm blaring. The wind slamming into the brick, like the Big Bad Wolf insistent on blowing Hudson's house down. Voices shouted at one another in the street, the soundtrack of Black Harbor.

"You, uh . . ." Hudson folded his hands in the space between his knees. "You wanted to talk off the record?"

Haven't we been, she wanted to say, but she swallowed her sarcasm. "He spray-painted his shoes," she said.

"Pardon?"

"The guy who shot your friend and stole my shit. His shoes were red, but he spray-painted them black."

Hudson leaned forward. "How do you know?"

"Because I could smell it. It was fresh. And I could hear it." Yes, it was coming back to her now. The sounds of shoes sticking to the floor.

"Red treads." He repeated her own words, the ones she now remembered saying over and over again as she'd rocked against the candy rack. *Red treads, red treads.* Hudson worked his jaw, as though literally chewing on this new information. "He could have paint on his hands. Under his nails . . ." He paused, and then: "Can I ask you something?"

Morgan lowered her cup, licked the sugar off her lip. "Shoot." She flinched, too late to catch her poor choice of word.

"What happened?" Hudson asked. "That night. When the suspect came in."

Morgan stared at him, tilted her head like a bird. Was he being serious? "Um . . ."

"I know. I mean, I know what ultimately happened," said Hudson. "But . . . order of events. The suspect came in and . . . held up the cashier?"

Morgan thought back to two nights ago. Hadn't she given her statement to the other investigator at the scene? Devine, was that his name? Apparently, he and Hudson didn't talk. "Yeah, he came in. He said something about money and . . . shot Officer Garrison." Her words fell to a whisper. "But he didn't take anything."

Hudson leaned a little toward her. "He didn't . . . what?"

"Take anything." She remembered it clearly now. The suspect had entered the store, all dressed in black. She'd heard the jingle bells clang against the glass door. The cashier called for Officer Garrison. And then five shots. The skull-splitting sound of bullets boomeranging off concrete walls. And then the ringing silence.

When she looked at Hudson again, she could almost see the gears turning behind his eyes. "It's weird. The suspect came in, asked for money or something, but then he didn't even take any."

"He just shot Garrison?" said Hudson.

She swallowed. Tears welled in her eyes as the memory of that moment came rushing back to her. Garrison bucking with the impact of the bullets. She couldn't look at Hudson anymore. She turned toward the TV. The news had come back on, showing an excavator dredging a rusted vehicle out of the lake. Clive Reynolds's photo appeared on the screen.

"Turn it up," she said.

". . . suspect the vehicle to have been down there since July of 2000," said the reporter, "possibly only days before the car's owner, Clive Reynolds, went missing."

Clive's photo filled the screen. He wore a suit and tie, arms crossed, smiling like a man on top of his world. A cold phantom hand gripped Morgan's spine and wouldn't let go. Her gaze flicked to the papers on Hudson's coffee table. Clive's name was all over them. She saw the photos of the drowned car, too. It looked like a tick, all turgid and white. There were bank statements and other boring white paper documents; glossy, grainy photographs; handwritten letters . . .

"No wonder you were so interested in me having been at the Reynolds residence." Morgan fixed her eyes on him and tried to hide the disappointment she felt, in herself, mostly, for trusting him.

"It's just . . . a connection I can't ignore," confessed Hudson. "Look, the county's dive team found Clive Reynolds's car when they were searching for the gun that shot Garrison."

"So, what do you think is my connection?"

"I don't know." The way he said it sounded honest, not dismissive. His eyes roamed her like she was a book. What kind of book was she? Horror? Psychological thriller? Whatever genre, she'd have a fucked-up beginning, middle, and end. But what was this? A little black book sat near the stack of reports, a faded red ticket stuck between its pages. The words ADMIT ONE stared at her in bold caps, and she knew the scripted font that would be on the other side.

"... *and for Eleanor Reynolds, the reopening of this case could either be the final turn of the key—or a cleared name. I'm Jada Taylor, and this is Channel 6* ..."

"Morgan."

His voice sounded like he was underwater. Her coffee cup crashed to the floor, shattered on the hardwood, splinters of ceramic bone. She was gone before he could hurt her.

Or before she could hurt him.

12

HUDSON

December 23 and it was raining. Raining. Hudson looked out the spattered window. On the other side of it, everything was blurry like a Monet painting. The interior of the Impala smelled like leather and three different kinds of cologne. The only woman in the car was Riley, who rode shotgun. Hudson sat in the back with Devine. Kole drove.

They'd met at the police department, all sworn and civilian personnel. He didn't know where the black umbrellas came from, but suddenly the parking lot was filled with them. He imagined from a drone's perspective they would have looked like a swarm of beetles, their backs slick and glistening. When he stood near the other investigators, Hudson was glad when Miserelli appeared by his side. Dressed in full uniform and eight-point cap, she held on to his arm and they stared stoically at Garrison's memorial. The signs were soaked. Blue and black ink ran together. The balloons were all deflated, the flowers sodden and encrusted in ice.

It was all in the rearview mirror, now.

No one spoke as Kole drove through the storm-darkened city. They passed the laundromat where the owner stood at the edge of the parking lot with his hat over his heart. In a residential area, people waved from their porches and wept. At the Fast Mart, the owner, José Guerrera, stood by the pump with a sign that said, *Ofc. Garrison—A True Hero*. Hudson's eyes burned and a chill grabbed hold of his spine. Bile surged up his throat as his gaze caught the air compressor where he'd vomited after first seeing

Garrison's body. Jesus, it hadn't even been a week ago. In some ways it felt like it had been forever, and in others, the wound was still fresh and searing. In the front seat, Riley stuffed her knuckles into her mouth to stifle a sob.

The tension in the Impala was thicker than concrete. Hudson knew it had to have something to do with his assignment of the Clive Reynolds case. Every chance he got, from telling everyone who would listen to knocking papers off Hudson's desk, Devine made it clear that the high-profile case rightfully belonged to him. Hudson was a rookie who wasn't cut out for detective work, and Devine was dead set on proving it.

And for perhaps the first time in his life, Hudson realized he was dead set on making sure Devine failed.

After Morgan had bolted from his house like a bat out of hell yesterday, Hudson scoured the contents of his coffee table, searching for what had caused her reaction. Rifling through the stacks of reports and Clive's old bank statements, he discovered his first potential break in the case. Perhaps it wasn't so much a break, though, as it was a new rabbit hole to explore: Every month, starting in September 1989 up until the time of his disappearance, there had been a withdrawal for ten thousand dollars. There was no check number to trace it to, no linked account. Every month, Clive must have gone to the bank and withdrawn the same amount of cash. For what, though? Had he been paying a debt? Paying someone off? Squirreling money away for his imminent departure?

Hudson would venture down the avenues of possibilities tomorrow. Today, he had to be present for Garrison's last day aboveground.

They'd been warned time and time again how hard today would be. Hudson was more than ready for it to be over. "Bittersweet" wasn't the right word to describe it. He imagined saying goodbye would feel like cutting off a gangrenous arm. It would be ungodly painful, but then there would be a degree of relief, hopefully, that it was all over. And in the days and months and forever that ensued, missing Garrison would ache like a phantom limb.

He didn't imagine it; rather, he knew it for a fact. Nan was one phantom limb, now Garrison would be another. Two significant parts of him existing on a plane other than this one. What was the point of him staying here at all?

Slowly, the caravan crested over a hill and entered through the iron gates. It was so silent, Hudson heard the sibilant sounds of the tires on the wet asphalt. The Ironside was shrouded in mist. A conglomerate of neo-Gothic buildings, all black brick and red-roofed, it was once an all-female boarding school. Now, it served as a venue for weddings, youth clubs, and funerals. Vines crept across most of the windows like periorbital veins.

The rest of the world was portentous and monochromatic. On his left, Lake Michigan threw her waves against jagged rocks. The tumult mirrored the nerves in his body, the buzzing of his blood, the trembling of his jaw. He felt suddenly claustrophobic and charged to run out into the rain, away from the herd of black umbrellas now parading toward the chapel. But where would he run? Home, where he could feel the looming presence of the police department and catch a glimpse of Garrison's ruined memorial every time he passed the kitchen window? To his mother's, where he'd have to tell the whole story of Garrison's demise only to give her the sick satisfaction of saying *I told you not to be a cop.* To Miserelli's? No. No, he couldn't go there.

The wind slammed into him as soon as he stepped out of the parked vehicle. It ripped the door right out of Riley's hand, too. She fought to close it, looking as if she wanted to punch it. They joined a two-by-two procession on the salted walkway and entered the chapel.

He expected it to be silent as a tomb. But inside, the chapel was anything but silent. His sense of hearing seemed suddenly heightened. Each note of the organ sent a vibration through his bones. The wind shushing through the vestibule prickled at the back of his neck. He heard crying, terrible sounds from deep in people's throats; the sharp click of heels on flagstone as visitors made their way up to pay their respects.

From where he stood in line, behind dozens of rows of pews, he could see the backs of Lilah and Noelle. Noelle's head was turned, her forehead pressed against the shoulder of who Hudson thought was her sister. Garrison's daughter, Lilah, sat as erect as though there was a rod in her back, forcing her to look in the direction of the casket. He knew her well enough to know that her fingernails were digging into her tights as she fought not to cry.

He wanted to comfort her. He *should* comfort her, he thought, but when he looked around, he saw that only family and civilians had gathered in their seating areas. The middle was empty, reserved for sworn personnel. He filed into one of the rows with Kole and Riley. Devine broke away and sat with Fletcher. Sitting with his feet planted firmly to the floor, Hudson looked around. The effect was dizzying. Two tiers above them held community members, friends, and law enforcement personnel from other jurisdictions.

Back on his level, he saw Miserelli with the rest of his and Garrison's old patrol squad. She caught his eye, but her expression remained frozen. His view of her was blocked when they stood again and assembled into a single-file line by unit and rank. The mayor led the procession and the aldermen came after him, then Chief Stromwell, who raised his hand in a salute as he approached the casket.

Hudson shuffled down the aisle with the rest of the Black Harbor Police Department. His throat tightened. He gasped, drinking in the stagnant air as he came within feet of Garrison's corpse. He glanced to his left at Noelle and Lilah. Their faces were puffy, their eyes raw and red. He managed a weak nod and then, biting his lip, looked back at Garrison. He looked a little better than he had the last couple of days. His makeup had been touched up. His arms were crossed over his chest, right hand placed on the brim of the eight-point cap that Hudson had only ever seen him wear in parades.

Hudson's hand trembled as he raised it to his temple in a farewell salute. The edges of his mouth pulled downward as though some invisible puppet master was contorting his face. His lip quivered. He felt hot, the grief he'd been keeping trapped inside all week finally boiling over. Tears burned wet, translucent trails down his cheeks.

Suddenly, he felt the comfort of arms around him. Noelle hugged him tight, pressed her forehead to his. She smelled pure, like lavender and eucalyptus. An unexpected observation occurred to him then: He didn't remember the last time someone hugged him.

"Brix loved you." Her words were hardly more than a breath in his ear. "He loved you like he would have loved his own son."

He wanted to say *I loved him, too,* but the words were stuck in his throat. A quiet, high-pitched whimper escaped him. He didn't even know he was capable of making a sound like that.

"You come see us tomorrow, okay, Ryan?"

"I will," he managed. He was aware again of the line behind him. But Noelle was Garrison's widow. Today, at least, the world paused for her. When Lilah stood, he turned to accept her embrace. He kissed the top of her head. He'd never done that before, to anyone, but it felt appropriate in this horrible, surreal moment. They didn't exchange any words. Sometimes words just weren't enough.

When he found his seat, he sat facing forward, his eyes closed, and willed his mind to drown out the sounds of the organ.

The pastor read John 15:13. Hudson knew the scripture by heart. His lips moved to the words, but no sound came out. *Greater love hath no man than this, that a man lay down his life for his friends.*

Chief Stromwell spoke next. "Officer Garrison was a hero," he said, and Hudson felt the word deep in his bones. It was true. Garrison had selflessly given his life in exchange for catching a dangerous criminal. He remembered the nights spent sitting in Squad #23, the two of them waiting for an opportunity like the one that finally presented itself to Garrison on December 19. He knew beyond a shadow of a doubt that they would have prevailed.

Jesus, Garrison. Why did you have to go after him alone?

Because he'd left him alone. That's why. And yet, what had Morgan said? That the suspect had just come in, shot Garrison, and left. What if it hadn't been an armed robbery attempt at all, but a premeditated homicide? With Garrison as the target.

Jesus, Garrison. He thought of the ticket that he'd found in his friend's trauma plate pocket and the recent PI job. *What did you get yourself into?*

The bagpipes commenced at the conclusion of the service. They exited the way they'd come in, with civilians leaving first, followed by the chief and his lieutenants. It sounded like a rushing waterfall, people standing from the pews and shuffling toward the vestibule. The pallbearers came and carried the casket down the aisle behind the bagpipers, and Hudson followed. When he reemerged to the elements this time, it wasn't the wind that rocked him, but the sea of flags and eight-point caps.

Sworn officers from every jurisdiction in the state, and some from across state lines, had come to pay their respects. They stood in formation, saluting the casket.

"Oh my God," he heard Riley breathe. She stumbled, her knees suddenly weak. Hudson caught her by the arm before she fell down the stairs.

"It's like a scene from a movie," someone else said behind him, and Hudson agreed. He had thought seeing them in the chapel was impressive, but to see them all here, sprawling across the lawn all the way to the edge of the water, was unbelievable. The mobile command center—a colossal black RV—was parked like a blockade. They helped one another down the steps to join the crowd, where they took their place in front of SWAT's armored truck.

During the honor guard performance, Hudson stared at the back of an officer in front of him, letting his mind get lost as he studied the half-moon-shaped reflection from the officer's flashlight onto his dark uniform shirt. The cold permeated the soles of his dress shoes, shooting pins and needles into his feet. Finally, a radio crackled to life over a loudspeaker. The Last Call.

"Radio Black Harbor 1978 . . . Radio Black Harbor 1978, do you copy? Black Harbor 1978 out of service. Thank you, Officer Garrison. We'll take it from here."

Someone next to him was laughing. Hudson turned, flush with anger, and realized that it was Kole. Except he wasn't laughing. His face was strained, the tendons in his neck taut. His shoulders shook as he wept. Hudson reached out and touched the sergeant's arm. Kole glanced at him and set his jaw, and they listened, then, as the waves crashed against the bluffs, taking more and more of Black Harbor with them. What Hudson wouldn't give for the lake to take him, too.

And there at the edge, by the wrought-iron gate, was someone who didn't belong. Someone who looked like he'd walked onto the set of the wrong movie being filmed. He wore a black leather jacket and black pants, signature black stocking cap. From far away, Hudson could see his tattoo like an inkblot on his neck. Tobias Shannon, better known as Hades.

What business would a convicted drug lord have at a cop's funeral? A person of interest in his murder, no less, and suddenly, Hudson knew.

Shannon had shot Brix Garrison and was here to see the results of his handiwork.

Despite the distance, and the mist, and the sea of people between them, Hudson caught Shannon's eye. The outsider gave a curt nod, then shoved his hands in his pockets and disappeared into the fog.

13
MORGAN

Morgan watched the televised funeral procession from the comfort of her parents' living room. She sat on the floor, legs bent like a frog as she hunched over the ottoman, sorting the marshmallows of her Lucky Charms: six hearts, six balloons, six clovers, and so on. Her dad was at the factory, picking up an extra shift. Her mom had gone to the store for almond extract. Grandpa Teddy lay in the recliner, eyes closed, mouth open for catching spiders.

She looked up from her sorting and saw the caravan of police vehicles. Hudson was probably inside one of them. She hadn't gotten in touch with him since yesterday. That would be counterproductive when she just wanted him to go away.

She didn't care about the $62,000 reward or whatever it was up to now. She didn't know any more than what she'd already told him. The person who shot his friend had been wearing all black, and he'd spray-painted a pair of red shoes. That's all she had. Sorry. See ya later. Have a nice life. Go fuck yourself.

The fact that Hudson had a ticket to The Ruins was all she needed to know about him. He was either: a sick, demented creep who didn't deserve to breathe; or a cop—maybe Fed-level—hunting her down.

The muscles in her stomach contracted. She couldn't be locked up again. Not again. Not again. Not again.

Her eyes scanned the individual piles of marshmallows, pausing on the red balloons, and she thought of the one that had waited for her, wavering in the smoldering haze of The Ruins. She'd been home for three months and was still no closer to finding the key's corresponding lock. Whoever had left it for her was probably growing impatient.

Had it been Hudson? Had he tracked her all the way here from Chicago, she wondered, remembering how the inside of his house hadn't seemed like his house at all. A woman should have been living there, not a single man and his dog.

But it had been his grandmother's house, hadn't he said? And the name "Hudson" was carved into the iron plate above the door.

She scooped up her marshmallows and dropped them into her bowl of milk, then sprinkled in the oat morsels and took a bite. It tasted like a lie. That was it. Hudson—or whatever his name was—had simply lied about his name and invented a backstory tied to the house.

Morgan twisted to grab her laptop from the couch. Opening a browser, she typed "Black Harbor Police Department Ryan Hudson" into the search bar. If nothing came up, well, she had her answer.

But something did come up. About 27,000 of them, actually. Of course, only a fraction would be pertinent to her investigation. The first hit was a LinkedIn profile. She clicked on it, but it wasn't finished. There was no profile picture, just his name, employer, and a graduation date of 2011 from the local university.

Exiting LinkedIn, Morgan scrolled down the rest of the page. The next link took her to the Black Harbor Police Department's Facebook. A gallery published four months ago showed Hudson dressed in a black suit, shaking the hand of the police chief as he received a plaque with his name on it. She zoomed in: RYAN HUDSON—INVESTIGATOR. The post above the gallery read: *On Monday, August 17, the Black Harbor Police Department recognized four promotions. Congratulations to Inv. Wyatt, Inv. Hudson, Sgt. Kepler, and Lt. Draves.*

The more Morgan surfed the internet, the more Hudson's legitimacy was confirmed, from mentions of his exemplary officer awards—six in the past six years—his volunteering at the local animal shelter, and his testimony in court regarding an investigation he'd conducted into a woman making her daughter drink drain cleaner. She clicked on the article. The trial had only happened a month ago.

Sheehan was convicted of physical abuse to a child when she forced her 13-year-old daughter to drink drain cleaner. Black Harbor Investigator Ryan Hudson testified in court on Thursday, stating: "A physical abuse charge is not enough. Sheehan has a history of manipulating others toward her own violent ends. This fact alone should prevent Sheehan from ever stepping foot outside a prison again. She should be charged with attempted homicide and no chance of parole. She's a villain." Investigator Hudson went on to show photographs of the victim's esophagus . . .

Morgan closed the article.

So, Hudson was who he said he was. And he helped people. Her nerves prickled. What would he see her as, though? A victim who deserved justice, or a villain who lured others to violent ends?

A pop-up appeared in the top right corner of her screen.

Hello, Morgan Mori.

It was Bennett Reynolds. Morgan bit the studs in her bottom lip, focusing on the sharp pain it sent through her jaw and down her neck. She would have to face the music sooner or later.

Hello, Bennett Reynolds, she replied.

14

HUDSON

On the nightstand, the face of his alarm clock glowed like a moon. Hudson squinted. It was 9:15. They'd passed out for almost an hour.

His mouth tasted smoky and sweet. It had seemed wrong, holding a plate of barbeque, drinking a beer, laughing with people whom he hadn't seen since his patrol days. Or nights, rather. At the dinner that followed the burial, he'd talked with the K-9 handler Chase and his wife for a while, and then Malcolm and Jiminez had joined the conversation. They were friends, he supposed, or they had been and were diminished to acquaintances now. People he saw only when the stars aligned, if they happened to be passing by the time clock on his way upstairs. He couldn't help but notice how friendly they were with one another. How comfortable. He felt the guilt of lost opportunity, of not getting to know them better. He'd never gotten very close with any of them because he'd never had to. He'd had Garrison.

The dinner was at Holy Smokes. He'd been there a handful of times with Garrison and the girls. Jesus, how old had Lilah been last time they all sat at the outdoor patio, beneath strings of Edison lights while enjoying heaping plates of cornbread and ribs? Thirteen, maybe?

After the dinner tonight, he'd sat with Lilah and Noelle for a few moments. It was a delicate dance, he thought, wanting to be there for them but not wanting to impose. And if he was being honest with himself, he hungered for their comfort, for their connection. To be next to the only people in the world whose pain surpassed his own. He'd lost a partner and best friend, and so had Noelle. And at sixteen, Lilah had lost her father. He'd wondered what thoughts zipped through her mind as she sat staring blankly across the room, a barbeque stain on the white tablecloth in front of her, and he couldn't help but remember Garrison's blood coagulating on the gas station floor. What future had she grieved, sitting there so silent with wet eyes, offering a twitch of her mouth when strangers walked by and touched her shoulder.

Tears came to Hudson now, as he thought back to her sitting there, alone in a room full of people.

A female sigh pierced the silence. Miserelli's copper tendrils spilled across his chest as she turned, the fragrant scent of her shampoo wafting over him.

He traced her spine with his fingertip.

"Mm." Miserelli moaned softly at his touch.

He liked to imagine she smiled a little, even if only the darkness bore witness. "We passed out," he said.

"We did."

"What time—"

"Nine seventeen."

She turned onto her back, lying on top of his hand. He felt her vertebrae press into his palm, and then she was facing him. Chaotic curls fell over her cheek; flames licking her skin. He wanted to touch one of them, hold it between his thumb and forefinger and study it for a moment, all the different glowing strands. But that wasn't what they had.

She flicked her green-eyed gaze to him. She was almost unrecognizable from her patrol self, the version of her with her hair pulled back in a low, bushy ponytail, ballistic vest beneath her uniform shirt to give her a boxy shape. Here, in his bed, she could be Julia Roberts's younger sister with her hair free and wild, barefaced, freckled shoulders, curves that disappeared beneath the crisp white sheet. "Something wrong?" she asked.

"No." The response was automatic. Garrison was in the ground. That was wrong. And Tobias Shannon had made a guest appearance at the funeral. That was wrong. And the two of them were in bed together, again. That was wrong. He was aware of its wrongness every time they found themselves in this situation, and yet.

And yet.

"You always grind your teeth after sex?"

"You tell me." She should know by now. They'd been doing the friends with benefits dance for the past six months—a secret they'd both kept from Garrison. It wasn't that Hudson had meant to keep it from him; it was just that he never saw a reason to tell him. Not to mention, he thought it would have fizzled out long before now. Miserelli probably had, too.

It did for a while after he got promoted. She was mad at him for leaving Patrol. Which was warranted in a way; he never told her he had taken the assessment. In fairness, she'd never asked about it, either. He'd be lying if he said the pressure of their secret relationship wasn't motivation to move upstairs. At work, they gave each other nothing more than curt hellos and polite nods, and then about a month ago, when the sky was still dark as coal, she'd wandered up into his bedroom. He'd had no idea anyone was in his house—Pip hadn't even barked—until he heard her duty belt fall to the floor. The stalemate was over, then, and they picked up right where they'd left off, with Miserelli coming over once or twice a week after her shift and getting into his bed. He was sure Garrison knew something was up, but if his partner ever suspected anything, he never let on.

Miserelli stared up at the ceiling and sighed. "Today sucked balls." Her words rode the wave of an exhale. "That fucking last call."

Hudson swallowed the lump in his throat. Eleven years on the force, and he'd never been so decimated over a radio call. *Black Harbor 1978 out of service.* Those words would haunt him forever.

The sworn officers of the Black Harbor Police Department were the toughest people he knew. They weathered bullets and hate on a daily basis, they took punches and kicks to the teeth . . . but he saw them crumble today. She was right. Today sucked balls.

"Have you heard anything yet? About the gun?" She didn't have to elaborate. They both knew which gun.

"No. It's Wesson's inves—"

"I just figured you might have heard something is all."

"And not tell you?"

The blankets shifted as her shoulders shrugged beneath them. "You're one of them now, upstairs."

Hudson rolled his eyes. If she had any idea how much of an outcast he was . . . "I haven't heard anything," he said firmly.

Miserelli cleared her throat. "So, what's up with the body in that car they dragged out of the lake? Is it Clive Reynolds or not?"

"No. I mean, I don't know yet. I'm waiting on the medical examiner's report to see whether or not it's him. But I don't think so," he added, remembering the Carhartt jacket and what Kole said about the length of the femur. He was careful not to mention anything that she wouldn't have already heard about at roll call or on the news. The torque wrench, for one thing.

"What kind of damage was there to the vehicle?" Miserelli was an evidence technician, which meant she photographed and collected the evidence at crime scenes. Things that were there and shouldn't be were always of special interest to her. If she were on the case, he knew she would salivate over the torque wrench and the fact that the driver's seat belt had been cut. She would probably have found other things by now, too. Things that wouldn't in a million years cross his mind.

"The passenger was still dressed?"

"Yes."

"Have you processed the clothing yet? For blood or fibers?"

"I sent the pull request to Grace yesterday." After Morgan abruptly left his house, he'd gone to work hell-bent on solving the twenty-year-old cold case. He emailed Grace, the evidence clerk, asking for the jacket, coveralls, and wrench to be sent to the state crime lab in Madison for testing. That was all he could do there. Then, he dove back into the box of mysteries, the one Sergeant Kole had hoisted up onto his desk just four days ago when he'd tempted him with the carrot of never having to work another Sensitive Crimes case again.

Miserelli blew air out her nose. She turned toward him, and Hudson felt a chill as the blankets shifted off him. He'd turned the heat down when he left this morning. "This is a twenty-year cold case, Ryan. You know how many people have tried solving this before you? Six. They all failed, by the way, too."

He caught himself from flinching. She did this when she felt threatened. Degraded him. Doubted him. It was why they weren't together. That and the fact that after this, she would zip up her pants and forget about him until loneliness got the best of her. It usually took about a week. "Lucky number seven, right?" he said.

She snorted. "You know why they assigned it to you, don't you?"

Because they feel sorry for me sucking it up in Sensitive Crimes. But Miserelli didn't need to know that. Hudson knew that although she was proud of him for getting promoted, part of her would be too happy to hear he hated it up there and wanted to come back to the beat. "Because they see my shining potential?"

"To get you out of the way. So you let Wesson PD do their job and find Garrison's killer. You're too volatile."

He knew that. Kole had told him as much. "I'm not volatile."

"Yeah? Tell that to my tailbone."

He inched away from her, felt the cold slip and settle between them. From the window, the weak, pallid light of a streetlamp leaked through. They'd been here, in this same situation, when Breaker called about Garrison. It was Miserelli's night off and they were enjoying a quiet night of sex and serial killer documentaries. She'd screamed when he relayed the message to her. That Garrison was dead. But when she'd leapt from the bed to get dressed, he'd stopped her. They couldn't show up together, in plain clothes, no less.

"Listen." Miserelli's touch brought him back to the present. Her hand was cool. "If we just lay low, you know, fly under the radar. You and me, we can—"

"There's nothing we can do, Joey. Garrison's case is *literally* out of our hands. You're right. We should leave it to Wesson PD." He looked at her to find her staring back at him, her eyes on fire.

"That's not what I'm saying. I'm saying you should cool your jets. Don't wear your emotions on your sleeve so much. Stop giving them a reason to want to distract you."

Now that she'd made him aware of his teeth grinding, he couldn't stop noticing it. She didn't believe in him. She didn't want him to succeed with this cold case or anything else.

Did anyone?

He'd fought through every step of becoming a cop. He had no support from his family. His mom would rather he dealt drugs than walked a beat. Less chance of being killed or sued. Even when he'd been promoted to investigator, there were people who didn't want him to move up—his friends, primarily. Current company not excluded.

"We know that area better than anyone," Miserelli said, and he knew she was talking about Sixth and Lincoln. "Better than anyone from Wesson. They didn't comb it well enough."

"They did. Trust me."

"Like you know."

He felt feverish. She was blaming him for not being there. For going upstairs and leaving Garrison to his demise. If she'd been so concerned, she could have left her partner and gone with Garrison. This wasn't all on Hudson's shoulders. "Look, this isn't the first time Wesson's investigating something like—"

"It's Garrison, Ryan. It is the first time." She rolled out of bed. The hardwood floor creaked as she shuffled around, kicking her legs through her uniform pants.

"What are you doing?"

"I've gotta go let my dogs out. I should have been home hours ago. I should never have—"

"What? Come over? You were the one who wanted to take this upstairs." He swung his legs over the edge of the bed. His toes grazed the cold floor.

"I was gonna say fall asleep. I should never have fallen asleep." She pulled her black tank top over her head, and threw her shirt on over it, leaving it unbuttoned.

"Listen. Can we talk for a second?"

"We've been talking for *minutes*." She said the word as though it were synonymous with "eternity."

He sighed. "I just think we should leave it to Wesson PD. I need to move on." He stopped. *Move on*. That wasn't what he meant. He would never move on from Garrison. Forward, someday, hopefully, but move on? Never.

Miserelli planted her hands on her hips, turned her chin up to the ceiling as she often did when a mope was feeding her a story she wasn't green enough to fall for. "What's so damn urgent now, Ryan? This case has been collecting dust before you or I even became cops. Probably before Garrison, even."

"This was Garrison's case," he said. "I need to finish it for him."

Miserelli picked her duty belt up off the floor and slung it over her shoulder. The new information didn't faze her. "I hope you know that if you had been shot, Garrison would be out there right now looking for that gun. Doing everything he could to track down that motherfucker and bring him to justice. Remember that."

The sentiment stunned Hudson into paralysis. His fingertips tightened on the edge of the mattress but that was all he could do. They stared at each other hard for a few seconds, before Miserelli turned and walked out. He heard her footsteps hurry down the stairs. She slammed the door.

Hudson sighed and fell back against the pillows, his heart racing. He closed his eyes, blocking out the light of the streetlamp, and behind his eyelids, saw Tobias Shannon as he'd stood outside the chapel earlier. Watching—and waiting for Hudson to fail. Like the rest of the world.

15
MORGAN

For the second time that week, the gothic iron gate of the Reynolds estate opened up to her. Morgan held her breath as the bald tires of her grandpa's Oldsmobile rolled over the packed snow. The sound made her teeth hurt.

She'd filled Bennett in last night on her current situation: cameraless, carless, and utterly mortified to explain to his mother that there would be no Christmas party photographs. He assured her everything would be all right, that it was *no big deal, seriously,* and invited her over. She accepted, only so she could return the money, and felt, now, like a rabbit hopping into a fox's den to be eaten alive.

Bennett's Porsche was parked in front of the guesthouse/garage combo. It was a modern iteration of Clive's 1978 Widowmaker—smaller, sleeker, sans whale tail spoiler—and newly waxed, not a speck of salt disrupting its rich midnight-blue finish. How did he keep it so clean, she wondered, as she pulled up next to it. She began to wonder if the Reynolds family— Don included—had invisible force fields that protected them and all their possessions from Black Harbor's grit and grime. Her own family did not have that immunity. She slammed the Oldsmobile's driver's side door and a clump of wet, grey snow plopped from the wheel well onto the cobble-stones. Point proven.

The Land Rover was here again, and a gunmetal Tesla that looked like a bullet. Great, more people to eat her alive.

The wind off the lake rocked her back on her heels, and the chill cut straight to her bones. She shoved her hands into her jacket pockets and approached the back steps. The keyhole screamed silently at her. Morgan froze. Only her eyes moved to shoot a quick glance over each shoulder. Then, she pulled the key from her wrist cuff and inserted it in the lock.

Her heart shot up into her throat as she gave the key a twist. It turned halfway and stopped. Morgan frowned and tried again. The key wouldn't turn any further. Her disappointment was palpable as a puff of vapor that hung in front of her face, taunting her. The excitement at the prospect of having an answer, a corresponding lock to this mysterious key, had built up more than she'd realized. Now that it was gone, she felt crushed. Defeated. Melancholic. And on Christmas Eve of all days.

She should leave. Just tuck the envelope under Bennett's windshield wiper. Morgan pivoted to head down the steps, when the door suddenly swung away from its frame. Bennett stood in its place, looking much more comfortable in his own skin this time. He'd exchanged the cable-knit sweater for dark jeans and a light blue button-up with the sleeves rolled. His hair was expertly pushed to one side, giving his Neptunian eyes free range to roam Morgan as she stood on the porch.

What was it about him that stopped her in her tracks, made her feel as though her soles were glued to the step? Perhaps it was the way his face morphed into Clive's when he smiled. "Morgan Mori. Long time no see."

"Bennett Reynolds. It's only been four and a half days."

"But who's counting?" He winked. The gesture made Morgan's knees weak.

"Are you going to invite me in, or is there a toll?" When he looked perplexed, she tilted her chin up toward the mistletoe suspended from the beam overhead.

"Oh." His cheeks colored when he followed her gaze. "There wasn't a toll, but if you're offering . . ."

"I'm not." She smiled, though, like she might consider it in the future, and let him hold the door open for her. They paused, for a moment, in the vestibule, and Morgan felt Bennett's hand slide down her sleeve. His fingertips found her hand then, and he tapped a subtle Morse code into her palm.

"I'm glad you're okay, Morgan Mori. I wish you'd have told me. I would have come."

And done what, she wondered. "Thanks, but . . . it became kind of a whole to-do. Cops wanted to talk to me, get a statement . . ."

Bennett nodded. He touched her cheek, then, and tucked back a piece of hair that had come loose from her red slouch hat. "Just promise you won't get caught in the middle of any more crime scenes." His voice was soft, sexy.

Morgan swallowed. She felt something stir inside her, a magnetic force, almost, pushing her toward him. She shivered, but not from the cold. If she kissed him, her life could change forever. And would that be a terrible thing? She stood on her tiptoes, a frog about to kiss her prince, when—

"Morgan!" Eleanor's voice rang like a bell, instantly shattering the moment. "What a joy!"

Bennett dropped his arms as his mother cut between them to give Morgan a squeeze. The gesture was unexpected. Morgan shot a glance over the top of Eleanor's head to catch Bennett's perplexed expression.

"Oh, Bennett, don't make her catch her death out here. Won't you come in for some coffee?"

Morgan nodded, although she didn't have much choice. Eleanor was already pulling her into the great room.

Bennett helped her out of her jacket before she could protest and hung it on an empty hook. She wasn't planning on staying long. She did take her boots off, though. She'd already lost the woman's photos. No sense adding insult to injury by tracking snow all over her floors.

The warmth and aroma of fresh-baked cinnamon buns greeted her as they entered the great room. Her stomach growled. All she'd had for breakfast were the remains of the Lucky Charms and the inch of dust that had collected in the bottom of the bag. Over the sound system, a melody of bells, guitar, and flute played a Celtic rendition of "God Rest Ye Merry Gentlemen." It was both ominous and beautiful; Morgan felt a little as though she'd just wandered through a wardrobe and popped out the other side, in a realm where people wore perfect, unfrayed clothes and sipped espresso.

The family was in the living room. They looked miniature in comparison to the tree, whose branches glistened and glimmered with crystal icicles and fairy lights. Eleanor, a vision in a gold-sequined sweater, had already cozied back up next to Don on the love seat. A white-bearded man sat on the couch across from them, his mouth curved into a grin as he watched Charlie play with a bright-colored keyboard. Cora sat on the floor beside her son, smoothing his wisps of blond hair.

"Morgan, you remember Don . . ." Eleanor rested a hand on her gentleman's chest. The man looked as dapper as he had Saturday night, and Morgan figured he was one of those people who always looked like that.

"Hello again, Morgan." His voice was low but soft, slightly ridged. The lights from the tree reflected in his rectangular lenses.

"And Christopher, aka Kris Kringle." Eleanor gestured to the old man in the blue turtleneck.

"Merry Christmas," said Bennett's uncle Christopher. "Tell me, young lady. Did you ever get your Butterfinger?"

The question immediately put Morgan back at the Fast Mart, reaching for the yellow wrapper when . . . *Pop!* Foil bags and windows and her eardrums all exploded at once.

Reassuringly, and out of anyone's view, Bennett pressed a knuckle against the small of her back. That little touch kept her from falling over, from curling into a fetal position and lying still until everyone disappeared. Play dead. That was how she'd always survived before.

"I—" Her voice shook. "I'm sorry." The warmth from the fire was suffocating. The edges of her vision blackened into tunnel vision, and she stared away from them, at a coat of arms displayed above the fireplace. It showed two tigers, mirror images of each other, claws poised to strike. A sword separated them, and at the bottom of the crest in gothic lettering was the name *Reynolds*. How pleasing and fearful it was to look at, perfect in its symmetry.

"S'okay," Bennett murmured. How close was she that she could hear him so clearly? Or, how silent had they all fallen?

"I, um—" She swallowed but her throat was dry. "I lost the pictures." The words spewed from her mouth like projectile vomit. "I— I was at the gas station when that cop got shot, and—"

"Oh my God, Morgan, for real?" Within seconds, Cora's cashmere scarf brushed against her cheek. The scents of vanilla and plum enveloped her. She had the same straitjacket hug as Eleanor.

To Morgan's disbelief, she tasted salt as tears streamed from her eyes into the space between her lips. She sniffled, and Bennett offered her a box of lotion-infused tissues.

She dabbed at her eyes, knowing full well that her eyeliner was probably smeared beyond repair. *Fuck, fuckity fuck.*

"Aw, my dear. Come sit." Eleanor patted the cushion next to her and Don, and Morgan was seated before she even realized she'd told her feet to move. "What happened, darling? If you want to tell us. If not . . . we understand."

Eleanor's soft words summoned a waterfall of hot tears to flood from Morgan's eyes. She hated herself for crying like this, in front of them, but then, this was good, wasn't it? She'd played the *woe is me* card and hadn't even meant to.

Maybe they'd go easy on her.

"You were there when that cop got shot." Cora knelt in front of Morgan, her hand on her knee. "How traumatizing."

Morgan nodded. "I'm sorry," she finally managed to choke out. "I was inside wh—" She drew in a deep inhale, let it out. Eleanor rubbed her back. "When the man shot him an-and stole my car. He shot him and he left and he took my car. I hadn't locked it because I was . . ." Why? Why hadn't she locked her car? She simply hadn't thought to. She'd only meant to get out and manage the whole transaction at the pump. She hadn't been prepared to go inside. Stupid. She was so stupid.

Her shoulders slumped even lower. "My camera was in the car, with all the pictures from Saturday night. I've been in contact with the police, but . . ." But nothing. It had been almost a week. Her car was gone. Her camera was gone. Eleanor's pictures, gone. She reached into her leggings' side pocket and extracted the envelope of money. She held it out toward Bennett, who stood near Christopher. "I can't accept your money. I ruined your Christmas."

Ruined. The word tumbled from her mouth without any warning. *My ruin.* Whoever had left her the key had known what she was, what she was capable of. She ruined things.

"Morgan, darling." Eleanor pulled her close and rocked her. She *rocked* her, like Morgan was a child and not a thirty-one-year-old woman. Headlines flashed through Morgan's mind, snippets of articles she'd read

over the years. MRS. REYNOLDS, MURDERESS; HOW TO GET AWAY WITH MUR-
DER: BE A REYNOLDS; MRS. REYNOLDS PROVES KILLING HUSBAND YIELDS BIG
PAYOFF, etc. How could any of them define the nurturing creature who
embraced her now?

"Bennett, would you please get Morgan a cup of coffee?"

"I'll get it." Don patted Eleanor's knee and stood. "How do you take
it, Morgan?"

Morgan sat up a little, wiped at her nose. "With whipped cream."

Everyone chuckled as though she was joking. Even Don, until he
paused and asked: "You're serious?"

A little sheepish now, Morgan nodded. She drank her coffee like most
people drank hot cocoa—with whipped cream and marshmallows and
cookie crumbles if there were any around.

Eleanor folded Morgan's fingers over the envelope. "Keep it. We had
you running around here like a madwoman."

Morgan fought a twitch tugging at the corner of her mouth. If only
they knew how mad she was. "Thank you," she said. Her eyes were still
wet, her vision blurry as she pulled away a bit so she could look at Eleanor.
"I wish there was some way I could make it up to you."

The lights from the tree sparkled in Eleanor's eyes. Her snowy white
brows peaked just a little when she said, "I have something in mind."

16
HUDSON

It was noon on Christmas Eve when Hudson pulled up to Garrison's house. Icicle lights hung from the gutters and there was a large wreath on the front door. A pair of wire reindeer stood in the yard. At night this time of year, Garrison's house usually looked spectacular, but in the daylight, Hudson saw the decorations for what they were: plastic and artificial.

Still sitting in his vehicle, Hudson took the key out of the ignition and stared at Garrison's hunter-green Ford parked on the slab beneath the basketball hoop. A good three inches of snow had collected on the windshield. He squinted to read a message written on the driver's side window. *I ♥ you Dad* cut through the frost, and he envisioned Lilah writing it with her finger.

Letting out a slow exhale, Hudson looked at the presents on his passenger seat: a red envelope and a bottle of wine in a shimmery bag. He'd never been good at gifts. That had been Nan's forte. Regardless, he grabbed them and walked up to the door, cringing at the way they felt like a pathetic consolation.

He knocked.

Seconds passed, enough for him to notice the many sets of footprints on the stoop. How many people had already come by for a visit today? Noelle answered the door, smile already queued up, but when she saw it was him, her eyes shone and her smile turned into a frown. She didn't have to put up a façade for him. He knew the weight of grief. How it made you feel like you owed it to the world to grin and bear it while even the smallest things seemed impossible. Like shoveling the walk. Folding the laundry. Putting a new bag in the garbage can.

Her face broke. "Ryan." She took his hand in hers then, and pulled him inside.

It was strange being in Garrison's house without him. He'd been over lots of times—with Nan and then without—so often, in fact, that Noelle and Garrison used to joke that Hudson was their son. Every time they'd mentioned it, he felt guilty for wishing it was true.

He stared past Noelle into the living room, half hoping to see Garrison sitting in his recliner and overhearing the explosions from his favorite Christmas movie, *Die Hard*. But all was quiet. It almost felt as if they were in an igloo, with snow blocking the sounds of the outside world.

"How are you?" he asked. A moot question.

She took in a breath. "A mess."

"Is there anything I can do?" Another moot question.

"You can sit down." A small smile curved her lips. She wandered to the kitchen island and Hudson followed, after slipping off his shoes.

Lilah came from down the hall, wearing pajama pants and an oversized sweatshirt. "I thought I heard you," she said.

"Merry Christmas." Hudson rose off the stool to put his arm around her. When he sat back down, he noticed for the first time the dining room table heaped with festive paper plates filled with cookies and brownies and bars of every assortment, all surrounding a centerpiece of what had to be at least five poinsettias. He warranted a guess most of it had come from the wave of visitors that preceded him.

"Can I offer you something to eat, Ryan?" said Noelle. "We have cookies and, well, more cookies."

"And if you're still hungry," added Lilah as she took the stool next to him, "you can add a side of cookies."

"Might need some wine to wash down all those cookies," he said, and slid the glittery bag toward Noelle.

She opened it and hugged it to her chest like a precious heirloom. "You know the key to a woman's heart."

"I thought you might be tired of lasagna."

Noelle smiled wearily. "I would have just dumped it down the garbage disposal once you left." She put the wine in the fridge where Hudson could see about nine different containers probably filled with homemade casseroles, lasagnas, and pasta salads. When Nan died, people brought tinfoil-covered pans to the porch for a month. He froze some of it, then eventually threw it out when every bite began to taste bitter—acrid like ground-up cigarettes. The worst part had been tracking everyone down to return their pans.

Lilah opened the red envelope he gave her, read the card, and thanked him for the fifty-dollar bill.

"We have something for you, too." Noelle nodded at Lilah, who disappeared around the corner into the living room.

"Oh, you really didn't have—"

But the sixteen-year-old had already reemerged, holding a box wrapped in blue-and-silver foil paper.

"We wanted to," said Noelle.

"Open it," prompted Lilah.

Hudson tore at a corner. The foil slid away to reveal a black wooden box with a glass top. He opened the lid, carefully, and discovered Garrison's eight-point cap. An invisible fist punched him in the chest and knocked the breath out of his lungs. His eyes burned.

He glanced from Lilah to Noelle. Noelle looked up at him from beneath dark lashes. "He would've wanted you to hold on to it."

Hudson felt his bottom lip quiver. Still gripping the box in his right hand, he pulled them into an embrace. He wanted to say *Thank you,* but the words that came out, instead, were, "I'm sorry."

"Sorry?" Noelle backed away so she could get a good look at him. "Ryan, what have you got to be sorry for? Brix *cherished* you. You were his *best friend.*"

Her words screwed into him like bullets. For best friends, they'd both kept serious stuff from each other. He thought back to finding the faded red ticket among the things Garrison kept in his trauma plate pocket. There was also the fact that, unbeknownst to Garrison, he'd been sleeping with Miserelli for the past six months.

"I should have been there for him," he said finally. "I should have—"

Noelle pressed her palms to his face, gently hooking her thumbs under his chin. "Listen to me, Ryan. My husband was a steadfast, smart-mouthed, stubborn son of a bitch. He had more honor and integrity in his pinkie finger than most men have in their whole beings—a lot of which came from the values you shared with him. If Brix was hell-bent on taking someone down, he was gonna get it done. No matter what anyone said. No matter where he had to go. So don't you believe for a second that you being there or not had any effect whatsoever on his death. Understand?"

No matter where he had to go. Hudson replayed her words in his head. A place like The Ruins, perhaps? And what did she mean about taking someone down? A new thought crossed Hudson's mind: Noelle Garrison knew things no one else did, things that could potentially lead to answers regarding her husband's demise.

Hudson's gaze drifted to Lilah, who'd gotten a cookie and was dunking it in a glass of milk. Now was not the time for an interrogation.

17

MORGAN

Morgan brushed crumbs off her desk. She'd swiped two Linzer cookies and brought them down to her basement lair, before her mom delivered them all to Silver Maple, the assisted living center where Grandma Daisy had spent her final days and where Grandpa Teddy still, as far as her parents knew, played cribbage twice a week.

Earlier this evening, the kitchen had been invaded by piles of sugar cookies and gingerbread men, peanut-butter blossoms, thumbprint cookies with orange marmalade, snowballs, fudge, and her mom's famous Linzers. Carved with Grandma Daisy's biscuit cutter, a primitive heart cutout in the top of the cookie to show off the bright raspberry preserves, and dusted with powdered sugar, Lynette Mori's Linzer cookies were the stuff of legends. They were Morgan's favorite, and had been the centerpiece of her mother's bakery, Lynette's Linzers. Now, her mom's baking had evolved into a black-market operation in her kitchen. Some residences in Black Harbor sold cocaine out the back door. The Moris' sold cookies.

Morgan peeled her eyes from her computer to look at her money, which she'd separated into two equal stacks, one on each side of her keyboard. Her trip to the Reynolds estate had panned out better than anticipated. Not only did she get to keep the money from the Christmas party, she had now gotten another inside look at the lives of Black Harbor's most mysterious family.

On the floor beside her was a large Rubbermaid filled with loose photographs and albums whose floral covers were faded like old wallpaper. Eleanor had been storing them for years, protecting them from oxygen and light in this forest-green tub. Now, she wanted Morgan to immortalize them—scan them onto a USB drive that she could keep forever. Some of the photos could use some restorative edits, Morgan diagnosed when looking over Eleanor's shoulder at the collection, but for the most part, they just needed to be scanned and organized into the appropriate folders: family vacations, parties, sporting events, etc. All things that Morgan had never had. She couldn't help but feel a little taunted.

An eerie thought wormed its way into Morgan's brain, then, as she considered how quickly Eleanor had pivoted from the lost Christmas photos to this project. What if the photos had been saved for her? What if Eleanor wanted Morgan to study them and learn her family's secrets?

Morgan crawled under her desk and plugged in her new toy: a scanner. Upon leaving the Reynolds estate, she'd mustered up her courage to venture to Walmart on Christmas Eve and purchase the only scanner on the shelf. The checkout lines were obnoxious. It had taken her almost an hour to get what she needed and leave. By the time she returned home, her mother had already begun her cookie delivery, Grandpa Teddy was asleep in his chair, and her dad was working overtime.

Now, it was late and Morgan had traded in the ambiance of the Christmas tree for the blue light of her computer and the infernal glow of her red lava lamp. She pinched a photograph between her thumb and index finger. In it, she recognized a young Bennett holding a line of fish caught off a dock. Clive was crouched next to him. There it was again, that twinge. She studied Clive's face: the proud smile, the laugh lines. His eyes gleamed and she could see the familial resemblance between him and Bennett. They had the same straight nose, the same hairline that was higher on the left and swooped down toward the right. They both looked at the camera as though they were the ones giving the photographer direction, not the other way around. A small shed stood behind them at the opposite shore of the pond. She wondered where the photo had been taken. It looked remote, in an intentional way. Not like Black Harbor, whose curbside appeal was attractive only to cretins and criminals looking for a place to hide.

She set the photo of Bennett and Clive aside and dug another one out of the container. This one was a family photo, showing Eleanor and Clive sitting on a blanket with all four children surrounding them. She studied the children. They looked to be a bit older here than in the mantel portrait. Carlisle stared lazily at the camera lens. Freckles dappled her bare shoulders; she had the full pouty lips of a preteen. Bennett looked awkward with acne and braces. Cora was slim with a stretchy elastic choker around her neck that, at first glance, looked like stitches. David raised an eyebrow. Eleanor's hair had tamed considerably from the do in the mantel photo, and Clive looked the same. He had one of those timeless faces. Judging by the ages of the children, the photo could have been taken just days before his disappearance. She looked at the back of the photo. *July 2000* was written in what she presumed to be Eleanor's loopy cursive. Morgan homed in on Clive again, the print mere inches from her face. So close she could smell the faint almond scent of the paper, she searched his eyes for a spark, a glint, an omen that he knew this was his last outing with his family. But the photo was grainy and of poor quality. His expression betrayed nothing.

If she scrutinized every photo like this, she would never make any headway on Eleanor's digitization project.

Okay, one more.

Clive and Christopher grilled burgers in this photograph. Although Christopher wasn't nearly as handsome as his brother, his muscles bulged beneath a "Kiss the Cook" apron.

How different he looked from the old man she remembered sitting on Eleanor's couch. Morgan barely recognized him. The Christopher Reynolds she knew was a shrunken version of the man in the photograph. His skin was wrinkled now, his muscles deflated. His hair, though thinning in the photo, had deteriorated into a spiderweb stretched across his mottled scalp.

She wondered what Clive would look like today if he were alive. Would age have been as harsh to him, or would it treat him kindly, as it had Eleanor? It was difficult to pair them together sometimes: Clive, who was forever frozen in his mid-forties, with dark hair and a bright smile; and Eleanor, silver and well into her sixties, though no less enchanting than the younger version of herself seated at the edge of the picnic table in the same photo. She stared at Clive with what appeared to be pure, unadulterated adoration. If Morgan could only be sure of one thing, it was the fact that if Eleanor really did kill Clive, she deserved a slow clap for her acting abilities.

In an hour, she had the whole album scanned and saved onto her computer, with each original photo returned to its designated sleeve.

Morgan cracked open the next album. It was wrapped in green leather. The smell of old books wafted toward her. The musky, woody, vanilla-y scent that reminded her a little of perusing a library. Not that she could remember the last time she'd engaged in that kind of behavior. Talking with Hudson the other day reminded her how much she missed the escapism books offered. The answers, the conclusions. Real life didn't offer any of that.

The photos in the green album showed rolling emerald hills, heavy rain-filled storm clouds, and the Reynolds clan all wearing slickers as they explored what appeared to be the ruins of an old stone castle.

Morgan flipped through the pages slowly, feeling a foreign longing for a home she'd never been to. Her fingers traced the letters of a wooden sign: *Welcome to Dublin*. FÁILTE ROIMH DUBLIN. Her lips stumbled over the letters, her tongue tying itself into a knot.

The ache in her chest spread. To her stomach, her shoulders, down her forearms. Her hands shook as she struggled to turn the pages, allowing herself the brief and false nostalgia of placing her childhood self at the pub table between Carlisle and Cora as they snacked on fish and chips. Running down a hillside beside Bennett. Hands cupped as she fed a baby lamb. Getting her face painted at a festival with David. Arm in arm with the Reynolds children as they posed for a photo with a raven-haired boy and girl. She slid the photo out of its sleeve and read the note on the back. Written in Eleanor's cursive was: *With cousins Saoirse and Cillian (Uncle Gerry)*.

So they had family over in Ireland. Cousins, at least. Must be Clive's side, she thought. Reynolds. That was an Irish name, wasn't it? And then she remembered the coat of arms she'd seen above the fireplace: two mirrored tigers, a sword separating them, and the name *Reynolds* underneath in gothic lettering. How she'd admired it for its symmetry.

Morgan turned her wrist and studied the top of the key. Three circles clustered together to rest above a diamond shape. It looked like a clover, something that belonged over in a place like Ireland or at least had come from there. *But how did you get here,* she wondered.

She flipped to the next page, determined to find out.

18

HUDSON

"—like a rat down a hole, you gotta flush him out."

That was the conversation Hudson walked into, when he'd arrived at the bureau with two plates piled high with baked goods. Noelle had insisted he take them to work. He'd obliged, dropping another three plates off in the roll call room for patrol and civilian personnel.

Devine and Fletcher had been talking about Tobias Shannon, aka Hades, whose presence at Garrison's funeral yesterday hadn't gone unnoticed. A grainy picture of him standing by the entrance gate was printed on computer paper and taped to the dry-erase board next to a figure written in blue: *$104,000.*

The reward for information leading to the arrest of Garrison's killer had jumped to over a hundred grand overnight. Hudson didn't know the community of Black Harbor had that much dispensable wealth. As far as Black Harbor citizens were concerned, Brix Garrison had been a favorite. Establishments all over the city, from churches to bars to the bowling alley, were pledging money with the hopes of persuading someone to come forward. On one hand, seeing the number as proof that Garrison had been loved caused his throat to tighten, his chest to ache. On the other hand, it scared him.

It was a call for vigilantism. For a chance at that kind of money, what civilian wouldn't see if they could hunt down a cop killer?

He wondered if Morgan had seen the updated reward. He hadn't communicated with her since she ran out of his house two days ago. She'd effectively ghosted him. And oddly enough, when he'd tried looking her up in Onyx, he'd found nothing attached to the name Morgan Mori. No criminal record, no calls for service, not so much as a seat belt violation. She had no social media from what he could find. It was as if she simply didn't exist.

It was after 10:00 P.M. now, and he was on his way to his mother's house. Normally, they ate dinner around six o'clock on Christmas Eve— *they* being him, his brother, his mother, and his nephew—but since he had to work second shift this year, his mom had agreed to delay the festivities. Not that it was ever all that festive, but still. It was more of an effort than she made the rest of the year.

According to Devine and Fletcher earlier, Wesson PD had Hades's whereabouts narrowed down to three places. There would be search warrants, he knew. Cops staking out each residence, waiting for Hades to emerge. Hudson clenched his jaw as he braked at a red light. His gaze drifted to the black box on his passenger seat, foil still stuck to it. *No matter where he had to go,* that was what Noelle had said. She knew something what Garrison had been up to; he was sure of it. He thought of the faded red ticket burning a hole in his memo book. He would ask Noelle about it. Not tonight, not tomorrow. But Boxing Day was fair game.

The light turned green and he crossed the intersection, fully aware that the cemetery where Garrison's body had been laid to rest was on his right, shrouded in dark. A light snow began to fall, dusting his windshield like a feather pillow was being shaken. Hudson squinted in his rearview mirror. A pair of headlights trailed behind him, but as he turned in to his mother's drive, the car passed.

His mother's house was the same one he grew up in, a tiny white ranch with burgundy trim. Tucked back about a hundred feet from the road, he'd seen garages—especially on the lakeshore—that were larger. Evergreens that he remembered push-mowing around when they were only waist-high now blotted out the blue moon. The kitchen windows glowed amber through the frosted glass.

A layer of ice coated the concrete steps of the porch. Holding his packages in his left arm, he raised his right fist to knock. The door opened before his knuckles touched it, and there stood Tobias Shannon, a copper-colored drink in his hand. A grin spread across his face and he stepped aside to let Hudson in. "Merry Christmas, brother."

"You shouldn't be here," said Hudson. He stomped his shoes off on the welcome mat.

"Merry Christmas to you, too," said Tobias. His eyes glittered over the rim of his glass.

"I'm sorry, it's just—they're looking for you."

"And in all the wrong places." Tobias gave a winning smile. His gold grillz glinted. It looked like a custom job. Hudson didn't want to know what he'd sold in order to pay for it. Although he'd be the first to admit his relationship with his brother wasn't even in the neighborhood of "close," he did know one discerning truth: Tobias loved to play stupid games and win big prizes.

"Hey, Ma." Juggling his gifts in one hand, Hudson leaned over to pull his mother into a hug. His chin rested atop her head and he noticed there were more silver strands amidst the black than the last time he'd seen her. Two months ago? He'd taken her out to lunch, where she'd cried, again, about his career choice dividing the family. He left her in tears and with the resolute fact that his pension was tied to the City of Black Harbor; if he left now, he'd lose everything. The way things were, he could retire in twenty years. That was more than a lot of people could say. Besides, he loved his job. It wasn't his cross to bear that his brother was Hades, drug lord of the underworld.

And yet it was, because Tobias's wrongdoings were Hudson's secrets to keep. He often felt they were like Dorian Gray and his painting. Tobias slithered around town, inserting himself in whatever criminal activity he could find and never incurring the consequences. Every bad thing he did, then, resulted in Hudson looking in the mirror to discover another blemish or a new knot between his shoulder blades.

Separating from him got easier after high school, when Hudson legally changed his name. He and his grandmother had been Hudsons. His mom and brother were Shannons, after his late father who'd died when he was two, entrenched in the same dastardly deeds Tobias was now. Hudson had no memory of his father; why should he have his last name?

But now their grandmother was dead and it was two against one.

His mother kissed his cheek, seemingly having let go of their last argument. For now. It was Christmas, after all. "Merry Christmas, baby." She squeezed him and Hudson felt his icy heart begin to melt at her touch.

"Smells good in here." He turned to hang his coat.

"There's some ham and scalloped potatoes I can heat up for you. You boys better not be arguing already, though."

Tobias went to the counter and began pouring another drink. "'Course not," he answered for both of them. Hudson glanced at the tree in the corner of the living room, with its sparkling white lights and plastic orna-ments. A paper angel perched on top. He took his gifts over to it and set them next to the others. Most were marked for his eight-year-old nephew, Elijah. He must be at his mother's.

"Ain't the same without you, Ryan," his mom said over the humming of the microwave.

"I know. I couldn't get off." He returned to the kitchen, hands in his pockets, taking one out to accept the drink Tobias handed him.

"You mean crime don't take a holiday?" Tobias clinked his glass to Hudson's. "Cheers, bro."

Cheers to what, Hudson wondered. Nevertheless, he took a sip. The bourbon burned his throat, cleared his sinuses. "I don't know, does it?"

Tobias raised his chin and smiled. His eyes were narrow slits; the snowflake on his neck pulsed as he took a drink. They'd shown a close-up of it on the news when introducing him as a person of interest. His brother's head was potentially worth over a hundred grand. Hudson let that sink in.

"They better not make a habit of you working the holidays," his mother said. She set to refilling her glass of champagne.

"It's just because I'm the new guy." Hudson lifted a forkful of pota-toes to his mouth. Blew on it. The aroma of melted cheddar cheese and caramelized ham almost sent his eyes rolling to the back of his head. "I'll be off next year." A promise he couldn't keep, but it bought him 365 days to figure it out.

"New guy?" his mother scoffed. "You've been at this for ten years!"

"New to Investigations," Hudson clarified. And it was eleven years. His mom shook her head, disapproving of it all.

"Listen." Tobias sat in a chair next to him. "I know we're supposed to be making merry and all, but . . . I'm sorry about your friend."

Hudson paused. His fork quivered three inches above his plate. "You can't be hangin' around, Tobias. People saw you at the funeral."

"No one saw me."

"*I* saw you."

"You're my brother. I wanted you to see me. To know I cared. It ain't always cops against criminals. Some of us are more alike than we think . . . or want to believe."

Hudson didn't like the way Tobias was looking at him. So sure, like he knew something Hudson didn't. They might have the same blood, but they were nothing alike. Tobias didn't have one good-intentioned nerve in his body. And Hudson, well, he had at least one. But there was another core difference between them that Hudson wasn't proud of: he lied, and Tobias didn't. It wasn't out of malevolence on his part, or reverence on Tobias's; rather, it was a matter of necessity and non-necessity, of having shame and not, of having everything to lose versus nothing.

Hudson had lied on his background check. He'd done everything he could to distance himself from Tobias, from changing his last name to making sure he graduated at the top of his high school class, and later the police academy. He volunteered at the animal rescue once a week, gave a percentage of his salary to support cancer research, and took three names off the Charity Tree for Christmas, buying gifts for anonymous children aged zero to twelve. He gave and he gave and he gave, for everything his brother stole.

Hudson lied because he had to. Tobias, on the other hand, never felt the need. Not even when they were kids and he left Hudson to drown by the pier. Afterward, when a cop brought Hudson home, wet and shivering and wrapped in a blanket, their mother asked Tobias why he'd walked away, to which he'd simply answered, "Because you love him more than me."

If that had ever been the case—loving Ryan more than Tobias—it ended that day for Phoebe Shannon. She made sure to shower Tobias with love—packing extra snacks in his lunch at school while Hudson got what was left. Stale Pop-Tarts torn in half. Popcorn, chewy from the night before. Once, he sneaked into the cupboard after school and bit into a processed Honey Bun. It was sickly and deliciously sweet, but when his mother found the wrapper in the garbage hours later, she scolded him for eating Tobias's food and made him fork over fifty cents to replace what he had eaten. "Stealing is a sin, Ryan," she told him. "You'll steal your way into Hell, you keep up this behavior."

Now, Tobias stole TVs, jewelry, and Hudson was pretty sure the Mercedes parked in the driveway was stolen and replated.

The only thing that made Hudson feel better was the theory that their mother really did love him more than Tobias, and she felt guilty. Giving in to his brother, then, was only her way of protecting them both—him from Tobias, and Tobias from himself. But, it was only a theory.

"It's dangerous for you," was all Hudson would allow himself to say. He pushed his ham around on his plate.

"The *world* is dangerous," challenged Tobias.

"You shouldn't have gone there!" The sharpness of his own voice startled him. His fist pounded the table, causing his fork to fly out of his hand. A crack across the cheek made everything go silent. His glasses crunched against the bridge of his nose and he knew they were broken.

Despite her barely five-foot stature, Phoebe Shannon had the ability to tower over anyone. Her chest heaved up and down, her jaw set. Her cheeks glowed as red as the ornaments on the tree. "What did I tell you boys about fighting?" she spat. "I'll have none of it. Not tonight. Now, if you can't love your brother for one night out of the year, Ryan, you'll have to go. And don't ever think about setting foot in this house again. Not 'til you quit with all this good guy, bad guy nonsense. God made you no better than the rest of us. It's time you learn that."

Hudson sat still. His feet felt cemented to the floor and his mouth filled with the taste of blood from having bitten his tongue. It had been years since she'd slapped him like that. But her words stung more. He righted his glasses as much as possible, then stood. His chair scraped across the floor. The snow had only just melted off his shoes when he shoved his feet back into them and grabbed his coat.

"Ryan—" his mom called, but Tobias stood and wrapped his arm over her shoulders.

"Let him go, Ma. He ain't one of us no more. Never fuckin' was."

19

MORGAN

Morgan sat at the breakfast table, bouncing her feet, both of which were engulfed in new Homer Simpson slippers. She'd opened them just twenty minutes ago, along with a set of pajamas, a bright red stocking cap with the *Duff* label stitched on the cuff, and a fleece blanket that looked like the quintessential big pink donut.

Every Christmas since she could remember, her parents had showered her with *Simpsons* stuff—likely due to the fact that it was Christmas morning when she showed up at the Moris' house all those years ago, with a secondhand jacket and a vise grip on her Bart Simpson doll.

She was adopted. That fact had never been kept a secret from her. How could it have been when she remembered sitting slumped in a pilled maroon chair in the caseworker's office, her swinging feet barely grazing the carpet. At the ripe old age of ten, she was planted on her new and improved mom and dad's doorstep. Ta-da!

She saw it immediately. Because although ephemeral, it was unmistakable. The slow pressing of the lips, the eyes that slipped into sideways glances, each parent blaming the other, as though to say, *You wanted this*. This bruised and brittle girl. This girl who bites and screams in her sleep. This girl who brings out the worst in everyone she touches. All this excitement built up and suddenly, here she was. The anticlimax, a firework that fizzled without even the smallest pop, a punch line that didn't land quite right.

Oh well, final sale. No returns.

She waited for her dad to finish with the silver shaker, then grabbed it and sifted powdered sugar on her waffle. From across the table, Grandpa Teddy's eyes crinkled at her. His freezer bag filled with watermelon Jolly Ranchers rested by his plate. It had taken Morgan six bags to complete. The other flavors were dumped in an old Halloween bowl downstairs. She still had to sort them.

To her mom, she'd gifted a new set of baking pans and a funny oven mitt. Her dad got a new wrench set and a bag of socks.

The whipped cream can crackled as she sprayed some on her waffle and added a swirl to her coffee. Grandpa Teddy held his mug out for her to do the same. He smiled like they'd just done something devious.

It was barely 8:00 A.M., but Christmas at the Mori household had run its course. They'd opened their gifts, said their thank-yous to one another, and folded the scraps of wrapping paper to be reused next year. After breakfast, her dad would go back to the factory, Grandpa Teddy would fall asleep in his chair, and her mother would fulfill some more last-minute black-market cookie orders.

Morgan wondered what the Reynoldses were doing. Eleanor would be perfectly put together, she was sure—all made up wearing diamond earrings and a silk pajama set she hadn't even worn to bed the night before. Don would be dapper, of course, at the breakfast bar making her coffee. Blake, Cora, and Charlie would coordinate in buffalo plaid pajamas; Carlisle would be in a festive adult onesie; David would be brooding in black; and Bennett would be dressed as if for a meeting—button-down shirt, black slacks, hair gelled and swept to the side.

Her heart palpitated at the thought of him and the moment under the mistletoe. He'd invited her over last night. His email popped up in the right-hand corner of her computer screen while she scanned. It had just turned midnight.

Merry Christmas, Morgan Mori.

Merry Christmas, Bennett Reynolds, she typed back.

I'm afraid we have a problem.

The statement had chilled her blood. What kind of problem could there possibly be between her and Bennett Reynolds? Did he want his money back? Because she'd already spent some of it on her family's gifts. The rest was stuffed in the Nestlé tin.

A new email appeared before she could respond: *Santa accidentally left a present for you here.*

Her stomach flipped. They'd gotten her something? How was she supposed to repay them? *Pretty sure I was on the naughty list this year, so . . .*

Come over in the morning, he said. *10ish?*

And so here she was, back at the Reynolds estate for the third time this week. Morgan deposited her grandpa's unintentionally vintage car between Bennett's Porsche and the Land Rover she'd deduced as belonging to Cora and Blake. Don drove the Tesla.

Bennett sat on the sun porch, his back to the window. She felt a little like she was sneaking up on him, stalking him. She knocked and watched as he turned, caught her eye, and disappeared. Within seconds, the door fell away and he stood before her, in all his primped and polished glory. Not a hair was out of place. Bennett Reynolds was a masterpiece. "Miss Mori. Merry Christmas."

Morgan smiled, attempting to mask her nervousness. What was it about him that kept her so on edge? Perhaps it was the ease with which he moved through the world. Or the way his eyes constantly scanned her, like she was a code he wanted to break.

"Can I interest you in a coffee? Espresso? Hot cocoa?" He threw the question over his shoulder as he wandered into the kitchen.

Morgan heel-toed her boots off and followed him toward the breakfast bar, her gaze settling on the fancy silver espresso machine. It looked like something out of a steampunk novel, with its myriad of gears and wands.

"How many shots?" Bennett was already behind the counter, sliding a cup under the machine's dual sprockets.

"Four?" She heard the inflection in her tone. Her normal shot count was six, but she should exercise some self-control. She was a guest in someone's home, after all. Then again it was Christmas, a day of merrymaking made possible only by shots—whether espresso or alcohol.

"You sure about that?" His eyes lifted.

"Unshakably."

"It's pouring six." When Morgan regarded him quizzically, he added, "Shot counts are like body counts."

"Body counts?" *As in bodies left for dead,* she wondered. What did he know?

"You ask a woman how many people she's slept with, you take her answer and add two. Guys, you minus two."

Morgan turned his words over in her mind. All was quiet inside the Reynolds house. And yet, a wake of warmth remained, as though the place had been teeming with warm bodies not so long ago. She and Bennett were alone. She could feel it. She kept her hand steady as she accepted the steaming cup. "So, what's your count, Mr. Reynolds?"

His keen eyes locked onto her face. "Two," he whispered, with a look that said he knew she didn't believe him for a second. He grazed her cheekbone with the edge of his thumb, then. It was an intimate gesture. She felt something stir inside her, something carnal and dark. If she was at The Ruins, she'd turn her head and let his thumb slip into her mouth. She'd bite down, just a little, so he knew she had teeth and that she was willing to use them. Then, he'd drop to the floor.

But they weren't at The Ruins. They were in the wolf's den. "You ready?" he asked.

Morgan was about to ask what for when she remembered her reason for coming over. "To see what Santa deposited under the wrong tree?"

They took their places in the living room, Bennett kneeling by the tree and Morgan sitting on the couch where Christopher had sat yesterday. She leaned forward, resting her elbows on her knees and breathing in the roasted aroma of the espresso. The place was already picked up from this morning's gift opening. They were a vanishing bunch, the Reynoldses. So alive and in command of the moment, and gone the next. "Where is everyone?" she asked, finally.

"Family snowmobiles. They hit the trail about an hour ago. Well, everyone except David. I think he's painting. Or brooding."

Family snowmobiles, what a concept. Of the people she knew, most of their family gifts consisted of a board game or a tin of popcorn. "You didn't want to go?"

"Had better plans."

She smiled appropriately, knowing that she was indeed his *better plan.* "So that's it, huh? The vagabond present that wandered under the wrong tree." There was, indeed, one lone gift wrapped in silver foil. A red bow perched on top.

"That's the one." He retrieved it from beneath the boughs and handed it to her.

The gift was about the size of a mailbox and weighed several pounds. She could tell by its weight that it was expensive. Tilting the box on its side, she slid her finger under a triangle of folded foil and began to unwrap. The foil fell away to reveal a white box with black and red type.

"You didn't," she said, stopping abruptly. The gift was still half-wrapped.

"You don't even know what it is yet."

"Bennett, I—" She what? Couldn't believe it? Couldn't accept it?

"Love it?" he finished hopefully.

Morgan sighed. She felt hollow. The stirring inside her was gone, evaporated. A new wave of feelings erupted in its place. Gratitude. Disbelief. Utter mystification. She finished tearing away the paper to reveal the newest Canon EOS 5D Mark IV, complete with prime lens.

"I know these things have a ton of gadgets, so there's a gift card, too." He pointed to a tiny red envelope taped to the top, inside of which, as promised, was a gift card for $2,500.

"Bennett, this is insane. I can't—"

"Process how happy you are?"

"Accept this. I'm sorry. I just can't."

The puerile light in his eyes extinguished. The color faded from his cheeks. Even his hair seemed limp. Morgan instantly felt regret, but it was true. She couldn't accept the camera, or the gift card.

Clearly unfamiliar with rejection, Bennett climbed up on the couch to sit beside her. "You can," he coaxed. He wrapped his arm around her. She breathed in his bottled scent of bourbon and smoke and felt cloaked in calm, like the feeling of a blanket settling over her or a drink snaking its way into her bloodstream. "Remember last week, when I told you I make a fuck ton of money? This didn't even cost close to that."

It wasn't so much about the money as it was the intimacy of the gift. To wield a camera again—one even better than the one she'd had before—was a revival. Of power. Of independence. Of a means to make her way in the world yet. "Bennett, we don't even know each other."

And she intended to keep it that way. She couldn't ruin him as she had so many others. What was that thing he'd said about body counts, add two? More like two dozen, in her case.

"I know everything I need to know." His fingertips walked over the back of her hand then, sliding into place between her knuckles. She felt him squeeze, felt a shot of endorphins rush through her, felt dizzy as he tilted his head toward her, his lips plush and inviting her to sink her teeth in.

The back door opened.

Cora's laughter echoed in the hall, followed by the sounds of boots thumping on the mudroom tile.

Relieved, Morgan broke free from Bennett, sliding over to the next cushion. Bennett looked away, nonchalantly raked a hand through his hair.

"Morgan!" Eleanor exclaimed. "What a joy to see you two days in a row. Merry Christmas!"

"Merry Christmas." Morgan waved as the long-lost Reynoldses filed into the kitchen area. Eleanor removed her earmuffs and her scarf and dusted the snow from Don's shoulders. Cora bounced Charlie on her hip; he looked like a snowbaby, all rosy-cheeked and bundled up in a white teddy bear suit. She heard a light banter, then, as who she guessed to be Carlisle and Blake hung up their jackets.

"Coffee or hot cocoa, anyone?" Don clapped his hands and set forth behind the counter.

"May I have a London Fog, darling?" Eleanor called. She smiled, showing her teeth, eyes shining brightly.

"Yes, love, but only because it's Christmas. You know these things are wretchedly tedious."

"I'll have one too, please, Don," said Cora. "Oh my God, Morgan, did you get Bennett to make you an espresso?" Cora shared a look with Eleanor, then turned back to Morgan. "He must really like you. Bennett lives to be served, not to serve."

Bennett rolled his eyes. "Look who's talking, Miss Can-You-Shovel-the-Walk-So-I-Don't-Get-Snow-on-My-Boots?"

Cora laughed and raised her right hand. "Guilty. But in my defense, Louboutins were not made for snow."

"They were made for *show*," added Blake. He'd taken off his jacket and Morgan startled at all the colorful ink on his arms. Now that he was only wearing a T-shirt, she could see that he was covered in tattoos. The edge of one even crept out from underneath his collar. They stopped abruptly at his wrists, though. Probably so he could wear a long-sleeve shirt and no one would be any the wiser. She hadn't been.

There was something different about all of them, wasn't there? Now that she was aware, she noticed the dimple piercings in Carlisle's cheeks, and where was her mane of blond hair? Surely it couldn't all be tucked into her hat.

"Thank you, honey." Cora leaned over to plant a kiss on her husband's lips. She entwined her arm with his then, and rested her head on his shoulder. With Charlie still on her hip, it looked as though they were posed for a family portrait, and Morgan was reminded again of her other camera, the one with all their Christmas photos on it. She looked down at the new hardware in her lap.

"Ooh, did you give it to her? What do you think, Morgan?"

"It's . . ." Morgan took a deep breath. "I don't know what to say. Thank you," she said for the first time, turning toward Bennett. "I'm . . ."

"In shock?" Cora laughed.

Morgan nodded. Yes. What was this strange new world into which she'd tumbled? Walking into the Reynolds estate really was like wandering through a wardrobe. Everything was better here. Nicer. Even the people. Who just gave someone—a stranger, essentially—thousands of dollars' worth of gifts?

"You really don't know what this means to me." A tear slipped down her cheek and she let it. She could help her parents catch up on bills. Buy a new car. Leave. "I don't know how I can ever repay you."

Don handed steaming mugs to both Cora and Eleanor. He returned to the espresso bar, pouring a shot of whiskey into his own.

"You could grace us with your presence again," suggested Eleanor.

When Morgan looked at Bennett, she added: "Come to the cabin with us. For New Year's."

"Cabin?" Morgan reached back in her memory for the last batch of photos she'd scanned, and thought she remembered catching glimpses of an A-frame structure in the woods.

"Aw, yes!" said Cora, as though speaking for Morgan. "That would be so fun. We go up every year. Well . . . we do now, again."

"It's a hike," said Carlisle as she hopped up to sit on top of the breakfast bar. She took her hat off to reveal a head of short blond hair, shaved on one side. And when David wandered in through the sun porch smelling of aerosol and standing next to her, she knew where she'd seen the two of them before.

The Ruins.

Carlisle's mouth twitched like she could read Morgan's mind. The key burned the inside of her wrist. It was possible that they had been the ones to leave it for her, Morgan thought. That the black sheep of the family had lured her home.

Suddenly, she felt Bennett take her hand. "Well, what do you say?" he asked.

How long had Morgan sat there, staring silently at the pair of them? Their presence awakened something inside her. Fear. Dread. A homesickness for a place she no longer had. The smell of spray paint took her back to the night of the shooting. *I found you*. Her head swam.

"Yes," she answered finally, only to appease the Reynoldses. She would cancel later. And as she gathered her things, she noticed how David's and Carlisle's eyes never left her. They weren't sheep at all. They were wolves.

20

HUDSON

The knock at his front door sent Pip bounding off the couch. Her nails clacked against the hardwood floors as she scurried through the kitchen, Hudson at her heels. He squinted through his taped glasses to see who was at his doorstep.

Miserelli's red hair looked like a firework, all kinked and shooting off in every direction, as it did when not tied in a low bun.

He drew in a deep breath and opened the door.

"Merry Christmas. Can we come in?" she asked, referring to her and the bottle of Jameson she held.

Hudson stepped aside and let her in. The crisp Christmas cold bit at his skin, needled at his bare arms, and made his nipples stand at attention beneath his T-shirt. He smoothed a hand over them so she wouldn't see. He wasn't in the mood for jokes. He wasn't in the mood for Joey.

Because this was what she did. She loved him, then she loved him not. Then she loved him again. Perhaps "love" was the wrong word. Wanted. She wanted him until she didn't.

He stood back, hands shoved into his flannel PJ pockets. He waited for her to speak, the cold floor kissing the bottoms of his feet through the holes worn in his slipper soles. Nan had bought him a new pair every year. Now that she was gone, whenever a new pair turned up as a recommended item online, he couldn't bring himself to pull the trigger. He'd slough around in these damn things until they disintegrated on his way to the fridge one day.

Did Miserelli see him, he wondered. Really see him for what he was—a man who spent Christmas morning alone but for his dog, who shuffled around the house in tattered slippers and pilled pajama pants, wearing a pair of broken glasses. On paper, he was a relatively intelligent detective with over a thousand criminal arrests under his belt. He could run a mile in under six minutes, outshoot just about anyone at the range (excluding SIU), and had earned the exemplary officer award for six years running. So which Ryan Hudson did she see, the flesh version or the paper version?

"Do you have shot glasses?" she asked, setting the bottle firmly in the center of the table. Whether it was meant as a peace offering or a Christmas present, all it did was remind him of how much he missed the other most important person in his life. Jameson was Garrison's favorite shot. Chase it with a bottle of Spotted Cow, and you had his favorite dinner.

His mind went to the Garrison household—Noelle and Lilah waking up in a chilly, cheerless house, the place on the couch empty where, every other Christmas morning, Brix would sit and laugh as he tore into something gimmicky—a custom bobblehead made to look like him or a hat with a bottle opener on the brim. The image dystrophied, drowned by the same deafening, disorienting silence that had befallen the chapel at the funeral. He wondered if they'd even put presents under the tree at all.

He grabbed two shot glasses out of the cupboard and ran them under the faucet to rinse the dust from them. Set them next to the whiskey.

"I figured we could toast to Garrison," said Miserelli.

Hudson nodded. He cracked open the bottle and poured them each a shot, slid Miserelli's to her.

"Thanks." She clinked her glass against his, and together, they tipped them back. Hudson watched her screw up her face. "Tastes like motor oil."

"It's not good," he agreed, wiping his mouth on the bottom of his T-shirt. He glanced up and noticed Miserelli staring at him, at his abdomen and the trail of dark hair that journeyed below his belly button. He fixed his shirt and put both glasses in the sink. He started to rinse them when he felt something against his skin, cold and light as a snowflake. The winter air clung to her clothes, her hair, her hands as she touched him. His entire body tensed, her familiar caress having turned him into a block of ice.

And ice could melt.

"How was your mom's last night?" she asked.

"It was good," he lied, and knew he didn't sound convincing.

"That's good." She rested her head against his back. He closed his eyes, giving in to her, to the whiskey that shrouded his mind in a dreamy fog. And for a moment, all his problems slipped away. He was a worry stone, worn so smooth after Garrison's death and being disowned by his family that nothing bad could stick to him anymore. For the first time in his life, he felt invincible, a little *come-what-may*.

Miserelli slid to her knees, taking his pants down with her. All he could see was her fiery crown moving back and forth as she began to blow him.

His hands gripped the edge of the counter. "Jesus," he breathed. When was the last time he'd gotten one of these? He went down on her almost every time they had sex, and yet, so infrequently did she return the favor.

"Don't stop," he said, and he said it again. His hands were in her hair, her wayward ringlets slipping in and out of his fingers, like melting embers. His muscles tensed, his abs contracted, every vein in his body swelled. If this was her way of apologizing . . . apology accepted.

He fell to his knees when he finished, his entire body racked with tremors. Miserelli straddled him. Her fingers made slow circles on the back of his skull that could send him into a coma. Even the slightest touch felt like a lightning bolt to him right now. She kissed him hard, and he kissed her back harder. His hands slid into the waistband of her jeans, finding purchase at the top of her butt. Her skin was velvet soft. Gliding his fingertips upward, he traced the calligraphy he knew to be inked on her spine.

Gently, he guided her to the floor. It wouldn't be the first time they'd had sex in the kitchen. In a push-up position, he leaned toward her and kissed her chin, planting a trail of them down the middle of her toned stomach. Sliding backward, he unzipped her jeans, his tongue tasting the vanilla lotion she'd massaged into her skin.

"Oh, Ryan . . ." Her voice was more soprano than usual. She arched her back, letting him slide her pants off over her hips and—

A rap at the door.

Panicked, Hudson looked up. Miserelli tore away from him and army-rolled into the living room. Pip barked. He stood, knocking his head on the countertop. He combed his hand through his hair. Fixing his glasses, he squinted to see who was outside. All he could see was the sleeve of a dark jacket.

Hudson opened the door. Nikolai Kole stood on his porch, casually, as though this were a friendly routine visit and not the first time he'd come to Hudson's house.

"Good morning, sir?" Hudson stepped aside to let Kole in, but the sergeant remained put.

"Hey, Harry Potter, your phone dead?"

"Uh, no, it's . . ." He trailed off, craning his neck to look behind him, as though he could see his phone that he'd left in the living room all the way from here. The outside air stung his skin.

Pip barked. He heard Miserelli try to shush her and had no doubt that Kole had heard it, too.

"Some baby cops picked up a guy for a disorderly. Fighting with his family, you know the Christmas tradition. Scored half an ounce off him. He's asking for a trade."

"A trade?"

"Information in exchange for a get-out-of-jail-free card."

Hudson furrowed his brows. His broken glasses slid down his nose. "What kind of information?" It wasn't a foreign concept. The underworld and the police department had their own economy wherein information was currency. The more serious the charges, the higher the price.

"He says he knows who shot Brix Garrison."

Hudson's heart stopped. Everything—frost blooming on windshields, plastic bags rolling across snowy streets, the lake effect whistling through brick houses and lean-to porches—it all stopped. When it started again a second later, he compared it to a video buffering. It felt like he was watching it, not living it: Kole standing on his doorstep, telling him it was over. They would finally arrest the piece of shit who put Garrison in the ground. Tears welled in his eyes.

A cloud materialized in front of Kole's mouth as he exhaled. "Kasper from Wesson PD's lead on this case. I called him down to do the interview. Figured you might want to watch in the—"

"I would. Yes. I'll be there in ten minutes."

Kole looked him up and down. He raised his brow as though doubting ten minutes was enough time for him to transform from his current state of undress. "Interview Room #1." He turned to leave and paused on the bottom step. "Oh, and Hudson."

Hudson paused in pulling the door closed. "Yes, sir?"

"Tell Miserelli she should park over on Locust next time. Less visibility from the PD."

21
MORGAN

The red letters of CANON MARK IV seared into her corneas like a branding iron. As she looked at the glossy white box on her passenger seat, she couldn't help but feel she'd made a Faustian bargain. Impossible. You needed a soul for a deal with the devil, and yet, she had made a trade. She'd agreed to go to the cabin all the way up in Who-the-fuck-knows-where-ville, and for what purpose? It was an event she wouldn't be getting paid to photograph. Rather, the Reynoldses seemed genuine about wanting her to participate.

It was a trap. Laid by Carlisle and David, and whoever else was hell-bent on taking her down for the things she'd done. The lives she'd probably ruined.

But what unnerved her most about going up north was that she wouldn't have the protection of hiding behind her camera. People might see the real her, the scared little girl beneath the sharp metal piercings and the stone-cold stare. Or worse, they might see the things she'd done, written on her face with ink that was invisible until she turned toward the light. *Torture. Blackmail. Ruin.*

That was why she had to cancel. She'd wait a day or two and then email Bennett that something had come up. Her grandpa had fallen on the ice. That one always got her out of obligations.

And yet, she couldn't deny she was curious about what else simmered beneath the Reynoldses' seemingly perfect surfaces. The Christmas party had been a performance for everyone else, with kraft-paper presents and flutes of effervescent champagne. But this morning, her third encounter with them, they'd begun to let their guards down, peel back the curtains. What would they be like off-camera, she wondered. Once the cable-knit costumes came off, would the claws come out?

The streets were empty, still. The plow must have come through not long ago. Piles of greyish snow butted up against yards, burying mailboxes. She watched a couple of kids in snowsuits dragging new plastic sleds before she veered left on Winslow Street.

Morgan stared through the windshield. In the daylight, the house at 604 was less intimidating. A dingy white with paint flaking off, it was camouflaged with its grim surroundings. She put the car in park, this time, and when she'd taken her new camera out of its box, clicking the battery pack and memory card into place, she did feel somewhat fearless.

"Focus," she whispered. She turned her wrist, then, ensuring the key was in its holster.

All roads lead back to home.

Well, she'd come home, now. Finally. Morgan drew in one last breath and exhaled before getting out of the car. She slammed the door. The sound was muffled, muted by the insulation of the snow. *How comforting,* she thought as she approached the front porch. If she screamed, probably no one would hear her.

The stair groaned as she put pressure on it. Gripping her camera tightly, Morgan skipped up the last three steps and squared up with the yawning doorway.

It was dark inside but for a ray of silvery light streaming in from a window. Her heart was in her throat, threatening to abandon ship if she didn't turn back now. But she couldn't. She'd come all this way with only the clothes on her back and a key that had become her everything—a hint, a hope, a promise—that there was life for her beyond Black Harbor. Whatever it opened could mean escape, the end of her sentence in this stark, coal-dusted prison.

And it was Christmas Day. Nothing bad happened on Christmas, right?

The wind whistled, rocked her back on her heels. A piece of hair cut across her face. Morgan pushed it away and, biting down on the studs in her lip, walked into the house that had shown her that Hell existed right here in Black Harbor.

Silence.

She'd wandered into a crypt. It was so quiet, the walls might as well have been poured concrete, marked by old graffiti. Drawings of pot leaves and pentagrams. Spent candles lay on the floor, their wax melted and hardened next to soggy pizza boxes, the remains of a seance.

The more Morgan looked around, the more her hope diminished. The cabinets were all opened and emptied, even the ones Bern had kept locked. The pantry had been pried open, the fridge lying faceup like a coffin. Her boots crunched on the pieces of a shattered crack pipe as she ventured farther in, toward Bern's bedroom.

The door was closed. Morgan drew in a breath before setting her hand on the cold brass knob and pushing it inward. She'd never stepped foot in this room before. It was smaller than she'd always imagined it would be. A full-size mattress lay on the floor, scantily covered by a stained sheet. The dresser drawers were pulled out. Someone had stolen all the clothes and knickknacks, whatever they had been. She didn't know what kinds of things Bern held dear, if anything at all.

The key was in her hand now. She tried it in anything that had a lock, seeing if she'd somehow overlooked the great mystery she'd been lured to discover. The bedroom door, the shallow closet, the top dresser drawer.

All empty.

She caught a glimpse of herself in the fogged mirror. She looked sad, on Christmas of all days, and small. Her glasses were too big for her face. Her jacket hung off her like a shirt on a scarecrow and her legs were stick thin, not even touching. Who did she think she was, honestly? That she could come in here and conquer her fears? She was nothing. Nobody. Just a scared little girl the world rejected over and over and over again.

The taste of salt made her tongue tingle as a tear meandered its way to her mouth. The image was achingly beautiful, in a way that she didn't usually consider anything about herself to be. Turning a smidge more toward the hoary light, Morgan chose a low aperture on the dial. Making eye contact with herself, she held the shutter down for a second until she felt the autofocus find purchase, and clicked. She took two more for good measure, already envisioning a black-and-white, grainy print she might make of it, when in the background, just over her shoulder, a spot of red peeked in and out of the frame.

Morgan jumped, dropping her camera onto the dresser top. She rescued it before it bounced onto the floor and clutched it to her chest like a newborn kitten as she tiptoed toward the hall.

The door to her old room was open. The edges of her vision darkened as she neared it. Her mouth felt dry. Her eyes watered as she fought the urge to cough, to not disturb the ghosts and the dust mites that had made this hovel their home.

She realized the cause of her tunnel vision now. Subconsciously, she'd lifted the camera to her face to only peer through the viewfinder. She gasped. A red balloon floated in the center of the floor, like the one that had waited for her in the smoky haze at The Ruins.

Morgan knelt. The balloon was tethered to a present wrapped in cheap holiday paper—white, patterned with the words NAUGHTY OR NICE in red calligraphy. A note was taped to the top of the box. It was a scrap of the same wrapping paper that had been folded, and on the blank inside was written TO: MY RUIN.

Her stomach seized. A cold sweat prickled at her hairline.

Morgan tore at a corner of the paper, wincing at how the empty house magnified the sound.

The box itself was nondescript, no name or shipping address to denote where it had come from. Inside, it held a black device. A portable DVD player, she realized, when she opened it. Stuck to the screen was a Post-it with two words that chilled Morgan's blood: *Wanna play?*

Her breath rattled in her chest. The sudden gust of cold that swept in through the busted windows dug into her shoulders, keeping her in place. She pressed Play, and watched as all the walls she'd carefully constructed since returning to Black Harbor came crashing down.

She recognized the room depicted in the video. The walls were painted matte black, mostly, but for a white orb: a skull missing its bottom jaw. Words were spray-painted in white in a scrawl-like fashion. *Shatter me. Beat me. Break me down.* A bench on a chain protruded from beneath the half skull where Morgan, herself, sat. Shackles glinted around her wrists.

The view was that of a first-person video game. The image moved as the person wearing the camera advanced into the room. She heard the door shut and she knew what was about to happen. In the video, Morgan wore a long wig, twisted into double braids, and lipstick the shade of blood. A plaid schoolgirl skirt left little to the imagination. She stared doe-eyed up at the guest, whose hand came into view as they peeled her bra strap down over her shoulder.

"Let's play," Video Morgan whispered. She offered up her hands, knuckles folded and pressed together in the shape of a heart, waiting to be undone.

"That depends," said the guest. "Have you been naughty or nice?"

Video Morgan gave her best catlike smize. "Naughty."

Before she'd finished saying the word, the guest grabbed her by the neck and squeezed. In the house on Winslow Street, Morgan felt heady, as though his hands were around her throat now.

"There's a wooden bat in the corner. Why don't you punish me properly?" whispered Video Morgan.

A carnal sound rumbled from the guest, a laugh. And then suddenly, it was cut by a yelp that evolved into heavy breathing. His hands let go of her, not by her command, but because he'd suddenly lost control of them. The camera lurched forward, showing Video Morgan expertly dodging out of the way as the guest's body crashed to the floor. A groan that sounded like white noise crackled in his throat.

Video Morgan disappeared off-screen.

Watching from her old bedroom, Morgan knew what came next. But she didn't tear her eyes away. She wanted to see what her guests saw in their final seconds before being marked forever, exposed to the world for what they truly were. Monsters. Wolves in sheep's wool. Ruined souls who ruined souls.

Video Morgan returned, wielding a glowing red branding iron. She straddled the paralyzed guest and, in her old room on Winslow Street, Morgan listened to the sibilant sound of scorching metal stamping into human flesh.

22

HUDSON

The funny thing about Black Harbor PD was that, although they had Interview Rooms #1 and #3, there was no #2. Interview Room #3 was reserved for children and victims of sensitive crimes. A blanket ladder leaned against one of the dove-grey walls, next to a basket of toys. The furniture was akin to what you'd see in someone's home: overstuffed chairs with ottomans, a matching couch. Beneath the window that over-looked the annex building and municipal parking lot, as well as his house, was a bookshelf filled with secondhand picture books. He'd spent a fair amount of time in that room, building rapport with children who were either too scared to speak or whose parents had coached them on what lies to tell.

Interview Room #1 was the opposite. Stark and windowless; the only break in the concrete block was a sixty-by-forty-eight-inch acrylic two-way mirror. It wasn't supposed to be comforting or calming. It was meant for interrogations. To break people down. To strip them of "nothing but the truth" until they had no option but to confess to their criminal mis-deeds: murder, rape, coercion. Hudson wasn't ready for that yet; however, he knew if he ever made the move to Robberies, he'd have to learn a thing or two about commanding that room.

It was an ironic commentary on Black Harbor. The fact that they only had these two spaces, for conducting either soft interviews or hard inter-rogations. There was no in-between. It was a black-and-white setup that forced people to be put in one room or the other, despite the fact that most people lived in shades of grey. Including Hudson, himself. And Kole, from what he'd heard.

The viewing room was the size of a narrow closet. It would be large enough for a twin bed and nothing else. There were two metal chairs facing the glass, neglected by the two people already in the room when he arrived. Sergeant Kole and Investigator Riley stood in identical poses, arms crossed, bodies squared up with the mirror. A pair of mint-colored headphones hung around Riley's neck. She leaned forward a bit, then, bouncing on the ball of her right foot, like a runner waiting for the sound of a gun.

Hudson pulled the door shut behind him and stood next to Kole. They were all three swathed in darkness now, the only light coming from the other side of the glass. At the stainless-steel table, a hulking figure sat, meaty hands folded. There was a bottle of water in front of him, and an unopened bag of chips. The man looked around, his gaze sweeping from the four corners of the room to the ceiling, like an animal surveying its cage. The rolls on the back of his bald head glistened with sweat. A bruise marbled his cheek.

An investigator who Hudson recognized from the roll call following Garrison's death entered the interview room. Dressed in jeans and a sweater, he looked as though he'd come straight from a Christmas party.

"Hi, I'm Detective Jerome Kasper from Wesson Police Department. I'm leading the investigation into Officer Garrison's death. How are you?"

The hulk shrugged his shoulders. It sounded as though he had cotton in his mouth when he mumbled, "Been better."

Kasper squinted, tilted his head as though assessing damage. "You might want to put some frozen peas on that. Stop the swelling."

"My cousin got me with a lamp."

Detective Kasper smiled. He had square teeth that were spaced apart, his mouth framed by a goatee. "You get him a shitty gift, or what? Sorry, bad joke." He cleared his throat. "My colleagues from this department said you've got some information concerning Officer Garrison, who was shot and killed just shy of a week ago."

The large man shifted. "Look, I can't go back to prison, man."

"No one said anything about you going back to prison."

"They got that dope on me, though. I swear—"

"Ronald, is it? Ronald Muntz?"

"Yeah."

"If you're about to tell me that half ounce of cocaine between your ass cheeks wasn't yours, you can save your breath. Now." Kasper walked closer to the table. "I could thank you for getting me out of my in-laws' place early, but I'm gonna catch hell from my wife when I get home. I won't get a lamp to the face, hopefully, but . . . you know how it is."

Hudson watched Muntz slump forward a bit, his back rounding.

"I'm gonna have to make it up to her," said Kasper. "Watch something on the Hallmark channel tonight. So you"—he pointed directly at Muntz's chest—"better make this worth my while. I don't wanna hear no *I know a guy who knows a guy* bullshit, all right?"

Hudson glanced at Kole. The sergeant cupped his right elbow with his left hand, his thumb hooked thoughtfully under his chin. His eyes swept back and forth across the two characters left to right, reading them.

"So, what have you got for me?" said Kasper.

"Look, man, you gotta swear if I tell, I ain't going back to prison. I can't do five more years, shit, I can't do five more *minutes* in that place."

"Ronald, I swear you won't go back to prison. Not for this. The fight with your cousin, that's just a disorderly conduct arrest. We'll get you out on a signature bond. And as far as the cocaine, we won't even mention it in the report. It's like you never had it on you—in you," he corrected.

"Okay." Muntz sighed. Hudson watched his shoulders rise and fall.

"You ready to tell me, then, who shot Brix Garrison on the night of December nineteenth?"

"Yeah." Muntz's breathing changed, sped up. From where he stood, Hudson could see more globules of sweat rolling down the man's stubbled head, trickling behind his ears and disappearing in the folds of his neck. "I just, uh, can I use the bathroom?"

"You serious, Ronald?" Kasper raised his brow.

"Yeah, I . . . I drank like a whole soda before they picked me up. I just gotta pee, that's all."

Kasper looked toward the mirror. Kole nudged Hudson. "Come on. I'll take the front. You watch his back."

Unsure what he'd just been volunteered for, Hudson followed Kole out of the viewing room, just as Detective Kasper opened the door to Interview Room #1. "This is Sergeant Kole and . . ."

"Hudson," Hudson offered. "Er, Investigator Hudson."

"Investigator Hudson," Kasper repeated. "They'll be your escorts to the bathroom."

Muntz looked at them each in turn. He was shorter up close, and more muscular. As Kole led the way through the bureau and down the hall with Muntz walking between them, Hudson could see clear over the top of his head. There were scars on it, dents. He would guess that today's scuffle wasn't the first fight he'd participated in. A gang symbol was tattooed on his neck. It looked like a DIY job, the ink all blued and blurred.

Once in the bathroom, Muntz went to the far urinal. Kole stood next to the paper towel dispenser, and Hudson took his place beside him. Muntz urinated for a long time. After about thirty seconds, Kole shared a look with Hudson. Muntz tipped his head back and closed his eyes, as though this was the first moment of peace he'd experienced all day.

"Jesus, you've got a bladder the size of a bathtub," said Kole. "How much soda did you drink?"

Muntz grunted. When he finished, he flushed the silver handle and zipped up his jeans.

"Hey hey hey." Kole blocked the door. "Wash your fucking hands, that's disgusting."

Muntz rolled his eyes and made a U-turn toward the sink.

If the reason for Muntz's being there hadn't been so grave, Hudson would have smiled. He knew Sergeant Kole was a bit of a neat freak. That fact was evident by the abundant supply of disinfectant wipes and hand sanitizer he kept in the bureau at all times, not to mention the man himself was immaculate. There was never so much as a hair out of place or a speck of lint on his clothing. How did he do it, Hudson wondered—have it all together in a place like Black Harbor?

The water shut off. As Muntz grabbed for a paper towel, Hudson noted he had the hands of a mechanic, the lines of his palms all antiqued with black, the same crud shoved under his fingernails.

They walked Muntz back to Interview Room #1 and returned to their positions in the viewing room.

"Better?" Kasper asked Muntz.

Muntz nodded and fell like a bag of sand into his chair. It scraped across the tile.

"Okay, now that you're more comfortable . . . tell me. Who shot Officer Brix Garrison on the night of December nineteenth?"

"I know a guy."

Kasper was already shaking his head. "I thought we weren't gonna do that."

But Muntz talked over him. "I know a guy. I bought dope from him. The stuff they found on me today."

"Okay . . . When did you buy it?"

Muntz sighed. His eyes darted to all the corners of the room as though someone else could have snuck in while he was gone. He looked at the window then, his gaze searching for where he knew Hudson and Kole to be, like a camera lens struggling to find a focal point.

"Couple days ago. Tuesday, maybe? He had a .50-caliber Desert Eagle. Black with a gold barrel. Was bragging about poppin' a cop a few nights before."

A storm cloud passed before Kasper's eyes. A crease cut severely across his forehead. When he lifted his gaze to meet Kole's, it was as though the two were telepathically connected, as though Kasper could indeed see Kole on the other side of the acrylic glass.

Hudson heard Riley inhale sharply, at the same time Kole whispered, "Motherfucker." They had him. The bullets that slammed into Garrison were .50 AE, 300-grain rounds for a Desert Eagle.

"You're sure?" Kasper posed to Muntz. "It wasn't like, a Glock 41 or . . ."

Now it was Muntz's turn to raise his brow. "Come on, bro. You don't mistake a hand cannon like that for anything else."

"You got a point. All right. So, who's your guy? The one who sold you the cocaine and was braggin' about poppin' a cop."

Muntz leaned forward in his chair, scraping it across the floor again. He hung his head. "I better not go to prison again, I'm telling you."

Kasper raised his right hand. "I swear on my mother's grave, you will not go to prison for this."

Muntz was quiet, as though rethinking his decision to come here.

"Ronald," prompted Kasper.

The giant man leaned forward so his forehead was on the table. From his vantage point, Hudson could see him kneading his hands. "You know he's gonna kill me for this, right?" His words were muffled, spoken to the floor. "He'll feed me to that goddamn snake of his or some shit."

"Sit up, Ronald." When the hulk didn't move, Kasper leaned hard on the table. The water bottle toppled off, bounced once when it hit the floor and rolled out of sight. "You have two seconds to tell me who shot Brix Garrison before I lock you back up in handcuffs."

Muntz finally looked up. He'd left a pool of sweat on the stainless-steel surface and Hudson could see that the back of his shirt was soaked through.

"One," counted Kasper.

Muntz shook his head. "I'm fucked."

"Two."

Suddenly, Muntz stood. A screeching metal sound tore through both rooms as he ripped the table out of the floor. Bolts bulleted in different directions, one nicking the two-way mirror. Riley yelled and covered her ears with her hands before darting after Kole, who had run into the interview room to assist Kasper. By the time Hudson made it in, Kole already had a Taser trained on the man.

"You pull a stunt like that again, Muntz, you're going to prison," said Kole. "I don't care whose grave I have to swear on."

"How about your friend's? Garrison, was it?" Muntz's breathing was heavy and labored. Flipping the table was obviously more exertion than he'd had in the past year or more. Riley and Kasper held him back.

The Taser in Kole's hand buzzed. The prods made an electrifying *clack clack!* Hudson felt his blood doing the same thing, electrifying. He wanted to punch Muntz square in the mouth.

"Hudson." Kole's voice snapped him out of his fantasy. "Call the jail. Tell 'em we got a new booking coming through."

"No!" shouted Muntz. He started to lunge at Hudson but Kole commanded him to his knees, the Taser still trained on him. "Tell us who shot Brix Garrison, Muntz. Now!"

Muntz let out a sob, and just as Hudson took his cell phone out of his pocket to dial the jail, he uttered a name that blackened the edges of Hudson's vision, like a page thrown into a puddle of ink. "Hades."

23
MORGAN

Morgan wandered out of the downstairs bathroom, towel-drying her hair and leaving wet prints that evaporated in her wake. In an oversized shirt worn thin by time, and a pair of boxer briefs, she plopped down on her mattress. Then, she reached for the bottle of Absolut wedged in the couch cushion and slugged it back.

The vodka swam between her teeth, scorched her throat on the way down. Upstairs, muted by the floor between them, she could hear the sounds of *A Christmas Story* as her mom curled up next to her dad on the couch, and Grandpa Teddy slept with his mouth open in the recliner. That was how they spent most Christmas nights, but this year, Morgan had excused herself as being sick—not a lie—and hoofed it downstairs, toting her two new gifts: one from a handsome and wealthy admirer and the other from a sadistic anonymous fuck who wanted to see her squirm.

The same sadistic anonymous fuck who'd left her the key.

She knew it without a doubt. The handwriting on both notes was the same. She set her presents on her desk, the camera on one side of her computer monitor and the portable DVD player on the other. Then, she sat on the edge of her mattress with her knees drawn up, and stared, daring either one of them to move.

When they didn't, her gaze slid to Eleanor's box of photographs, on top of which lay a duplicate portrait of the one she'd first studied on the mantel. Her eyes burned a hole in the picture as she dared to imagine how different things would have been if she'd been born a Reynolds. If she hadn't been "the ruin," "the little wretch" as Aunt Bern had called her.

Left in her clutches at four years old and for four more years thereafter, Morgan had always thought Bern had been named for the scars on her face, the puckered flesh that made striated rivers on her skin. Legend had it she'd knocked a scalding kettle on her head when she was young. Or her sister—Morgan's mother, Ava—had. Both women told different stories, apparently.

The people paid her aunt cash, mostly, but sometimes they presented little baggies of what looked like snow in exchange for twenty minutes, forty minutes, an hour—depending on the amount—with Morgan. There was no set menu. It was à la carte. They could do whatever they wanted to her in the allotted time, so long as they did not kill her.

That didn't mean some of them didn't come close.

They wore hoods, or what Morgan later learned were balaclavas. Black wool hoods that concealed everything but their eyes, and even that space had a mesh insert. They could see her, but she couldn't see them. A man beat her with a belt. Another strangled her with his tie. A woman hurt her with a corkscrew. But the worst were the plastic bags from the liquor store. Cloudy black things and vaguely translucent, they always looked to Morgan like skin shed by a snake. They slipped them over her head like a bonnet and knotted the handles around her neck. She screamed. Not because anyone would save her, but as her sentence dragged on, she learned that screaming made her black out faster, so she didn't have to be lucid for the horrors that ensued.

And then, one morning just weeks after Morgan's eighth birthday, all was quiet. She didn't hear the growl of the coffeemaker. Or the shuffling of Bern's slippered feet across the kitchen floor. She didn't hear the dreaded knocks on the door, or the whisper of a jacket sliding over the back of a chair.

The only sounds came from outside. Cars shushed past. A shovel scraped against a sidewalk. A dog's metal tags tinkled. A shrill scream scared the birds from the power lines. An icicle fell from the gutter and splintered.

When the police came, they wrapped Morgan in a blue fleece blanket.

They muttered words like "Jesus Christ" and "house of horrors." They asked if she had family, to which Morgan shook her head.

Bern had been her only family. Her mother had run off years ago. She'd disappeared so effectively, in fact, that Morgan had begun to doubt her existence at all. All she had were vague memories and the Bart Simpson doll she'd given her before dropping her off at the house on Winslow Street, never to be seen or heard from again.

The investigation revealed that Bern had slipped and fallen on her way to the mailbox. Cracked her skull on the sidewalk. The cops told her not to look, but Morgan stole a glance out the window and saw Bern lying there. Her eyes looked frosted over, like a windshield in December. The blood had already frozen around her head.

After, Morgan's homelife became a kaleidoscope of different families, different houses. She never stayed in any one place too long; her ways of staring for hours on end and arranging everything in perfect symmetrical formation, from Legos to books to knives in the cutlery drawer, had a tendency to scare people. Especially adults. The children seemed more or less intrigued, but as soon as they began to mimic her behavior, she was cast out like a package delivered to the wrong address. Return to sender.

That was how she ended up almost exactly where she started, in Black Harbor, no more than ten blocks from where she'd lived with Bern. Lynette and Bruce Mori were a childless couple who'd been on the list for over a decade. And so, one monochromatic Christmas morning, she appeared on their doorstep—the gift they'd always wanted, but made with broken parts.

The social worker said it was a clean start. But even then, Morgan knew better. She was like a memory card. You could do your damnedest to erase all the images on it, but they were all there underneath it all, waiting to be recovered.

She was small and uncivilized. When she eventually started school, only the faculty were wise to the fact that their first grader was ten years old. She got her driver's license at twenty, and graduated at the age of twenty-two. She was careful not to make any friends through it all. Or perhaps it had been less effort on her part and more the natural aversion of her peers. We learn from a young age to stay away from things that look like they could hurt us.

She didn't hurt anyone until later.

The Ruins. She'd named it that herself, after hers truly. A nod to Bern, it was her way of telling the universe that she hadn't forgotten about what happened to her in the little slanted house in Black Harbor. Like her, The Ruins began as a blank space. It had previously been a department store with bright lights and whitewashed walls. Women in heels and black slacks offered perfume samples and makeup trials. There were jewelry cases and racks for scarves and handbags and unnecessary accessories. And when the mall went bankrupt and the store went out of business and purged all its finer things, Morgan leased it for pennies on the dollar.

Her thesis: What would humans create, if unbridled? If fear of judgment wasn't part of the artistic process, what would they bring into the world? The left side of the brain is limited by the right side's fear, but without that fear factor, without dreading rejection, how far would people go?

The Ruins opened up to a dozen art students who brought friends—filmmakers and models and photographers, creatives who wanted to live in and make use of the space. And within a few months' time, it had become a burgeoning and wonderfully weird community. People from the outside were invited in. They paid monthly memberships that helped keep the lights on, the events going, everything from New Year's parties to film festivals and poetry slams.

In the center of it all was a fountain that had long since been drained. A tree made entirely of Mylar foil sprouted from it. Thousands of feet of fishing line draped from its branches, to which Polaroid photos were clipped. In its trunk was a hollow that held an exposed, anatomical heart that had a battery pack and a mechanism inside so it beat sixty times per minute. Beneath the tree was a light that could be changed to red, yellow, blue, or magenta to manipulate an ambiance.

There was a garden of flowers made from thrift store dishes. Mannequins dressed to kill, frozen in mid-strut down an aisle fashioned into a mock catwalk. They wore electrical tape and barbed wire, a dress of singed one-hundred-dollar bills. One was clothed in a sleek black dress with a sleek black heel, her other foot being devoured by a grisly hunter's trap, the chain trailing in her wake like a shackle. Carlisle's mannequins. That was where she'd seen her and David before—gluing spikes and feathers and adding finishing touches before the pieces came to life on the catwalk.

Stairwells were covered in graffiti and palindromic poetry and each room had its own atmosphere. They were named for tragic women: Hester, Sybil, Ophelia, and Lenore. Sometimes, people just called them by the colors of their walls: scarlet, grey, violet, and black.

Morgan's favorite haunt was Lenore's room, with its matte black walls and sculptures of ravens diving from the ceiling. That was where she waited for them, the guests who paid not to create but to destroy, on a white bench at the base of a skull mural. It extended from the wall like an unhinged jaw.

She waited for them as she had at the house on Winslow Street, twenty years before. Only now, she had better clothes. She wore ribbed over-the-knee stockings and a short leather skirt. A torn T-shirt or a lacy bralette. One shackle encircled her left ankle, another for each of her wrists. But they were only for show; never locked. Her pulse pounded whenever someone entered. Excitement mixed with nostalgia, and of course, a dash of fear. That she'd fail. Be overpowered again.

Their breathing was always the first thing she heard. It was heavy and hurried, stifled somewhat by the black hoods Morgan doled out as courtesy. Everyone took her up on it. In the underworld, anonymity was valuable, and once you lost it, there was no getting it back.

Their energy matched hers when she patted the bench beside her. Excited. Nervous. They thought they were there to meet a fifteen-year-old girl. That's what she'd told them online, and she looked young enough to play the part. Some of them had done this kind of thing before; others were exploring the darkest parts of themselves for the first time.

Morgan always made sure it was the last time.

She let them touch her. Some, she even let them press their lips to her neck, slide their hands up her shirt. She never let them get too far, though, when she'd straddle them, slip her chains over their shoulders, and jam the needle into their neck.

The ketamine only took a few seconds to do its thing. She liked the sound they made when they hit the floor. All that dead weight, crashing down. Some of them had to have broken bones from hitting so hard. She never found out, though, because once she pressed the hot iron to their necks to expose their ugliness to the world, she never saw them again. Her henchman—a mute giant of a man—came in afterward and hauled out the trash.

When they came to in an empty, half-dilapidated parking garage hours later, their only memory took the form of their new status burned into their flesh, defined by a single word: *Ruined.* Going to the police would require them to admit what they'd been doing in a place like that. And the police might dig. Exhume things they didn't want pulled to the surface. Like the fact that the complainant was under the impression they were going to The Ruins to engage in violent sex with a minor.

It had been the perfect business model.

Until it all disintegrated. Poof. Nothing left but a key and that goddamn note. *My Ruin: All roads lead back to home.*

Whoever had burned down The Ruins was watching her. They knew who she was and that she would eventually summon the courage to return *home*—to the house on Winslow Street. They'd planted the portable DVD player, and not long before she'd gone there. The balloon had still been afloat. In this cold, a balloon wouldn't last more than a few hours.

It could have been the person from the video. They'd been wearing a camera, obviously, to catch her in the act.

A cop?

The man had been white or at least light-skinned, so it hadn't been Officer Garrison despite the fact that he'd been looking for her. And Hudson . . . she'd seen his neck. The smooth, unmarred skin. It wasn't him.

Then who? Who was haunting her? Hunting her?

Her eyes scanned the piles of photos on her desk. She went over to it. Pinched between her fingers was a picture of the Reynoldses all sitting at a pub table in Dublin. Could it be one of them, she wondered. But what ties would any of them have to her? Her focus homed in on Carlisle and David. They'd visited The Ruins as artists, attended her swanky soirées. They would know what she was capable of, what she did in those back rooms named for tragic heroines.

She picked up another photo. And another. In each, David and Carlisle stared at her—through her—their looks taunting her with what they knew.

"No," Morgan breathed.

She rifled through Eleanor's box of paper memories, searching for a photo where they didn't have a damning glare, and came upon a copy of the family portrait she'd first seen on the mantel less than a week ago.

The Carlisle and David in the portrait didn't know her. They were young, six and thirteen. But they stared at her as though they could see through her, as though they understood. Perhaps because they weren't so different from her, with their love for macabre things. Carlisle with her singed dresses and bear-trap heels. David with his aerosol portraits of human pincushion dolls in the stairwells.

Morgan, at least, had an excuse. Bern had made her into what she was, a misanthropic vengeful creature. What was theirs? While their dad had disappeared without a trace, there had to be more to it than that. Something more depraved.

She moved whole albums out of the box, turning over every picture of David and Carlisle, until at last her fingernails scraped the bottom. Something cold knocked loose from the corner and rolled toward her.

It was a film canister. Curious, she held it up to the light of her lava lamp. It looked old. The orange label had begun to peel. And then, she dropped it as though it had started on fire. It clinked and rolled across concrete floor, circling back toward her like a planchette on a Ouija board. Morgan picked her feet up, hugged her knees to her chest. She might as well have been communicating with a ghost; she felt the blood drain from her face, her lips go numb, as even in the dim light of her parents' basement, she saw the handwritten initials on the canister: *M.R.*

Her lips moved soundlessly. *My Ruin.*

24

HUDSON

"I ain't a cop killer, Ryan. Come on. You know me."

Hudson scrutinized his brother through a thick glass partition. Tobias looked as rough as he'd ever seen him, though in his line of work as a drug dealer, Hudson supposed he must have had days when he'd woken up in worse shape. At least here, in Sulfur County Jail, he was safe. Although—he threw a glance over each shoulder, noting the cops guarding each exit—if he really killed Garrison, he might not be.

He'd sat in his car for a full five minutes before drumming up the courage to go in. The possibility of someone recognizing him scared the hell out of him. While Hudson had never worked in the jail, it was attached to the law enforcement center, a concrete building that, with all its fissures, looked like a skull being forced out of the asphalt. Patrol officers transported prisoners here. Luckily, he still knew very few people on first shift. If he was with Garrison, it'd be a different story. Garrison had been a local celebrity. But without his larger-than-life partner, Hudson was essentially invisible. It worked in his favor, he thought as he finally got out and slammed the door. He paid the meter, cursing Tobias for making him his one phone call.

Now, he stared at Tobias behind a sheet of glass. His skin was sallow. Purplish half-moons cupped his eyes. Stubble covered his usually smooth face and neck. The center of his snowflake tattoo pulsed as he swallowed.

"You think I did it." Tobias turned away, cut his chin on his shoulder. Sniffed. "Is that why you didn't warn me?"

The phone caused his voice to echo. It sounded as though they were miles, rather than inches, apart. Hudson's heart began to hammer, and he reminded himself that Tobias couldn't hurt him. Not like all the other times, like when they'd been kids and Tobias pushed Hudson off the pier, or later, in high school, when he got his cronies to zip-tie Hudson to the urinal so he could beat the shit out of him.

Where were his cronies now, Hudson wondered. His friends.

Nowhere to be found, that was where. Hiding in their hovels and drug dens, probably more than content to know that Hades was locked up and off the streets. Out of sight, out of mind. He wasn't a drug lord anymore. He'd been dethroned, pitched from his status in Black Harbor's underworld. The man who sat on the other side of the glass partition from him was nothing more than a lowly drug dealer.

Hudson sighed into the plastic receiver. The phone smelled like cheap perfume. He wasn't obligated to help Tobias, who had committed his life to terrorizing him. But, he didn't have it in him to not help him.

When Muntz gave Kasper the address last night—corroborating one of the three places they'd been looking into—police had moved quickly. Kole wrote the warrant while Kasper called Wesson PD's SWAT team to dress and assemble. And Hudson had been powerless to stop any of it. He stood in the bureau like a buoy in the climax of a storm, the waves tossing him this way and that, struggling to stay above water.

He knew they'd seize Tobias's phone. A call or text from Hudson would have been damning for both of them. He wouldn't have had time to drive over there if he'd wanted. And had he even wanted to? He wondered if he'd play it all differently now, after seeing his brother shrunken in his jail jumpsuit, the fabric faded to the color of the Ruins ticket.

No, he decided. He wouldn't have done anything differently. Because if Tobias killed Garrison, he should rot in prison. And if he didn't, then the truth would set him free.

And yet, the truth, like killing two birds with one stone, could destroy them both. Hudson knew that. He'd known it since eleven years ago, when he first submitted his application to the Black Harbor Police Department. Being exposed as the brother of the city's most notorious drug dealer would end his career and put Tobias in a body cast, or worse.

He'd be labeled a snitch, which was just about the worst thing a guy could be.

"You know, he saved my life once, your friend." Tobias's dark eyes held on Hudson's like magnets. "Saw me at the edge of Forge Bridge, one foot already off the railroad tie." He set his elbow on the counter, pinched the bridge of his nose, driving his knuckle into his brow.

Hudson had never seen Tobias like this, so vulnerable and defeated. He furrowed his brows, trying to make sense of the pitiful man on the other side of the glass. It had to be true. Tobias never lied. "Tobias, I never knew. You never said anything . . ."

"You never asked. But we're not really that way, you and me, are we? We're brothers, but we've never been brotherly." He smiled, though it wasn't a happy smile. "Not like you were with him, that Garrison character. I hated him for it, a little. The affection you showed him and not me. The way you looked up to him like he was some kind of god. But I understood. We were who we were. Or . . . are who we are," he corrected. He mashed the heels of his hands in his eye sockets, smoothed out the lines of sleeplessness that creased his forehead.

"When?" In his mind, Hudson saw Tobias staring into the cruel black water below Forge Bridge, where countless bodies had bobbed to the surface, bloated and nibbled on by fish. He remembered, not too long ago, one corpse was recovered with a plastic bag in its throat. As if smacking the water and drowning hadn't been bad enough, the poor bastard had had to choke on garbage, too.

In this frozen, coal-blackened city, everyone knew someone who jumped.

"Four years ago . . . ish," replied Tobias. "Shayla had just taken Elijah. Filed for a restraining order. I couldn't come within a hundred feet of my own kid."

"Did you hurt her?"

"Used to." He sighed. The crackling in the earpiece made Hudson flinch. "Just . . . either I wouldn't be home when I said I'd be, or I'd be cussin' her out, calling her every name imaginable. Cracked my hand across her cheek once. Split her lip." His gaze was razor sharp, daring Hudson to judge. "I never said I was a good guy. That was my main reason for being up on that bridge. I thought it might not be such a terrible thing if a guy like me wasn't walkin' around no more."

Hudson knew the feeling. He'd never thought of himself as a bad guy, like Tobias, but he'd contemplated the second part—the "not walkin' around no more" part. Sometimes the will to quit was stronger than the will to live, especially when you came home in your funeral blacks to a cold, silent house. "You said Garrison stopped you?" he asked. "How?" He envisioned Garrison parked in the vacant lot in front of the bridge, typing up a report in his vehicle when he saw a shadowy figure on the wrong side of the railing. The image felt like more than something he was conjuring in his own mind, and he realized, as it took the shape of a memory, he'd heard Garrison tell the story. He just hadn't known the man he'd yanked from death's doorstep was his brother.

Neither had Garrison.

"I was gonna do it." Tobias frowned. "Just step off the edge like you're walkin' onto an elevator except there's no elevator there and you fall down the shaft. And I heard a voice. *Son.*" His own voice broke. He bit his bottom lip to stop it from quivering. Took a deep breath. "He called me son, and the first fucked-up thought that entered my mind was Dad. I wasn't really in a right state of mind. I thought Dad had come from the other side or something, come to stop me from going the same way as him, but . . ." He trailed off and swiped away a tear that rolled down his jaw. "It was like I was already in mid-step, and when I tried to go backward, to undo what I'd just done, it was too late. I fell. And I don't know how in the world he was so fast, he was like the Flash, but he caught me by the collar of my jacket. He was the only thing keeping me up, keeping me alive. I swung under the bridge some and smashed my face on the rails. Knocked out a few teeth. But he pulled me up and other than that I was fine."

Jesus, Garrison. He was suddenly overwhelmed by the urge to hug him if he were here, were he still alive. But for what? For saving his brother who might have come around four years later and shot him?

As if Tobias could read Hudson's thoughts, he said, "Now, how could I do it, bro? Kill a man who saved my life? Who called me 'son'? Who let me spend at least four more birthdays with my little boy? Four more Christmases?" He shook his head. His face contorted into something anguished, compressed, like a can being crushed. "I know I'm not a good guy. But I'm not a monster."

Hudson put both of his elbows on the counter and leaned forward until his forehead nearly touched the glass. He closed his eyes and pictured Tobias standing on the outskirts of Garrison's funeral. What investigators had mistaken for a killer assessing his damage was really a man in mourning.

That is, if Tobias really was telling the truth. As if he had a second phone up to his other ear, he heard Sergeant Kole's voice, reciting the golden rule of Investigations: *Everybody lies.*

He sighed. "The gun that killed Garrison was a fifty-caliber Desert Eagle. Why would it be in your apartment?"

"I swear to you, Ryan, I've never seen that gun in my life."

He heard Kole again, chiding. *That's what they all say.*

"Then how'd it get there? People said they saw you with it. Waving it around. Bragging about . . ." He cringed. ". . . popping a cop."

Tobias rolled his eyes. "People are liars. You oughta know that by now." He paused to lick his chapped lips. "Who's *people,* anyway?"

Hudson pictured Muntz sitting in Interview Room #1. The feeling of a fist squeezing his intestines returned, the cramping he'd felt in that instant that Muntz had uttered the name Hades. "It's confidential."

"Are you fucking serious, bro? I'm about to fry for murder and you're worried about protecting some code of ethics you got?"

"You're not going to fry," Hudson assured him. Wisconsin had abolished the death penalty in 1853, and the electric chair was a southern thing. It was this sort of know-it-all-ness that had always gotten Hudson punched when they were younger.

"You believe me, don't you?" Tobias looked desperate, and for the first time in his life, powerless.

Hudson straightened up. He raked a hand through his hair and scratched at the back of his head. "Who else was in your place recently?"

"You mean who could've dumped the gun?"

"Yeah."

"Shit, people in and outta that place all day. Alice—this new girl I got—she's chummy with some seedy characters."

Hudson raised a brow.

"You know what I mean. I'm shady but these people are . . ." He sucked his teeth. "They leave a bad taste in your mouth, you know what I mean?"

He did, actually. He and Garrison arrested a woman once, who was so grimy, so nasty, so sour with the smell of tobacco that his mouth tasted like he'd smoked a pack of cigarettes afterward. "What do they do?" he asked.

Now Tobias fixed Hudson with a raised brow, a look that said *You've been walking a beat for over a decade and you don't know what people do around here?* "Lie. Cheat. Steal. You know the drill."

"Steal? Like rob places?" While Morgan had dismissed the narrative that the suspect had come in to rob the gas station, Hudson hadn't. Witnesses messed up their accounts all the time. It had all happened so fast; how would she have known whether he pointed the gun at the cashier or Garrison first?

Tobias shrugged. "Some, yeah. Shit, Kai's last name is 'steal.'"

The name hit Hudson like a kick to the stomach. "Kai Steele was in your place?"

"Like a rat in the goddamn walls. Motherfucker never left."

"Doing what?"

Tobias shrugged. "Smokin'. Chillin'. Gel'in like a felon."

"And if it was Kai's gun—which you say you've never seen before—your DNA won't be on it, right?"

"I don't see how it could be."

"You never held that gun?"

"Nah, bro, I'm telling you right now, I never even saw it."

Hudson's mind reeled. The gun had been swabbed for DNA, but the process of getting results back could take a few weeks. And there was no guarantee the findings would be conclusive. But if he could get the police to look into Kai Steele again, and find evidence to prove the gun belonged to him, Tobias could be cleared of murder charges. He would still do three or four years for the four ounces of cocaine the SWAT team found in his toilet tank—unless they could trace that back to Kai, too—but after that he'd be a free man . . . again.

"Who else?" asked Hudson. "You said there were seedy characters in and out of your place all day."

"Shit." Tobias blew air out of his mouth. "Guy named Ruiz. I think he's an informant, though, so I quit sellin' to him about a week ago. Destiny, she's one of Alice's friends. Lives above the Moonlight Market on Main. Ronald, he stays in the back of the old martinizing shop. He's a real piece of shit."

Hudson tried on his best poker face. He was willing to bet that the Ronald Tobias mentioned was Ronald Muntz. If Tobias found out he snitched, he could send someone after him and ruin any chance he had of getting out of here. "How so?" he asked.

Tobias's face darkened. "Don't you investigate crimes against children, bro?"

"Generally, yeah." Hudson had to admit, he was surprised Tobias knew that. He'd never mentioned his assignments to his family, which meant his brother kept tabs on him.

"Tell me how you feel, then, about a grown man raping his niece. Who's ten, by the way. Or hiring sixteen-year-olds for sex."

Hudson clenched his jaw. He'd searched Muntz's name in Onyx, and although he hadn't come across charges for the crimes Tobias was talking about, it didn't mean they didn't happen. He just hadn't been caught. *Absence of evidence is not evidence of absence.* And yet, Tobias could be misinformed. Or reaching. His brother was drowning, and drowning people will always pull someone else under to save themselves.

"Detective, you almost done?" He felt the presence of one of the correctional officers.

"Yeah." Hudson scraped his chair back across the floor and reached to hang up the phone.

Tobias's voice was muffled on the other end. "Hold up. Do me a favor, would ya?"

Dread folded over Hudson like a weighted blanket. He brought the piece back to his ear. "What?"

"Feed Persephone while I'm gone? There's some mice for her in the freezer."

"Persephone is your . . . cat?"

"According to my rental agreement."

Hudson hung up the phone. He stood and slung his messenger bag over his shoulder. As he turned to go, a knock on the glass made him turn back around. "You believe me, yeah?"

He nodded despite himself. He wasn't sure what to believe. Possibilities ripped through his mind. The only solid, indomitable fact was that Garrison was dead, and if his brother had in fact killed him, then Hades himself would have hell to pay.

He would make sure of it.

25

MORGAN

The orange film canister stared up at her from the shallow depths of her purse, a reptilian eye waiting in its cave. Or perhaps it was more of an uncharacteristic sunburst, a splash of color Morgan wouldn't normally have in her possession. The only bright shade she liked was red, like the Duff hat that nested on her head and the lava lamp that currently sat shotgun. She'd buckled it so it wouldn't roll onto the floor. Globules of red paraffin wax collected at the top.

Once more, her eyes scanned the handwritten *M.R.* initials on the canister's curved body. She closed the flap of her purse, then, like tucking an unwanted message away in an envelope.

"My Ruin" was what Bern had called her. No one else. But for all of Morgan's spelunking into the caverns of her mind, she could not recall her aunt's handwriting. Had her *u*'s always had the perfect symmetry of a hook at the beginning and end of the stroke? The *n* was the same, a precise transposition of the *u* that preceded it. If the canister belonged to Bern, what was it doing among Eleanor's things?

There was only one way to find out.

She had to develop it.

She peered through the windshield at Exos Labs. It was a sprawling campus planted just off the highway. In the center was a glass tower she assumed was the main office building. The way the other buildings stretched out brought to mind bacteria under a microscope, spreading, spreading, until it took over all the wooded area and fields that bordered it.

Morgan slammed the car door. Her boots clicked on the snow-blown walkway toward the glass building's entrance. It looked like a fortress, somewhere a villain would stand on the top floor and look out at what lands he was about to conquer. Or like a contemporary Mount Crumpit from *The Grinch*.

But Christopher Reynolds was no grinch. He'd been jolly both times she met him, once as Santa Claus and once as himself at Eleanor's. She wondered if he would be at the cabin later this week.

The lobby was a rotunda, wherein sat a receptionist with sideswept hair. He wore a charcoal sweater over a collared shirt. Morgan pegged him as an intern, probably a college kid earning a few paychecks during Christmas break.

"Who are you here for?" he asked, hardly looking up from the book he was reading.

"Christopher Reynolds." Her voice sounded less authoritative than she'd meant it to. She was out of practice. She'd hardly said a word since yesterday, only to inform her mother she'd be gone on a shoot all morning and afternoon. She kicked herself almost immediately after choosing that specific brand of lie, of course; there would be no money shoved into the Nestlé tin to show for it.

At the mention of the CEO's name, the receptionist dragged his gaze from his literature and looked her up and down, from her pilled wool scarf to her intentionally ripped tights. "Do you have an appointment?"

"He knows I'm coming." Not a lie. She'd sent an email this morning to the address noted on Christopher Reynolds's business card, the subject titled *Curiosity re: chemicals,* and asked if the company might have some hydroquinone, metol, sodium sulfite, and borax that she could purchase— essential components to a DIY photo-processing kit. To her delight, he'd responded that yes they would, and no purchase was necessary. *Come by the lab at 9,* he replied. *I'll have them ready for you.*

The intern raised a skeptical brow. Then he sighed, closed his book, and picked up the phone. After dialing an extension, he said to Morgan, "What did you say your name was?"

"Morgan Mori."

"Morgan Mori says she has an appointment with you, sir." He hung up and returned to his book. "He'll just be a moment. You can sit over there." He gestured with a limp flick of his wrist toward a row of seats in front of the window.

Morgan nodded a silent albeit insincere thanks and mentioned, "Dave dies at the end." She took pleasure, then, in the twin creases that formed between his brows.

"Excuse me?"

Poorly imitating the limp hand gesture he'd just made, she motioned toward his book.

"It's a whole Schrödinger's cat thing." She felt his eyes burn into her back as she took a seat and smiled to herself. Fuck him.

True to his word, Christopher Reynolds jogged down a winding staircase a moment later. Morgan stood and greeted him with her most winning smile. "Hello, Mr. Reynolds."

"Oh, please, call me Christopher. Lovely to see you again, Morgan."

Dressed in a black turtleneck beneath a navy-blue suit, Christopher Reynolds looked every bit the CEO. Although almost double the age Clive had been when the last picture of him had surfaced, she could see the brotherly resemblance. It was in the eyes, mostly. Christopher's were a rich, dark brown—the shade and shape of chocolate-covered almonds.

Morgan offered her hand for him to shake, and he pulled her into an embrace. He was stronger than she'd expected, his seventy-year-old sinewy muscles activated around her. "It's a cold one out there today," he said. "Did Alvin offer you anything, coffee, tea?"

Alvin. Morgan fought the urge to turn out her bottom lip in a teasing puppy dog frown. With an unfortunate moniker like that, no wonder the kid was a pretentious dick. "No, he didn't," she said, "but it's okay. I'm good."

Christopher side-eyed his lowly intern. "Okay. So long as you're . . . good. Shall I give you a tour? After all, you'll likely be coming to photograph the place in a few weeks."

A few weeks? That was news to Morgan. When Christopher had mentioned corporate photography and headshots at the Christmas party, she'd assumed he meant sometime in the summer when the grounds were green again, the courtyard in bloom. But winter was perfectly fine with her. She could put Bennett's gift card toward some fancy lights and be ready for action in a week or less.

Outside, light snowflakes swirled against a gunmetal sky. She kept a stair behind him as she followed him up the curved staircase, but when they arrived on the catwalk that extended over a laboratory, she fell into step beside Christopher. Morgan had a bird's-eye view of people in yellow hazmat suits. About fifty feet and a glass ceiling separated her from them. "What are they making?" she asked.

"Have you ever heard of Prozac?"

Heard of it? Back when she'd been able to afford it, she could have been its brand ambassador.

He pointed to the vats that made Morgan think of Mr. Burns's nuclear power plant. "They're full of hydrofluoric acid."

Morgan looked at him, incredulous. She'd binge-watched *Breaking Bad* back when it had been a new Netflix sensation. "Is it really strong enough to—"

"—dissolve bodies?" He laughed. "Eh. You'd need a lot of it. And it'd be rather messy. Lye is much more effective in that regard. It essentially strips it down into either water or water-soluble molecules that can be flushed down the drain."

"You sure know your body dissolvents."

"Keeps life interesting." He winked.

The tour continued through various labs and sterile rooms. "We put in an ISO 4 clean room last year," Christopher narrated as they passed over an all-white room with what looked like a glass garage door. Morgan didn't know what he meant, but he added, "NASA standards. That means there are less than ten thousand particles per cubic foot of air. Which, compared to half a million to a million particles per cubic foot in a regular room . . . is pretty significant."

Morgan nodded along in agreement. She got the gist of what he was telling her. This place was hella expensive. Reynolds Capital had invested a lot of money to keep this portfolio company up and running, and more sterile than a bottle of Absolut.

His office was in the middle of a narrow hallway, down a wing in which the walls were no longer made of all glass. He unlocked the door with his thumb and Morgan followed him into a large, spartan room. One entire wall was devoted to a window that overlooked a frozen pond surrounded by stalks of ice-encrusted cattails. It was beautiful. The black-and-white landscape resembled an Ansel Adams photograph.

The chemicals, contained in various jars and bottles, were on a countertop, a black reusable bag pooled around them. All she had to do was find the handles, pull them up like a drawstring, and away she could go. But Morgan didn't want to be rude. He seemed to enjoy her company, or at least the fact that he had a non-work-related visitor.

A black-and-white framed photo of a ribbon of water snaking through a valley hung on the wall above a spider plant, the only splash of color in the entire office. Morgan wandered closer to it, and observed what appeared to be Christopher Reynolds's signature scratched in the bottom right corner. "You took this?" she asked.

"Guilty." He nonchalantly traced her footsteps, one hand tucked in his pocket. "Had to get up at three A.M. and hike up before the sunrise."

"It was worth it."

Christopher beamed at the compliment. Morgan meant it, though. She would never be that skilled with a manual camera if she practiced from now until the end of her life. Another photograph, this one nearer the door, featured a sailboat. Its ghost trailed in its wake, a hazy impression of where it had been. The water was an ethereal sheath. "Ten-minute exposure," offered Christopher. "I've got a little Pentax K1000 I've had since the seventies."

"These are . . ." She was lost for words. "You should submit them to a magazine."

The old man looked down at the floor as though embarrassed. He wore the emotion unnaturally, like Bennett in that cable-knit sweater. Reynoldses weren't cut out for shyness or humility. "I've had a few published. By nature magazines and whatnot. I shoot for myself, though. It's amazing how all the world's secrets reveal themselves if you're patient enough."

"And if you look in the right places," Morgan added. "When you said you dabbled in photography, I didn't realize you were so . . ."

"Old-school?" He laughed.

"Talented."

"You're too kind."

She almost laughed herself. She really wasn't. *Tell that to all the people with "Ruined" branded on their necks,* she thought. But they deserved it.

Christopher walked over to the counter, pointed to a plastic spool and the canister amid the chemicals. His eyes twinkled. "I figured you might be able to use these," he said. "They were just in storage. I have so many I'm tripping over them."

"Thank you," Morgan said, and she meant it. She figured she'd have to rig something up on her own, but an actual developing reel and tank would make things a lot easier.

"What film camera do you shoot, by the way?" he asked. "I don't know if you ever mentioned it."

"Oh, I don't." When Christopher regarded her curiously, she added, "I found a roll of film among Eleanor's things. Thought I would develop it for her as a surprise, if it isn't corroded."

"Did you, now? Well, how 'bout that." He smiled, but his bottom lip quivered, revealing a row of coffee-stained teeth.

Morgan paused as a chill gripped her spine. Was it the note of intrigue in his voice that caused it, or the fact that he looked like them— white-collar moguls from Chicago's business district who escaped their corporate constraints for an hour to visit The Ruins. The same kind of people who entered the house on Winslow Street, trading cash and cigarettes for time alone with a little girl who learned not to cry or show weakness until after they had gone.

Morgan swallowed the lump in her throat, suddenly intensely aware of the absolute silence. It was so quiet, she could hear the snowflakes kissing the glass. Mechanically, she skirted around Christopher and scooped up the darkroom supplies. "I should be going," she said, "I, um, have a shoot in less than an hour. Thank you for this."

"Oh, okay then." Though he seemed taken aback, he recovered quickly. "I'd love to see them sometime."

Morgan stopped, her hand on the door handle. "See what?"

Christopher chuckled. His lips stretched across his teeth as he smiled. "The secrets Eleanor's been keeping in that canister."

26
HUDSON

His brother's last known address was a literal hole in the wall. Hudson parked across the street and two houses down, his SUV sandwiched between two cars with illegal window tint. He didn't have long before someone started sniffing. His vehicle was too clean, too prim for this part of town. How funny it was, then, that *this part of town* was only a four-minute drive from Hudson's own place, and therefore, the police department. He thought of the neighborhoods in Black Harbor like cancer cells. Once one got infected with poverty and violent crime, it spread to others.

He couldn't see anything of Tobias's dwelling, only an alley disrupting two houses with flaking paint from growing together. It was tucked back there, Tobias had assured him, at 1104 Northridge Drive. That was the address he remembered Muntz telling Kasper yesterday.

Now, he waited outside for a sign of Kai Steele. It was a long shot that he'd be there, but it was the only shot he had at the moment. Hudson tore his eyes from the alley and unlocked his phone. He scrolled through Kai's social media, not knowing exactly what he was searching for, but searching nonetheless.

Red treads. Red treads. But even if he could find a picture of him with red shoes, or even better, spray-painting his red shoes black—the equivalent of expecting a lobster dinner at a Denny's—it wouldn't prove anything. The only thing "red treads" corroborated was a witness statement, and with each day that passed, Hudson was becoming less and less sure about Morgan Mori. He hadn't spoken to her since the eve of Garrison's funeral.

A person in a black, salt-stained jacket walked past, eyeing him through his windshield. Hudson gave a polite but dismissive nod and turned back to his phone, his gaze following the pedestrian until he turned the corner. Kai wasn't here; Hudson could feel it. And he might never return. It had been a fine hideout until yesterday, when the police busted the door off its hinges. Now the place was violated, sullied, ruined.

He seemed to have deleted his social media accounts, too. It was more likely he'd changed his name and started fresh. Kai Steele was an alias anyway. Which meant Hudson would have to invent another attractive woman to send him a friend request once he found him again.

If anyone knew Kai's most recent activity, it would be the guys in Robberies. Trying one last thing before he called it quits for today, he found Fletcher's number in his phone and dialed.

Three rings and a voice. "Hello?"

"Hey. Dan?"

"Yeah."

"It's Ryan."

"Ryan?" He held on the second vowel, buying him time to match a face with a name. All cops' numbers came up as "Unknown."

"Hudson."

"Oh, Hudson! Holy shit." His voice quieted. "Hey man, just the guy—"

"Has Kai Steele been up to anything lately? Has he hit any more gas stations, or . . . ?"

"Steele? Nah, we haven't seen neither hide nor hair of him in shit, must be three, four weeks. Can't even say if he's still alive."

Hudson sighed. The pause in the conversation allowed him to rewind to when Fletcher had first answered the phone. "*Just the guy who* what, by the way?"

"Huh?"

"When you picked up. You said I was *just the guy*. What's that about?"

"You don't know?"

"Know what?" Hudson suddenly tasted the faint metallic tinge of blood. Had he had any water at all yet today? No. He'd completely forgotten to eat, too. Ever since Tobias had called him at 4:00 A.M., he'd stopped functioning on a basic human level.

He heard shuffling on the other end of the phone. It sounded like Fletcher was on the move, to a more isolated area, perhaps. He must be at work.

"Everyone's talking, man. Are you really Hades's brother?"

He'd heard the expression before, but until now, he'd never literally felt the blood drain from his face. He swallowed. The action felt like razor blades in the back of his throat. "No. I—" He huffed and his breath fogged the driver's window. "Where'd you get that from?"

"Like I said, everyone's talking."

"But who did you hear it from, Dan?" His voice was harder now, louder. Each word was its own cutting syllable.

"I can't— I can't tell you. It's true, isn't it?" He could envision Fletcher shaking his head, his viking mohawk swishing back and forth. "Jesus Christ. How the fuck—"

Hudson ended the call. Before his screen faded to black again, a text message came through. This one from Miserelli. *Hades? Really, Ryan? WTF!*

Another from Malcolm. *Hey bro, what's going on?*

And Chase. *Just heard. Is it true?*

Resisting the urge to throw his phone through the passenger window, Hudson whipped it into the seat instead. It bounced, ricocheted off the dash, and landed on the floor with a thud. It kept buzzing with a barrage of text messages. Cranking the key in the ignition, Hudson tore out of Hades's neighborhood.

When he pulled up to his drive, Morgan was waiting on his porch like a bad omen. *Jesus Christ, what now?*

Hudson got out, slammed the door. A clump of slush dislodged and fell from his wheel well, onto his shoe. He closed his eyes for a second, forced himself to take a long inhale as the cold seeped through his sock.

Morgan stood as he approached. She looked like a renegade orphan in her tattered jacket and bright Duff hat, combat boots too big for her spindly legs. It was below freezing. Why hadn't she stayed in her car? He didn't care. *He didn't care.* Morgan Mori was a mess and he had other messes to clean up at the moment.

"Hello, Morgan."

A black tote bag hung from her forearm. "Hi."

"Do you want to come in?"

She nodded, her chin tucked into her scarf. Her cheeks were red, wind-bitten. How long had she been out here?

He didn't care.

Hudson walked up the steps past her and plunged his key into the lock. His house wasn't much warmer than outside, he lamented as he tossed his messenger bag on the table. It slid into the peacock butter dish, knocked the top askew.

Morgan crept in behind him like his shadow.

Pip erupted in a series of high-pitched barks and skittered into the kitchen. Not in any mood to have his eardrums shredded, Hudson scooped her up, opened the sliding door, and plopped her in the backyard. She sank in the downy snow, her ginger puffball tail protruding like an antenna.

He heard Morgan shut the door, and then . . . nothing. No phone alerts. No Pip barking. Just. Silence.

Finally, Hudson let out the breath he didn't realize he'd been holding. The kitchen chair was still pulled away from the table from when he'd sat there to put his shoes on this morning. Earlier this morning. How was it only 10:00 A.M.? He felt like he'd lived a few days in a matter of a few hours, and yet, the morning still pounded away at him like waves smacking into the pier. *Why was Morgan here? What did she want?* He wanted to ask her. Another part of him just wanted her to go away.

Taking his jacket off, Hudson tossed it on the table and went to sit down. The chair slid away from him and he fell to the floor. His tailbone hummed. The snowmelt from his shoes soaked into his pants. He let his head fall back and knock against the table leg. Maybe if he just threw in the towel, went to bed, he would wake up and everything would be back to the way it was before. When he and Garrison were living it up on patrol together, and no one knew his brother was Black Harbor's most dangerous drug lord. Nan would be here. Maybe Miserelli would even be talking civilly to him, because they never would have complicated their friendship by sleeping together. Was it too late to make a Christmas wish?

Notes of honey, pear, and whiskey stirred him awake. A pale hand held the open bottle of Jameson in front of his face. Hudson took it and tossed some back. The alcohol tore through his throat and burned all the words away. He handed it back and Morgan took a drink. "So, how was your day?" she asked.

27

MORGAN

The stairs to Hudson's basement were a steep descent into a mouth of shadow. Morgan clutched the straps of the mesh bag so tightly her knuckles might have split through her chapped skin.

Hudson reached across her to flip the light switch. At the bottom of the stairs, a lone bulb glowed. She followed him down to a porous concrete floor, past a boxy washer and dryer set, above which hung a clothesline with black socks and undershirts. The walls were old stone with roots poking between. He hadn't exaggerated when he said his basement was fit for horror films. To her left was a shelf system with jarred pickles, beets, and salsa. Interesting. He didn't seem the canning type.

At the back of the labyrinthine room, on the opposite end of a storage area housing plastic totes and Christmas decorations, was a sink. Perfect.

Despite still wearing her jacket and hat, Morgan shivered. The dampness of the basement penetrated her layers and took up residence in her bones.

Upstairs, when she'd taken the film canister out of her purse, Hudson had looked sucker-punched. His eyes widened as they read the initials scrawled in black marker. "M.R.," he said. "Who is M.R.?"

"It's a long story."

"Where did you find this?" he asked, and she told him about her scanning project for Eleanor.

"Do you have everything you need?" Hudson asked now, when Morgan set the bag on the counter by the sink. She took out the chemicals, placing them alongside the tape he'd snagged from a drawer upstairs, and asked him for three painter's trays.

"Three?"

"Yeah." She ran through the process again in her mind. They would need one tray each for the developer, stop bath, and fixer. None of it meant anything, of course, if the film inside was corroded.

Hudson went to find three clean painter's trays. Even if they weren't clean, though, Morgan thought, they would do. She wasn't aiming for any award-winning prints here, especially with this thing. From her backpack, she removed a crude homemade enlarger. A Frankensteined Lucky Charms box, the contraption was two rectangular pieces that fit together. A square window covered with tracing paper was cut in the end of one, a circle in the other.

Hudson returned with the trays still in the packaging. He tore the plastic off and set the accompanying rollers and brushes on the washer for the time being. Next, Morgan sent him off to fetch a cardboard box to complete her enlarging station, and an extension cord. "What else?" he asked once he procured them.

"Your glasses."

"My what?"

She paused, midway through extracting a package of photo paper from her backpack, staring at him and his taped-together glasses. "You're farsighted, yeah?"

"Yeah."

Morgan knew the searching expression he wore now; he was wondering if he'd ever told her that detail. But she could tell by the way his lenses magnified his eyes. "Well, I'm nearsighted. We need a convex lens, i.e., yours, to act as a magnifying glass."

"For what?"

She set the photo paper down and held up the cereal box enlarger. Her finger tapped at the circular opening. "Ideally, when we shine a light through this contraption, it will travel through the negative and be magnified and sharpened by your lens on the other side, which can then be exposed on the paper."

Hudson frowned. "Have you done this before?"

"I took a film class in high school, once. But we didn't do it like this, no."

"Then how—"

"YouTube. Don't worry, I don't need them right this second. We have to process the film first."

"How long will that take?"

Morgan shrugged. "Five minutes? You got somewhere you need to be?"

Hudson shook his head. "I'm off today. Where'd you get all these chemicals?"

"I know a guy." She tried not to let her hand shake as she mixed the components for the developer and poured it into the little black tank. Lastly, she pulled the lava lamp from her bag of tricks. It was red and would work as a safe light for when the film was ready to be developed into prints. Unwinding the cord from its aluminum base, she plugged it into the female end of the extension cord and handed the male end to her male counterpart. He should know what to do with it.

"You know a lava lamp guy, too?"

Morgan smiled. "This is from my own private collection. It's vintage, so don't break it."

Hudson disappeared over by the washer for a moment as he connected the cord to an outlet.

They stood back, surveyed their workspace. The little orange canister waited front and center, before an ensemble of painter's trays, chemicals, scissors, and the enlarging contraption. The trays were empty; they would mix the chemicals later, after the negatives had developed and dried. "I think we're ready," said Morgan.

"Ready for what, exactly?"

Morgan reached above her head and tugged on the short, beaded chain. "Lights out."

It was so dark she couldn't see her hands in front of her, and deathly quiet. All Morgan heard was the sound of Pip's nails clacking on the hardwood floor above and Hudson's shallow breathing next to her. She should be more nervous, in the dark and underground with a man she barely knew. But she did know him, kind of. She knew he was a good cop. That he volunteered at animal shelters. That he worked on cases to rescue kids like her. And perhaps most important of all, while he had a ticket to The Ruins, there was no mark on his neck.

She'd made a mental map of where everything was. Her fingertips closed around the film canister and, using the scissors like a wrench, she twisted off the top. The film was so cool it felt wet as it spilled from its prison.

Blindly, she found the plastic reel and fit the film into its grooves.

"What's that clicking noise?" Hudson asked.

His voice was disembodied. Morgan imagined they'd fallen into another dimension, one where people weren't people; they were just thoughts and souls in a world so deep, light couldn't get through. The concept was oddly comforting. If she was bodiless, no one could hurt her. And she didn't have to hurt them in return. "I'm winding the film on the reel so I can put it in the developing tank."

"You need help?"

"It's kind of a one-person job."

"I see." He sighed and she could feel his breath against her cheek. She startled; she didn't realize they were so close. He probably didn't, either. "So, what else was in Mrs. Reynolds's collection?" he asked. His voice was low, almost a whisper. "Besides the film canister. Were there any other photographs of interest?"

"Pictures of them at the cabin, mostly. Old pictures. Some of Clive and his car."

Funny how she felt him nod, felt the almost imperceptible movement in the air. "Cabin? They don't seem the type to rough it in the great outdoors."

Morgan shrugged, an automatic response. He couldn't see her. She agreed with him, though; she suspected the Reynoldses' cabin was more like a mansion with some rustic features. "It's in some place called Loomis, three or four hours north of here," she said, recounting what information Bennett had shared with her since the invitation.

"Are the dates printed on them by chance?"

She liked the sound of his voice, she realized. It held a quiet calm, not like one before a storm but the steady, consistent calm of a rainy afternoon.

He must be good with talking to child victims, she thought. Not like the abrasive detectives who'd spoken to her during the days after being rescued from the house on Winslow Street. If Hudson had asked her for her name and to tell him what happened to her in that room, she felt sure she would have told him every horrifying detail. Instead, she'd been too scared. Scared the detectives wouldn't believe her. So she kept it inside, until the monster she'd been unintentionally nurturing reared its ugly head in The Ruins.

Morgan turned the secured container upside down again. "Some," she said finally, remembering the photo of Clive and Bennett catching fish in front of the pond. She couldn't put her finger on it, but there was something magnetic about that picture, that place with the beached canoe and the woodshed in the background, an ax leaning against its wall.

Leaving the top secured, she poured the tank into the sink. She felt for the faucet, then, and turned it on, letting the water fill the tank through the aperture in the lid, rinsing the film clean. She repeated the ritual five more times.

Cold water droplets stung her hands as Morgan unscrewed the cap and pulled out the reel. She unraveled the film and wandered to the area of the clothesline. End to end, she clipped the film to the cloth rope. "Moment of truth," she said, and flipped on the lava lamp. Their immediate area was bathed in a stygian glow. The rest of the basement remained inked in shadow.

Dread twisted Morgan's stomach into knots. She was afraid to look, to see a strip that had been devoured by time. But she crept closer, and instead, saw blank frame after blank frame after blank frame. Fuck. The film hadn't even been shot.

Her heart thrummed so hard it echoed in her head. This was it, a story not erased but unwritten.

Beside her, Hudson gasped. "Oh my God." He went toward one end of the strip and positioned it toward the light. Morgan followed. She clutched his forearm like a child tiptoeing to see out an overlook, and there they were. Ghosts. That's what they looked like as her brain worked to process the negative's inverted highlights and shadows. Evergreens were white, their tops spearing an expanse of mercurial sky. A lake was a great blank swath that swallowed an entire frame. Then there was a house—a large,

A-frame cabin—perched on a bluff. A woman in a triangle bikini lounging on a lawn chair, a drink and a magazine beside her on a resin table. The invertedness of the negative made her large sunglasses look like headlights. Judging by the clothes and the level of corrosion on some of the photos, the woman could have been the same age as Eleanor, but she wasn't Eleanor. Her face was too soft, hair too tame and straight. It looked white as snow in the negative, which meant it must have been black.

There was a girl, too. She was young, maybe only three or four. Chin-length hair as silken as the woman's. The same soft, egg-shaped face. The girl built sandcastles. Ate a snack. Held a phone up to her ear. Morgan squinted at that last one. The girl was in the middle of the woods, it appeared, someone lifting her to the height of a random . . . pay phone? The whole composition of it looked surreal.

Holding the negatives within inches from her nose, Morgan scrutinized every line, every shadow, every blown-out highlight. It was the eyes she found most unsettling. All white and eerie, it looked as though they'd been intentionally carved out of every photo.

Another character appeared, then, when the woman, the girl, and a man all sat in a canoe. The woman and man faced each other, and the girl sat on the man's lap. He wore shorts and a T-shirt. Morgan read the strip like a book. In some photos his face was partially obscured by the little girl's head as he leaned to whisper something in her ear. In others, he cradled her close, his chin resting on her hair, and smiled at the woman seated across from him. Morgan's breath hitched. She would recognize that golden Hollywood smile anywhere. Clive Reynolds.

And then, looking more closely at the little girl, she saw it. The girl sat next to it during story time, she carried it by its arm as she collected stones from the lakeshore, fished with it by the edge of the dock. Her Bart Simpson doll.

The girl in the negatives was her.

28

HUDSON

"Are you sure it's you?" Hudson asked. They were in his living room now, sitting in the same positions as last time. Pip perched on a pillow beside Morgan, her tongue out, beady eyes bright, tiny head jerking from one human to the other, not bothering to disguise the fact that she was eavesdropping.

He asked the question, but he knew. The girl in the negatives was the woman sitting diagonally across from him. And she was the key to everything.

Clive Reynolds had a secret daughter.

Morgan Mori.

Or rather, Morgan Reynolds.

He did the math, his gaze drifting and zeroing in on the photograph they'd just exposed and brought upstairs. If Morgan was thirty-one now, then those photos had been taken more than twenty years ago. She couldn't have been more than four years old in them.

He studied her now. The bite marks in her lips, her chewed-to-the-bone fingernails. She was the same girl; she'd just been frozen in time, hidden away from the world in a little orange capsule. And then deposited here, in Black Harbor. Right back where she'd started.

She stared at the black memo book on the coffee table. Slowly, so as not to startle her, Hudson leaned forward and grabbed the book. He turned his knees toward her then, and opened it between them. The faded red ticket lay on the pages like a fresh scar.

Welcome to The Ruins, where your true self dwells. He didn't need to read it to know what it said. He'd learned the inscription by heart. This ticket, this scrap of paper, was the reason she'd run out the other day. "What is this place?" he asked.

Morgan didn't meet his eyes. She stared at the ticket, her lips parted as though exhausted from keeping her story in all this time. "It was mine," she said finally. And she told him. Everything.

He should have recorded her, considered for a second setting the video on his phone. But she was like a fawn in an open field. She'd let him observe her, but the second he made a move, she'd bolt. She'd done so once already. He knew her well enough to know her presence was fragile.

He came to know even more about her as she narrated the abuse at the house on Winslow Street. The sharp objects, the suffocation, the whispers in the dark. If Hudson had been the one assigned to her case, he didn't know if he would stay in Black Harbor—if he even could—knowing the horrors that happened beneath the surface when the rest of society walked on a hair's-breadth sheet of ice above it.

"And The Ruins?" Hudson asked. "It was a . . . *creative warehouse,* you said? Where people would pay to torture you?" It made sense in a sick, twisted way. Morgan had simply imitated her aunt's business model.

Morgan nodded. She pulled her knees into her chest so her heels dug into the edge of the couch cushion. Her stockings were slightly askew. She paused to straighten them. "Different strokes for different folks. That's the thing about creative endeavors. They're subjective." She told him about the rooms named for tragic literary women. The Lenore room with its skull and matte black walls, the bench with shackles. The branding stove.

"How did it work?" he asked.

"How did what work?"

"All of it. If I wanted to . . ." How did he put this? If he wanted to get his rocks off by torturing her? ". . . fulfill a creative endeavor."

He watched her shoulders rise and fall as she took a deep breath and lowered her feet to the floor again. She reminded him of the numerous children he'd spoken to in Interview Room #3. The ones who could never meet his gaze. They stared beyond him, as though there was someone else in the room, digging their toes into the carpet or picking at their cuticles.

Morgan was doing the same thing now. Her glassy stare fixed on some-thing on his mantel. A photo maybe, or one of the many glass peacock figurines he'd neglected dusting since Nan died.

"They got ready in a separate room," she said. "Some changed their clothes. Others just wore what they wore to work. Suits. White-collared shirts. The occasional pencil skirt. I gave them hoods to put on."

"Why?" he asked, and immediately wished he'd kept quiet. She was finally opening up. Decades had passed since her rescue, and the victim from Winslow Street was talking to him. He'd better shut up and not fuck this up, as Kole would advise.

To his relief, she answered. "Both parties got something out of it. They got to keep their anonymity and I didn't have to see their faces. And . . ." She wet her lips. "It felt a little poetic, I guess." She cut her gaze over to him and seemed satisfied with his undivided attention. "The guests at the house on Winslow Street used to tie black plastic bags over my head while they hurt me. I got to not minding it. Actually, I preferred it because I'd almost always pass out before things got too bad."

Despite Hudson's expectations, telling her story had a calming effect on Morgan. She stopped bouncing her foot. Her breathing normalized. He stared hard into her eyes that were the lightest shade of green, the color of a bottle lost at sea, and wondered what message they held inside.

She was relaxing a little, letting her wall down. And yet, she wrung her hands, her long fingers entwining her wrists. "I wanted them to feel everything," she said, finally.

He chanced one more question. "Did anyone refuse the hood?"

Not breaking eye contact with him, Morgan shook her head. "People are cowards. They all took me up on it."

Hudson nodded. He hadn't realized he was still holding the memo book. He was afraid to shut it—that closing the book would close her, too. But to his surprise, she kept talking, the words pouring out of her. Not smooth, but steady enough. "I'd be sitting down. Shackled." She held up her arms as though the restraints were still there, and he noted as he had before that each wrist bore a matching black leather cuff.

She patted the empty spot on the cushion next to her, between her and Hudson. "They'd sit. And then. I'd play. Just for a minute or two."

On his couch, Morgan hiked up her skirt. Her tights were ripped in all the right places, if that was possible. His gaze followed one tear from her knee all the way up to where it disappeared in the apex between her thighs. He swallowed. His mouth was dry, his shirt collar suddenly too tight as he watched every minute movement she made. She had him, and she knew it.

She crossed her right leg over her left, turning her hips toward him. In one swift motion, she rolled off the couch and onto his lap. Her body was quick and light, like a bird's. "Let's play a game." A ribbon of light danced behind her eyes. She looked wicked and simultaneously innocent. They were so close, he could see the dash marks her top teeth had left in her bottom lip.

Instinctively, Hudson held her. His hands cinched her waist, beneath her rib cage. She draped her arms over his shoulders, her fingertips swirling his hair. Her shirt hung loose, revealing pasties made from electrical tape and between her breasts, the delicate lines of a serpentine tattoo. The rapid pulse of her heart that matched his own beat beneath translucent skin. She smelled faintly of chemicals and something sweet.

"What kind of game?" His breath was more of a gasp.

The snakebite piercings in her lip glinted like snowflakes, beckoning him to press his mouth to hers. He wondered if she tasted like sugar.

No. This was wrong. She was a person of interest in more than one high-profile case. Hudson started to pull away when she began to move her hips back and forth, sliding against him. *Jesus*. He let his head fall back and felt her press her fingertip to his neck, like a gun.

"Hide the needle," she whispered in his ear. Holding on to his shoulders, she leaned back, and Hudson caught a fleeting smile.

"You inject them?" he said. "With what?"

"Special K."

"Ketamine?"

She nodded. "You'd be down by now," she said, throwing a glance at the floor.

"And then what would you do?"

The smile was back, only barely. "Poke them with a stick." She pressed her thumb to his neck. It hurt.

He turned his head but she didn't stop. "Okay," he said. But her eyes had gone onyx. She pressed harder, promising to leave a bruise with the whorls of her fingerprint. "Morgan, stop it!" He grabbed her arm.

She jerked, suddenly, as though she'd just touched a hot burner. When he looked into her eyes this time, he saw that they'd lightened back to their original jade. A teardrop fell from her lashes and slid down her cheek. She started to shiver.

"I made them symmetrical," she said softly. The teardrop disappeared in the space between her parted lips. "As ugly on the outside as they were on the inside."

Suddenly, Hudson understood. He thought back to his interviews with traumatized kids, the way they stared past him to mentally rearrange the objects in the room to achieve symmetry. Morgan had done the same thing with people, making their outsides match the depravity they hid inside themselves. Cautiously, he wiped away another teardrop. His thumb grazed the corner of her mouth. She opened it as though to speak, but no words came out. He leaned in to her, listening. She touched his neck again, gently this time, as though to assess what damage she'd done. Her cold fingertips slid under his shirt. He inhaled sharply at the sensation. The hair on his arms stood on end. He couldn't help it. He leaned farther, desperate to be in her orbit.

"Don't get too close," she warned.

"Why?" But even as he asked it, he was beyond the point of no return.

With her mouth touching his, she whispered, "Because I bite."

29
MORGAN

Morgan. My darling, my ruin.

Clive had a deep voice. Gravelly. She remembered now. It was as though all his sentiments had expiration dates; his voice started so far down inside him that by the time the words exited his mouth, they'd already begun to fade. An incessant reminder that her time with him was temporary. He would never spend more than a couple of hours with her and her mom. Except the one time they had gone up to the cabin in Loomis.

It was no wonder it felt familiar from the photos. She'd been there before, once. She was almost too young to remember, her mind a palimpsest of fond childhood memories buried by darker ones.

Her past came back to her like old scars being torn open.

At her mother's apartment, he read Morgan books and brushed her hair. If he stopped by after work, he brought Chinese food—noodles in brown sauce, chicken with a sweet, fried skin. He bought her presents and taught her to ride a bike. And when she fell and scraped her knees, he wiped the tears from her cheek and told her everything would be okay.

But it wasn't. She didn't know that the last time she saw him was the last time she would ever see him. If she had, she would have begged him not to go. Would have promised to be a good girl so he would stay or take her with him. She would have asked what she'd done to make him want to never come back. And then her mom left, too, and it was just her and Bern and the strangers who put the black bags over her head.

He'd called her *My Ruin*. That's where it had come from. Morgan had never thought it anything more than a pet name. But now she knew he'd meant it as a jab, a verbal knife poke in the ribs. Call a spade a spade, right? A pet name when she hadn't known any better; now, she canonized it among the classic nursery rhymes, a sinister tale masked with a light-hearted tune. Jack busted his head falling down a hill. Humpty Dumpty broke his shit. The ring around the rosie was a bubonic lesion, and pockets full of posies covered the stink of rotting flesh.

The picture of her with Clive and her mother surfaced in her memory. The negative transformed the photo into an x-ray, stripped them down to their barest essentials. They were made of the same stuff. The girl with the Bart Simpson doll, the woman with straight hair, the handsome man with a winning smile—underneath it all, they were three identical skeleton keys. Like the one that itched her wrist.

Had he been the one to leave it for her? Could Clive Reynolds—her father—be alive and searching for her?

Morgan awoke, disoriented and out of place. The world around her was unfamiliar. Where were her glasses? She couldn't have fallen out for more than ten or twenty minutes, and yet it felt like she'd just taken a flight around the world. And landed right back here in Black Harbor. For it was Black Harbor, still, without a doubt. She felt its wintry breath seep in through the cracks in the windowsill. Detected the dusty smell of coal to which people become nose-blind, the stannic scent of fish blood and scales, of soil frozen under layers of ice and snow. She heard the wailing of sirens in the distance, muffled, like someone screaming into a blanket. The walls of Hudson's old house groaned, as though they were in the belly of some sleeping beast.

The flannel sheets grazed her skin. She was naked but for the electrical tape Xs on her nipples. Turning over, she felt a stickiness between her legs, a diminishing burn. She snaked her arm out from under the blanket and reached for the nightstand, blindly searching for her glasses. She felt their round, cold frames lying atop a book. Squinting, Morgan read the spine: *East of Eden,* by John Steinbeck. So Hudson was the read-in-bed type.

His back was to her. She turned toward him again and counted his vertebrae, lightly tapping each one with her fingertip. He spasmed at first, as though he, too, had just woken up without sense of time or place or notion of who was in his bed.

He moaned quietly and turned over. He was so clean, so free of marks. And yet, she knew that inside, he was battered and scarred, with wounds old and fresh. It had only been a week since his friend's murder, after all. And he clearly still mourned for his dead nana. Morgan suspected he hadn't changed the house since she'd left it. A transient thought passed through her mind: Would anyone ache for her when she was gone, the way Hudson ached for his departed loved ones? Would anyone even notice if she was no longer sucking air?

"Hey," said Hudson, sounding half-asleep. He wasn't wearing his glasses, either. Seeing his eyes without them was like noticing them for the first time. They were rich, espresso brown, not anything like the empty eyes of the people in the negatives. Morgan smiled, half of it disappearing into the pillow.

"I didn't mean to fall out," he admitted.

"Blame it on the Jameson," she said.

He laughed softly.

"You like that stuff?" she asked.

"Not really," he said, and then: "There's a time and a place for it, I suppose."

"Like where?"

The corner of his mouth quirked upward, tugged by a dream. "Like a pub in Dublin on a rainy day." He drew his arm out from under the blanket, reached toward her, and she flinched like a dog anticipating a smack. His face fell, and he touched her hand as softly as snowflakes lighting on a windowpane. She exhaled, convincing herself that he wouldn't hurt her, and wanting to believe it. She watched his eyes flicker as he studied her, from her pale skin to the two-headed snake that slithered between her breasts.

"What's this?" he asked, after another moment of them sharing the silence.

Morgan felt him touch her wrist where she kept the blackened key. "It was a gift," she said, and she told him how it had been the only thing left on a pile of smoldering concrete, when The Ruins had burned to the ground.

"All roads lead back to home," repeated Hudson. "And it was addressed to M.R., the same initials as on the film canister."

She nodded and recited what she knew the initials to stand for. "My Ruin."

"Or Morgan Reynolds."

The name hung in the air above them. She'd never considered it until this very moment, but Hudson was right. She was Morgan Reynolds.

Which made Bennett . . . her half brother.

A chill crawled up her spine and she whispered a silent thank-you to the universe for never kissing him under the mistletoe.

"Whoever took the photos, then," noted Hudson, "must have known. Could it have been Clive, himself? It would have been around 1993. Did cameras have delay timers then?"

Morgan scrunched the blankets up over her shoulders, then put a hypothesis out into the ether that she'd been developing since this morning. Cameras have had delay timer capabilities since the 1950s, some even before that. The memory of a statement made earlier today resurfaced in her mind. *I've got a little Pentax K1000 I've had since the 1970s.*

Christopher had seemed to come a little undone when she'd told him the film was in Eleanor's private stash. She uttered his name, even more sure of it when she said it a second time so Hudson could hear. "Christopher Reynolds."

"Clive's brother? But why—"

Morgan couldn't hear him anymore. Her mind was loud with the cacophony of things shattering and clicking into place. She thought of the negatives hanging up in Hudson's basement. The photos of Ava sunbathing in a lawn chair, of Clive with a young Morgan on his shoulders. Of all three in the canoe, Clive leaning over to whisper something into Morgan's ear. The white that crept like fingers into the frame.

And she understood. The white blurs at the edge of every photo were foliage. Evergreen boughs, cattails, waist-high blades of grass—wherever Christopher had been hiding to get the shot. The subjects hadn't once looked at the camera. Because they hadn't known it was there.

It's amazing how all the world's secrets reveal themselves if you're patient enough. Christopher's words echoed in her head. "Blackmail," she whispered. Although she knew it to be the answer, she wondered why Christopher had wanted to expose his brother's secret family. Perhaps it had been a ploy to secure his position as CEO of Exos Labs. And yet, the film had remained undeveloped in Eleanor's collection . . .

Hudson lay back, his head sinking into his pillow. He rubbed the heels of his palms over his eyes, his forehead, smoothing out the lines of consternation. On the floor, his phone emitted a muffled buzz. He leaned over his side of the bed and rummaged through his jeans pockets. As he did, Morgan noted the sheen of sweat that suddenly broke out on his back. He tossed his phone toward the bottom of the bed then, and with his nose pointed up toward the ceiling, he spoke. "You wanna hear something fucked up?"

"Why stop now?"

"My brother is the biggest drug dealer this city has ever seen." And he began to laugh.

30

HUDSON

"Well, do you think he did it?" Morgan asked. They were sitting in Hudson's living room again, digging through the cold case box. He'd changed into quintessential Saturday attire—sweatpants and a T-shirt—and Morgan had done the same. When they crawled out of bed, she'd simply followed him to his closet, grabbed a black BHPD T-shirt, and slipped it on as though she owned it. She sat on the armrest of his couch now, clutching a cup of coffee with a jumbo marshmallow floating on top, and bounced her bare foot on the edge of the coffee table.

"I don't know," he said after a moment. "I really don't know." It was the honest-to-God truth. As much as he wanted to believe Tobias wouldn't have shot Garrison, he couldn't give his brother his complete vote of confidence. He'd seen what people were capable of when their backs were up against the wall. Tobias killing Garrison could have been as simple as owing someone a favor. Who, was the question. Tobias was Hades, Lord of the Underworld. But even the real Hades had Zeus to answer to.

"He let me drown, once, when we were kids." The confession was a prisoner suddenly left unguarded. The words tumbled from his lips, tasting freedom. "Well, I didn't drown, obviously. But almost."

Morgan's head tilted. "What happened?"

Hudson sat on the floor, the coffee table at chest height and his elbows planted on its surface. His fists formed a *V* under his chin. "We were playing on the pier. I must've been seven, or so. Tobias nine. It was getting dark. The pier was half sunk with these concrete posts jutting upward; it looked like a key. We started to head back, hopping from post to post, and I missed. I fell into the water. Jesus, it was cold." Hudson heard his own voice; it sounded to him like someone else was telling his story. The words were a wave, slow at first and gathering speed until they crested and began to decrescendo. He exhaled, his breath ragged. "It felt like arms dragging me under," he remembered. "Like the whole pier was on top of my chest. I fought to break the surface, and when I did, I saw Tobias looking down at me. I reached for him and he—he walked away."

"He left you?" said Morgan. "When you were drowning?" When Hudson set his jaw, she added, "That's hard core. How'd you get out?"

Hudson was shaking his head. "The mercy of God, I suppose. A wave came and lifted me just enough that I could grab a piece of the broken slab and pull myself up."

"And you walked home from there?"

"Someone heard me yelling and called nine-one-one. A cop found me clinging to the pier. He wrapped me up in a blanket and brought me home."

"Makes sense." Morgan sipped her coffee. The warmth steamed her glasses.

"What does?"

"You." She gestured to him with her free hand. "Law enforcement. Good cop. The whole bit."

Hudson furrowed his brows. He wasn't playing a bit. And yet, perhaps she was right. He was so desperate to put distance between himself and Tobias that he would do anything, including lie on his background check, to do it.

"Do you have a picture of your brother?" Morgan's voice brought him back to the here and now.

"Just old ones," he said. "Us as kids." He stood and walked over to the mantel. Sucked in a breath. Two years had passed since he'd ventured over to this side of the room. The mantel was just as Nan had left it, albeit covered in dust. What would she say about the inch of debris that blanketed the Cream City brick, the stack of leather-bound Aboriginal poetry collections, the blue and bronze peacock statues, their wedding photo? He wore a tux and she a backless white gown; they sat at the head table, arms linked, each holding a glass of champagne. He supposed, deep down, a part of him was hoping the dust would bury the photograph, like he'd buried his wife.

Nandalie. They'd been married less than a year when she'd gone out to get the mail and never came back. A twenty-year-old kid had been driving high on his way to an interview. Two years later, Hudson still couldn't get the image of her black hair encrusted in the windshield out of his mind.

A screw twisted in his stomach. He passed over the photo for a different one, and blew dust off the glass as he handed it to Morgan. It was a portrait of his mother, him, and his brother. Phoebe wore a red turtleneck and held him—then two or three—on her lap. Tobias, who had to have been about five at the time, stood next to her, his head tilted toward hers, a shit-eating grin plastered on his face as though he'd just lit a fire and was waiting for the alarm to sound.

"Here, this one's more recent." He showed her his phone with Tobias's latest mug shot. It was the same one featured on every local news station.

"I just—" She sighed. "His face was covered. His hands. All I remember were the spray-painted shoes. I'm like one of Pavlov's dogs when it comes to spray paint."

Hudson believed her. After spending so much time in a place like The Ruins where it sounded like every surface was coated in aerosol, she wouldn't have mistaken it.

"And there's no video?" When he shook his head, she remarked, "How convenient."

"Most of the establishments around here either don't have a working surveillance system or they don't know how to turn it on. I'm serious."

"So, I could walk into just about any gas station, steal a year's supply of Butterfingers, and get off scot-free?"

"Probably."

"Don't cops wear body cams?"

"Yeah, but Garrison was just buying a cup of coffee. He didn't have a reason to turn it on."

Morgan set the framed photograph next to the box containing the CliffsNotes of Clive Reynolds's life. "You know, for a cop, you hang around some pretty shady characters. Present company not excluded."

Hudson had to laugh a little at the irony. "I know."

An abrupt knock at the door sent Pip pouncing off her pillow and racing into the kitchen. Darting a glance at Morgan as a silent command to *stay put,* Hudson followed in the Pomeranian's wake. The window by the kitchen sink was too frosted to see who was there. It was probably Miserelli. Jesus, that was all he needed right now.

But, maybe it was, actually, just what he needed. The time for them to end things was long overdue. Bracing himself for the impact, Hudson opened the door. Déjà vu hit him. Sergeant Kole stood on his doorstep as he had almost exactly twenty-four hours ago.

"Sir." His breath issued a cloud that hung between them for a second and disappeared.

Kole looked as stone-faced as Hudson had ever seen him. "Do I look like a lobster to you, Hudson?"

Hudson squinted as he knit his brows. Despite the negative temperature, Kole did look a bit red. Beads of sweat clung to his hairline, frozen into ice crystals. "No?" he said.

"Then why are you putting me in hot water?"

Hudson opened his mouth to say something—though he hadn't made his mind up as to what—but Kole cut him off. "Tobias Shannon makes you his phone-a-friend and you come running? Are you shitting me? You didn't belong there, Hudson. He might have killed Garrison, for Christ's sake, and you—"

"He didn't!" He felt spit fly off his tongue, and shock at the sheer volume of his voice. He'd just shouted at his superior. But at least he knew the answer to the question Morgan had asked five minutes ago. The answer was no, he didn't think Tobias killed Garrison. And he would put all of his energy into proving everyone who thought otherwise, wrong. Including Nikolai Kole.

"I didn't say he did." Unfazed, Kole stepped toward him. One foot crossed the threshold, then the other, and suddenly he was in Hudson's kitchen, shoving him into the wall. Hudson felt a burning pain in his ear as Kole drove his forearm against the side of his head. He heard his glasses crunch and all he could think of in those seconds of being forced to eat the paint off his kitchen wall was *These are my only pair.* He bucked and went to elbow Kole in the ribs. But with his free hand, Kole grabbed Hudson's wrist and muscled his arm down. Hudson felt defeated as Kole managed to secure both his hands behind him. He braced himself for a knee in the back or another destabilizing move that would bring him flat to the floor.

But it never came.

Instead, he felt Kole's breath hot against his neck, though it was Garrison's words that he heard. "Jesus, Hudson."

For a split second, Hudson wondered if he'd blacked out. If he did, he came to as soon as Kole released him. Stumbling forward, he caught his balance after knocking into a chair and realized the sole reason Kole had let him go. Standing in the entryway in just his T-shirt, Morgan took a sip of her coffee.

"You've got quite the front, Hudson," Kole said. "You hiding some serious equipment or what?"

Morgan raised her hands and spaced them about a foot apart.

Kole, shaking his head, laughed. And had he not been mortified by the consequences he was undoubtedly facing, Hudson might have laughed, too.

"Hello, Morgan," said Kole, and when Hudson shot a look at him as a silent *You know her?* Kole gave him half an eye roll that said, *Please.* "I'm Nik. His supervisor."

Morgan raised her hand in a subdued greeting.

"I intend to stay awhile." Kole took off his jacket and draped it over a chair. "If you wanted to put pants on or whatever."

The two men watched, then, as Morgan grabbed the chair that Hudson had caught himself on seconds earlier, and sat down with her legs apart, toes pointed like a ballet dancer. She set her mug on the floor and leaned forward, her palms pressing into the front of the seat, fingers gripping the edge as she had gripped the sheets upstairs. The T-shirt pooled like a scant loincloth between her legs.

"Or whatever." Kole's eyes rested on Morgan for a moment, this Coraline-esque character in Hudson's kitchen. When he turned back to Hudson, he said, "I don't think I even need to tell you, but just to kick things off, your name's getting thrown around the PD like a hot potato. And I haven't even been in at all today, that's just my phone blowing up with everyone and his brother asking if I knew you'd been to see Tobias Shannon. Speaking of brothers . . ." He fixed Hudson with a deadly stare.

"Who told?" Hudson asked, remembering the conversation with Fletcher earlier this morning.

"Irrelevant. Tobias Shannon is the prime suspect in the murder of an officer. You don't think his calls and visits are being monitored?" He shook his head. "I'm sorry, but you're a moron. On top of that, you're the lead—forget that—*solo* investigator on the highest-profile case this city has ever seen. New recruits come to Black Harbor PD with the hopes that someday, they'll get a chance to put the Clive Reynolds mystery to rest. And you're blowing it. All you had to do was stay away from Tobias Shannon and not sleep with the key witness. So far you're zero for two."

Hudson sighed. He leaned against the counter, his arms folded tight across his chest. Kole had him pegged. If he closed his eyes, he would think they were across the street in Interview Room #1. "How long have you known? That he was my brother?"

"How long you been at the PD?"

"Eleven years."

"Then I've known for eleven years and a few months."

"But how—"

"I did your background check. It actually wasn't that hard to dig up. Found your records of when you legally changed your last name at age eighteen from Shannon to Hudson and worked backward."

Hudson was at a loss for words. Kole had known this whole time, and never said anything? "They still hired me, though. How come you never told anyone until now?"

"Whoa whoa whoa, let's get something clear. I still haven't told anyone. I kept your secret for you; it was you who fucked it up. And I never said anything back then because I wanted you to have a chance. I figured there was a possibility you were joining law enforcement at your brother's behest—though he wasn't Hades back then, just a lowlife—so he'd have an inside guy lookin' out for him, getting rid of his scent. But when I looked at your college records and all that volunteer work, you just didn't seem the type."

"Thank you." He wasn't sure if his gratitude was for what Kole had just said, or for the fact that he hadn't stood in his way of becoming a police officer. "Is that why you assigned me the Clive Reynolds case? So I could . . . prove myself, or something?"

"There was that, yeah. And it was a good distraction from Garrison's investigation. Plus . . ." He paused, and for the first time since Hudson had known him, Kole looked unsure.

But Hudson hadn't come this far—screwed up this royally—to let Kole's reasoning remain a mystery. "Plus what?"

Kole tilted his head to one side. He raised an eyebrow at Morgan, who raised one back. He regarded Hudson again. "You want the good news or the bad news first?"

"The good news."

"Okay. You don't belong in Sensitive Crimes."

Relief washed over Hudson. He'd felt almost certain that at the very least, Kole was going to pull him from the cold case and toss him back into his current assignment. He couldn't do it anymore, especially not after knowing all that had happened to Morgan as a child. He was afraid to ask, but there was no avoiding it. "And the bad news?"

"Look, I know you don't want to hear this, but you don't belong in Robberies, either."

The statement hit him harder than the blow Kole had just dealt him with his fist. "But Garrison and I—"

"What? Spent the last four months of your patrol career tracking a string of convenience store robberies. You make any arrests?"

"No, but we got some leads." He thought of Kai Steele holing up at Tobias's place. Police had been so close to bringing him in last night. If only he could catch him, so many questions would be answered.

"Leads don't put the bad guys away," said Kole. "Arrests do. And even those don't stick half the time. The truth is, Garrison was good at a lot of things. But detective work? There's a reason he was never promoted."

"He never wanted to."

"Really? Is that why he took the test?"

"What?" In all their years together, Hudson had never heard Garrison utter anything but disdain for the bureau. Surely he wouldn't have taken the investigators' exam.

"Not the one you took. But four years ago, yeah, he took it." Kole paused for a beat and then added the obvious, "He didn't pass."

Hudson shook his head. He felt hollow inside, duped, and cheated, as if he hadn't known the real Brix Garrison at all. It was his friend's unapologetic disdain for the bureau and all the people in it that compounded Hudson's guilt of going upstairs. That and leaving him in Patrol alone. "I just don't understand," he said after a moment. Garrison had been a lot of things. Husband, father, brother in blue, life of the party. But the last thing he'd been was a hypocrite. "Why would he hate on it so much if he'd wanted to go there once himself?"

"Why want something you can't have." It was a statement, not a question.

"So, what now?" Hudson asked. "If I don't belong in Sensitive Crimes or Robberies, what's your plan for me?" He dreaded Kole's answer.

Kole was quiet. He stared in the direction of the living room, but not really at anything at all. The light from the kitchen window reflected in his frost-colored eyes. Finally, he spoke. "What did I tell you when I assigned you the Reynolds case? I stuck my neck out for you, Ryan."

The nearly imperceptible quiver in his voice had Hudson almost wishing he was back with his face being smashed into the wall. He deserved it, anyway. He didn't know whether *I know* or *I'm sorry* would be a more appropriate response, so he said nothing.

"You got involved, after I distinctly commanded you not to. All you had to do was keep your eyes on your own paper and you'd have solved the Reynolds case by now. People would be passing your name around for a whole different reason." He sighed so heavily his shoulders rose and fell. The black chain around his neck caught the light. "You realize I could get sent back to Patrol for this. Which, hey, if that's a guy's cup of tea then good for him. But it ain't mine. My heart's in Investigations. Running that bureau and steamrolling lying motherfuckers in that interview room. I've worked too damn hard . . ." His jaw tightened.

Kole was right, Hudson realized. After this debacle, he might not get banished immediately from the bureau, but command staff would be less likely to align with him on any further matters of importance, including when it came time to either grant him an extension in Investigations or send him back to Patrol. Hudson felt like a cockroach. He'd screwed over the one person who had given him a chance, not just with the Clive Reynolds case, but with his entire career. "What can I do?" he asked.

Slowly, Kole straightened up. He rolled his neck from one shoulder to the other, working out a kink. Still not looking at Hudson, but staring outside where the snow came down in fat flakes, he said, "Look. You and I both know that Ronald Muntz is a lying piece of shit."

The statement felt like a splash of cold water. "We do?"

"If he's saying Hades shot Garrison and you're saying he didn't . . ." He turned his palms over and lifted them like he was weighing both options.

"He didn't," Hudson confirmed.

Kole turned his chair around with his jacket draped over it and sat backward, making good on his intentions to stay awhile. "Okay. Then tell me who did."

Suddenly, Hudson was back in the Fast Mart, staring at Garrison's body on the floor. Shards of potato chips were littered everywhere like shrapnel. Morgan was to his right, rocking back and forth against the candy rack, talking to Devine about the shooter's *red treads*. Bursts of blinding light popped from camera flashes. Yellow placards marked the location of casings. Fingerprint powder coated the countertop, the door handle. He was back there wiping the vomit from his chin, his eyes watering, weeping, his tears frozen to his face. He was crouching down, sliding the faded red ticket out of Garrison's trauma plate pocket, tucking it out of sight when the medical examiner arrived.

The Ruins. The ticket. How Garrison had come by it was still a question mark, but it led to Morgan. What had Kole just said, he'd worked *backward* to find out Hudson's connection to Tobias? Hudson had to work backward from Morgan, and as he did, like a game of Tetris, everything started clicking into place. And then Morgan, bless her blackened little soul, spoke two words that would derail everything. "I lied."

31

MORGAN

"Lied about what?" said Hudson.

Both men stared at her. Morgan dug her nails into her forearm and scratched. "On Wednesday when you interviewed me in your car, you asked if Garrison had said anything to me."

From her peripheral vision, she saw Nik shoot Hudson a disapproving look at the mention of an under-the-radar interview. "And you said he didn't," Hudson reminded her.

Morgan sat still. She was painfully cold all of a sudden. The tip of her nose, her lips, her fingertips. Her toes felt wooden as she pressed them into the floor. Her jaw tightened. She was clamming up. It used to happen to her as a child, when the detectives would talk to her about the things that happened at the house on Winslow Street.

"Morgan."

She couldn't tell which one of them said her name. Only that it sounded far away. Like she was locked in a box and they weren't.

The weight of a hand on her shoulder. She startled.

"Morgan." It was Nik. Her gaze traveled up his arm, from winter-bitten skin on his hands to the charcoal thermal long-sleeve shirt he wore, the top two buttons undone to reveal a black chain. A five-o'clock shadow masked the lower hemisphere of his face. His skin was clean but for a few longitudinal lines in his forehead and a small arrow-shaped scar beneath his right eye. He was handsome, she supposed. Not Hollywood handsome like Clive, but attractive for Black Harbor, albeit a little overdramatic. His voice had an edge like a knife, which she liked. "Morgan. What did Officer Garrison say to you?"

The words were there, three little snowflakes swept up in the flurry that raged in her mind. She kept losing sight of them, watching them swirl round and round. *I found you.*

"It's okay," Nik said. "Just, think back to that night. When you walked in the door. Did Garrison say anything to you then?"

Her breath slowed as she inhaled. She felt the cold on her face as she had on the night of December nineteenth, remembered tripping over the mat as she'd walked into the building. "He caught me," she said. "I—I tripped on the rug. And he asked if I was okay. And then I went to the candy aisle. I was . . . looking for a Butterfinger." How stupid it sounded, especially now when she played it back for an audience. Her candy cravings had landed her in the middle of a murder scene.

"And then what?" Nik asked.

Without moving her head, she lifted her gaze to Hudson. Over the rim of her glasses, he was just a blurry figure looming over her. As she inhaled again, the scent of her coffee brought her back to that scene, the ear-shattering *pop!* after *pop!* and the chip bags exploding. The sound of bullets punching through skin and lodging in arteries. Two hundred pounds of flesh and muscle and bone crashing to the floor, blood reaching toward her like crimson fingers. She heard the screeching of her own car like a horse being stolen from its post and driven into the night's unknown terrors. She felt paralyzed again, powerless to move, to run, as she watched Garrison's head roll unnaturally on his neck, his empty eyes staring at her, lips stuttering as they formed the words . . .

"I found you," she whispered.

"Say again?" Nik leaned in.

"I found you," Morgan said, louder. A moment of silence followed, so heavy it crushed her eardrums.

"Jesus H. Christ," said Nik.

Morgan looked at Hudson. He'd gone ashen as a corpse. Even his lips were blue.

"That's why he had the ticket. He'd been looking for me." She strug-

gled to keep her voice steady. Here she was in a room with two police officers, about to spill every last vile secret she'd so meticulously kept locked
inside. It was all so off-brand for her. Of course, she'd already told Hudson
most of everything, but that was different. They'd been alone, and he was
like her. Strange. Adrift. Misfit. He wouldn't throw her in an institution,
but Nik—

"Hold up, what ticket?" said Nik.

Without a word, Hudson stood and walked into the living room. He
returned with his black memo pad, opened to the spread with the faded
piece of paper.

Two deep creases formed between Nik's brows. He stared, but didn't
touch it. "The Ruins," he read. "I don't get it. What is this place?"

Morgan looked at Hudson. He held her gaze for a beat, as though
trying to decipher what she was thinking. With a sigh, he turned to Nik.
"How long have you got?"

Having risen to get a better look at the evidence, Nik settled back
down. He rested his chin in his hand, the attentive listener. "All day."

For the second time in a handful of hours, Morgan divulged her life
story, starting from the beginning. She told him that her father was Clive
Reynolds, and her mother a woman named Ava, whose name she only
knew as a curse from her aunt Bern's lips.

"Who took these?" Nik held the razor-thin strip of negatives that
Hudson had retrieved from the basement. From where she sat, Morgan
could barely make out the figures that she knew were her family—and
her.

"Christopher Reynolds," said Hudson. "We think."

"Blackmail?"

"Probably."

The strip curled on the kitchen table as Nik scrutinized every photo,
then went back a second time. And a third. "Son of a bitch," he whispered.
His eyes flitted back and forth to Morgan, comparing her to the child in
the negatives. "I remember you. That Bart Simpson doll. You wouldn't let
it out of your sight." The two men shared a solemn look, and when Nik
turned back to Morgan, he said, "I'm sorry." She watched his face cave in
a little. His brows formed a *V* and his mouth became a severe line. "Jesus,

I wish we'd have found you sooner. That your aunt hadn't had to drop dead before someone rescued you."

Sorry. The word felt like the tip of a hot blade poking a blister. Had anyone ever said it to her before? When she'd been young, people had either regarded her with pity or not at all. She was a ghost, a creepy little thing that haunted the corners of people's vision and unnerved them when they noticed her. Later, the pity morphed into fear. She'd worked hard to make it so. Because if people feared her, they didn't hurt her. They just . . . stayed away.

"Thank you," she whispered, though she didn't need saving anymore.

Next, she gave him the abridged version of her life after Winslow Street. She went to live with her now parents, Lynette and Bruce Mori. She grew up. She went to school in Chicago and worked at The Portrait People in the mall to pay the bills. And when the mall was all but bankrupt, the opportunity to lease a department store was too tempting to resist.

"That's this place?" Kole tapped the ticket.

"Yes."

"And you said Garrison had this on him, when . . . ?"

Morgan looked at Hudson.

"How are the three of us poring over this thing and it isn't in Evidence?"

"I reacted," Hudson confessed. "If it was something bad, I didn't want Brix's family to know about it. Not from a report, anyway."

"Well, was it?"

"What's that?"

Nik rolled his eyes. "Something bad. I assume you've done some research and haven't just been using it as a bookmark this whole time."

Morgan felt Hudson's gaze shift to her. The Ruins was not his secret to tell. And for all that she'd told him, there was still more.

Nik dialed his sights on her, too. "What kind of seedy operation were you running?" he asked. "And why would Garrison have gone there?"

"He was a PI," said Hudson. The admission sounded abrupt, as though he'd been holding it in for some time.

"A PI? Brix Garrison?" Morgan was sure that if Kole had been drinking coffee, he would have spit it out.

Hudson's voice was distant, like a computer with a dozen other programs running simultaneously. "We talked maybe four or five months ago. About his plans for after retirement. He said he had an offer."

"Jesus." Kole scratched his head, then rolled his eyes up toward the ceiling in a *Lord help me* moment. "Okay. And he went to The Ruins, or he was looking into it at least, because of you." He pointed to Morgan. "The secret Reynolds kid. This is easy."

Hudson furrowed his brows. "It is?"

"We need to talk to Eleanor Reynolds."

32

HUDSON

The reward for information leading to the arrest of Garrison's killer had frozen at $132,000 when, in the early morning hours of Boxing Day, Tobias Shannon was booked in. After a call to an inside connection at Crime Stoppers, Kole had unearthed the fact that over half of the money had been put up by a generous private donor.

Clive Reynolds's widow, Eleanor.

They were on their way to the Reynolds estate now, driving along the crumbling edge of the lakeside road. Hudson had never been in Kole's personal car before. It smelled like Armor All and artificial lemon scent. A black corded bracelet with beads that spelled the name *Hazel* hung from the rearview mirror.

The Reynoldses' mile-long driveway was the sole reason their house was one of few remaining on the bluffs. The others had been vacation homes, mostly, owned by Chicago fat cats hell-bent on evading Illinois's crippling property taxes. If they only stayed on this narrow strip of Black Harbor—with their supper club and boat slips just down the quay—and didn't venture into the city, they could pretend their vacation destination wasn't a coal-blackened slum rife with murder and mischief.

Hudson never came this way, himself. He had no business here, and he doubted Kole did either. The same could not be said of Garrison, however. How many times had Garrison driven this same route, navigating this disappearing road? How many times had he entered through the monogrammed black gate? And how many times had he parked on the cobblestone drive and knocked on Eleanor's back door, just as Hudson and Kole were about to do now?

Kole pressed the keyless start button. There was a *tick, tick, tick*ing noise as the engine powered down. The vehicle quieted. "You ready to do most of the talking?"

Hudson stared out the windshield that was already beginning to fog. Through it, he could make out the shape of a fountain in the yard and a trellis covered with cedar boughs. "It might be best if you start," he suggested. "Since you have—"

"—charisma?"

"I was going to say since you have a rapport with her, but sure."

Kole got out and slammed his door. Hudson followed suit and fell into step with him. The walk had been snow-blown and salted, revealing the black and grey cobblestone pavers underneath, like miniature gravestones pushing up through the snow. White Christmas lights twinkled in evergreen garlands and red ribbons that spiraled up the pillars. The decor seemed long past its due now, but it was only the twenty-seventh—the beginning of the purgatorial week between Christmas and New Year's. He noted the smithwork on the heavy oaken door. The doorknob protruded from an ornate iron backplate. Looking closely, he saw that it was a relief sculpture, with antlers that swirled like filigree and met at the crown of a stag. A keyhole was punched into the animal's chest like a bullet wound.

A fleeting thought dashed across his mind, like a deer sprinting into the grass; he wondered if Morgan had tried her key in it. He'd already put together that her being hired as the Reynoldses' photographer was anything but happenstance, but which one of them had lured her home? She seemed to favor David and Carlisle, but if she really was Clive's secret daughter, any one of them could have a vested interest in bringing her back to Black Harbor.

"Hello!"

A voice projected behind them and startled Hudson. He and Kole turned to see a man jogging up to them. He wore a heather T-shirt over black running tights with a reflective stripe, and gold running shoes with

red tips that didn't look at all comfortable to be running in. Despite it being a whole eighteen degrees out, trails of sweat dripped from his hairline
and collected on his stubbled chin.

"Good morning," said Kole. "I'm Sergeant Kole with the Black Harbor
Police Department, and this is Investigator Hudson. We're here to speak
with Eleanor Reynolds."

"Yes, of course. Eleanor mentioned you were stopping by." The man
smiled, issuing a cloud of steam through his perfect white teeth. "I'm Don,
by the way," he said, confirming Hudson's suspicion. He stepped forward
and shook both of their hands, then skipped up the porch steps past them
and opened the door. "Come in."

"You're pretty hard core, Don," said Kole as they entered what appeared to be a mudroom of sorts, though it was the nicest mudroom Hudson had ever been in. "How far you run?"

"Oh, just a quick six." Don slipped out of his shoes, stowed them away
in a low cubby beneath a built-in bench.

"You training for anything or just stayin' in shape?"

"Keeping up." Don grinned like guys do during locker-room talk.
"Eleanor's got enough stamina for both of us."

"Quite an age gap between you two, yeah? Fifteen, twenty years?"
Kole asked.

Don's smile diminished. "No one would care if it were the other way
around," he said. The rebuttal was polished, concise, as though he'd had
quite enough time to think of it. Nevertheless, Hudson couldn't help but
agree with him. Women who dated men younger than them were cougars,
while men who dated younger were simply adhering to the status quo.

Don called for Eleanor then, who floated into the common area from
down the hall, and Hudson discovered that "silver fox" didn't even begin
to describe Eleanor Reynolds. She was radiant, enchanting in a teal top beneath a sparkling cashmere cardigan. White pants. Fuzzy Fair Isle socks. A
soft halo of light illuminated her hair, twinkled in her eyes. She was a star.

Hudson pulled his gaze from Eleanor to survey the rest of the house.
How many people would kill to be inside of this place? To be this close to
Clive Reynolds's widow, to peer inside her world. He felt a little like how he
imagined Larry King must have felt when he got to interview O. J. Simpson,

and he understood, in those seconds, the allure of being a reporter. The thrill of being granted access to a story or a new angle that hasn't broken yet. He was more cut out for a profession in journalism than he was law enforcement. Reporting the facts instead of hunting them down. It would have made his mother happier, at least.

A Christmas tree that rivaled the size of the one in the square downtown stood in the corner of the living room. There was a mantel with framed photos on top, expensive-looking couches, and to his left he could see a winding staircase that climbed up to the second and third floors. The kitchen was open concept with a granite island beneath pendant lighting, a silver espresso machine, and a cozy breakfast nook. In a cove between floor-to-ceiling cabinets was a desk with a chair and a rotary phone. He pictured Eleanor sitting there every July 15, waiting for the call that her husband had been found.

"Sergeant Kole," Eleanor said. She shook his hand. "What a treat. We don't typically speak in person."

"Hello, Eleanor. This is Investigator Ryan Hudson. He's the lead detective on your husband's case."

"Pleasure." Eleanor offered her hand for Hudson to shake, and as he did, he glanced at Don. The word "husband" didn't seem to affect him.

"I'm going to go take a shower, darling." Don planted a kiss on Eleanor's forehead. His gaze didn't leave the two policemen in his kitchen, though, until he'd disappeared down the hall.

"Would either of you care for a cup of tea? Espresso?" asked Eleanor.

"We're fine without, thanks," Kole answered for both of them, and Hudson knew that he wanted to get in as many questions as possible before Don made his valiant return. He was thinking the same thing.

"Is there a quiet place we can talk, Mrs. Reynolds?" Hudson asked. "We have a few clarifying questions regarding some new information in your husband's case." He wasn't sure what exactly Kole had told her when he'd set up the meeting, but it had likely been along those lines.

Eleanor touched the back of her neck. She looked lost in thought. No, he realized. She was listening for Don's footsteps to fully dissipate. "I'm feeling a little flushed, gentlemen," she said. "Might we talk outside? It's actually quite a nice day out."

They put their shoes back on and Eleanor guided the way through a winter garden. Cedar boughs hung low with oversized ornaments. Lights twinkled like fireflies. The snow-covered grounds blending into the sky made the Reynolds estate look infinite.

Hudson walked with his shoulders hunched, his fists balled in his coat pockets. Eleanor carried a muff of faux silver fox fur. Kole kept pace with her, his hands naked and exposed to the elements. He didn't seem affected by the cold at all; the promise of impending answers was enough to keep him thawed from the inside out.

A cardinal perched on a crystalline birdbath, a spot of blood against the white backdrop. "They say cardinals are spirits." It was the first thing Eleanor said since they'd been out here. "Although, ask me who *they* are and I couldn't tell you."

She'd offered the branch. It was up to them to grab hold. Hudson stole a glance at Kole, ready to follow his lead. But, the quiet lingered for a few seconds more. Hudson listened to their footsteps crunching on snow, the wind whispering through the trees. His heart pounded in his ears. Should he say something?

Just when he opened his mouth, Kole asked: "Who could this one be, specifically?"

Eleanor slowed her walk. She turned to look at Kole. "Well, I've got plenty of dead relatives but I know you're not here to ask me about any of them. Of course I'm talking about Clive."

"You think he's dead, then?" Hudson's bluntness surprised even himself; reminded him a bit of Morgan's communication style. But they didn't have time for niceties. The way the narrow path forced him to walk two steps behind Eleanor and Kole, he couldn't help but feel like a tag-along little brother.

Eleanor sighed. "I understand the probability of Clive showing up alive after all these years would be quite slim. And if I'm being honest, perhaps it wouldn't be such a good thing. After all, it's not as if we could pick up where we left off."

"Don seems like a catch," said Kole. "How long have you two been an item?"

He could only see a sliver of her face as she turned to Kole, but Hudson noticed a demure smile. Her lips were closed, but the pointed tip of an eyetooth peeked out. "Officially? Thirteen years this New Year's Eve."

"That's coming up," Kole remarked. "What about unofficially?"

"Excuse me?"

"You said you and Don have 'officially' been going out for coming up on thirteen years. How long have you unofficially been . . . more than acquaintances?"

Hudson swallowed. He clenched his fists tighter in his pockets and was glad for no one paying him any mind. There was something about Eleanor Reynolds. Perhaps it was part of her enchantment that she reminded him of an icicle—delicate enough to shatter, sharp enough to kill. He didn't want her to do either, right now. He just wanted her to talk.

"Don was my daughter Carlisle's youth basketball coach," she offered. "He's been a friend of our family for . . ." Her eyes rolled upward as though the answer lay in the vacant sky. "Twenty years? Give or take."

"Twenty years," repeated Kole. "That's a long time. So, you knew him pretty well before . . ."

"Yes."

"He was there for you when Clive went missing?"

"Don is a very kind soul. It's why we're together now, but . . ." She stopped in her tracks. Turned to face both of them. "Detectives, I hope you didn't come all the way out here to insinuate my boyfriend might have had something to do with my husband's disappearance twenty years ago. Because I can assure you, that simply is not the case."

"No insinuation at all, Mrs. Reynolds. Just making small talk."

Hudson sighed. Eleanor had a point. Don seemed protective of Eleanor, sure, but probably because he knew better than anyone the damage the investigation had done to her privacy, her character, her surefootedness in the world. For the past two decades, every move she made was analyzed by public scrutiny. On the other hand, there were underground fan clubs for her, women who admired her—first for killing her husband, and second, for so flawlessly getting away with it.

"Cops don't make small talk," Eleanor rebutted.

Kole smiled. "All right, we'll cut to it. Why'd you hire Brix Garrison to investigate your husband's disappearance?"

The corner of Eleanor's mouth twitched. "Because I wanted it solved, why else? After twenty years, gentlemen, I'm sorry, but a woman could get the idea it had fallen from your list of priorities."

And she'd be right, too, thought Hudson. Such was the nature of cold cases. They were reassigned only when new information was brought to light, and pending a lull in active cases. Which, for Black Harbor, was about as common as a total solar eclipse. But for someone close to the subject of a cold case that had been shelved and collecting dust, he imagined the pain must be like the persistent ache of a phantom limb. It had the power to drive people insane, and yet, Eleanor Reynolds was expertly composed. She'd had twenty years to practice, after all.

"Brix Garrison was a patrolman," said Kole. "He didn't do investigations."

"He never forgot about me," said Eleanor. "Which is more than can be said of anyone else." She began to walk again, toward a brick shed. The stones were mottled cream and black; Hudson wondered if the black was part of the brick, or if it was spores from coal dust. The extinct coal industry left a gritty film over every inch of the city, from which even the Reynolds estate wasn't immune.

"Do you know he called every year on the anniversary of Clive's disappearance?" Eleanor said, not looking at either of them. "That old rotary phone in the kitchen. That's why I've always kept it, as much of an eyesore as it is. I know I could have given him my cell number and disposed of the thing, but . . ." A puff of air issued from her mouth. "I guess there was something ceremonious about it. Early on, in the first weeks, even months, since Clive's disappearance, I used to imagine the phone ringing. I'd pick it up, and Officer Garrison would tell me that my husband had been found—alive—and I'd be so overwhelmed I'd fall into the chair by the desk." She shook her head, turned slightly to glance at each of them. "Foolish, I know. How fantasies change when your husband disappears into thin air. And now they're both . . . gone. Clive and the one person who knew his case as well as I did. And poor Morgan was there. How terrible."

"Speaking of Morgan," said Kole, "how did you connect with her? We know she photographed your Christmas party."

"Her services were a gift, from my son, Bennett. He knows my penchant for photographs. He's taken quite an interest in her."

"What do you mean by *interest*, Mrs. Reynolds?" Hudson felt Kole's side-eye like a laser beam.

"They went for a drink after the party," obliged Eleanor. "And he certainly didn't object to her being invited to the cabin for New Year's. I'd say that qualifies as interest, wouldn't you?" They arrived at the garage. She punched in a four-digit code on a stainless-steel keypad.

Hudson's ears pricked to the sibilant sound of locks disengaging. Kole followed Eleanor inside, but he hung back for a moment, frozen in place. Morgan never told him she'd gone out with Bennett that night. In fact, when he'd interviewed her in his car, she'd insisted she was at the Reynolds estate the entire time, up until stopping at the Fast Mart for gas. Everything in him wanted to ask Eleanor if she knew where they'd gone, but Kole might actually kill him for straying too far off the topic of Garrison and how his death could link up with Clive's disappearance.

He would have to ask Morgan later, and pray she didn't run off and ghost him again. At least he could take comfort in the fact that she didn't have the means to leave Black Harbor.

He stepped into the garage and pulled the door shut behind him. They'd exited the winter garden and ended up in a showroom. There had to be a dozen or more classic cars, all covered by protective tarps. The sight was a bit unsettling. They looked like mummies kept in an aboveground tomb. An immaculate workbench and pegboard of tools spanned the east wall.

"Holy shit," breathed Kole.

How much money was parked in this garage, Hudson wondered. Eleanor was sitting on a fortune.

"You know, the Widowmaker wasn't Clive's only love," she said. Her heels clicked on the epoxied floor as she walked a few paces in, turned around so she held both of them in her sights. "She was his favorite, sure. His go-to. The one everyone knew about. But . . . she wasn't the only one he kept close."

As he listened, Hudson got the feeling Eleanor wasn't just talking about Clive's classic car collection. And if he'd picked up on it, then Kole definitely had.

"Mrs. Reynolds, are you saying Clive had a mistress?" The antiquated word tumbling from his mouth and the company of vintage cars discombobulated Hudson. He felt as though he'd time traveled backward to a different decade.

Eleanor smiled as though he'd said something cute.

"How'd you find out?" Kole said.

"Oh come on, gentlemen. A woman knows when her husband has stepped out. Especially one like Clive. The formerly inattentive husband is suddenly the doting partner and adoring father, taking his family out to dinner so the public can see the Reynolds clan, so happy and harmonious. Buying diamonds for his wife, horse riding lessons for Cora. A basketball court for Carlisle, an in-ground pool for Bennett. Even a car for David—a Mustang. Plus, there were the calls to the house." She shrugged. "Landlines have their perks. If I had a nickel for every time I picked up the phone in the den and listened to him talking to a husky-voiced harlot, I'd be a rich woman." She paused, angled her chin as though reminding herself that yes, she was a rich woman.

"Sounds like Clive wasn't too good at covering his tracks," remarked Kole. His voice sounded farther away. Hudson hadn't noticed he'd moved to stand next to a car. His hand was poised to lift up the covering. "Chevy Camaro. My grandpa used to have one of these. May I?"

Eleanor nodded.

Kole peeled away the tarp, revealing a cerulean blue finish and a stripe of chrome at the bottom of the frame. He whistled. Hudson didn't know Kole to be a car guy, but then, there was a lot he didn't know about the sergeant. Why he chose to waste his life in Black Harbor, for one thing—reliving a Groundhog's Day of crime, drugs, and lies over and over again. For what?

He supposed he could be asking the same of himself.

Then, Kole reached into his back pocket for his cell phone. Either someone from work was trying to get a hold of him, or something in the Reynoldses' garage had caught his attention.

"Back to the night of the nineteenth, Mrs. Reynolds," said Hudson. "You didn't notice anything . . . out of the ordinary, perhaps?"

"You mean besides having forty people inside my house?" Eleanor shook her head. "You know, it's usually rather quiet around here. Just me and Don, and Bennett if he's visiting a portfolio company in town. He stays in the guesthouse, though. We don't often have guests, but I suppose it's fun to pretend, once in a while, that things are a certain way. Especially during the holidays." She sighed. The shadow that darkened her face was gloomy. For once, under the bright white lights, she looked her age. Wrinkles branched from the corners of her eyes.

Hudson knew what she meant. The first Christmas after Nandalie passed, he went to the tree farm like they used to, picking out the perfect Douglas fir while Pip bopped around in the snow. He decorated it with the ornaments from the basement, strung lights across the mantel, and sipped hot cocoa while watching *National Lampoon's Christmas Vacation.* He'd been more aware of Nan's death that day than he had throughout her entire funeral. Without his wife, Christmas was a joyless, lonesome time. Eleanor had a family to be strong for, though. And Hudson—he had nobody. Especially now that Garrison was gone, too.

"I know what you're thinking," Eleanor said. She looked pointedly at both of them. "From your perspective, a woman I hired to photograph my Christmas party became a witness to the murder of a man I also hired to put my husband's cold case to rest. Is that it?"

"You hit the nail on the head," confirmed Kole, who had returned to stand next to Hudson.

Eleanor nodded. "And you think they're connected."

"'Think' is a strong word," said Kole. "We're exploring whether or not they could be."

"Tell me. What connections are you *exploring,* then? Do you believe it's possible that whoever killed Clive—if that's what happened—shot Officer Garrison, too? All these years later?"

"We don't know," Hudson said, honestly.

"The cases are more than likely connected," said Kole. "For all we know, Clive's been alive and well all these years, caught wind of Garrison sniffing around, tracked where he'd be, and . . ." He snapped his fingers to mimic a gun going off.

It wasn't the first time Hudson had heard that particular theory. They'd discussed a half-dozen scenarios on the short ride over. Eleanor didn't appear to be rocked, either, and Hudson suspected the same scenario had crossed her mind, if only fleetingly. And yet, "You arrested someone, though," she said. "Shannon, wasn't that his name? Toby or Taylor . . ."

Hudson bit his tongue. *Tobias,* he wanted to say, but uttering his brother's name would feel like locking him in his cell for good.

"We're not convinced he's our guy," said Kole.

Eleanor nodded. "If you're seriously exploring the possibility that Clive is alive and . . . did away with Officer Garrison," she said, "then you know the human remains found in the Porsche do not belong to my husband."

"We're still waiting for the results—" started Hudson, but Kole talked over him.

"Not a chance. We're waiting for confirmation on the identity, but the long bones are too short to belong to Clive. Which, since we're here, we might as well ask: Do you have any idea who it could be?"

"The victim in Clive's car?"

Hudson and Kole both nodded while Eleanor slowly shook her head.

"Think back," said Kole. "I know it's a long time ago, but did Clive have any enemies? Friends who he might have gotten into a tiff with?"

"Besides his brother? No."

"His brother?" said Hudson. "Christopher?"

Eleanor began to pace leisurely across the garage floor, as though window-shopping for a new car. "You know, Clive wasn't my only one, either." One hand out of the silver muff, she caressed the taupe covering stretched over a hood. "I was with Christopher for three months before Clive swept me off my feet. He never forgave him for that, and yet . . . if we were meant to be, we would have been. They were like that, though. Clive and Christopher. Always wanting what the other one had. Diving to whatever depths to get it." She considered her smartwatch. A tennis bracelet glimmered beside it, and Hudson wondered if it was the "diamonds" she'd mentioned earlier. A gift from her cheating husband.

"Look, gentlemen, I have to wrap this up. But I'll leave you with this: I know no marriage is perfect. Mine and Clive's was far from it. But for all its flaws, I still loved being married to him. And I loved *him*. I loved what we'd built together."

Hudson and Kole exchanged glances. She walked past them, toward the door, and reached for the handle.

"Just one more question." Kole's voice prompted her to pause. "Why didn't you say anything? When Officer Garrison was killed, why didn't you come forward about hiring him as a private investigator instead of waiting for us to connect the dots?"

Hudson held his breath.

"Because I knew you would," said Eleanor. "For years, I've been blamed for my husband's death. I am the black widow of Black Harbor. Whether he's dead or alive, Clive isn't coming back. And now with another dead body discovered in the Porsche and the knowledge that my desire for answers could have led to Officer Garrison's death . . . I just wanted to wash my hands of it. I know it's selfish. But I hope you can understand."

"We can," said Hudson, for both of them.

Eleanor nodded a silent thank-you. They followed her outside, back into the biting air. It felt even colder now than it had fifteen minutes ago. Falling into step behind Eleanor and Kole again, Hudson looked toward the house. The windows were portals into empty rooms. Broken clouds reflected in the glass, giving them a similar inverted effect as the negatives. He squinted. The skin on the back of his neck prickled as his eyes made out the silhouette of someone watching them from the guesthouse balcony.

33
MORGAN

Morgan shivered. She'd been cold since leaving Hudson's house the day before. Invisible pins punctured her skin as though she were a voodoo doll. It didn't matter how many scalding showers she took. The winter was inside her, freezing her from the inside out.

She sat in her parents' basement, burritoed in a pilled blanket, surrounded by Eleanor's albums and bathed in the ruby glow of her lava lamp. Loose prints were stacked in neat, symmetrical piles. Leather albums whose covers were worn by time lay closed, each one waiting to be read like a book.

Morgan selected a print from the top of the pile and pinched it between her fingers. A sudden tremor caused it to shake like a dead leaf on a branch. He looked like them. Clive. The man who had made her and left her. He'd swaddled her in wool and then abandoned her to the wolves. She studied this picture of him at a black-tie affair, holding a martini, Eleanor a vision beside him, and wondered, *Had he been one of them?* Well dressed and inconspicuous, he looked like everyone who'd ever paid her a visit at The Ruins— corporate moguls who loosened their ties and went to abuse someone on their way home from work. She imagined him with a black hood over his head, touched his neck where she would have seared the mark.

She didn't realize she'd crumpled the photograph until she felt the cramp in her hand. Her nails dug into her palm. Morgan unfurled her fingers, revealing the ruined picture.

She tore it in half, then. And quarters. Ripped it again and again until it was a mosaic that could not be pieced back together. She sprinkled the shards on the floor. Her heart pounded. She could feel her pulse beating in her throat. Her blood warmed with the electric current that coursed through her veins.

Now, Morgan stared at the shreds of paper on the floor, piled up like the dirty slush that lined the curbs outside. Her gaze drifted across her desk, where stacks of more memories waited to be scanned. Hurt welled inside her.

Her hand hovered over one. She grabbed the top-most photograph. It was another one of Clive and a young Bennett at the pond, kneeling behind a row of fish spread out on the dock. In the background was a little shed, a stack of firewood leaning against it. Bennett smiled, missing his two front teeth as he held up an invisible line with a bluegill hooked in the mouth. Clive's arm was around him. To their right, dragged up onto the bank, she recognized the canoe from the negatives. The one in which Clive had held her and whispered baseless nothings in her ear. A whimper escaped her mouth. She sounded like a wounded animal.

She tore the picture of Clive and Bennett in half. Quartered it. Scattered it on the floor. The piles were uneven now. Biting her lip, Morgan grabbed a picture from the top of the next pile, this one of Clive pressing his thumb to the nozzle of a hose while Cora and Carlisle danced in their swimsuits. She ripped it. Scattered it. Grabbed the next one.

A trail of tears burned down her neck and soaked into her shirt as she destroyed one after another of the Reynoldses' memories. A silent scream welled up inside her. She hated Clive. Hated him for leaving her to rot in a room while he traveled the world with his other family. While they toured Roman ruins in Bath, she was being ruined in a house of horrors in exchange for cigarettes and little blue pills. And while they fed little lambs in the emerald hills of Galway, she was a little lamb being fed to the wolves. While they lay atop matching blue-striped beach towels on the white sands of Mykonos, she curled into a fetal position on a hardwood floor, praying her door would remain shut for the night.

How could he have abandoned her? His own blood. His flesh.

His ruin.

Suddenly, everything stilled. Her chest heaving, Morgan looked around her. Little shards everywhere. Kindling.

Dread bloomed in the pit of her stomach, paralyzed her. Eleanor's photos were destroyed beyond repair. She couldn't explain this. Warmed by her hatred of herself and for the villain she had become, Morgan threw herself on her desk, her body racked by sobs. She couldn't face them now, or at the cabin, or ever again. As if the Reynoldses hadn't had a trying enough past, she'd gone and obliterated every glimmer of a happy memory within it.

Clive and Bern were right. She was a ruin. Fragile like a bomb, she destroyed everything she touched.

When she finally peeled herself off her keyboard, bits of paper stuck to her arms and forehead, she shot an email off to Bennett. *I can't make it to the cabin. I'm so sorry, explain later.*

She wouldn't, of course, explain later. She would never talk to him again. Besides, she didn't belong at the cabin, with him. He was her brother. Well, half brother.

Morgan dragged her arm across her mouth, wiping away tears and mucus. She drank in deep breaths, attempting to compose herself. She had to clean up this mess.

From upstairs, a knock sounded at the door. She knew it was Hudson before her mom even called down to her.

34

HUDSON

"I'm the black widow of Black Harbor." Kole looked professorial as he repeated Eleanor's words, standing in front of a makeshift suspect board. The three of them—he and Kole plus Morgan—were in Hudson's living room again. Kole tapped on Eleanor's square on the wall, which he'd drawn with a dry-erase marker. "Think she was trying to tell us something?"

Beside him, perched pretzel-legged on the back of his couch, Morgan crunched down on a piece of pepperoni pizza. He'd picked her up a half hour earlier. She left her house wrapped in the same afghan she'd worn the last time she was in his car. Her eyes were red-rimmed, her cheeks tearstained. But when he asked what was wrong, she wouldn't answer. She was so cold and so quiet on the ride back to his place, he thought he might have dreamt up the events of yesterday—when he'd led her upstairs and she'd ridden him like a wave and sunk her teeth into his collarbone.

"That she killed her husband?" Hudson took a bite of his own pizza, leaned forward to catch the slipping cheese with his plate. The Dominos box lay open on the dining room table; it was the first time in two years it had been used for anything besides storing Hudson's folded laundry and whatever he didn't feel like putting away.

Kole shrugged. "That's the definition of a black widow, right? A lady who keeps killing her husbands-slash-male-suitors?"

"Are you saying Don might be next, then?" He hoped that's what Kole was alluding to, and that he wasn't about to construct a theory regarding a romance between Eleanor and Garrison being the reason Garrison was in the ground. If Kole thought that could even be a remote possibility, then he hadn't known Garrison very well at all.

"Of course he could be," said Kole, and Hudson felt the tension in his shoulders release. "Anyone could be. Or no one. It's also possible that Garrison and Eleanor were knocking boots and Don hired someone to put an end to it. He doesn't exactly look like the type of guy who's going to do his own dirty work."

Hudson winced. He felt his cheeks redden, his palms sweat. "No, it isn't possible."

"Look, don't fall into the trap of mythologizing someone because they're dead," warned Kole. "We're exploring all avenues, remember?"

Quiet fell. Hudson glanced at Kole and noticed how his gaze had cut to Morgan. She'd hardly said a word since she got here, except to Pip, who she'd bent down to coo at before even taking off her boots.

Now, he looked away from her and locked onto her square on the wall instead, drawing an imaginary dashed line between hers and Bennett's. She'd lied about going out for a drink with him that night. Why was she protecting him? What was she hiding?

Finally, Morgan spoke. "Didn't she get, like, a ten-million-dollar life insurance policy after Clive died?"

"Eleven," Hudson and Kole offered simultaneously.

She let a beat of silence pass, and then: "What happens if you take out a life insurance policy on someone and they turn up alive? Do you have to pay that money back?"

Kole's brows scrunched toward each other. "Good question. I know you can legally declare someone dead after seven years—you know, if there's no hide nor hair of them—which is what Eleanor did, obviously."

While Kole talked, Hudson searched on his phone. He read out loud: "If the person who was declared dead is later discovered to be alive, the insurance company has the right to reclaim the death benefit proceeds . . . plus interest."

Morgan cringed. Kole fiddled with the marker like it was a fidget spinner. "If Clive really is alive," he said, "I'd say the prospect of losing eleven million dollars would be a pretty compelling reason to shut up the only person who knew about it."

"Garrison." The name tumbled from Hudson's mouth. He looked up, catching Kole's eye, and he knew they were on the same page.

Kole turned toward the wall. "Scenario One," he said as he wrote it to the left of the boxes. "Clive ran off with his mistress—your mom"—he looked at Morgan—"and the two have been living it up in Belize or wherever all these years." He jotted down *Clive + Ava* and drew what Hudson assumed was supposed to be an island. "Garrison discovers that Clive is still alive, communicates this to Eleanor, who then tells Don. They take care of Garrison so the information never gets out."

Hudson nodded along. It was plausible; of course it was. His mind went back to the cold case box stuffed full of Clive's financials; the monthly withdrawals for ten thousand dollars and the one that had been skipped around the same time he'd reported his Porsche stolen. He'd be willing to bet the withdrawals were money orders sent to Ava to keep her quiet about the affair—and their shared child. But why had he stopped? Had Eleanor found out? According to his bank statement, it certainly didn't look like he'd run out of money, but Hudson also knew that just because a bank account looked in the black, didn't mean there wasn't a sucking hole of debt in a different one.

"The Widowmaker," he said.

"What about it?" Kole asked.

"Do you think it was really stolen?" He filled Kole and Morgan in on what he'd just run through in his mind concerning Clive's recurring withdrawals.

Kole turned to the wall. He tapped Clive's square with the marker. "You saying our boy Clive might have committed insurance fraud?"

Hudson nodded. "Eleanor's a smart lady. I doubt she gave Clive total control of the accounts. She would have caught on to the fact that a mysterious ten grand was disappearing every month. After all, she knew he had mistresses and that Ava wasn't the only one. But money orders are near impossible to trace. He might have been sending it to Ava to keep her quiet."

"Hush money," said Kole. "Sounds about right. So, Ava ditched Black Harbor, leaving little Morgan with her POS sister, and demanded Clive send the money directly to her account so he wouldn't know she skipped town."

"Right," said Hudson, though he was still working through the scenario. The pieces seemed to fit.

"And you think Eleanor found out?" Kole asked.

Hudson shrugged. "Something threw a wrench into it." As soon as he said it, he thought of the torque wrench in the back of the Porsche. Could Clive Reynolds have killed the victim in the passenger seat? And if not Clive, then who? He pushed the question aside for a moment and caught his bearings. "Something happened. Perhaps Clive decided he needed Ava out of his life for good, so he was going to pay her off. Or maybe Ava found out about another mistress and gave Clive an ultimatum. Either way, the most likely scenario is that Clive needed a large amount of money to send to Ava." He glanced at both Kole and Morgan to check that they were in agreement. "If you owe money, the easiest and quickest way to raise it is to cash in on your most valuable asset."

Kole was nodding. "He knew no one would believe he'd sold that Porsche. So he phoned it in as stolen."

"He was up at his cabin at the time for the Fourth of July. He made the insurance claim on the fifth, after they returned to Black Harbor."

"So, who'd he get to do his dirty work?" Kole asked. "You know, drive the car into the lake."

Hudson's eyes roamed the squares on the wall. Christopher. Blake. Bennett. Don. David. He wasn't trying to be chauvinist, but he didn't find it at all likely any of the women could have beat a man to death. And yet, Eleanor had been quite the athlete once. In the 1970s and '80s, she'd been the star hitter for an All-American women's softball team, according to what he'd dug up in several online articles. If she could swing a bat, she could swing a wrench.

But Eleanor had been up at the cabin that weekend—there was photographic evidence to prove it. And so had Clive, David, and Christopher. Bennett was simply too young to have done such damage, and neither Don nor Blake was in the picture yet. His gaze drifted lower, to the bottom left corner of the wall, where Muntz's and Tobias's squares buddied up next to each other. Ice formed in the pit of his stomach. Tobias had been walking the razor's edge of the law since the day he was born. Hudson wouldn't put it past him to have taken a payout in exchange for dumping the Porsche.

But, was Tobias capable of murder? Before Hudson even finished asking himself the question, he remembered the sensation of drowning and seeing Tobias stand over him on the broken pier. The answer was crystal clear. *Yes.*

"So, our hypothesis is that Clive needed a large chunk of money to pay off Ava," Kole recapped. "He committed insurance fraud by hiring someone to get rid of his Porsche and then reported it as stolen."

"Yes," said Hudson.

"Not bad. I'm with you."

"Unless he wasn't paying her off," said Morgan. She unfolded her legs and let her stockinged feet swing over the floor. "Maybe he was cashing in so they could start a new life together."

Kole exhaled, nodded. Hudson could see his eyes moving swiftly across the board, working to break its code. He uncapped the marker and wrote *Scenario 2.* "Or," he offered, "let me take you back to circa the year 2000. The world has just avoided Y2K, crime in Black Harbor is steady but rising to the force of nature it is today, and Eleanor's getting hot and heavy with Don. She wants her husband out of the picture, but she also wants to keep his money and not destroy her family. She takes out the notorious eleven-million-dollar life insurance policy on Clive, Don takes care of him, and seven to eight years later, once he can officially be declared dead, they cash in." He paused to finish drawing arrows and Xs and dotted lines. "If—twenty years later—Garrison caught on to the fact that Don killed Clive, well, that would be reason enough for Don to kill Garrison." Finished, Kole wore a triumphant smile.

"You seem dead set on Don having killed Garrison," observed Morgan.

"I don't know about dead set," said Kole, "but pretty damn close, yeah."

"Why?"

Kole glanced at Hudson. "Shit, we forgot to show her what we found." He walked over to Morgan and held out his phone, showing the last photo in his camera roll. Hudson leaned over her shoulder to study the picture again, recognizing the epoxied floor in Clive's classic car showroom. There, next to the tire of the Chevy Camaro Kole had pretended to admire, was a light spray of black. So close that they were touching, Hudson felt Morgan stop breathing.

It was the silhouette of a shoe.

"Is that . . . ?" she asked.

"Yep," said Kole, zooming in to show the flecks of spray paint. "Let me ask you this, Morgan. If I lift my foot up like this to paint my shoe," he picked up his foot, "where's some of the paint gonna go?"

"On the floor, probably."

"In the shape of . . . ?"

"Your shoe."

"Exactly." He slid his phone back into his pocket. "Don has a motive to kill Garrison. And a means to do it."

Hudson considered Don's running shoes: gold with red tips, they resembled bullets with tracers. If all of his shoes were as conspicuous, he might have spray-painted them to avoid recognition. Criminals covered up logos and identifying marks all the time.

"If Clive is alive, Don has a motive," said Morgan. "But if he's dead . . ." She shrugged.

Hudson watched Kole chew on that. Morgan was right. Don's wealth was fragile and dependent on Eleanor. But if Clive was dead and the life insurance policy secure, Don might just be sitting pretty. It would be in his best interest to simply lay low and enjoy a life of luxury.

"If Clive is alive," repeated Hudson, "couldn't *he* have killed Garrison? If he knew he was on to him."

"That's interesting," said Kole. He tapped the marker cap to his chin. "That's really fucking interesting. He might still know the code to his own garage, too. If Eleanor didn't change it after all these years."

"Or had someone else do his dirty work for him," suggested Hudson.

"Talk to me, Goose. Who you thinking?"

Hudson wet his lips. "Bennett."

Kole wrote *Scenario 3* on the wall and Hudson heard Morgan's sharp, almost inaudible intake of breath, and he knew he'd done it; finally tugged on the right thread to get her to tell the truth about that night. He thought back to their first conversation in his car, when she'd lied about Garrison saying something to her. She'd lied again, when she'd omitted the part about going out with Bennett after the party. Eleanor had dimed her out this morning.

Morgan held his gaze. He could see a tremor course through her body as she fought the urge to run. He wouldn't let her, not this time.

"The way I see it, there are two hypotheses." Kole jotted down bullet points beneath Bennett's square. "Like Don, Bennett is dependent on Eleanor's wealth. Who knows how much debt he has wrapped up in his private equity business. If he catches wind that his dad is still alive, he might want to get rid of Garrison before he brings this fact to light, and all that life insurance money goes bye-bye."

"Plus interest," added Hudson.

"Plus interest. Or," added Kole, "Clive is alive and begged a favor of his favorite son."

"He didn't, though," said Morgan.

"How do you know?" asked Kole.

"Because we were together, at Beck's." Morgan shot Hudson a look that hovered between apologetic and annoyed. "He asked me to get a drink with him after the party that night. I did. And his shoes weren't spray-painted then. According to your picture, the suspect spray-painted his shoes in Eleanor's garage."

Kole closed his eyes, massaged his temples. "Why are we just hearing about this now?"

"And then you stopped to get gas on your way home from the bar," said Hudson.

"Yes."

"But there are three different gas stations between your house and Beck's." The volume of his voice surprised him. "You went clear across town to go to that specific gas station. Why?"

He watched Morgan dart a look at Kole to save her. But Kole just stood in front of the suspect board, working his jaw. His eyes looked softer though, less frosted over. When had the two of them switched roles of good cop/bad cop?

"I . . . took a detour," Morgan stammered.

"To where?" he asked.

She turned her wrist over to reveal the top of the skeleton key, and he knew. "Home."

The house on Winslow Street was Morgan's home, thought Hudson, no matter how hard she tried to forget it. And someone knew. Someone wanted her to go back there.

"I just waited in my car," said Morgan. "I thought about going inside. But I couldn't do it. Not in the dark. And then, on Christmas Day . . ." She leaned over the edge of the couch and reached into her canvas bag, extracting what looked like a portable DVD player. She handed it to him. The thing felt like a block of ice.

"The Ruins is outside your jurisdiction?" she asked.

Hudson nodded.

"What is this, 2001?" said Kole. He crept closer, his eyes no doubt fixing on the Post-it note stuck to its base. *Wanna play?*

Facing them, Morgan snaked her pale arm over the screen and hit the Play button.

"Jesus," Hudson whispered when it was over. Kole pressed Play again and watched it a second time. "What'd you stick him with?" he asked, his eyes not leaving the screen.

"Ketamine," she answered.

"Branding iron?"

The hiss of the man's flesh was audible again. "Yes."

"You always brand them on the neck?"

Morgan nodded. "What harm is there to being branded if no one can see it?"

"He had a mark on his neck." Kole's soft tone implied he was talking to himself, but Hudson recalled the description given by the Fast Mart cashier; that, along with Muntz's statement, was enough to arrest Tobias, whose throat was inked with a snowflake tattoo.

"I think what Morgan's trying to tell us, Hudson, is that whoever shot Garrison could very well be the person in this video. Is that correct?" Kole's eyes flicked toward Morgan, who shrugged. "So, the question we need to answer is: Who goes to this place? Had to be either a cop or a criminal."

Hudson frowned. "He was wearing a camera."

"One of those button cameras, I bet." Kole turned to Morgan again. "We use them over in SIU sometimes. Our informants wear them. It fits in the buttonhole of your shirt."

"That's why I thought it might have been one of you," Morgan admitted. "A cop, like, shutting me down or something."

"Well, he was white, or light-skinned," said Kole. "Which rules out Garrison." Hudson flinched, again, at the heinous consideration of Garrison setting foot in a place like The Ruins. "And it definitely wasn't either of us." He tugged down his shirt collar to reveal the unmarred skin. Hudson considered doing the same, but stopped. She knew what he looked like.

"It might have been David," offered Morgan. "David Reynolds. I've seen him and Carlisle at The Ruins before."

"The black sheep." Kole scratched his chin with the marker cap. "Clive Reynolds's scorned son, passed by for heir to the family business."

"He didn't want it," said Hudson.

Kole tilted his head. "Even if that's true, it doesn't sound like Clive even asked him."

"But why kill Garrison?" Hudson asked. "What would have been his motive?"

Kole looked at Morgan. "That's what she's going to find out. That invitation to the cabin still open?"

Morgan shook her head. "I emailed Bennett just before I came here. Said I couldn't go."

"Well, tell him you had a change of heart."

"I'm not going with him. He's—"

"Your half brother, I know. Just don't fuck him and you'll be fine. As for us . . ." He turned back to the whiteboard. "There's someone else we've been neglecting."

Hudson's gaze followed Kole as he tapped on Muntz's square. "Someone on this wall coerced this asshole to frame Hades. Now, who was it, and how are we gonna get Jabba the Hutt to talk?"

The idea that came to Hudson was so absurd, yet so perfect, it almost took his breath away. "We're going to squeeze him."

35
MORGAN

"You're gonna need more than caffeine to get through this weekend." Bennett grinned at Morgan from the driver's seat as she lowered the Starbucks cup from her mouth.

She smiled back, trying to mask her nerves. They'd just pulled onto I-94, the beginning of a 190-mile stretch of highway between Black Harbor and Loomis, Wisconsin. The Reynoldses' cabin overlooked a 2,400-acre body of fresh water named Lake Noquebay. It was remote. It was wooded. And according to Google, it was twenty degrees colder than even Black Harbor.

You Reynoldses like to settle on lakes, Morgan noted when Bennett emailed her the details last night.

Lol it's where we dump all the bodies, he replied.

I'm sure it will be great, she typed back. *I always wanted to do something like this.*

Investigate your family. See what makes you people tick. Although it was *our family,* technically, wasn't it? And she was one of the *you people.*

But Bennett didn't need to know that. Suddenly, she felt her stomach drop as he sped up to get around a semi. She watched the yellow lines on the road zip by like lasers. Riding with Bennett felt like being in a space capsule. He weaved expertly in and out of traffic. The speedometer read 86 mph. At this rate, they would arrive within the hour. "Do you have a secret identity as a race car driver or something?" she asked.

"In my head, yeah." He grinned, reminiscing. "My dad and I came up here a lot when I was young. He used to let me drive when we got farther north and the freeway quieted down. A secret he took to his grave, I'm sure. My mom would kill him to this day if she found out."

A knife of silence sliced between them. Bennett looked suddenly sullen, as though the memory had taken something from him. He swallowed, and then: "I'm really glad you decided to come. Usually everyone's paired up but me."

"Really?" Morgan knit her brows. Bennett was handsome, with a full head of hair, a winning smile, and money in the bank. How was he as single as she was? "But Carlisle and David . . ." she pointed out.

"Are basically a couple," he said, and Morgan was jarred with the memory of the two of them holding hands at the Christmas party. "Then there's Blake and Cora, Mom and Don, and me. Sometimes Uncle Christopher shows up, but . . . he's not exactly who I want to ring in the New Year with, if you catch my drift."

Morgan forced a smile. "Well, you don't have to resort to Christopher this year."

"Yes, and thank you for that. Speaking of, what made you change your mind?"

"About . . . ?" She was buying herself time. She knew what he was asking. He wanted to know why she'd emailed him yesterday to tell him: *Plot twist. Turns out I can go up north with you after all. If the invitation is still open?*

"You know," said Bennett. "The plot twist."

"Oh." She looked away, touching her chin to her shoulder. A piece of hair fell over her face and he tucked it into her cap. The gesture was soft and sentimental, and wrong. But he didn't know. And that made it a little heartbreaking, too. If they weren't brother and sister . . . would she? Cocksure and charismatic, Bennett was the antithesis of herself. Morgan knew that if other women were to see her with him, their claws would come out. She had to admit she liked the thought, a little bit—that someone else could want something she had. Not that she really had him, but still. He didn't know that.

And then there was Hudson. Moody, mercurial, and so damn unsure of himself. So like her. The two of them were more like siblings than she and Bennett and yet, when she was with him, they made a symmetry together she couldn't explain. Everything felt at equilibrium.

He'd become less pathetic to her since she'd discovered Nan was the name of his dead wife and not his dead nana. Not that losing your grandmother wasn't traumatic, but it was a little more expected than losing a spouse. Now that she knew that dark, depressing detail about him, it was impossible not to see it in everything he did and everything that surrounded him, from the peacock ornaments to the dusty wedding photo on the mantel.

"Hey."

She raised her eyes to look up at Bennett. He should have been focusing on the road, but instead, he was focused on her. "You okay?"

"Yeah." Morgan shook the unsorted thoughts from her head, forcing them to scatter. "I'm sorry . . . for the plot twist."

"You keep me on my toes. I love that about you."

Love. She withered at the word.

Evergreens frosted in purest white snow drifted by. A winter wonderland. Sometimes it was easy to forget there was a whole beautiful world not far beyond Black Harbor. She couldn't help but wonder who she might have become if she'd grown up here, just a few miles out of the city.

"So, do you still have that stellar brown-and-orange ski suit?" She recalled a photo of Bennett posing in a retro ski suit, no doubt a hand-me-down from someone who'd been alive in the 1970s. The photos, along with 479 others that she hadn't torn to shreds, were all digitized and saved onto a crystal USB drive; the originals were separated into black photo-safe boxes in Bennett's trunk. She was done with the Reynolds family after this weekend.

"I guess you'll have to wait and see." A corner of Bennett's mouth lifted. "You know what's crazy," he said after a minute. "I feel like I've known you. You know there are some people you meet and you just feel this instant . . . connection?"

Every nerve in Morgan's body twinged. "Déjà vu?" she suggested.

"Yeah, kind of. There's just . . . this voice in my head that *insists* I've seen you before. I don't know. Maybe I'm crazy."

"Or maybe we were snails together in another life."

Bennett laughed. "Could be." His eyes glittered as he scanned her from her combat boots to her stocking cap. She wondered what he was thinking, but then, she really didn't have to wonder. Ever since the knee brush at the bar, the near kiss under the mistletoe, and not to mention the expensive new camera, Bennett Reynolds had made his intentions quite clear.

Just don't fuck him, and you'll be fine.

She bit her lip and stole a side-eyed glance at Bennett as he drove. There was no doubt in her mind he'd been looking forward to getting her alone and seeing what she was made of. And if Morgan was being honest with herself, she was, too.

It was only 4:00 P.M. when Bennett's Porsche wound whisper-quiet down snaking, curling roads, and yet, the sky had darkened to the color of a bruise. The stars startled her. Morgan tilted her head, staring out her window at the millions of pinpricks. She'd never seen so many stars. Although perhaps she had when she'd come up here with Clive and Ava. Not that she would remember. Until the film roll she'd developed in Hudson's basement four days ago, her life had always begun at the house on Winslow Street. Just her and Bern and the strangers who came to bargain their souls for a piece of hers.

Now she had none. Not a shred, or a molecule, or the most infinitesimal atom of one. It was how she could do the things she did. Or used to do.

"Here we are," announced Bennett. He slowed before a grove of snow-laden pines. "Your home for the weekend."

Home? She couldn't see anything. But then his headlights shone on a gate—these people liked their gates—and a snowcapped rock stamped with *The Reynolds Family, est. 1992.* Bennett pressed a remote clipped to his visor and the gate swung aside like an arm beckoning them forward. The driveway wended through skeletons of birch and ash and cedar boughs. It might have been longer than their driveway in Black Harbor, though it was tough to gauge in unfamiliar territory. And in the dark.

"Is this where you take me to kill me?" Morgan asked, in jest of

course, but a little curious. No one would ever find her in this sleepy, se-
cluded town, if it could even be called as much.

She detected a shadow of a smile on Bennett's face, and then he explained: "Believe it or not, this used to be a happening place. Some of these
streets are all overgrown now."

"In the 1800s?"

"Probably," he laughed, coasting to a stop beside Cora's Land Rover
and Don's Tesla. Morgan breathed a silent sigh of relief, taking solace in
the fact that they wouldn't be there alone. Not that it mattered. She was
sure this place—like the Reynoldses' actual home—was large enough to
get lost in.

It was. What the Reynoldses had humbly dubbed their "cabin" was a
multimillion-dollar lake house. Morgan said a silent R.I.P. to the hundreds
of cedar trees that had died to build this lakeside mansion. Triplet peaks
pierced the night sky. She recognized the A-frame structure from the negatives. How much larger it looked in real life, when she could step back
and take in the whole picture. Snow dust fine as powder cocaine sifted
off the banks and boughs, swirling and glittering around her. Before she
could retrieve it from the back seat, Bennett slung her duffel bag over his
shoulder and grabbed his roller case from the trunk. "I can—" Morgan
started, but he waved her off.

"I got it," he said.

"I'll get the door," she offered. In-ground lights illuminated a freshly
snow-blown stone pathway, and Morgan wondered if the Reynolds family
had landscapers up here, or if they drew fancy gold straws to decide who
would take care of the walkway. She knocked twice and pushed the door
open without waiting for an answer. A vast rotunda opened up before her.
The sound of her boots on the hardwood floor echoed. A chandelier, made
from antlers sawed off the skulls of twenty or more bucks, suspended from
the ceiling's zenith. Cedar beams crisscrossed above; overstuffed couches
and chairs created a semicircle around a crackling fireplace. Across the room
was a wall of windows that overlooked the lake. Here in the Reynoldses'
glass house, Morgan felt exposed, vulnerable, like an amoeba under a
microscope.

Blake and Cora greeted them. Eleanor and Don followed in their wake, doling out one-armed hugs without letting go of their crystal stemware. Carlisle and David arrived together shortly after, and Morgan's pulse quickened as she noticed David did not take his scarf off with his jacket. He kept it on over a tight black sweater, and when he caught her staring, she felt her cheeks burn.

They ate dinner—fancy shepherd's pie with rosemary sprinkled on top, red wine, and a decadent Bailey's cheesecake for dessert. Morgan wondered who made it. Perhaps there was kitchen staff off-site or down a separate wing. She didn't think anyone in the family was a gourmet chef, and yet, she was learning that there was more to these people than meets the eye.

After dinner, when they all retired to sit near the fireplace, she watched each Reynolds character shed their skin. Blake had changed into pajamas, his T-shirt revealing fully inked sleeves on both arms. His pants were cinched at the ankles and the ends of tattoos poked out there, too. *They must cover his entire body,* she thought. Tendrils of ink climbed up past his collarbone creating wisps of ivy on his neck. Morgan wondered if that's what the cashier had seen.

He sat on the sheepskin rug with Cora. The couple looked younger without their toddler, and Morgan saw, now, that the eldest Reynolds daughter had tattoos on the insides of her arms—a harp and a tree of life whose bowing branches gave it the illusion of a screaming skull.

David and Carlisle disappeared for a while, and when they came back in through the front door, they smelled like weed. Morgan inhaled deeply, hoping for a secondhand high.

Eleanor wore a silk robe tied over matching pajamas. The fabric clung to her, showing the sinewy muscles the woman was made of. She had the body of a swimmer, Morgan thought, with muscular shoulders and a long, triangular torso. Don stood behind her, swirling a glass of cognac. Without his glasses, he looked frighteningly plain. His IQ dropped at least twenty points, and Morgan saw him for the mooch Kole and Hudson had pegged him as. He'd hitched his wagon to Eleanor thirteen years ago—allegedly, although probably longer than that—and was now in her rustic-inspired mansion, drinking expensive liquor and smoking even more expensive cigars. Not bad for a former intramural basketball coach.

Cora clapped her hands together, demanding everyone's attention. "Let's play a game," she announced.

The words raised Morgan's hackles. She stood so close to Bennett that she felt his body heat more than she felt the fire, imagined sparks dancing off the staticky fibers of his sweater onto her. She knew there was more to this game than Cora was alluding to; just like the entire glass wall, the Reynoldses did nothing small. And then she felt the gentle caress of Bennett's finger against the inside of her palm and she knew there would be only one objective in this weekend-long game: hunt or be hunted.

36

HUDSON

The serrated, high-pitched sound of a zip tie splintered away the silence. Hudson set the duffel bag onto the floor. His shoulder burned from having hauled it the two and a half blocks from where they'd parked. It was minus twenty-seven without the wind chill. The tip of his nose was ice-cold, as well as his fingers, but the rest of him was thawed from the exertion. He looked down, his eyes having adjusted to the dark now, and hoped his cold-blooded cargo hadn't frozen to death.

As if in answer, the bag moved.

"What the fu—"

Another whine of a zip tie.

Kole grabbed a T-shirt from off the floor and stuffed it in Muntz's mouth. The large man writhed and kicked his bare feet against the mattress, but he didn't scream. Not that anyone would hear him if he did. Muntz lived in the back entrance of a martinizing shop. It was midnight and the place was well past closed.

His door had been unlocked. Now, Kole leaned in, closer than he would have if Muntz's mouth wasn't full of cotton. "You know what they did to liars in medieval times, Ronald? Oh, sorry. I guess you can't really talk. Just nod for yes and shake for no. Got it?"

From where he stood at the foot of the bed, Hudson saw beads of sweat swell on Muntz's forehead. When Muntz didn't move, Kole flicked his ear. He nodded fervently, prompting Kole to continue with his lesson.

"They used something called a pear of anguish. It was this metal contraption that looked like a pear—thus the name—and they'd shove it in your mouth, busting up your teeth on its way in."

The lump in Muntz's throat bobbed. He squeezed his eyes shut and started to groan. Kole flicked his ear again. "Hey, listen up. I might have a pop quiz for you, later. Now this pear, right? It had a screw, and when you turned it, these sharp petals unfurled that would rip your mouth apart. You follow?"

Muntz nodded emphatically. His eyes widened then, darting around, searching for the device.

"Relax," said Kole. "We didn't bring one. We brought something else. Which, if you tell us why you planted a Desert Eagle in Tobias Shannon's place—who you might know better as Hades—we won't have to use. Okay?"

Muntz nodded again.

Kole and Hudson made eye contact. When Hudson gave the command, Kole yanked the shirt out of Muntz's mouth. The man gasped like he'd just spent the last several seconds underwater.

"What do you want with me?" he yelled. The metal bed frame protested as he tried to wrench his wrists free. The bed would collapse before that happened.

Kole cocked his gun and pointed it between Muntz's eyes. "How 'bout you chill the fuck out for a second. We're gonna try this interview thing again, and this time, Investigator Hudson's gonna ask you some questions."

"I don't know shit about Hades—"

"Bullshit." The word was sharp off Hudson's tongue. He felt suddenly hot, his blood carbonated as it pumped through his veins. "You lied in the interview room. Why?"

Muntz spat, and Hudson heard the wet discharge slap against Kole's cheek. Kole pushed the barrel of the gun to Muntz's forehead. Muntz laughed, showing a mouthful of cracked, tar-stained teeth. "How's your friend? Still deader than a doornail? Killing me won't bring him back, you know."

"Why did you lie, Ronald?" Kole pushed through.

Hudson was shaking. He was glad it was dark, that Muntz wouldn't see the trail of sweat sliding down his jawline. The muscles in his arms burned. The duffel bag had to weigh thirty or more pounds. And she was starting to get restless.

"I don't know what you're talking about."

"The asshole who shot Garrison spray-painted his shoes," said Kole. "We saw the black under your fingernails when you were washing your hands."

Muntz's laugh sounded like a cat being strangled. "You think it was me?"

"Congratulations on putting two and two together," said Kole.

Now that his eyes had adjusted to the dark, Hudson scanned the room. It was spartan, with empty beer cans and chip bags strewn about. A grease-stained take-out bag slumped on a Formica countertop, adding to the place's stink. On a ratty old recliner rested a laptop; a jar of Vaseline and crumpled tissues on the end table. He remembered, suddenly, what Tobias had said about Muntz soliciting sixteen-year-old girls for sex, and wondered if he was staring at the scene of a crime. If only Muntz would have run into Morgan posing as an adolescent; she would have branded him for the ruined and ruinous thing he was.

"What's the matter, four-eyes? You never seen a fifi before?"

"A what?" Hudson's eyes roamed the table again, this time landing on a cylindrical object that appeared to be made from washcloths and duct tape.

"It's a masturbation device," said Kole. "They make 'em in prison."

"You wouldn't last ten seconds inside," Muntz chided Hudson. "Skinny thing like you'd be bitched up so fast—"

For perhaps the first time in his life, Hudson felt pure, unadulterated rage. He thought of Garrison lying faceup on the grimy gas station floor. Of Tobias sitting behind a glass partition. Of a young Morgan crying herself to sleep in her childhood torture chamber.

His sweet Nandalie lying lifeless on the concrete.

The anger awakened every cell in his body, compelled him to hoist the duffel bag onto the mattress, drag the zipper across it, and let the ten-foot-long serpent spill out onto the rumpled blankets.

Persephone was a boa constrictor, pale as moonlight with rivers of black creating a diamond pattern on her scales. When Hudson had coaxed her into the bag with a frozen mouse back at Tobias's place, all he could think of was how her skin reminded him of Morgan—white as snow, smooth as a scar, black ink on her flesh.

Muntz shrieked and began to kick wildly. The snake recoiled, only to wrap around his thick ankle. "Get it away from me!"

Kole stuffed the shirt back into Muntz's mouth, kept the gun trained on his forehead.

"Her name is Persephone," said Hudson. "And she isn't too happy that Hades has gone away. If you help us clear his name, maybe she'll forgive you."

"The black under your fingernails. Was it spray paint, Ronald?" asked Kole. He yanked the shirt out of Muntz's mouth. "Talk."

"Spray paint?" Muntz's forehead wrinkled. His eyes swept back and forth, searching his memory. "No, it's grease, man. I'm a mechanic."

"And a hit man."

"A hit man? No, you got it all wrong."

"You know, Persephone can smell a lie. You feel her tongue flicking against your skin?"

On the bed, Persephone undulated like a wave. She was one long muscle, tightening and curling, slithering under the blanket. Muntz's planet of a face imploded. He looked like a jack-o'-lantern two weeks after Halloween.

"It's grease!" insisted Muntz. "I work on cars and shit!"

"I didn't know a practicing mechanic was eligible for unemployment," said Hudson. He'd done his homework earlier, going through the recycling bin Muntz had dragged to the curb. The guy was collecting six hundred dollars a week, and spending it on Cheetos and malt liquor, apparently.

"I work off the books, at my buddy's garage." Something changed in Muntz, then. A delayed reaction to knowing he'd been caught, perhaps. "That's where he found me. I guess all these years later, he knew I wouldn't be good for nothing more than fixin' cars."

"That's where who found you?" Kole still held his gun, but it wasn't trained on Muntz anymore. The barrel was lowered toward the edge of the mattress.

"Mr. Reynolds."

"Clive?" said Hudson. Jesus, he knew it.

The wrinkles in Muntz's forehead deepened. "No. Christopher."

The name slammed into Hudson like a bullet. Vertigo claimed him. His chest heaved beneath his jacket and his head felt fuzzy. The room began to tilt as pieces of the investigation fell into place. He heard Kole speak, but it sounded like they were underwater. Every word had a muffled, disorienting quality.

Of course. Christopher had taken the photos of Clive with his secret family. Suddenly, he saw his life flash before his eyes—not his own life, but Clive's—all his memories, his secrets immortalized in tiny purple negatives.

"—opher want with you?" He caught the end of what Kole was saying.

Muntz shook his head. "Get it out of here, please!" he shouted.

"As soon as you talk, Persephone goes back in the bag."

Hudson watched Muntz's Adam's apple bob in his throat. He half expected him to spit again. Instead, he said, "He said he needed a favor. Gave me a gun and the address of where to plant it. I thought that was it. Then the day after I'd done it, he came to me again and said I had to tell five-o that it was Hades who shot that cop." He closed his eyes, no doubt trying to shut out the feeling of a boa constrictor entwining herself around his legs. "He said to get in a fight or something so I could make a bargain. He didn't want me just going up to the counter and confessin'. That would have raised a red flag, he said."

"Why would you do all that for him?" Kole asked. "Why not just head outta town and turn him in?"

Muntz laughed. "Where'm I gonna go? And who would believe me? That's how he got me after he killed Dez."

"He killed who?" said Hudson. "When?" He searched his memory, trying to recall what Christopher Reynolds looked like. He had to be in his sixties by now, if not older.

Fat tears rolled down Muntz's cheeks. His face, neck, every inch of exposed skin glistened in the hoary moonlight that filtered in through the shoebox-sized window. "He came to the shop I was working at . . . twenty years ago. Needed to get rid of this Porsche, a classic, 1978 Widowmaker.

He wanted to sell it for parts." He bit his lip, fighting back a whimper as Persephone began to coil around his leg. "My buddy, Dez, noticed a pair of panties on the floor by the passenger seat, and a training bra, like, for a younger girl." He writhed as the snake tightened. The zip ties cut into his wrists. "Dez threatened to call the cops, turn him in for child molesting. We both knew who he was. I mean, Clive Reynolds was the only guy rich enough within a thousand-mile radius to own a Porsche 930 Turbo, and his brother was never far from him. Classic coattail rider. So, Dez made him a deal. He wouldn't tell if Chris left him the car. He'd have sold it out of state, I'm sure, made a mint." He sighed, hot air and phlegm rattling in his throat.

"I take it Chris didn't like the ultimatum," said Kole.

Muntz shook his head slowly. His eyes glazed over as if he'd slipped into a trance. He opened his mouth, but his words hung suspended for a moment, his memories from one single day twenty years ago coming back together. Hudson had no doubt it was the first time he'd recounted it out loud. "He snapped," he said, finally. "It was like the devil suddenly possessed him. His eyes . . . they were dark and bright at the same time. He grabbed a torque wrench from the bench and bashed Dez's skull in. He hit the floor like a ton of bricks. Blood sprayed everywhere."

Hudson glanced from Muntz to Kole. The sergeant didn't move, didn't breathe, even, as though he feared the slightest sound would cause Muntz to stop talking.

Muntz squeezed his eyes shut again as Persephone made a ripple under the blanket.

"Then what?" Kole dared, when Muntz went mute for thirty seconds. The silence pulsed. "Ronald?"

"He told me to make it all disappear," Muntz blurted. "The car, the wrench, the blood. He said if I didn't, he'd tell police I killed Dez. Because who would they believe?" His eyes were wild as he regarded each of them in turn. "A poor kid like me who had a few misdemeanors on his record, or him? So, I waited 'til dark and drove it into the lake. Turned off the lights. Launched it right off the pier." He sighed. His jaw tensed. "I let the car sink all the way to the bottom, waited until it was fully submerged. Then I climbed out the window and swam for my fucking life." His whole body was racked by sobs as the repressed terrors of that day came flooding back.

"You're telling us you squeezed out of that tiny opening?" tried Kole, and Hudson remembered leaning half in, half out of the driver's side window when the Porsche was in the impound lot. The edges had cut into his shoulders, and he was much thinner than Muntz.

Muntz sniffed. "It was twenty years ago, man. I ain't what I used to be. Keeping a secret like this . . . it packs on the pounds."

Kole gave Hudson a look that said *He ain't kidding*, but Hudson was preoccupied with putting the pieces together. The edges of his vision darkened. Black filled the room, making way for an imaginary film reel of incriminating images to be projected over the shadows.

The young girl's underwear on the seat of the Porsche. Christopher Reynolds smashing the witness's head in with a torque wrench. Sending the other witness to his probable death. And yet, he knew Muntz had survived the lake.

Because he'd waited for him.

Just like he'd waited in the weeds, snapping photograph after photograph of Clive with Morgan and Ava.

It was exactly how he must have waited at the smoldering remains of The Ruins, watching to make sure Morgan found the key that would lure her home to Black Harbor. *M.R.* Besides Clive, Christopher might be the only person on earth who knew her as Morgan Reynolds.

"I always knew it would come back to haunt me." Muntz sighed. Fat beads of sweat glistened in his forehead creases.

"He pay you?" asked Kole. "To frame Hades."

"He said there'd be reward money and that I could collect it. Get out of town. Finally start clean."

"But why him?" Hudson wondered. Of all the criminals in this place, why did it have to be his brother who was framed for his best friend's murder?

"In case you forgot, this is Black Harbor. Nothing's sacred. He knew Hades's brother was a cop. Said you were diggin' too deep." Muntz cracked an eye open to peer at Hudson. His cheeks were red as Persephone began to tighten around his neck.

Hudson pressed his cold fingertips to his temples, fighting a wave of nausea. His brother's incarceration was his fault. He should have listened to Kole and stayed out of the investigation of Garrison's death. Because now, his disobedience had planted himself directly in Christopher Reynolds's sights. And who knew what else the old man was capable of?

37
MORGAN

Morgan's eyes shot open. Her heart raced. She hadn't planned on falling asleep, here in the den of wolves, and yet—she patted her body—she'd woken in one piece. She didn't recall going to her room. She'd been drunk on wine; she remembered stumbling down the hall, her socks slipping on the hardwood floor and Bennett catching her. His rough, stubbled cheek against her neck as he laughed. She'd smelled the bourbon on his breath, felt the heat. He hadn't kissed her, had he?

She touched her fingertips to her lips, as though she'd be able to feel the imprint of his mouth there. No. The last person to kiss her had still been Hudson. What she wouldn't give to roll over and find him lying beside her. Maybe he'd notice her looking at him and he'd wrap his arms around her and she'd feel safe, for once in her life.

That was a new feeling—*wanting* someone.

Outside, a light snow fell. It was prettier here than it was at home. In Loomis, it actually looked like snow, whereas in Black Harbor, she'd always thought the flakes looked like ash. She turned toward the window, smoothed the comforter over the vast, virginal expanse of bed, expecting to feel the chill of the morning air woven into the blanket's fibers.

She jerked her hand away as though she'd touched a hot burner.

The bed was warm.

Reaching toward the nightstand, she grabbed her glasses and put them on. The world was still bathed in a pearlescent early-morning glow. The view out her window revealed bars of birch, black-and-white striations that hinted at a divide between her and all that lay beyond these walls. Her heart racing, she stared at the other half of the bed where, faintly, she could make out the impression of a body.

Someone had lain next to her. Perhaps only a moment ago.

And they'd left something behind. A string tied around a notecard folded in half. She knew before looking up what the string was attached to. Fighting back a whimper, Morgan tilted her head. Above her floated a red balloon.

Every muscle tensed. The culprit could still be in the room. She hugged her knees to her chest and held her breath, listening for the sounds of someone else breathing, of fingernails on the hardwood floor. What if they were under the bed? Morgan clenched her jaw, battling every childhood nightmare of a hand shooting out and grabbing her ankle.

But no one else was here. She could feel it.

Swallowing back her fear, she reached for the notecard and opened it. Inside was a limerick, written in black pen.

Li'l lamb, li'l lamb, who can you be?
We're made of the same stuff, can't you see?
You are his ruin,
And I—his undoing,
Both lured by the call of a skeleton key.

She read the fourth line again. *And I—his undoing* . . . Were they talking about Clive? Had whoever left this note for her done away with him?

Goose bumps erupted on her arms as she realized the person could still be near, perhaps just down the hall. Sucking in a deep breath, Morgan launched herself off the mattress and leapt toward the door. To her relief, it swung open. She shut it behind her and held the knob.

She half expected the knob to turn from the other side, but it didn't. Her throat burning, every nerve ending in her body electrified, Morgan hurried on cat's feet down the corridor.

The doors to the other bedrooms were closed, not even cracked.

It was dead quiet in the house. She was both glad and unnerved for that. The kitchen didn't smell like roasted coffee beans and there was no fresh fruit on the island. She passed through the living room where, just hours ago, they'd played Never Have I Ever, and stared out the towering picture windows. In the light, now, she could see the expanse of the frozen lake. It was a grey-and-white world out there, with a smattering of evergreens. Birch trees, although probably stunning in the fall, looked like bones jutting out of the snow.

The silence was so absolute it was suffocating.

The west wing opened up to her like an invitation. She vaguely remembered Bennett's tour from last night. The study and the sauna were both down this way, and Eleanor and Don stayed in the last room on the left. Perhaps one of them had crept down to her room and left the limerick. Laid down beside her.

Before she realized it, Morgan was halfway down the wing, edging closer to a thin blade of light that shone on the floor. Across from the study, a bedroom door was ajar. She heard a shuffling sound from inside. Someone sliding something across the floor.

Tucking herself into the shallow alcove of the study, Morgan gripped the edge of the wall and stretched her neck to see into the sliver of the adjacent room. A man was up and getting undressed. She just saw his back at first, as he pulled off a woolen sweater over a pale blue dress shirt.

She had no idea who it could be. Everyone was accounted for in the opposite wing, unless, perhaps, Blake had not slept upstairs in the loft with Cora. Trouble in paradise?

But this man was too broad at the shoulders, too compact in the torso. That ruled out David, too.

Bennett?

Morgan squinted and leaned a tiny bit closer, careful not to lose her balance and fall on her face as she rubbernecked.

He pulled the sweater completely over his head, and a tuft of white hair popped up.

Christopher.

He must have arrived sometime in the middle of the night, or even within the hour. His muscles sagged beneath his white undershirt. He patted his hair down and leaned over a bureau to consider the old man in the mirror.

Morgan held her breath. She watched as he prodded and pinched at the crepey skin around his eyes as though willing it to firm. Then he turned his head and dragged a finger down the side of his neck. She suspected he'd cut himself shaving, but then she saw it: the pinkened, puckered skin and the word "Ruined" seared into his flesh.

Have you been naughty or nice?

She heard his voice clear as a bell, now. Remembered it like a wound that wouldn't heal. He'd asked it of her in The Ruins, and again at Eleanor's party, when she'd sat on his lap and wished for a Butterfinger. Of course she hadn't seen the mark, then. It was covered by his Santa Claus hair and beard. And later, when she'd gone to see him at Exos Labs, he'd worn a turtleneck.

Outside, the winter wrapped wraithlike arms around her. The ground was so cold, it felt as though she were standing on nails. Morgan squeezed her knees together, jammed her hands into her armpits. In the drive, she noticed Christopher's blue truck, its windshield the only one not frosted over. He must have arrived only twenty minutes ago or so. She imagined him entering the house, slipping off his shoes, and slithering onto her bed to lie beside her. It reminded her of a story she'd watched on the news where a woman let her pet snake sleep with her. She thought it was cuddling, but it was really just sizing her up to eat her.

Her memory flashed back to the video in The Ruins and the conversation she'd had with Nik and Hudson about the buttonhole-sized camera. The answer was clear. Christopher had known who she was the whole time—his brother's secret daughter—and he'd planned to do one of two things with the video: expose her for the ruinous thing she was, or rewatch the video to satiate his lascivious appetite later.

Morgan half turned, her eyes scanning the expanse of snow and ice and skeletal trees. Running wouldn't get her far. She'd freeze before she made it to the main road. Although it had been dark when they arrived last night, she hadn't seen another residence for miles before Bennett turned onto their sequestered property. She wondered if the Reynoldses owned the entire town. She was on their turf now, without another soul in sight.

"Morgan!"

A voice calling her name ripped her from her frightening reverie. Through the fog of her own breath, she saw Bennett standing in the open doorway. He was shirtless, wearing flannel pajama pants and slippers. She was in his arms before her brain had a chance to decide between fight or flight.

"What are you doing out here?" His hands encapsulated hers.

Her teeth chattered. "I— I must have been sleepwalking."

"Come on." He started pulling her toward the house. "You'll catch your death out here."

But he was wrong, Morgan knew as she was hauled helplessly to the Reynoldses' front door out of which she'd burst just a moment ago. Her death awaited inside, and he'd been waiting for her for a long, long time.

38

HUDSON

He hadn't been to Garrison's house since Christmas Eve. Now, less than eight hours after returning Persephone to her terrarium, he was sitting in an old computer chair, in the spare bedroom that doubled as a home office. Pictures stared at him from the shelves. To his right was a photo of Garrison's motorcycle parked in front of Hart's Pass, where he'd almost lost his life six years earlier. On his left, a photo of Hudson and Garrison with their wives at a backyard party, all holding bean bags. Who would have thought when that photo was taken, that two of them would be dead?

Life had a way of surprising you.

Noelle leaned in the doorway. She wore a flannel shirt rolled at the sleeves that he recognized as Garrison's. Lilah was at work. "Are you sure I can't make you a cup of coffee, Ryan?" The ceramic mug she cradled in her hands was white with the type *I ♥ meetings*.

"No thanks," he said again. If Noelle had been at the Fast Mart, and smelled the coffee mixed with Garrison's blood, she'd never touch the stuff again either. But who was he to take that away from her? Coffee was probably one of few comforts for her nowadays.

She'd asked him three times if he wanted coffee in the ten minutes he'd been there. "Widow brain" it was called, the brain's built-in coping mechanism for protecting people from more pain than they can bear, such as the loss of a spouse. He'd experienced it after Nandalie. Many days, he still felt the familiar fog settle over him, felt as though he were moving through life blindly, arms stretched out in front so he didn't run into a wall. But it did nothing to save him from falling into a hole like the one he found himself in now. A hole Garrison had dug, no less.

Hudson jiggled the mouse. The computer woke slowly. A blank box prompting for a password appeared on the screen. "Can you get into his computer?" he asked. After interrogating Muntz last night, a new urgency to look deeper into Christopher Reynolds burned a hole in Hudson's head. He'd started backtracking, ruminating on what he would have done if he were Garrison investigating Clive's case. He would have started as he had, checking the old reports for who had been interviewed and who hadn't, for anything that might have been missed or misconstrued. Everything Hudson had had been given to him by Kole, inherited from the investigators before him. But now that he knew Garrison's connection to Eleanor, he knew that Clive's widow must have given Garrison something that put him on a path to The Ruins.

Biting her lip, Noelle came forward. "Let me tell you something about my husband," she said, picking up the keyboard and flipping it over. The flat underside revealed a notebook page cut in half, with every login and password Garrison could ever have used, taped to it. "He absolutely hated remembering passwords."

Hudson shook his head, allowing himself a small smile. "So old," he chided. The desktop faded in, with all of Garrison's browsers, applications, and folders. Some folders were labeled with various vacations: *Cabo, San Lucas, Seattle, Italy, El Rey.*

Hudson repeated the last one under his breath. "El Rey," he said, then, to Noelle. "Is that the name of a place?"

Her brows knit. She frowned. "Nowhere we've been together."

Hudson clicked on the folder. It held dozens of documents—old photographs and newspaper articles. He opened an article that filled the entire screen with a grainy black-and-white photograph of Bennett Reynolds dressed in a suit and tie, sitting with his hands folded in front of him at a long, sleek desk. The headline read REYNOLDS ROYALTY: THE RIGHTFUL HEIR CLAIMS HIS THRONE.

"Eleanor Reynolds," he whispered, putting it together.

Bennett looked hardly old enough to have graduated college in that photo, and yet as his eyes skimmed the columns of text, Hudson learned that Christopher Reynolds had acted as interim CEO of Reynolds Capital between the years that Clive was gone and Bennett was ready to step into his father's shoes.

"What's that?" Noelle's voice jarred him from his reading.

"El Rey is code for Eleanor Reynolds," Hudson explained. He paused, and then, "You knew he was working this for her, didn't you?"

Noelle looked a little ashamed. She sighed. "I'm sorry, Ryan. He asked me not to say anything. To anyone."

"No, I'm not—" He wasn't . . . what? Blaming her? Mad at her? Upset with Garrison for keeping this secret? How could he be, when he'd been sleeping with Miserelli for the past six months? But this was different. Garrison was dead because of what he'd gotten himself into. And Hudson was . . . well . . . he was alive for now.

"It's bad, isn't it?" Noelle chewed on her lip. "He was finding some pretty crazy stuff. Dark stuff."

"Like what?"

"He went all the way to Chicago one day. Came back with this ticket . . ."

Hudson's pulse quickened. "The Ruins?"

She nodded. "What is that place?"

"Like you said, dark." He didn't have time to explain it all now. He needed to know something from her, though. "Did he ever say if he'd gone in there?"

"The place was burned from the inside out, I guess. He found the ticket in the parking lot."

Hudson nodded, her statement confirming his belief that Garrison wouldn't have ventured into that kind of place on his own. He scrolled through endless rows of documents. There were bank records and statements, insurance claims . . . He clicked on one that showed Clive filing for bankruptcy on one of his portfolio companies. And then a month later, another one. A month apart, every single portfolio company of Reynolds Capital had folded. But before that—he clicked to open another file—in April of 2000, Eleanor had purchased an eleven-million-dollar life insurance policy on her husband.

"Jesus."

He was so enmeshed in the computer files that he hadn't realized No-elle was reading over his shoulder. The smell of her coffee made his head swim, but he fought through it. "What is it?"

Hudson squinted, zoomed into a space on the scanned-in application form where Garrison's handwriting noted: *Clive's password red_canoe78, Eleanor's password red_canoe78.*

"What does that mean?" Noelle asked.

"It means Brix was on to something," Hudson breathed. "He was go-ing to prove Eleanor Reynolds was innocent of her husband's murder."

The discovery made him feel weightless, like he could rise right out of Garrison's chair. How Garrison, the old dog, had gotten around to match-ing Clive's passwords with the same one Eleanor had allegedly used to set up an online purchase of his life insurance was over his head. Apparently, old dogs could learn new tricks after all.

"For hating passwords as much as he did," Hudson explained to Noelle, "it looks like Brix figured out Clive's go-to, and matched it with the one used to purchase the life insurance policy."

"Which means . . ." He could see the gears turning behind her brown eyes. "Clive purchased the policy, not Eleanor."

Hudson nodded.

"So, Brix knew that Eleanor was innocent, and someone didn't want that information to get out."

"It would seem that way, yes." He mentally retraced his steps, back to the person-of-interest board Kole had drawn on his living room wall. The only one who made sense was Christopher, who, between killing Gary Hernandez and making Muntz dump the Porsche in the lake, had a few things to hide. He was safe, as long as Eleanor was the top suspect in Clive's disappearance. Unless . . .

"Why would Clive do that, though?" Noelle wondered. "Why go through all the trouble of creating a false account in Eleanor's name instead of just purchasing the policy on himself?"

Hudson thought for a moment. Aside from the paperwork he'd com-pleted through the police department, he'd never taken out a life insurance policy. He'd received money when Nan died, yes, but after myriad medical bills and funeral costs, he'd barely inherited enough for a car wash and a tank of gas. If he were to die now, everything he owned would go to his mother. How difficult could it be to essentially commit identity fraud and take out a life insurance policy as someone else? What would you need besides their name, social security number, and date of birth? All of which, as Eleanor's husband, Clive would have had access to.

"He knew he was going to die." The statement surprised him, stepping so surefooted from his mouth, but as soon as the words held purchase, he knew them to be true. Whether by his own hand or someone else's, Clive Reynolds knew his days were measured.

His phone rang. The ID came up as "Unknown" but he knew it was Kole. "Hello?" he answered.

"We've got a fucking mess on our hands now." Wind severed his voice. He sounded like he was on the move.

Hudson heard a door slam, the engine start. "What are you talking about?"

"Someone just blew Muntz's goddamn brains all over the place."

39
MORGAN

For breakfast, Morgan nibbled on dry toast and water, despite the smorgasbord of eggs, sausages, and fresh fruit.

"Wine get you, too?"

"Huh?" She looked up and saw Cora tilt her chin toward her plate.

"Oh, yeah." Just thinking about seeing her own handiwork on Christopher's neck was enough to make her stomach turn.

"It's all downhill after thirty," Blake quipped, scooping two sausage links onto his own plate.

Morgan forced a smile as, warily, she let her gaze slide over to Eleanor, who sat at the table next to Don and across from Christopher. But he wasn't looking at Morgan. Instead, his eyes drilled into the center of the table where Don held Eleanor's hand. Morgan watched him watching them. As though he could sense her stare, he refocused, like a camera lens, onto her. They locked eyes. Now that she'd seen it—the ruined patch of skin peeking out of his turtleneck—she couldn't miss it.

His mouth twisted as he opened it to speak. "Say, Morgan."

Her blood froze. Hearing his voice for the first time since knowing where she'd heard it before felt like a knife in her ear. She leaned forward just a little, inviting him to go on.

"How did your little darkroom experiment go?"

Eleanor looked from Morgan to Christopher, back to Morgan. "Darkroom experiment?"

"Yes." Christopher chuckled. "Quite ingenious, really. She stopped by the lab to pick up some chemicals to develop a lost roll of film she'd found. It was in your collection, I think, didn't you say, Morgan?"

Eleanor tilted her head. "Oh, well that's exciting! How did they turn out, Morgan?"

The weight of all the Reynoldses' eyes on her was crushing. "They didn't," she lied, and summoned an appropriate frown. "The film was corroded, unfortunately."

Eleanor nodded, but there was a darkness to her tone when she said: "Well, sounds like you gave it a college try."

"I did," Morgan assured, and then she felt the light pressure of someone's hands on her waist, gingerly pushing her aside.

Bennett tugged on the silverware drawer and grabbed a fork. He was freshly showered and smelled of his signature cologne. "You all thawed out from your morning walk?" he asked.

Her cheeks were hot, suddenly, as Cora's and Blake's attention turned to her. Even Carlisle stopped kicking her feet and stared.

"You went for a walk?" Cora asked. "Where?"

"The driveway." Bennett laughed to himself as he scooped some scrambled eggs onto his plate.

Morgan shrugged. "I sleepwalk sometimes."

"Oh dear," Morgan heard Eleanor breathe. "Are you all right, Morgan? No frostbite, no . . . ?"

"I wasn't out there long," Morgan promised. "Probably only thirty seconds before Bennett found me."

"I heard the door shut," said Bennett, and Morgan remembered he'd pointed out his bedroom was the first one down the hall when he'd given her the grand tour yesterday.

"Thank goodness," said Eleanor. She pressed her hand over her heart.

"Sounds like someone's getting locked in her room tonight."

Morgan didn't have to look to know who'd spoken. She'd know Christopher's voice anywhere.

"Miss Mori, your chariot." Bennett gestured to a two-toned blue Yamaha Sidewinder. For all her years spent in snowy Wisconsin, Morgan had never seen a snowmobile up close, let alone ridden one. It looked like a guard dog with its chest puffed out, and yet its skis lighted atop the snow as though it weighed as much as a dragonfly.

"Damn, why didn't you get the big one?" Morgan said as she straddled the behemoth. She put on a bulbous blue helmet and for a second, indulged her imagination in pretending she was an astronaut, exploring the planet Neptune, where the lakes are cold enough to shatter bones.

Bennett climbed on and sat in the space in front of her. He flipped the switch and the machine purred.

Morgan looked around. The Reynoldses were a caravan of matching snowmobiles. She wasn't the only one riding doubles; Eleanor hugged Don from behind, her cheeks already rosy from the cold.

Could he really be a cold-blooded killer, this man whom Eleanor cozied up to, she contemplated, thinking back to two days ago, mapping out possible scenarios in Hudson's living room. Could he have done away with Clive all those years ago?

And what about David? Although he didn't fit the description of the man who had killed Officer Garrison, Eleanor had made it apparent in her conversation with Hudson and Nik that there was no love lost between David and his father. Perhaps he had murdered Clive in a fit of rage.

Christopher wasn't outside the realm of possibilities, either. She remembered the old photographs of him. He'd been larger than Clive, back in the day. Making up for what he lacked in looks with muscles. She wondered if his jealousy of Clive stealing Eleanor had finally reared its ugly, homicidal head.

"Morgan?"

She shook herself back to now.

Bennett laughed. "You ready?"

She gave him a thumbs-up and they took off.

Could you outrun the cold? It was a legitimate question she grappled with as she and Bennett flew through the trees faster than the speed of sound. Although perhaps her retained warmth had something to do with the many layers she was wearing, including a pair of Bennett's sweatpants over her leggings. She wondered how long they would be out here. With all its ice and snow-laden boughs and sticks thrusting upward from the banks, this place was a hazard. She didn't know much about nature, but she knew its golden rule: the more beautiful something is, the more deadly.

Up ahead, she saw Carlisle's toboggan hat whipping behind her like a flag. Cora and Blake were too far ahead, blue dots in the distance. Eleanor and Don brought up the rear.

"Come on," Bennett yelled into the air, as though she had any choice but to move with him. "I know a shortcut."

He dove down a short but steep slope. Above them, Morgan heard Eleanor and Don whiz by. She mimicked Bennett's movements as he leaned left and then right, dodging brambles and branches. Adrenaline surged through her body. She held on tight, probably squeezing the air from his lungs, to keep from being flung off.

"You okay?" Bennett called.

She nodded, though she didn't know if he could see it. "What's that?" she asked, suddenly pointing up ahead to a small building that looked like it was made of Lincoln Logs.

"An old post office," Bennett explained. "This was all a little town once."

"What happened to it?"

She didn't have to see him to know his face was split into a wolfish grin. "People like me."

"Private equity guys?"

"Businesspeople who saw an opportunity for profit. The county makes more off the taxes on these lake houses than they ever did with the whole town."

"So money really can buy everything?"

"What do you think, Morgan Mori?"

"I think I'm in the wrong line of work."

Bennett laughed. "After the holidays, I'll take you on as my apprentice, how about that?"

She forced a grin and for a moment, the wind froze her face that way. They sped on through the graveyard of a town where he pointed out an old, dilapidated bait shop, a hardware store, and a library. Then, something appeared that felt like an unsettling brand of déjà vu to Morgan. She knew this place. A frozen pond with a dock and a little lean-to shed.

It looked smaller in real life than it had in the photographs. A pile of logs was stacked along one wall, a long-handled ax splitting the top-most one, as though whoever had last swung it, called it a day and simply never came back.

"This is your pond," she said, remembering scanning old photos of Clive and Bennett, holding up fishing lines of bluegill and perch.

Bennett laughed. "Sure is. Man, we used to spend a lot of time out here."

"You and your dad?"

"Yeah."

A canoe that might once have been fire-engine red was beached on the shore. It looked cut in half, its tail end stuck under the ice. Who knew how long ago the little boat had been abandoned, left to the weather and the elements and the solitude. Morgan felt sorry for the thing, and then, as they continued to careen through the woods, she was struck by a memory so vivid, so real, that she almost fell off the machine, for all by its lonesome, amidst the birch trees, stood a blue box.

It looked like a vintage parking meter, and yet, she remembered being lifted up as a child, someone's hand guiding hers as she dialed a number on the keypad. The memory was immortalized in a negative, even. Clive had taken her there.

"What is that?" she asked Bennett, pointing to the thing that was now behind them.

"What?" He turned to look over his shoulder.

"That blue box back there."

"Oh. I think it's a call box or something. For police, back in the day."

"There's a phone in there?"

"Probably not anymore." He laughed as they blasted through a mound of powder. "Why, you wanna call in to report a crime? Perhaps someone's stolen your heart, Miss Mori?"

Something like that.

Morgan brushed the joke aside with another forced smile and took note of her surroundings. Her wrist itched where the key was kept. She would come back later. Alone.

40

HUDSON

Hudson was disoriented. It felt as though he'd never left Muntz's apartment, and now he was back in the dingy unit, the reek of blood and feces potent enough to choke. His eyes watered, blurring the scene before him. Ronald Muntz had devolved into a gelatinous pool on his mattress, his left eye socket blown out by a .45-caliber bullet. A matte black Glock lay on the floor, just beneath Muntz's meaty hand that hung off the mattress, his fingers bloated to resemble blood sausages.

A camera flash lit up the scene as an evidence technician photographed a note scrawled on a tear-away receipt book. *I have seen and said too much.*

ME Winthorp stood next to the corpse, measuring the state of decomp. He heard her say the words "possible suicide," and "self-inflicted gunshot wound."

Kole stood beside him. "Self-inflicted, my ass," he muttered. He sounded rough, like he'd swallowed a cup of sidewalk salt. "This is not good."

Hudson shook his head, agreeing. "At least there's the interview with Kasper," he suggested. It was their one saving grace. People would focus on the incident of Muntz's arrest and subsequent snitching, which would all lead back to a motive of retaliation—the suspect being someone who wasn't too happy about Hades's incarceration. Because in Black Harbor, snitches got more than stitches. They got splattered on the walls.

The buck would stop at a motive for vengeance; no one would have to know that he and Kole had scared the truth out of Muntz just hours prior. It was selfish, he knew, but Hudson couldn't help but feel relief in knowing the law's eyes would be on someone in Tobias's circle instead of himself. And then, like the answer to a math equation suddenly clicking into place, he knew that this was the kind of thinking it took to survive in Black Harbor.

Dog eat dog.

"Christopher?" Hudson whispered, out of earshot of the others. He and Kole had receded to the edges of the scene.

"That'd be my bet," replied Kole. "I already sent Fletcher and Devine to bring him in for questioning."

"But won't they ask—"

"I'm their boss, Hudson. You know, not *everyone* questions authority figures. Believe it or not, some detectives actually just do what they're told."

Hudson winced. If he'd stayed away and hadn't wandered off the rails of the Reynolds cold case into Garrison's investigation . . . Muntz might be alive. Tobias might be free. And yet by the same token, if he'd assumed the same tunnel vision as the investigators before him, the case would be no closer to being solved. Garrison would still be dead. Morgan would still have been victimized. Clive Reynolds would still be a mystery.

Muntz and Tobias had themselves and the lifestyles they'd chosen to blame. He was tired of being held accountable for the way other people messed up their lives. *That* was self-inflicted.

A ringtone that Hudson recognized from *Guardians of the Galaxy* alerted Kole to an incoming call. "Hey," he answered, and paused for a beat. "Shit. Okay. Thanks. Bye."

"He isn't home?" Hudson asked. He knew it had to have been Fletcher on the other line.

"Son of a bitch."

"What now?"

"Damned if I know," said Kole. He looked like he wanted to kick something.

"Did they check his work—"

"Riley's on her way with McKinley. My bet is on him not being there, though."

"Then where—"

Kole let out an exasperated sigh. A plume of fog issued from his nose. "You tell me, Sherlock. Christopher's proven at least twice now that he'll kill whoever fucks with him. Who do you think is next?"

Ice melted in the pit of Hudson's stomach as he thought back to Muntz's account of Christopher with the girl's underwear on the passenger seat of Clive's Porsche, and suddenly, he knew him for what he was: the man in Morgan's video. *Have you been naughty or nice?* Christopher had gone to see her at The Ruins and she'd branded him.

He had a mark on his neck.

Christopher Reynolds had shot Brix Garrison at the Fast Mart on the night of December nineteenth. The shoe print in Eleanor's garage made sense. Something had set Christopher off at the party. He had too much to lose, too much to hide if the case of Clive's disappearance were to be reopened. So he left the party, in his haste forgetting he was wearing a pair of conspicuous red Santa boots, and spray-painted them black. Then, he drove to the place he knew Garrison would be. Where he always was that time of night—watching the Fast Mart at Sixth and Lincoln. What he hadn't anticipated was for the one person Garrison had been tasked to find being there as well.

"Morgan." Her name was a ghost that evaporated almost as soon as it left Hudson's lips. He was back in his vehicle, tearing out of the lot before the subzero chill could even nip at his ankles.

"Ryan, what is going on with you?" Miserelli's knocks punctuated the last three words.

Jesus, could people stop spontaneously showing up at his door? He had to get on the road, drop Pip off with Noelle, and book it up to the middle of nowhere. Morgan still didn't have a phone, which meant he had nothing to ping. He might have to find her the old-school way—going from house to house. He hoped Loomis was a typical northern town with a sparse population, though he expected the Reynoldses' place to be sequestered; he wouldn't be surprised if they had their own island.

Pip spun off the couch in a frenzy, her nails clacking across the floor as she raced into the kitchen. Hudson stayed where he was by the sink, popping the top off a bottle of Excedrin. He refrained from washing it down with the half-drunk bottle of Jameson on his counter. He needed his wits about him. Now more than ever.

"Ryan!" Miserelli pounded again. Her fist was in mid-strike when he opened the door. She fell into his kitchen rather than walked in.

"I don't have time right now, Joey."

"You don't have time?" She sounded erratic. She *looked* erratic, he noted as he spared her a glance. Her coppery coils atop her head looked as though she'd stuck her finger in an electrical socket. Her eyes were wild, her face as gaunt as he'd ever seen it. When was the last time she'd slept, he wondered. He could probably review all her unrequited phone calls and text messages and find the answer to be not in the past week.

"You don't have time?" She laughed. "You don't have time? Ladies and gentlemen, the ever evasive—"

"What do you want?"

She charged him, backing him up against the wall as Kole had done on Saturday. It was Thursday now, New Year's Eve. "I want to know what the hell is going on. First off, your brother? Tobias Shannon? Hades? Are you effing kidding me?"

"I wish I was."

"And you and Kole, working together in some sort of good ol' boys thing, what the hell is that about?"

"I honestly don't know what that's about."

"Come on, Ryan. I'm not a baby cop. People have seen you and Kole gettin' cozy more than once this past week."

Did nobody keep their eyes on their own paper? He knew the police department was a breeding ground for gossip, but until recently, he'd never been the subject of it. To his knowledge, anyway. "He's helping me with the Reynolds investigation. It's a lot bigger than we thought, Joey."

"Try me."

So, he did. He tried her with the fact that they'd just about replaced Hades as the suspect in Garrison's death with Christopher Reynolds. He told her about Ronald Muntz giving a false statement to Wesson PD's Detective Kasper, the dirt under his nails that pegged him as a mechanic and linked him to the body in Clive's drowned Porsche. He saved the snake for last.

When he was finished, she stared at him like he'd just relayed the whole thing in tongues. She knit her brow and spoke three words. "Who are you?"

Hudson set his jaw. Who was he? He was Brix Garrison's best friend. He was the brother of Hades, Black Harbor's most notorious drug dealer. He was the widower of Nandalie, his beautiful wife who lay beneath ten feet of snow and frozen earth. And he was perhaps the only person who had a shot at rescuing Morgan from an ending as torturous as her beginning.

He grabbed his jacket and shouldered past her. "Someone with a cold case to solve."

41

MORGAN

It was cool in the cabin. Dark as a cave. The only light that permeated the vast windows was the faint, pearlescent haze of the moon. In the living room, the fireplace glowed with the low, barely breathing embers of a fire. It was past midnight. The house was asleep, but for her own footsteps creeping toward the front door, and the silhouette of someone sitting on the couch.

Morgan jumped, clutching her chest. The strap of her duffel chafed her neck as it shifted.

The glow of an iPad illuminated Eleanor's face, made her look like a ghost. She wore a long pale nightgown, and Morgan was reminded of the wolf disguised as Little Red Riding Hood's grandmother.

"Sleepwalking again?" she asked. "At least you'll be prepared this time." She raised a brow, noting the fact that Morgan was dressed in her winter coat, hat, and scarf.

Morgan bit her lip. She pressed her palms against the wall, felt the cold soak into her skin. "I was—" She stopped. She didn't have an answer other than the truth.

"It's okay, Morgan, I won't stop you." Eleanor's voice was composed, gentle. "It's just . . . I never thanked you for the scanning project you did for me. The USBs look wonderful."

Morgan clenched her jaw. Nodded.

"It must have been hard for you. Having to touch all those photographs."

Morgan's brows knit. There was the softest click as she powered off her device and set it on the end table. The fire rimmed her profile, the rest of her face a mystery. "Seeing Clive with us," she added. "With his wife and his other children."

The word "other" hung like an icicle between them. Every nerve in Morgan's body went numb. "You know who I am?"

"My husband's daughter? Yes, I know."

Morgan lowered her duffel bag to the floor. Her shoulders burned. "How?" she asked, and when she looked up, she discovered that Eleanor had begun to approach her. In a moment, they were but an arm's length apart. With Eleanor's back to the only light source, Morgan knew that the woman could see her face, but for Morgan, Eleanor was only a shadow.

"It's in the eyes," said Eleanor. "Only Clive had eyes that light shade of green. Like sea glass. In fact, I loved the color so much I convinced him to let me have the whole house painted that color."

Morgan recalled the first time she'd driven up to the Reynolds's sea glass–colored mansion and couldn't help but feel a little foolish. How often, over the past three decades, had she looked into the mirror, wondering who made her, when, according to Eleanor, Clive Reynolds was written all over her face.

"There are certain mannerisms, too," said Eleanor. "The night of the Christmas party, I watched you straighten the picture frames on the mantel, and I wondered. He used to tidy up those photos like it was his job, making sure each corner of each frame was perfectly in line with the next."

Silence fell like a blanket of snow. The fire hissed.

"The film roll wasn't corroded," said Eleanor. "It showed Clive and you . . . and your mother, didn't it?"

Nearly paralyzed with apprehension, Morgan nodded.

Eleanor sighed. "You know, Christopher gave me that film roll over two decades ago and I told him to stick it where the sun doesn't shine. I guess I thought . . . I hoped . . . that if I didn't see it, it wouldn't be true. That I could keep on pretending Clive was the devoted husband and the doting father to his four children that everyone believed him to be. And I did pretend, for quite a while after that, actually. I almost believed it myself."

"When did you stop?" Morgan chanced. Her voice came out as a whisper.

"The day he disappeared. Honestly, I knew. I *knew,* then, when the police arrived at the house to take my statement, that he wasn't ever coming home. That his past had caught up with him and not even that damn Widowmaker could have outrun it."

"I'm sorry," said Morgan.

"Don't be sorry over something you've got no control of, darling. You might as well be sorry for the rain."

"What can I do?"

"You can answer one thing."

Anything, Morgan was about to say. It was the least she could do. After all, she had ruined this family: Eleanor, David, Cora, Carlisle, and Bennett. Jesus, Bennett. She would have to vanish from his life as swiftly and surely as their father had. But, her mouth remained shut. She couldn't even form one single word.

"What happened to him?" Eleanor asked, and her voice sounded like ice breaking.

Morgan withered and felt akin to the dying embers in the fireplace. "I don't know."

Eleanor sighed as what was perhaps her last hope was extinguished. "That's what I expected. I just . . . I thought that if anyone had seen Clive one last time, it might have been you."

An invisible screw turned in Morgan's gut. She wished she could remember the last time she'd seen Clive, but her brain had blocked out every shard of memory he was in. All she knew was the house on Winslow Street and the horrors that happened in the dark—the horrors that still haunted her every time she closed her eyes. She didn't realize a tear had slid down her cheek until she felt Eleanor's cool fingertip there to catch it.

"I'm sorry." She whispered it like a secret shared between just the two of them. It was her last goodbye to Eleanor Reynolds, the fabled black widow of Black Harbor, before she slipped out the front door into the cold, starlit night.

Morgan shot a wary, wild-eyed glance over her shoulder as she turned the key in the snowmobile's ignition. It was a sharp sound, at first, that softened into a purr as the engine warmed up.

Around her, all was still. Even the wind ceased to swim through the trees. But for all she knew, Christopher could be throwing his boots on right now, ready to chase her down. She was doing exactly what he'd hoped for all this time, she realized. He'd burned down The Ruins and left her the key, lured her home. And she was about to find out what the hell for.

The tracks from yesterday were still visible. She followed them, wending through birch trees and evergreens, her ears on high alert for the sound of another engine.

But it was just her. Alone in this treacherous winterscape.

She glided past the snow-covered ghost town. Past the library, the bait shop, and the post office. The shed, the woodpile, the half-sunk canoe. It was close. When she'd come here earlier it seemed only seconds had passed between the canoe and the call box.

And then . . . yes.

A swath of moonlight, dappled through the trees, shone down on it. She slowed the snowmobile, left the engine running as she hopped off and sank into knee-deep drifts. She was so filled with excitement that she didn't even feel the cold as she waded through the snow. She tore off her glove and slid the key out of her cuff, closing her fist tightly around it. Now less than two feet from the call box, and her eyes having adjusted to the dark, she read the embossed print on the metal: GAMEWELL CO., LOOMIS POLICE DEPT. A keyhole stared at her. Dared her to try the black skeleton key.

Morgan plunged it into the aperture and turned. The tumblers were rusted, but as she turned harder, with a noise that sounded like a yawn, the door opened to reveal an old phone and a pad of curled paper. Her stomach lurched. The notepad was blank. She could hurl into a snowbank right now. She'd come all this way, gone through all this trouble, for what? An antique?

With frozen fingers, Morgan flipped through the pages. Empty. Whatever, if anything, had been written, had been erased by time.

She picked up the phone, held it to her ear. Not even a dial tone.

Her rage thawed her from the inside out. She slammed the phone receiver down. It was so cold it shattered. And then, a little black panel fell forward.

Bricks of faded green lined the box. Twenty stacks of hundred-dollar bills. Morgan's mouth fell open. There had to be at least $200,000 here, in this random box in the middle of fucking nowhere. She blinked, half expecting it to disappear, but it didn't. She noticed a black Moleskine journal tucked in the corner. It reminded her of Hudson's memo pad, the one he kept the Ruins ticket in as a bookmark.

She flipped it open to the first page and read:

Morgan. My darling. My rúin.

The hair on the back of her neck stood on end.

You remember what it means, don't you? Rúin. It's from an Irish song; we used to listen to those a lot, you and me. It means "secret," like a secret treasure, something precious. It means you, my perfect girl. My secret daughter.

If only I could have kept you.

I'm sorry, Morgan. For everything. All that money I sent your mother, I thought she was using it for you—to buy you clothes and food and books. I didn't know she'd left the country and abandoned you to the care of your aunt. And I use that word "care" ironically, Morgan, I do.

I'm a ruined man, Morgan. Not a rúin like you, but a devastated husk of a man. I have nothing. I am nothing. All I can leave you is the value of my last earthly possession: a 1978 Porsche 930 Turbo. Use it to see the world—and live. Live the life you deserve.

Love eternal,
Dad

Her teardrops froze on the letter. Had she misinterpreted his words all this time? She wasn't a ruin or a wretch; she was her father's *rúin*, his secret treasure. Bern had misconstrued the words, made them into something twisted and ugly.

"Morgan!" Her ears pricked at the sound of her name ricocheting off the trees. It was Bennett. She could barely hear him over the purring of the snowmobile. "Morgan!" He was getting closer.

Shoving the journal back in the box, she slammed the door and turned the key in the lock.

"Morgan! Please, stop!"

The key was stuck. She jiggled it but it wouldn't budge. Fuck.

"Morgan!"

She turned. He was closer than she thought and closing in. He stopped in his tracks, like a hunter who's just startled a fawn. His skin was pale in the moonlight, his hair matted to his forehead. He'd left the house in such a hurry he hadn't even zipped his jacket. His pajama pants were tucked into his boots that were now filled with snow.

But he smiled. It was a slow smile, aged like a fine wine.

Horror set into Morgan like rigor mortis in a corpse. He'd been waiting to break out that smile, she realized. Ever since he'd tied the key to a red balloon and left it on a smoldering stairwell. She realized something else, too: she'd been played—hard—and she'd lost at her own fucking game.

No. It never was her game. It was Bennett's. It had always been Bennett's.

He paused in his advance. They were within spitting distance of each other now. "I see you've finally claimed your inheritance. Took you long enough."

Inheritance. The words struck a chord. "You knew."

"For a while now, yeah." Bennett swiped away a piece of hair that had fallen into his eyes. "Remember when I told you we didn't come here for a long time after he died? When we finally reopened the cabin two years ago, I found an envelope shoved in the back of the mailbox. The little red flag must've blown down or something." He smiled again, remembering his good fortune. "The mailman never picked it up. So there it waited, this envelope that held nothing but an address and a key, for . . ." He blew out a breath that suspended in front of him for a second before dissipating. "Eighteen years?"

Morgan thought back to the envelope with the note written on the back. *My Rúin. 604 Winslow Street. Black Harbor.* So, he'd known where to look for her. Or, where to start, at least.

"But, how did you—"

"—know you existed?" He shrugged. "My father was a better businessman than a con man. He couldn't cover his tracks to save his life. When I found the envelope, I started putting the pieces together. Knowing you'd once lived there, at that shack on Winslow Street, didn't do me a whole lot of good, for a while, anyway. I did my research and found out you went into the foster care system. Changed your last name. You're kind of a ghost, you know?"

Morgan swallowed. She liked it that way. No paper trail. And yet, he'd still managed to track her down.

"And then I found the video on Christopher's desktop," Bennett went on. "It's amazing what turns up when you stop searching." He laughed and rolled his eyes as though to say, *Oh, that Uncle Christopher.* "I had a sneaking suspicion he was up to some shit, so I hacked into his computer. The son of a bitch has been embezzling from the family business for years, paying for prostitutes and setting himself up for a nice oceanside house in Switzerland. Gave a shady Investigator Gauthreaux a fat payday, too, a while back. My guess to abandon the case and get the hell outta Dodge."

Morgan's mind raced. Hudson had mentioned there were investigators before him who had tried and failed to solve the Clive Reynolds case—there had to have been. Christopher had paid at least one of them off to drop the investigation and disappear. She remembered the photos of the drowned Porsche on Hudson's coffee table. The body in the passenger seat with the busted eye socket, and she knew, with the same certainty that Christopher had been one of the monsters who paid Aunt Bern to do unspeakable things to her as a child, that he had put him there. Why else would he care about police digging into his brother's life? Unless he had ended that, too.

"The video file was right there," said Bennett, "even labeled *Morgan Reynolds*. I saw you incorporated the whole 'ruin' thing in your branding. It really has become your identity, hasn't it?"

"Who set the fire?" Morgan asked. "You or Christopher?"

Bennett elevated his brows as if to ask whether or not she knew him at all. She didn't, but she was getting to know him, now. "I made Christopher do it. Who knew all that spray paint on the walls would be so goddamn flammable. Then I made him sit, watch, wait until the fire department had put out the flames, so he could leave a little message for you."

All roads lead back to home. "You were blackmailing him." The answer was obvious now. Bennett had obtained the video from his uncle's computer, and used it to become his puppet master. Then, he'd burned it onto a disc and put it in a portable DVD player for her to find.

Bennett's mouth was open as though poised to speak—or strike—and then it twisted into a smile. "I'm a man of opportunity, Miss Mori. I told you that."

"Just like you blackmailed him to kill that cop." It was all falling into place now. *He had a mark on his neck.* Her mark. The one she'd seared into his flesh.

Slowly, Bennett clapped. "Did anyone ever tell you you're not as stupid as you look? Convincing him was too easy. Uncle Christopher's become gullible in his old age."

"What did you tell him?"

"I told him that my mother had employed the services of Officer Garrison as a private investigator to solve my father's cold case. Which was true. And cops are creatures of habit. It didn't take a genius to figure out he parked at that old furniture store every night. Why do you think I bought the property? Couple weeks of watching him on surveillance, and I had his routine down to a T."

Morgan didn't realize she was biting down on the studs in her lip until she tasted blood. "What did you tell Christopher that wasn't true?"

"That my father was alive. Trust me, Dad's return from the grave would not have been good for old Uncle Christopher. He'd tried to sexually assault his daughter, for one thing—how'd you like the video, by the way? Little graphic for my taste, but it held my attention. And for another, he was stealing from the family business. Not to mention, I'm sure there were other things Christopher didn't need coming up to the surface."

"Did you kill him?" she asked, though she knew the answer. "Clive?"

"He was going to do it himself. I just gave him a little push."

Morgan's head was shaking, shivering like a pine cone on a branch. "Why?"

"Why'd I push him or why did he hang a tire chain around his neck and walk to the end of the dock? Because he knew he'd fucked us over, that's why. And because he was a coward. He couldn't face his own music—divorce, prison, all of the above." Bennett shook his head. "He didn't get to go out like that. On his own terms. Not after what he did to our family."

He'd created a monster, that's what he'd done, Morgan thought. *He'd created me.* "How did you know, though?" she asked, her teeth chattering. "That he had . . . m-me?" The cold was so intense, her fingertips were on fire. She'd been out here more than fifteen minutes already. Frostbite could be setting in.

"You've seen the red rotary phone in the kitchen?" Bennett's eyes were a pair of frozen moons as they locked on to her. The tendons in his neck went taut as he fought against the cold. "I used to pick it up after he'd been upstairs for a while. See if I could hear voices on the other line. Nine times out of ten he was talking to her—Ava. She made a lot of threats. Said she'd go to the press. Show up and drop you off at our doorstep, which . . . I mean, I guess you eventually did yourself. With some guidance."

Morgan stood still. She was a doe, locked in the hunter's sights.

"They were at Carlisle's basketball tournament that day," Bennett explained. "Mom, Cora, Carlisle, obviously. David was in his room, doing emo shit, like always. Dad said he was gonna run errands. I told him I was going to my friend's house, but I just laid down in the trunk of the car. It was too easy. I slept most of the way." He smirked at how cool he'd played it then, as a twelve-year-old, hitching a ride to murder his own father.

"Did you know?" Morgan asked.

"Know what?"

"That you were going to kill him?"

"Actually, no. I was just curious. I wanted to know where he was off to. I didn't think about it at all, in fact. It just . . . happened. You should've seen the look in his eyes. Just . . . fear. As pure as I'd ever seen it. And then a little confusion crept in, as he recognized my face, I suppose. He reached for me, but . . . I wasn't really in a mood to help him out."

"You let him drown."

"Like I said, he was gonna do it anyway."

Morgan's breath hitched. He'd brought her out here to do the same thing. To do her in like he'd done their father twenty years ago. "Is that why you gave me the key?" she asked. "To lure me here?"

"Honestly, I just wanted to know what the hell it opened. I've spent the last two years opening every door, every drawer, every lockbox I could find. You were my last resort. I figured if anyone could figure it out, it would be you. And I was right. It's funny how mnemonics work, isn't it? You'd forgotten everything and suddenly, when a stranger gives you a key, you remember you had a whole other life."

Morgan was dizzy. She felt the weight of the sky pressing down on her and yet her feet almost lifting off the ground. Everything she'd been searching for—the lock that fit the key, the answers to who she was, the mystery of Clive Reynolds—all led to here, a northern nowhere. *If you scream in the woods but there's no one around to hear you, did you make a noise at all?*

"How'd you know I'd go back to the house on Winslow Street?"

Bennett shrugged. "Because I'd have done the same thing in your shoes. We're made of the same stuff, Morgan, you and me." She recognized the line from his limerick. "Just like David and Carlisle. Only, you and I are too dangerous to coexist." The snow crunched beneath his boots as he took a step toward her. He curved his arm, as though to coax her into a hug. His other hand was in his pocket. "Thank you, Morgan," he said softly.

"For what?"

The bullet was hot when it slammed into her chest. She catapulted backward. Her ribs shattered. She coughed and blood sprayed the snow. The shot woke the entire woods. Suddenly, she heard what sounded like thousands of birds screaming. They evacuated from their branches in what looked like a plume of black smoke, the collective movement of their wings causing snow to plummet all around her.

Snow cradled her skull. Morgan stared up at the stars above, the evergreen spires making the sky into a jagged cutout. She gasped. Her throat made a hissing sound. So, this was what dying felt like. She thought she'd experienced it before, with all those plastic bags over her head, but this was different.

She heard footsteps crunching on snow as Bennett approached her. Heard his excited breathing, his lips peeling back as he grinned. The metallic sound of a spring as his finger squeezed the trigger.

And then, like a wounded doe always does, she shot upright and ran toward the water.

42

HUDSON

The crack of a gunshot caused Hudson to slam the brakes. His vehicle spun around once, twice, and butted up against a snowbank. The seat belt cut into his collarbone as it saved him from catapulting through the windshield. Thank God the airbag didn't deploy.

Hudson punched the button to turn the flashers on, then unbuckled himself and tumbled out of the SUV. Morgan was in those woods. He knew it.

Entering the woods was like plunging into a dark, soundproof room. Insulated by snow and pine needles. The air was heavy here, like a weighted blanket tempting him to lie down and go to sleep.

But he had to find Morgan. He hadn't driven all night to lose her.

His legs burned as he waded through the drifts. The smell of gasoline bled into the air, and within a minute, he discovered the source: a snowmobile with the engine running. The machine looked expensive, like something a Reynolds would have. He turned his head right then left, frantically scanning the trees for its operator.

A figure appeared not two feet in front of him. Hudson doubled back, aiming his gun. He exhaled when he realized it wasn't a person, but . . .

What was it?

He took a few steps closer. It was a police call box—an antique—like the ones he'd seen in downtown Milwaukee. The door was partially open, stacks of what looked like cash lining the interior. A skeleton key was stuck in the lock.

Morgan.

Hudson touched the key, and immediately jerked his hand back. His skin shone red. Signs of a skirmish made themselves plain to him as his eyes roamed the forest floor. Drops of gore spattered the snow like someone had shaken a can of crimson spray paint.

She'd either injured someone or was injured herself. Up ahead, he could see a break in the trees, a clearing, maybe, where the snow leveled off. The blood spatter went that way, too.

He followed it like a hunter tracking a wounded animal, stopping, suddenly, when he heard a voice. Fighting his way closer, he saw a dock and a weathered canoe that matched the ones in the negatives. A shed leaned against a stack of old grey logs and in front of it, about thirty yards away, was Morgan. He saw her red stocking hat first. Then her scarf that trailed behind her like a slick of blood, and finally, he noticed how compact and slumped forward she was. She'd fallen to her knees on the frozen pond. A thin sheet of ice was all that prevented her from an excruciating death.

His gaze slid to the right, where Bennett Reynolds stalked out of the trees. Hudson held his breath, and when he turned, he looked straight into the barrel of Bennett's gun. He ducked and the bullet careened into a tree behind him. Shrapnel of bark flew in all directions. Hudson dove into the snow and rolled onto his side. He squeezed the trigger and fired off three rounds, then sprang to his feet and ran for cover.

Bennett fired again.

Hudson felt the bullet zip through the back of his boot. He kicked it into high gear, his lungs searing. He spun around and shot twice, missing Bennett by an inch. The next one of Bennett's bullets was destined for him. Fire exploded in his shoulder. His bones splintered. Hudson cried out and went down like a bag of cement. His gun flew from his hand as he somersaulted. The world spinning, he clambered to his feet and fell again.

He had to get up. Had to get to Morgan. The snow stung his hands. His whole body vibrated. Hudson ran until he felt the unforgiving planks of the dock beneath his feet. He had nowhere to go, and yet Bennett was advancing. The planks groaned, counting down his final seconds.

"You're out of your jurisdiction, Detective." He trained his gun on Hudson.

Hudson stole a half glance over his shoulder. He couldn't tell if Morgan was still there or if she'd fallen through. He thought he could see her hat, but his vision had become a kaleidoscope of shapes and colors. Fireworks of reds and yellows. Flares of blinding white. It was beautiful, and he'd be okay if this was the last thing he saw before he died, even if it was the capillaries bursting in his eyes. "Let her go." Those three simple words stole the breath from his lungs.

"You've got a stain on your shirt," said Bennett, and Hudson suddenly became more aware of the blood leaking out of the sucking wound in his shoulder. It spread like a red wine stain, soaking his flannel.

"You ready to see your friend again?" Bennett crept closer. "Your wife?" He must have registered the shock in Hudson's eyes, because he added: "I conducted my own investigation on you, Detective Hudson—or should I say, Shannon." His mouth twisted into a grin. "Who do you think tipped off your little friend, Devine, about who your brother was? Did it spread like wildfire? The truth about who and what you are?"

Hudson's breath flared hot out of his nostrils. "How?" he managed.

"I know every plot of land within a hundred-mile radius of Black Harbor. Your mom has lived in the same run-down shack for the past forty years. I'll tear it down, soon enough. Her house is a shithole, but it's sitting on some prime real estate. It's funny; no matter what we do to distance ourselves from our family throughout the year, we always return home for the holidays."

Hudson remembered. The headlights in his rearview mirror on his way to Garrison's on Christmas Eve. The lone car besides his own on the road to his mother's house. Bennett had followed him.

"Face it," said Bennett. "You're a criminal. And you come from a long line of criminals."

"No!" On his knees now, Hudson lunged at Bennett. They slammed onto the dock and rolled, ice cracking and chipping and stinging. It was all a blur. The lenses in Hudson's glasses spiderwebbed. Bennett got on top and, straddling Hudson, held him by the throat with one hand, and dug the other one into the wound in his shoulder.

The pain was blinding. Hudson tried to scream but he couldn't breathe.

The veins in Bennett's forehead popped, the muscles in his neck straining. "Brings back memories," he said, almost wistful. Then, he smiled. "I gotta hand it to you. For a skinny guy, you put up a better fight than Clive. Maybe you've just got more to lose."

Hudson kicked and tried to wrestle out of Bennett's grip, but Bennett was larger and stronger. When he tried to push his head into the boards to gain leverage, he felt nothing but cold air. His shoulders were off the dock, floating above the ice.

This was it. This was his end. He'd failed to finish Garrison's unfinished business. He'd failed to save Morgan. His killer's wild, bloodshot eyes would be the last thing he saw before he died. And then the light that shimmered behind them flared, like stars exploding. Suddenly, Bennett's grip relaxed from his neck, and as he lurched forward, Hudson saw a wood-handled ax sunk into the back of his skull.

Flecks of red spattered Morgan's snow-white cheeks. Her dark hair was matted to her face, her lips were blue. A stain plumed on the front of her jacket, soaking her sleeve, he noticed as she reached for him. But it was too late. Bennett's body fell forward, taking Hudson down with it.

They crashed through the ice, and all 206 bones in Hudson's body shattered. Every molecule of oxygen in his veins froze. He'd never known cold or pain like this. Drowning, now, was different from drowning off the pier in Lake Michigan. It was still, here. Quiet. There were no waves to thrash him about, no riptide to pull him under. Just darkness and stillness. He was in a vacuum, a black hole where light and sound didn't exist, and when he began to think that perhaps this was death—that he'd taken his last breath on the dock—he hit the bottom. Bennett landed beside him, his weight freeing sediments that had long since settled on the floor of the pond. Hudson kicked away from him, and reached into the weeds, blindly searching for anything to gain purchase, when his fingers closed around the rusted links of a chain.

43

MORGAN

She was a snowflake. Cold. Pale. But not dangerous, not anymore, she thought as she lay on the dock, staring upward at the star-spangled sky. The precipitation lighted on her lips, her skin. It didn't even melt. She could lie here and let the fresh snow be her burial. It wouldn't be the worst way to go. Not after all she had done.

Bennett was dead. She'd felt his life drain from his body the second she drove the ax into his skull. He shared the same watery grave as his father now. Their father.

We're made of the same stuff, can't you see?

No, they weren't. Clive Reynolds hadn't made her what she was. The house on Winslow Street had. The Ruins had. Her real family—her parents and Grandpa Teddy—had. She would miss them terribly. She wondered if they would miss her just as much.

And Hudson. Had he died on impact, or was he still down there, fighting for breath?

With all she had left to give, Morgan tugged her scarf out of her jacket. The effort pulled tears from her eyes. The pain was enough to make her scream, but her voice was gone. Blood dripped from her jacket onto the wood as she crawled to a post at the end of the dock. She tied her scarf around it, letting its end fall into the water.

He would see it, hopefully. And if he wanted to live in this frozen, fucked-up world, he would grab hold.

Winded from the exertion, Morgan lay back down. Her mind slowed. Sleep was taking her, the forever kind that made her feel as if she were floating above the snow and the evergreens and the frozen fishing pond that had swallowed three bodies. What would the Reynoldses think when they all woke up, she wondered. Would they be shocked? Or, perhaps they had known all along who she was and they were simply waiting for her and Bennett to destroy each other.

Eleanor had certainly known. As had Christopher. And Bennett. They had all known, she realized, and they'd simply watched and waited for her to crack.

Well played.

They'd find her, eventually. Then, they'd divvy out the cash in the call box and it wouldn't even make a difference to any of their lives.

A faint smile tugged at Morgan's mouth as she thought of what she would have done with it. She would have bought her mother's bakery back; a stair lift for her grandpa so he could have his own space in the basement; money in the bank for her dad so he could quit killing himself with long shifts at the factory. A tear slipped from the corner of her eye. It was too late for all of that now.

Her head rolled on her neck so completely that the ice on the dock kissed her cheek. She thought of Garrison staring at her from the floor. *I found you.* He had found her, the key to everything, and more. She felt a pain so sharp it took her breath away then, and for the first time, Morgan saw nothing when she closed her eyes.

44
HUDSON

"He knew too much."

Those were the first words out of Christopher Reynolds's mouth on January 3, when Hudson and Kole stood behind the two-way mirror in Wesson PD's investigations bureau, listening to the events of December 19 finally unravel.

"When you say 'he,' are you referring to Officer Garrison, who you shot in cold blood on December nineteenth, or Gary Hernandez, whose skull you bashed in with a torque wrench circa July 2000?" asked Detective Kasper, who sat across from the old man. Christopher Reynolds was barely recognizable in an orange jumpsuit. He'd shed his high-falutin' attire like an expensive snakeskin, and sat with his forearms on the stainless-steel table, wrists linked by handcuffs.

"It's a fair question," Kasper pressed when Christopher had the audacity to look annoyed. "For the record, Mr. Reynolds: Who knew too much?"

"Officer Garrison." Christopher's voice was rough. Hudson watched the blue veins in his neck pulse beneath the puckered scar. That mark told them what they needed to know: that Christopher Reynolds had gone to a place called The Ruins with the intention of having sex with an underage girl. Instead, he'd been met by a woman—his niece—who stuck him with a needle full of ketamine and branded him for the ruined piece of shit he was. Hudson and Kole had filled Wesson PD's Detective Kasper in on the backstory. He would need it to put together an accurate portrait of Christopher's motivations and offenses.

"Why that night?" Kasper asked, going back to the nineteenth. "What happened that you decided to leave the Christmas party, go to the Fast Mart, and shoot Garrison?"

"I saw Eleanor on the phone with him," said Christopher.

"How did you know she was talking to him?"

Christopher raised a white, wiry brow. "It was the red rotary phone in the kitchen. She only ever spoke to him on it. Twenty years she's sat at that damn desk, by that damn phone . . . delusional that he'll call with different news than the year before. That Clive would be alive and well and coming home." His bottom lip curled in distaste. "I knew who Morgan was the second I saw her at the party. She's my brother's daughter, for Christ's sake. The one I'd tried for years to convince Eleanor existed."

"Even going so far as to stalk her and photograph her. And give Eleanor a roll of film that she never developed . . . but Morgan did."

Christopher looked up, his gaze sliced in half by the rims of his glasses. It was news to him that the pictures had been developed. Kasper laid each freshly printed four-by-five on the table like he was dealing a hand of cards.

The old man's tongue peeked out between his cracked lips as he studied the photographs. Hudson knew them by heart. He'd picked them up from the lab earlier and watched as the processor lifted each one from the drying rack. The figures looked less ghastly in the actual photographs than they had on the strips of negatives in his basement. There was Ava with her dark hair holding a young Morgan to her chest as Clive leaned in for a kiss. There were the three of them on the canoe, the photo partially framed by cattails wherein Christopher had crouched, unseen. There was the picture of Clive holding Morgan up to talk on a telephone in the middle of the woods. Even through the film grain, he could read *Loomis Police Department* on the front of the call box and see the tiny aperture meant for a key.

It was how he'd known where to find her, after all. Like Bennett, he'd dived deep into his own research after seeing the picture, and found an historical map of Loomis that depicted all the locations of the police call boxes. There were only two in the whole town, and he'd chosen the one nearest the lake as his destination.

"So, walk me through that night," said Kasper. "You show up at Eleanor's house to do the whole Santa charade. You hand out presents. Ask kids what they want for Christmas, the whole shebang. In that time, you recognize Morgan as . . . your niece. The one who branded you at The Ruins."

Christopher nodded.

"And you tell Eleanor, who, for the past, what, thirty years, has been ignoring your accusations of her husband having a secret family. I mean, she wouldn't even look at the photographic evidence you captured. And now here was Clive's secret daughter in her living room. It couldn't have been easy."

Christopher tilted his head and Hudson got a good look at the brand on his neck. The puckered skin, the white scars. If this was Kasper's attempt to empathize with Christopher, he thought, it wasn't working. And yet, the old man issued a gravelly question. "What's that?"

"Hmm?" Kasper seemed almost disinterested.

"What wasn't easy?" pressed Christopher, and Hudson realized that Christopher was as eager as they were to put all the pieces together. For Hudson, this mystery had lasted only a matter of weeks, but Christopher Reynolds had endured decades of unanswered questions. He'd had no better idea than the police on what had become of Clive, and seemed appropriately distressed at the news of Bennett's guilt and death. And relief. There would be no more blackmail, no one watching his every move and snooping on his computer. Not that Christopher would have access to any of that. He was going to prison for the rest of his life. Which might not be all that long. Hudson knew all too well what they did to baby touchers in the clink.

Kasper had completed a slow circle around the table. "I was gonna say, getting that evidence, all those years ago when you spied on Clive taking Morgan and Ava up to the lake house. Pretty impressive, I gotta admit. You got pretty close."

Christopher shrugged.

Kasper paused, his hip level with Christopher's shoulder. "But maybe it was seeing Morgan that wasn't easy. On your family's turf. Your two worlds crashing into each other. Would she tell them that you'd gone to a place called The Ruins with the intent of torturing her? Of course, she'd have to explain what she, herself, had been doing there. And would she even recognize you?" The detective took a step, and then another until he was across the table from Christopher Reynolds. "You couldn't help yourself, could you? Once a perv, always a perv, right? You called her onto your lap. And when you realized she had no idea that you were her father's jealous brother, or that you'd paid her a visit at The Ruins, you gave her your business card. To keep her close, I'm sure. To get her to trust you. You knew she had nothing; could tell just by looking at her that she would take any job that came her way. What did you have planned for her, Christopher? Or were you just enjoying watching Bennett toy with her? You know, it was his little game of cat and mouse that led Morgan—and the police—to you."

Suddenly, Hudson had a flashback to Morgan sitting on the back of his couch, eating pizza and swinging her stockinged feet moments before she showed them the footage from The Ruins. How he missed her now that she was no longer in his orbit. Her disappearance felt like another death.

"Let's dial this back, huh," said Kasper after a beat. "So, when Morgan Mori showed up to photograph the Christmas party, did you believe that Bennett hired her on purpose?"

"One hundred percent," said Christopher. It was the most direct answer he'd given since entering the interview room.

"To fuck with you, or what?"

Christopher cracked open the water bottle on the table and took a drink. "Everything Bennett did was by design. He always had the ability to think light-years ahead." The words came easier now. It was as though each one he spoke was a weight lifted from his chest.

"Good quality for a private equity guy," noted Kasper. "And once you recognized Morgan, you told Eleanor. Who got on the phone with Officer Garrison."

Christopher nodded.

"You said earlier that Garrison knew too much. What do you mean, exactly?"

"Everything," said Christopher. "The Porsche, how it got in the lake . . ."

"How did Clive Reynolds's Porsche end up in the lake?" asked Kasper.

Hudson listened, then, as Christopher Reynolds confirmed Muntz's story—omitting the detail of the young girl's underwear. It began with insurance fraud. Clive needed money to pay off his mistress, Ava, but he didn't want to leave a paper trail and he'd already embezzled enough from his own business. So, he turned to his brother, Christopher, for help.

Christopher, who despised him.

Christopher, who wanted everything Clive had: wealth, status, Eleanor.

"He asked me to make it disappear," said Christopher, "while he went up north with Eleanor and the kids for the Fourth of July weekend." He dragged a nail at the label that had been softened by condensation, and began to peel it off the water bottle.

They all knew what happened afterward. "You could have burned it," said Kasper. "All your DNA and fingerprints would have been scorched off by the time anyone showed up to investigate."

A light smile tugged at Christopher's mouth. His whiskers bristled. "I could have."

"But you got greedy."

Christopher shrugged, but as Kasper went on to give details about Christopher's escapade in the Porsche, his face reddened. Hudson watched the old man's pulse beat in his ruined neck. "You took the Porsche for a ride," said Kasper. "Enticed some young female to ride shotgun, according to her story, anyway." When a pair of vertical creases appeared between Christopher's brows, Kasper added: "The victim's come forward. She saw on the news that you were in custody and she came down to the station. She was fifteen at the time. Fifteen when some dude pulled up to the curb in a black Porsche and offered her fifty dollars for a hand job and to sniff her panties."

Christopher didn't look up. He kept picking at the label until it was shredded on the tabletop.

"Then you drove it to a chop shop to sell it for parts. Be honest, Christopher. Did you go there looking for a fight? Chop shop in this area—did you honestly think they'd be able to afford a car like that?"

Christopher said nothing, and Hudson feared he was done talking.

Kasper switched gears. "How old were you when Clive asked you to get rid of his car? Mid-forties?" He slid a photo out from underneath the pile and dragged it in front of Christopher. Hudson squinted to see a photo he recognized from Eleanor's stash—they'd gone through the entire thing in the time that had transpired, piecing together a mosaic of Clive Reynolds's life and death.

It was the photo of Clive and Christopher grilling burgers, where Christopher wore a "Kiss the Cook" apron and was undeniably in peak physical condition.

"Sure," said Christopher.

"In pretty good shape, yeah?" Kasper paused for a beat. "People say you have anger issues."

Christopher's head jerked in the detective's direction. "Who says?"

"That's unimportant."

"Who says?" Christopher's voice grew louder.

But Kasper pushed through. "So, you're in good shape. You've got some anger issues. Now you're forced to do your brother's dirty work and you can't even get a decent price for the Porsche he wants you to dump. And on top of *all that*, there's the whole blackmail thing, right? Gary Hernandez saw the underwear and threatened to tell police you were soliciting sex from underage girls. Lucky guess, or had you earned a reputation, Christopher?"

Silence. In the observation room, Hudson stole a glance at both Kole and Riley who both held their breath, listening.

"I mean, you had no choice but to bash the guy's face in with a torque wrench, right?" pressed Kasper.

When Christopher said nothing, Kasper asked: "What did Clive say, when you eventually told him? When he realized that his little scheme cost a man his life. Maybe two. You didn't know Muntz would make it out alive, after you made him dump the car in the lake, did you?"

Christopher's side-eye told Hudson that he knew he did. "I watched from the pier."

"And you didn't finish him off?"

"Some people are worth more alive than dead. I'd already put fear in him. He was mine."

The last three words sent a chill down Hudson's back. *He was mine.* Ronald Muntz had been Christopher's puppet, just as Christopher had become Bennett's.

"You thought a lowlife like Ronald Muntz could come in handy," said Kasper. "Like when you needed him to dump the gun at Tobias Shannon's place. Interesting that you chose Shannon, of all the criminals in this city. How did you know he was related to a cop?"

Christopher leaned back in his chair. His shackles scraped across the floor. "It's a small town. Detective Hudson was the common denominator, with his connection to Officer Garrison, the stolen Porsche, and to Morgan. I watched her go up to his house once. I knew there was something going on. So, I asked around. All information has a price. It's just that sometimes only the rich can afford it. I found out that we had something in common, too. You see, I, too, know what it's like to have a brother you hate, and yet, for whom you'd do anything."

Hudson felt the weight of the words settle on his shoulders. Christopher had him pegged, and he despised the fact that they indeed shared this similarity. He waited for Kasper to throw a glance at the two-way mirror, but he didn't. "So, you gave Muntz the gun to plant, and then you killed him when he was no longer of use to you."

"He said too much," replied Christopher, and Hudson was reminded of the decoy suicide note in Muntz's blood-spattered room. *I have seen and said too much.*

"Take me back to that night," said Kasper. "December nineteenth. What happened between you leaving Eleanor's Christmas party and showing up at Muntz's place with a gun?"

Christopher sat forward, laced his fingers. He looked up at Kasper and took a breath, as though he was finally ready to reveal the crux of why he was there. He licked his lips, but he didn't speak. Moments of the same stinging silence passed by.

"Tell me what happened."

To his credit, Christopher divulged every damning detail of that night. How he'd hurried from Eleanor's to take care of Garrison before he could connect with Morgan and tell her who she was—and what was rightfully hers. "Who knew what the girl was entitled to," he said. "What she could take. It was a concern of Bennett's. He obsessed over it, always thinking about that strange key and the money it had to lead to."

He'd been right about that, at least, Hudson thought as he remembered the stacks of bills that had been in the call box one moment and gone the next.

Christopher had changed out of his Santa Claus getup only to realize he hadn't brought a change of shoes. In a hasty effort to disguise his rather conspicuous red boots, he went to the garage, where he knew David would have a collection of spray paint. His account aligned with the order of events that police had assembled upon unearthing Morgan's car buried in the local salvage yard.

The owner called in a complaint after noticing his gate had been busted while he was out of town for the holidays. Surveillance video showed Christopher depositing the Civic and being chased down by the junkyard mutt. He lost a boot in the skirmish: red suede, spray-painted black. The contour matched the outline Kole had photographed in Eleanor's garage, and Hudson's lucky, educated guess at the code granted the police entrance: 1978, the year of Clive's Widowmaker.

A good year, as Garrison would have said.

"The Fast Mart is, what, four miles from the estate?"

Christopher shrugged. "Give or take."

"But Garrison wasn't in his vehicle like you expected him to be?"

"No."

"He was inside the store. Getting a coffee."

"Yes."

Kasper paused at the front of the table. "Let me take a wild guess. Disguising the homicide like a robbery wasn't premeditated, either. Spur-of-the-moment logic, right? Because who would suspect a Reynolds of robbing a gas station? You people wipe your asses with hundred-dollar bills when the rest of us—" He stopped, perhaps startling himself with the volume to which his voice had risen. "You know, I guess the rest of us don't have it so bad, either," he said quietly. "At least when I go home, I don't have to worry about a knife in the back." He slapped the tabletop twice. "Just say it for the record, Christopher, and we can be done. Did you kill Brix Garrison on the night of December nineteenth?"

Christopher dragged his gaze toward the two-way mirror. He wasn't stupid; he knew people were behind it. The unseeing look was the same one Hudson had become accustomed to in Sensitive Crimes, when his subjects stared through him, as though there was someone else in the room. This time, there was. Kole stood beside him, jaw clenched, as they both held their breath and listened for the confession all of Black Harbor had been anticipating.

"Yes," said Christopher.

The word set Hudson free. He exhaled and felt the tension he'd held for the past two weeks uncoil inside him. Kole set his hand on his shoulder. They'd done it. Not only had they cracked Black Harbor's most notorious cold case, they were about to lock away one of the city's seediest characters for good. Black Harbor would never be Mayberry, but it was better off without Christopher Reynolds stalking its streets.

"Just one thing." Kasper's voice was less stern. Instead, there was an inflection that only accompanied genuine curiosity. He turned off the recording device. "Off the record. Why didn't you lawyer up?"

Christopher sighed. His breath rattled deep in his chest. "Because I'm just so goddamn tired." And Hudson thought it might be the truest thing anyone in an interview room had ever said. He sank to his knees and knew nothing, then, but the sound of himself weeping and Christopher Reynolds's shackles dragging across the linoleum.

Now, Hudson stood in a place he'd never been before. Pebbles skittered down a steep slope before disappearing into a vast canyon. Evergreens grew out of the cliffside, their roots thick and rippled like muscular arms thrust into the rock and hanging on for dear life. The air was heavy and laced with fog. From his vantage point in the Okanogan-Wenatchee National Forest, he could see the verdant mountains that Garrison had never gotten to.

Garrison's Harley-Davidson leaned against its kickstand, parked in front of a grove of trees. Hudson walked away from it, taking in the beauty of the forest and the rivers that wound through the foliage thousands of feet below. He understood, now, why Garrison had come out here. People didn't go to Hart's Pass to die on its precipitous roads over six thousand feet above sea level; they came here to live. To see nature and the wonders of the world unfold before them. To realize how small we all are in the story of the universe.

He'd driven for two straight days, spending a night each in Minnesota and Montana, and finally he was here in Washington at the state's highest point reachable by car—or motorcycle. In that time, he'd thought a lot about what had happened in the past six months.

Almost immediately following Christopher's arrest—being arraigned on three charges of first-degree intentional homicide, grand theft auto, and multiple charges of sexual assault dating back to July 2000—Tobias was cleared of homicide charges. He was still doing time for dealing cocaine, but as long as he behaved, he wouldn't be in for more than a few years.

Hudson unbuckled the leather saddlebag by the bike's back tire and withdrew a black box. He opened the lid and touched the fabric of Garrison's eight-point cap. "Leave it to you to have unfinished business all the way out here," he said. He knelt, then, laying the box at the base of a tree. "Rest in honor, old friend."

A tear trailed down his cheek as he stood and returned to the bike. Reaching back into the saddlebag, he felt the familiar weight of his black memo pad and thought about Morgan running out of his house that day when she'd seen the faded red ticket tucked between its pages.

She was the reason he was still alive. The memories of that morning came back to him like images broken into shards of ice. He saw the light flare in Bennett Reynolds's eyes again like a blown fuse, and then the tops of the evergreens getting smaller as he fell backward, crashing through the frozen pond. And then darkness, broken only by blades of moonlight. A rusted chain. Morgan's bright red scarf floating like a gash in the water. He'd grabbed hold and pulled himself up into the freezing air. But where he'd expected Morgan to be, her heels dug into the dock as she strained to pull him up, was only a post, and a bloodstain quickly being overwritten by fresh-fallen snow.

Later, when Kole and Kasper came to collect him from the local hospital where he'd been stitched up, they informed him a snowmobile had been discovered abandoned at the Canadian border. Months passed without seeing hide nor hair of her while Hudson settled into his new position in White-Collar Crimes, until a few weeks ago, when her mother reopened her bakery, Lynette's Linzers.

And then, something had arrived in his mailbox, just before he left for Hart's Pass. Standing at the top of the world now, Hudson opened his memo pad to reveal a plane ticket, tucked inside like a bookmark.

45
MORGAN

Black combat boots tapped on rain-washed cobblestones as Morgan walked in step to the music that percolated through the streets of Dublin. The city had an earthy smell, just minutes after the rain, and she was soaked through. Her clothes were damp beneath her anorak and water dripped from the ends of her dark hair. The sun was shining again, though, bright as a pot of gold and dappling the colorful buildings. A faint rainbow of red, orange, yellow, indigo, and violet ribbons shimmered, showing her the way.

She knew she could find them here, at Dogg & Duke's, a nondescript pub off the district's main drag. The cobblestones were worn a little smoother down this way, the buildings characterized by cracks and chipped roofs and the odd graffitied poem now and again, which she loved. It felt like home.

The bar had a teal door and a brass tiger head for a knocker. She paused before touching it, as though it might bite. But in the past six months, she had explored and experienced more of the world than she had in her thirty-one years before, and it would take more than an inanimate object to scare her. Instead, Morgan took two steps back, raised her camera, and took a photo. She'd taken thousands of photos in the time she'd been away. And when she rode on dingy subways and slept in spartan hostels, her photographs of doors and their locks and their keyholes were all she had—and all she needed.

Lowering her camera and closing her eyes for just a moment, Morgan breathed in her new life. It smelled of butter and battered fish. It sounded like fiddles and flutes and pipes. It tasted of freedom.

The warmth of the pub cloaked her like a blanket, fogged her glasses. Entering this new world within a world, she took off her anorak and folded it over her arm as she swam through a crowd that had gathered to hear the band.

Finding a high-top table, she watched and listened, enchanted, as two men and a woman began to play a haunting air. The man with a grey ponytail strummed on a harp. The younger man—raven-haired like the woman—whispered into a flute. Melodic notes transported Morgan from the noisy, humid pub to rolling hills and salty waves crashing against crags, and when the woman sang it sent a shiver down her spine.

Her lips moved in memory to the lyrics: *Siúil, siúil, siúil a rúin | Siúil go socair agus siúil go ciúin* . . .

It was the song Clive had sung to her, lost amid years of nightmares and forced forgetting. She wanted to remember now, though, for out of flames fueled by torture and pain had she been fearfully made. And she had nothing left to fear.

Few souls could say as much.

When the set was over, Morgan wiped her eyes, careful not to smudge her mascara. She ventured toward the stage area, and the woman, Saoirse, immediately embraced her as though they were long-lost friends.

"Morgan," she cried. "This feels like a dream."

Maybe it all was, Morgan thought, letting her mind wander for a brief passing moment. Maybe all we are and were was but a dream. Within a dream, within a dream.

"This is Cillian," said Saoirse, once they'd parted.

Morgan nodded and shook the younger man's hand. His fingers were calloused.

"And our dad, Gerry."

Morgan stepped toward the older gentleman who was tall and burly. She offered her hand and her name. "Morgan Reynolds."

Her Uncle Gerry smiled as he took her hand, then pulled her into an embrace. "There are no strangers in Ireland," he said. "Certainly not among the Reynoldses. You're staying with Saoirse, then, for a while?"

Morgan nodded. She'd found Saoirse Reynolds as all people find one another these days: on Instagram. She showed her the decades-old picture of Saoirse and Cillian with the other Reynolds children, explaining who she was afterward, of course, and, since she was exploring France at the time, less than two hundred dollars and two hours later, she was here, in Dublin.

"Will you join us?" asked Cillian. "We're headed over to Johnnie O's as soon as we pack up."

Morgan looked at each of them, her family, and felt her heart constrict, swelling against her rib cage. "I will," she promised. "But I have to meet someone here, first."

Saoirse shared the address with her, and Morgan returned to the high-top table, extracting a book from her backpack, nestled next to her Bart Simpson doll. The cover was softened and it had a few more tears than when she'd bought it at a bookstore in London to read on the train to Paris. Setting the copy of *Fight Club* on the table, she ordered two pints of Guinness and two shots of Jameson, and waited for Hudson to walk through the door.

ACKNOWLEDGMENTS

"What happens to them after?" I asked.

The sunlight streamed in through the living room window, creating a gauzy effect around my friend's silhouette. My fingers hovered over the keyboard as she paused in thought, and said, "In a lot of cases, victims of abuse will continue to be victims . . . or they will become the perpetrators of it."

It was this thread that began knitting the story of *The Widowmaker.* I would like to thank Sergeant Sarah Zupke of the Racine Police Department for sharing her knowledge as a former Sensitive Crimes investigator. Her insight helped shape Morgan and Hudson in ways I wouldn't have been able to accomplish otherwise.

In fact, there are many people without whom this book wouldn't exist. Sharon Pelletier, for one, who is my wonderful literary agent and voice of reason. Her confidence gives me confidence, and without her, I would never have connected with my fearless editor, Leslie Gelbman. Not only did Leslie take me on during one of the most unprecedented times in history, she championed this book on the sheer belief that I could write it, and she didn't run for the hills when, after being left to my own devices, a first draft popped up in her inbox that was simply "too dark and too weird"—a critique I adored so much I had it made into a neon sign.

St. Martin's Press and Minotaur Books have been incredibly collaborative and supportive. Thanks especially to Kayla Janas and Joseph Brosnan for connecting me with exciting opportunities, Lisa Bonvissuto for her keen eye and ability to tug on the right threads, and David Baldeosingh Rotstein for absolutely killing it with the cover design for *The Widowmaker* as well as *Hello, Transcriber*.

I'd like to thank my fellow authors who shared a quote and who, over the past couple years, have shown me that people who write murder mysteries are some of the nicest, most genuine humans on the planet.

Thank you to Allied Authors of Wisconsin. Not only did we survive a global pandemic, I'd say we thrived with the introduction of virtual hangouts. And to my longtime critique partner, Alissa Stormont: I'm so glad we met in the slush pile all those years ago.

To anyone who has ever come to hang out and ended up musing at my murder board: Erin Nachtigall, Liset Herrera, and Elenna Garrett—you're the real deal. Thanks, also, to Nikki Sharon-Schultz, who can always help me identify that special something.

I'd be remiss if I didn't mention Investigator Rob Rasmussen. His insistence on including a detective who wears snakeskin cowboy boots led me to writing one of my favorite scenes.

Thank you to my Barnes & Noble friends. I always tell aspiring writers to work at a bookstore; these booklovers have your back for life. Speaking of booklovers, thank you to all booksellers big and small, bookstagrammers, book lenders, and bibliophiles. Your love of literature keeps us all going.

I want to thank my family for their evergreen encouragement. Words are hard, sometimes, and they let me talk about fictional people like they're part of the family. Thank you to my husband, Hanns, who answers my morbid questions while he's getting ready for work, role-plays interviews with me—as long as the Packers aren't playing—and inspires me every day with his relentless mission to do good in the world. And of course, the daily word count would be an awfully lonely endeavor without my chubby little 5 A.M. warriors, Griswold and Muffins. Banana loves you.

Finally, to my law enforcement family: Thank you for your service and sacrifice. I have the privilege of writing for Band of Blue, a nonprofit organization that helps families of fallen officers. This cause is near and dear to my heart, as on June 17, 2019, we lost one of our own, Officer John

Hetland, who gave his life to stop an armed robbery. It is out of immense respect for John, his family, and all fallen officers that I wanted to write about the devastating impact a line of duty death has on the community and that officer's loved ones. I hope my words have done justice. R.I.H.